GRUNT AIR

John R. Taylor

ibooks

New York

ibooks

1230 Park Avenue
New York, New York 10128
Tel: 212-427-7139 • Fax: 212-860-8852
bricktower@aol.com • www.BrickTowerPress.com

Library of Congress Cataloging-in-Publication Data

Taylor, John R.
Grunt Air
  ISBN-13: 978-1-59687-851-8
  ISBN-10: 1-59687-851-7
    Library of Congress Control Number: 2007937274
    Fiction/Suspense, Adult/General
    Military/Adventure

Fisrt Edition
November 2007

10 9 8 7 6 5 4 3 2 1

Dedication

The Rules of Engagement (ROE), a manual of authorized military combat actions established by the Johnson Administration in the early part of the air war in Southeast Asia, had, by the 1970s, become fatally outdated. The ROE had not been revised to account for effective improvements in enemy equipment and combat tactics or setbacks in the political and diplomatic arena. As a result, American forces suffered significant and unnecessary losses of combat aircraft and aircrews throughout Southeast Asia. Concurrently, with the war winding down, U.S. war protests heating up, peace negotiations at a stand still, and the Administration impatient for an exit strategy, the North Vietnamese figured out they could hold American POWs as pawns in their strategy to win a favorable peace treaty. The fate of American POWs stranded in Laos and Cambodia became ever more perilous.

General John Lavelle brought these life-or-death issues to the attention of his higher headquarters, the Pentagon, Congress and the White House. At every level, he was rebuffed by those who lacked the personal courage to secure the changes necessary to protect the troops who stood in harm's way. General Lavelle resolved not to sacrifice his men in combat, not to abandon those missing in action or held captive in the "bush" simply because of the unfavorable political and diplomatic climate above him. General Lavelle kept faith with his men using deceptive official reports and subtle, unauthorized modifications to the ROE and the prisoner recovery policy. In doing so, he put his own military career on the line. John D. Lavelle was a true combat leader. He is a man who will not be forgotten by those of us who live today thanks to his personal character and selfless leadership.

This book is dedicated to the late General John D. Lavelle, the distinguished Commanding General of the Seventh United States Air Force in Southeast Asia, August 1971 to March 1972.

Acknowledgements

It is traditional that this section be set aside for the author to recognize various people, publications, books, etc., for their contribution to the author's work. It is generally the shortest and most overlooked chapter of a book. In books like this one, the acknowledgement should be the longest and most revered chapter since I, as well as all other Americans, should thank the members of the armed services who stood a post in Vietnam for their service to our country. My personal thanks to my comrades, and **welcome home.** In gratitude, I should list every man and woman who gave his or her life in the war in Southeast Asia, but that has been done for me by the "Scar," also known as the Vietnam Memorial.

Then there are those who didn't come home, but remain "over there," still serving their country as prisoners of war. These men find themselves abandoned by their country. At the end of the day, lame governmental excuses and hollow rationalizations are but empty words when it comes to their abandonment. What is important is that we remember and forever commit their personal sacrifice to our nation's history and moral fabric. We must never let their memory fade from our heritage and national resolve. Across America we have a legacy given to us by those who forever will stand silent sentinel for this country. We must keep the faith with them in our hearts, as they have for us.

Writing this book was a labor of love. I originally decided to write the story on the Freedom Bird coming out of Saigon in 1972. Like so many things in life, it got shuffled to the rear by other personal priorities. I had a burst of renewed desire back in 1985-1987, when I met Red and Dorothy McDaniels and personally became involved in Red's efforts to get our remaining POWs back home. That is a story by itself. Red's story about his six years as a POW in the infamous Hanoi Hilton is a real motivator. His book compelled me to write the Grunt Air story and I started my initial outline, but the business of living once again overtook a good idea. While I didn't write the book at that time, I mentally designed the book. I wanted to tell the story like it was, but even that changed with the broadening scope of the material. What started as a story became a novel so that I could cover many details, aspects and actual events in a more entertaining way. Also, by writing a novel *based on actual events*, I could write with an easy conscience and not with the fear of going to

Leavenworth Prison. I could also depict some of the real scumbags I ran into while serving overseas. Jim Blackmore kept hounding me to get off my butt and write the book so, on 30 November, 2001, I took the first step. I wrote a letter to Dr. Eric Carlson, who heads up the Special Collections Department of the University of Texas in Dallas. He has developed a wonderful collection of documents, films, pictures, and memorabilia from the days of Air America. It is a fantastic collection and was, other than my memory, a primary source of information for this book. Thanks to Carole Thomas who helped me focus my research there. Going through the archives brought back a great number of old memories. It was like a reunion without people. The more I researched the archives, the more involved I became. I was emotionally ready to write the book.

First, I went back and reread cover to cover both Red McDaniels' book, *Scars & Stripes*, and his wife's story, *After the Hero's Welcome*, about her life and her problems as the wife of a POW. Both books are a must read. Their stories will touch your heart and make you feel good about being an American and the responsibility that goes with that privilege.

I also reread my friend David Christian's book, *Victor 6*. I was hooked now! I couldn't remember squat about our Recon Team operations. My memory has become so bad that I can now hide my own Easter eggs. I had to get back up to speed mentally in this area, as well as with the details of POW life, so I read several related books for research and pleasure. The battle for Laos was best presented by two absolutely outstanding books: *The Shadow War* by Kenneth Conboy with James Morrison, and *Shooting at the Moon* by Robert Warner.

Two other outstanding books about the POWs in Southeast Asia were, *Honor Bound* by Stuart I. Rochester and Frederick Kiley, and *Code Name – Bright Light* by George J. Veith. Both books are excellent to read and the authors really did their homework. I also read a number of other excellent books on the topic that I highly recommend to you. They are, *Air Commando One* by Warren A. Trest, *The Phantom Warrior* by Gary Lenderer, *SOG* by John L. Plaster, *Maverick* by Dennis J. Marvicson with Jerold A. Greenfield, *The Ravens* by Christopher Robbins, and *Firebird* by Chuck Carlock. I want to thank all of these fine authors as a reader, and as an author, for the pure enjoyment and mental stimulation they provided.

During my youthful years I should have been cutting my literary teeth on *The Hardy Boys* or *Tom Sawyer*, but I didn't. I found myself focused on *Flying* and *Professional Pilot* magazines and the works of Ernest Kellogg Gann. I loved *Fate is the Hunter* and, most of all, his book *The High and the Mighty*. In this aviation thriller, the main character is an aging World War II pilot who had been relegated by age and time—and a traumatizing aviation accident in South America that killed his wife and son—to the position of co-pilot on a commercial airline flight from Hawaii to San Francisco. After saving a flight from ditching and safely landing the plane, the vet goes off into the night, leaving the reader the impression that a forced retirement was inevitable. The aging pilot was named "Dan Roman." As my personal thanks to the late, great Mr. Gann for his fine work and personal inspiration, I have chosen to carry on *The High and the Mighty* legacy by giving a life after flying to the aging "Dan Roman." A life that includes a career in the oil business, a second wife, a daughter and two sons, one of which is named Daniel James Roman and who is destined to carry on in his father's flying footsteps.

No author actually writes a book alone. Yes, it may be one person's creation, but it is the help and support of others that ensures the final product. That is certainly the case here. Without the support and guidance of Earl W. Green, a screenwriter and successful author himself, this book would have crashed on takeoff. Many thanks to my longtime friend Earl who helped me keep this book flying in the right direction. Earl and I go back a long way together in this and other works focusing on military leaders of our time. Jerold Greenfield was a major part in the refinement and editing of my work. He was more than an editor to me. He was a compass to the professional format and design. Deep, heartfelt thanks to Cindy Rybarczyk who proved to the world that modern day hieroglyphics, in the form of my handwriting, could be deciphered. Her personal dedication to the timely completion of the book, penetrating observations and storyline perceptions were invaluable. Now that the book is completed I can reintroduce myself to that woman who is often referred to as my wife. Thanks, Addie, for putting up with me during this personal stroll down memory lane.

The list of others that had a part in this effort goes on beyond the covers of this book. Thanks goes to Ron Pauluh who kept reminding me of the limitations of man and machine when we were flying together in the military. Ron, also known as "Mr. Black and White," always gave me clear and concise advice then and now. A special thanks goes to the late Anabelle Hardy who taught me how to put meaning into words. While at St. Johns, I was frequently challenged to higher achievement by a real dynamic administrator and mentor, Keith Duckers. Every time I slowed down, or just kept pace with other cadets, Keith would fire me up by giving me a very difficult leadership challenge. This passion for challenges continues to this day thanks to him. Last but not least is the late Russell L. Guernsey, former Commandant of Cadets at St. Johns Military School in Salina, Kansas. A decorated hero of WWII in his own right, Russ instilled in me and countless other cadets the wisdom and discipline we needed to understand and live by the words:

"Duty, Honor, Country"

Prologue

Above the U Minh Forest, South Vietnam
November 7, 1971

It is about an hour after sunrise, and the jungle glistens wetly below. The crew chief of the Huey called Outlaw Three throws a yellow smoke grenade out the cargo bay door and watches it stream downward to mark the landing zone. Seven other Hueys are on the way.

In the left seat, Captain Dan Roman pulls the chopper back up to a thousand feet, placing himself in position to control the insertion of the second and final load of ARVN troops. Below him is a small hole in the jungle at the far south end of South Vietnam. Charley lives there, deep in the brush, with all his relatives. The 175th Assault Helicopter Company is dropping over a hundred troops here, just 36 klicks to the south of Quan Long airfield.

Roman is operating on the assumption that a platoon-size Viet Cong unit hides somewhere in the area. According to the Intel staff at MAC-V headquarters, they are guarding a small supply cache hidden in the jungle between two major streams. One of the waterways, which the VC used extensively to move men and supplies, is on the south side of the jungle area, and the other runs to the west. Rice paddies fill in all the space between. Before Vietnam, Roman hadn't realized there was so much rice in the world.

It is Roman's second mission of the day, and the sun is barely above the treetops. Earlier, he and his platoon had left three machine-gun teams at the junction of the two streams to cover the VC escape route in that direction. Minutes later, with the element of surprise on their side, the first load of new troops arrived and deployed without incident on the east side of the jungle. Now the second load was due. So far so fucking good.

Above Roman, four Cobra gunships circle at 2,500 feet waiting for the worst to happen.

U.S. ARMY AVIATION RECON TEAM - LIMA

GRUNT AIR

DAN ROMAN
COMMANDER

FIRST SERGEANT: L.C. WOODS
CLERK: SP5 SEACREST

MAJOR FITZMORRIS
7th AF LIAISON

INTELLIGENCE
CW4 ABEEL (SPHINX)
SP5 DUNCAN (MR. TOUCHDOWN)
VIETNAMESE INTERPRETER
LAOTIAN INTERPRETER

COMMUNICATIONS
SSG NELSON

SUPPLY
CW4 GEDEON
SSG CAMPBELL

MAINTENANCE
CAPT TOM RYKER
SSG NOLAN
3 MECHANICS

OPERATIONS
CAPT JAN TOOTHMAN
SFC HARDY
SP4 CHOATE

COMMAND AND CONTROL

ARCHANGEL
CW4 DOUG ALBERTS
CPT. U. MUANG (RLAF)
1 LT MIKE JENNER
CW2 TRACY KELLOGG
SP5 BURKE (CREW CHIEF)
SSG RAY BLANTON (RADIO/INTERP.)
SGT DO KA BOUNG (RADIO/INTERP.)

AVIATION PLATOON

CALL SIGN:	**11**	**22**	**33**	**44**	**55**	**66**	**77**	**88**
PILOT:	LT. DITTON	CW4 DONOVAN	CPL. TOOTHMAN	LT. LEE DAVIS	CW3 HETLER	1 LT. DORSEY	CAPT. RED STAGGS	CAPT. ELDON BARNES
CO-PILOT:	CW2 REDINGS	CW2 LAWRENCE	CW3 FONDREN	CW2 ROBINSON	CW2 DODSON	CW2 BRAD CARTER	LT. GIL GILLESPIE	CW2 DEAN KELLY
CREW CHIEF:	SGT. ENGLAND	SGT. ROBBINS	SGT. FASTIC	SGT. KELLER	SGT. DECKER	SGT. FARRIGNO	SP5 JOE ESPINOSA	SP5 BILL COX
DOOR GUNNER:	SP4 ZAHN	SP4 TAMASHIRO	SP4 PRINCE (CPT. TRIPP)	SP4 SHACK	SP4 WIGGS	SP4 JANZ	SP5 CHARLIE DAY	SP5 JIM BURWELL

RECONNAISSANCE PLATOON

CO: CAPT. JASON BEST
NCOIC: MSGT. PANFIL

TEAM: **ALPHA**
TEAM CHIEF: CPT BEST
NCO: SFT LUJAN
INTEL SPECIALIST: SGT WALLS
LAO/VN INTERPRETER: CPL MUONG KY

BRAVO
GY SGT THORNHILL
SGT GRYNER
SP5 BRINDLE
SGT MONA TONG

CHARLIE
SFC RICHARDSON
SSG RAMIREZ
SP5 SCHWARTZ
CPL WANG SING KHAN
SSG MASON

DELTA
SSG KRUMINS
SSG BOYNTON
SSG PRIEST
SGT. THENG PAO YAP

ECHO
1 LT CHRISTIAN
SFC ANDERSON
SFC STIBBENS
SGT YONG TON PAO

"There they are," Roman says to his copilot, a new young recruit named Ragland. The men squint into the dawn, shielding their eyes. The Hueys float down in trail formation like descending a staircase in the air, making a straight line of black shapes in the bright sky.

Roman keys his mike. "Outlaw Lead, confirm smoke at far end of LZ. You are to make a Hot LZ approach and insertion from three five zero degrees and depart zero seven zero."

"Outlaw Lead rogers yellow smoke at south end of the Hot LZ with an inbound from three five zero and zero seven zero outbound," replies the voice of Roman's flight school crony, Jan Toothman. Briefly, Roman reflects on one of Toothman's famous Axioms of Combat. "If your attack is going really well, it's probably an ambush." Jan had other poignant mottos of the same variety, like his paraphrase of Rudyard Kipling. "If you can keep your head while those about you are losing theirs and blaming it on you, you obviously don't know what the fuck's going on."

Just as Roman completes his thought and turns into his next orbit of the LZ, the enemy takes the opportunity to prove Toothman correct. Heavy machine guns, small arms fire, bright twinkles from the deep jungle, swarming all around the Hueys, low and slow and vulnerable.

A dozen lines of machinegun tracers come out of the woods. A lot more than a platoon down there, Roman suddenly realizes. "God damned staff," he mutters to himself.

"Outlaw Three, this is Lead, we are taking fire ... hell of a lot of fire." Toothman's voice goes up a step in pitch as it always does when people shoot at him. This is understandable because he is looking directly at a steady stream of tracers reaching upward to his Huey. He shuts his eyes and his left hand grips hard on the collective pitch lever as the hard hollow thumps of the rounds echo around him. Then they stop. He opens his eyes. Still alive? Yes. So is the bird. No angry red lights on the Master Caution Panel.

"Dan, this is bad shit down here," reports Toothman. "I'm taking lots of hits!"

"Abort! Abort!" Roman shouts. "Lead, give me an orbit at 1,500 feet two klicks north."

Things start happening. Toothman pulls hard on the collective to increase rotor thrust, throws the cyclic pitch lever hard left to tilt the rotor in that direction, and leads his flock of Hueys out of range — but not before the enemy rounds leave their mark.

A voice crackles on the radio. "Hood! Watch out! RPG at your three o'clock."

Hood pays attention. He jerks his head to the right, eyes locking on the stream of smoke coming up to him from perhaps 40 or 50 yards away. That close, it would take an idiot to miss a shot like that. He is a dead man and he knows it. In a split instant, his bladder joyfully relaxes in anticipation of the long, dark peace to come, warmth spreads through his flight suit, the screams of his crew chief ring in his ears in spite of his headset, and he looks over his shoulder just in time to see the rocket-propelled grenade zip into the chopper through the open right-hand cargo bay door … and zip out through the left. A swish and in an instant, it is gone. Life would go on for the crew of Outlaw Two Three.

Others are not so lucky. The brash 19-year-old door gunner in Outlaw Two Two has had his reddish blonde hair and freckled face completely wiped out by a burst of machine gun fire from the ground. Headless, his body hangs out the door, secured by his safety harness.

The ARVN troops sitting next to him start to blubber and stutter and groan, horrified by the sight, until the VC gives them something else to think about. Tom Futch, the Huey's copilot, watches his right leg get shredded by another burst from the machine gunners on the ground. His body jerks in the seat, he slumps forward over the controls, grabbing his painful wounded leg, while the pilot struggles to fly the chopper and push him back. He looks bad, but he will live. The firing stops as soon as the formation of Hueys is out of range.

Roman keys his mike once again, calling on the Cobra gunships above, just waiting for their turn.

"Bushwhacker Six, make me some widows and orphans."

"Roger Three," responds Bushwhacker Six. The platoon leader of the four Cobra gunships rolls his machine hard over on its left side, a sickening drop toward the tree line. Two others roll in the opposite direction to work the area just short of the canal. The fourth follows the leader. Noses down, the Cobras expel rocket and minigun fire furiously at the tree line surrounding the clearing and at the jungle a short distance away, trying to pick up any troops that might think of retreating.

No use. Roman knows from unsavory experience that VC have evaporated into the jungle. With Ragland flying the ship, Roman flips a switch, changes to a new frequency, and makes another call.

"Black Pony, Black Pony, this is Outlaw Three on Victor."

"Good morning Outlaw Three, this is Black Pony Four. What can the Air Force do for the Army today?" The Air Force Forward Area Controller, orbiting at altitude, sounds in a jovial mood. That's because he is at altitude and no one is shooting at him.

"Black Pony Four, we have a large concentration of VC in a forest area north and east of two streams at the following coordinates. We need you to flush them out of the woods to the north so we can play with them."

"Roger Three, I have four Air Commando One Trojans in the area. Wait one." Roman waits. "They're rolling hot west to east in zero two mikes. Have your ground troops on the east side get down and pop smoke."

Two minutes. Plenty of time.

"Roger Four." Roman relays the order to the ARVN observer in the back of his Huey. In moments, red smoke appears on the ground.

The first of the AT-28 fighters comes into view from the north, hurtling along above the treetops. Two canisters drop lazily from its belly. The jungle erupts in hellish orange flame, greasy black smoke, and fury. Right behind him, the second fighter lets loose two 250-pound bombs to help spread the flames.

"Bushwhacker Six," calls Roman, "watch the north side if Charley starts to run."

The third AT-28, low-winged and snub-nosed, makes the next bombing run, his 800-horsepower engine pulling him through the air at over 250 knots, releasing his napalm just north of the previous strike. When it hits, huge fingers of fire and smoke shoot into the sky just in front of the fourth aircraft in the flight, which drops a few more 250-pound bombs. Another explosion. And then, somehow, a third, even larger.

The silver and white plane jerks in the sky, shudders, rolls over, drops, the pilot struggling for control. Just above the trees it comes straight and level. A hard pull on the stick by the scared pilot causes it to nose up and escape into the sky.

"Holy shit!" Ragland stares at the huge balls of flame. "What was that?"

"Must've hit an ammo dump," says Roman.

"We hit an ammo dump," says the Forward Air Controller.

"Air One Delta's been hit." It is the pilot of the fourth AT-28, who has just barely survived being swatted out of the air by the exploding ammunition.

"Reporting wrinkles in my left wing skin and my right side windshield is smashed."

"Did you take any hits?" asks the FAC.

"I'll say. There's a tree limb sticking clear through my right wing. It must be three inches thick. I'm losing fuel because of the damned thing. I'd better head back to Soc Trang."

Roman looks below. The remaining VC are scampering out of the burning woods, some on fire, some running in crazy circles. The Cobras pull up, turn and go back in again, firing deadly bursts of bullets into the enemy. Minigun fire and rocket blasts rip up the clearing, along with any VC in the open.

"Okay Lead," Roman calls to Toothman. "Insert your load so we can get your wounded back to Quan Long."

"Futch is doing okay," reports Outlaw Two Two. "Davis stopped his bleeding and put him in la-la land with morphine. He'll need a medivac to Saigon."

"Roger that." Roman watches as the rest of the Hueys drop their ARVN troops in the LZ and head back to Quan Long. He calls the Forward Air Controller, thanks him for a great show.

They stop at Quan Long to refuel, and get Futch off-loaded and on his way, by the faster fixed-wing aircraft, to better medical care than he could get in the field. Ragland, Roman's copilot, watches stone-faced as the medics pull Futch and what is left of his leg out of the Huey and place his semi-conscious body onto a stretcher, rushing him across the field to the medivac aircraft. He hadn't said a word on the flight back to Vinh Long.

WO1 Miles Ragland was fresh out of flight school, flying his first Combat Assault since arriving at the 175th three weeks before. Roman generally took the responsibility of giving the new pilots their familiarization rides, demonstrating combat procedures. He always took seriously their inevitable reactions of shock, bewilderment, and fear after they'd seen the Real Thing for the first time. He remembered how he had felt.

"Relax, Miles," he says, sitting next to him on the lip of the cargo bay, the inevitable dust blowing around at their feet. "Here's what they say about combat missions. A good one is when you come home alive, and a great one is when you can use the aircraft again. We did both. Even poor Futch."

Ragland gives no sign that he had heard.

"Look Ragland, people die in combat. That's why they call it war. General Patton was right. The name of the game is not to die for your country, but to make the other poor bastard die for his.

"Meanwhile, as long as we're in this shit, we're all brothers. We all defend each other, stand up for each other, and we never leave anyone behind. You may not know any of these guys very well right now, but you will. And you'll become closer to them than you ever thought possible. This is a brotherhood that will last a lifetime."

Ragland just stares into the late morning sun. He is realizing his life has changed forever, and it isn't even lunchtime yet.

1

Archangel, We Have A "Positive"

Laos
November 7, 1971
Early morning

While Captain Roman was conducting his mission in the Delta, Lieutenant Alan Christian crawled soundlessly through the dense jungle undergrowth of Laos, somewhere between North Vietnam and Thailand, raised his binoculars to his eyes, and was horrified at what he saw.

The weather was good now that the rainy season was over and the drenching monsoons had stopped, so the image was cruelly vivid. About a hundred meters in front of him, bright and clear in his sight, was the dusty courtyard of a POW camp known to Americans as the Homestead. Two Caucasian prisoners of war and one South Vietnamese were kneeling on the ground, being subjected to the dubious hospitality of an NVA officer and an overly large guard. The guard was behind one of the Caucasians, doing something to the man's wrists. Christian couldn't see exactly what it was, but he clearly saw the result and it made him sick.

"Son of a bitch," he whispered. The man on the ground had his arms and wrists tied behind his back by a length of rough cord. The guard had pushed a stick through the ropes, twisting it to tighten the bonds, like a tourniquet. The man's face twisted in excruciating pain, his cries reaching Christian's position. The Lieutenant had to look away, then, he had to look back.

The NVA officer asked the prisoner a question, didn't like the answer, and nodded to the guard. Another cruel twist of the stick, another cry of pain lost in the jungle. Apparently, the officer didn't enjoy the suffering screams either because he abruptly stuffed a rag in the man's mouth. The screaming stopped, but the blood didn't. The ropes began to drip red where they cut into the soft flesh of the man's arms and wrists.

It was all Christian could do to keep from reaching for his weapon and squeezing off a few rounds into the courtyard. It would be so easy to wipe out that NVA bastard and his brutal buddy with the CAR-15 rifle he carried, but that was not his mission this day, and it probably wouldn't change the situation that much, anyway. There were other guards in the compound, other officers, and he'd probably wind up a prisoner himself, on his knees in the same situation. Better to just do the job he was sent to do.

Along with the other members of his Long Range Reconnaissance Team, code named Echo, Christian was assigned to locate and identify POWs, not rescue them. So he tried to avoid looking at the suffering that was taking place before his eyes and concentrate instead on the general layout of the camp. That was more critical at this point. When they came back with the rescue team – and they would very soon – his diagrams and information would be indispensable in the planning and execution of the recovery mission.

He lowered his field glasses and began to draw a careful sketch of the camp, noting every detail of the compound: the number and location of the guards, where the cells were located, the type and configuration of the fences around the camp, cover and concealment points and the most direct ways to get in and out. Finally, he concentrated on the prisoners themselves. The long, low building that ran along the back of the courtyard seemed to hold six or eight South Vietnamese prisoners, along with the two Caucasians. They'd probably kill the Vietnamese as soon as they talked, he guessed, or send them north to be "re-educated."

The man with the bleeding arms, who was trying his hardest to scream, could have been an American. His uniform had, at one time, been Army jungle fatigues but were barely that now. Christian strained harder to make out the collar insignia, but it wasn't easy. The man was twisting and bobbing in the dirt trying to escape the pain of the tightening ropes. He appeared to have been tall and rugged, but now was much reduced, dirty, thin, and dripping with blood.

"He's a major," the Lieutenant murmured to himself as he recognized the oak leaf symbols on the collar of the man's tattered fatigues. The branch insignia would be more difficult to recognize since it was in the shade. Then, just as though the prisoner was reacting to a command, he turned his head and torso to his right, letting the sunlight hit his branch insignia.

"Air Defense Artillery? What the hell is he doing out here in the bush?" No time to worry about that now, though. Concentrate on the most current problem: get out, meet up with his recon team, then to headquarters. He'd let the brass figure out how to handle the rescue.

But first, he had to find out more about the second Caucasian POW and the hapless Vietnamese, now face down in the dirt. The other Caucasian's uniform was in better shape, so it was at least a little easier to identify him. He appeared to be an Australian officer. Christian could tell that he was a pilot by the shape of the wings on his tattered shirt, but couldn't determine his rank. Probably a field grade officer.

The third man wore a South Vietnamese Air Force uniform. Just as Christian got a good look at him, he jerked up, the instant result of a vicious whack with a bamboo stick by the meaty guard. A full colonel. "He's fucked," Christian speculated. "They'll beat him till he breaks, then shoot him. We'll have to get him out, too."

He quickly sketched in the rest of the details on his map, lay down on his stomach, grabbed his rifle, and eased himself silently out of sight of the camp. His life and the life of his team members depended on how quiet he could be. Staying in the shade and underbrush, he made his way back to the rally point. His team, which had also looked over the camp and the surrounding area, was waiting for him. Each one had crawled just as silently to the other sides of the camp, made their sketches, and were undoubtedly ready to make a complete report to command. The last thing you wanted to do was get sent back to pick up some small but critical detail you should have gotten the first time around.

When he approached the team's rally point deep in the overgrown brush, the first thing he saw was the impressive bulk of Sergeant First Class Anderson. The bastard was built like a linebacker's nightmare, huge through the chest and shoulders, meaty and strong in the legs. He was on his third tour in long range reconnaissance, and he'd probably do another one if his bravery and ferocity didn't get him killed. But then, Christian remembered, Anderson had grown up in the absolute worst part of Harlem, so a jungle full of enemy troops wasn't all that uncomfortable for him.

"He should be leading this mission instead of me," Christian thought as he made his way through the dense dry underbrush. It wasn't that long ago that Christian himself had been a staff sergeant. But they'd promoted him after the disastrous recon mission into the Vinh area of North Vietnam.

"A major success," the generals had said. "Brilliant job." Sure, if you think it's brilliant to lose four of your six men. Christian had saved the other two somehow – he truly couldn't remember everything that had happened— so General Abrams gave him a battlefield commission to second lieutenant, personally pinning the bars and the Silver Star for Valor on him during a ceremony at MACV Headquarters. He still had nightmares about the troops who hadn't made it. They did manage to leave a phone tap on one of the NVA's main telephone lines. Pretty ballsy move, but they had paid dearly for it.

Anderson caught sight of him and gave him a quiet, deliberate nod. No fast moves out here. No noise, either.

Christian saw Stibbens next, the team's Intelligence specialist, as he sat up from behind a fallen tree and smiled.

They all crawled to a point farther into the woods so they could stand up unseen.

Before Christian could speak, the fourth member of the team, Laotian Army Sergeant Yong Ton Pao, appeared almost magically at Anderson's side. He was smiling.

Pao was a hell of a story, and a hero in his own right. Three years of study in Singapore had taught him fluent English. Best of all, he was a Hmong tribesman and could follow trails through the jungles where there weren't any. He was also the only Laotian member of all the recon teams who had chosen to wear American jungle fatigues instead of his traditional Hmong clothing. He was proud to be a part of the unorthodox American unit.

"Looks like we hit the jackpot," Stibbens whispered.

"I guess so," Anderson said. "An American POW in the middle of Laos. Damn."

"The sooner we report this, the sooner they can extract them," Christian said. "The NVA are gonna move them soon, no question. Once they're up the Ho Chi Minh trail moving toward Hanoi, we'll lose them for sure."

It was a grim thought. Everyone in the group knew what happened to POWs who went up the Trail into northern Laos. Beaten and tortured every step of the way, with the camp commanders and guards trying to pull every bit of information out of them they could. A lot of the POWs never made it all the way.

If they did actually get there, to a place like the infamous Hanoi Hilton, the North Vietnamese would use each little piece of information to develop a comprehensive picture of the prisoner and his military career. Then the interrogators would use the information as a wedge during questioning, trying to open the prisoners up even more. There was lots of face to be earned for the "confessions" they obtained, especially if the prisoner was an officer, or better yet, an aviator. The NVA and their Russian cronies had a wish list, and people like a Navy electronics-jamming air-crew were right at the top. So were fighter pilots and F-105 Wild Weasel personnel.

"Did you get it all?" Christian asked the group. "Does anybody need to go back?" The smiles and nods gave him the answer he was hoping for. Mission accomplished. Well, mostly accomplished. They still had to get back to base.

"Okay. Let's start for the pickup point. Can we do three and a half kilometers in five hours? We need to be there while it's still daylight. Stibbens, you take the point."

Stibbens looked quickly around and moved off through the brush the way they had come. He'd been an up-and-coming fashion photographer back in the States, but decided to enlist because it was the best way to avoid being convicted for assault. His explanation: "The model's husband came home a little too early. All I did was to defend myself." The evangelical Christian judge thought that the aggrieved husband's fractured skull, shattered kneecap and three broken ribs added up to a bit more than simple self defense, and had been ready to put Stibbens in a small room for a long time. Vietnam was a compromise, but the ex-photographer seemed to have a talent for covert operations.

Stibbens was one of those people—and Vietnam was full of them—who felt at home the second his boots hit the tarmac at Tan Son Nhut. Since he knew that people would be shooting at him on a fairly regular basis, he figured that long-range reconnaissance patrols were the best place to be. At least he'd get the training that would help him survive.

He'd been out of sight for almost a minute when Christian followed him in the slack position. Anderson was a minute behind him. Pao would wait several minutes and then take up a position to detect any "followers."

They were a problem. If the enemy ran across a recent manmade path in the jungle underbrush, they'd follow it, then report back to their unit. Before long, a force of NVA combat soldiers would pour down the trail, catch up with the Americans, and take them.

Pao was good at detecting enemy trackers. When he spotted one, he'd ease up behind and send him to his ancestors before anyone knew what happened. He'd been credited with 45 kills, not counting the ones he'd accomplished in actual combat. He moved through the jungle like the ghost of a ghost, ridding his native land of the godless monsters from Hanoi.

The four men humped in a generally northeast direction, 20 to 30 meters east of the small creek that snaked through the marsh area joining the POW camp. The Homestead camp had a code name assigned to it for simplicity's sake, as did all the other major camps. It was easier to remember than numbers. The Americans were imaginative in their nomenclature. There was Disneyland, the Big Casino, and, of course, the world-infamous Hanoi Hilton.

Once they started up the side of the limestone hill that overlooked the camp, the team took a break and formed a circle as a defensive position. They had plenty of time to meet the Grunt Air chopper that was due to extract them at 1600 hours. Christian could see the excitement on the faces of his men, because he felt the same exhilaration. They were finally going to get an American out of Laos. It was more than a mission for them—it was a personal goal. Every rescue mission before this had failed, but they were determined not to. Quietly, they took out their notes and went over them, adding little details they remembered.

A few minutes later, they moved off again, keeping to the high ground as much as possible. The moldy odor of the jungle came to them as did the fragrant smell of the numerous tropical flowers, but they paid no attention. They were used to it, and besides, they were too busy watching for followers.

Stibbens spotted them first, four of them, coming down what was called the high speed trail—a well-traveled path through the brush. It went from the long, flat top of the hill down to the creek where the NVA would get their water, and that's where they were going. The NVA had water bottles hanging around their necks, and based on the number they were carrying, they were part of a squad-sized unit. Not good. If the chopper showed up and the enemy opened fire, the Grunt Air pilots would have to back off and leave them there. So said Lt. Colonel Whaley's hallowed Rules of Engagement.

Stibbens signaled Christian to halt, holding up four fingers. Anderson found a spot off the trail uphill of Christian. Stibbens did the same. Nobody knew were Pao was, but he had found a spot further downhill where he cut the top off a small tree with his machete, bent it over, and made the top into a spear. It took all the strength he had to bend the young tree over, but he had done it before. He waited.

The first NVA soldier wandered up the trail and lost his head to Christian, who sprang up and gave him a two-handed backhand with the machete. Anderson and Stibbens got two more the same way. The fourth soldier, far to the rear, almost tripped over the headless bodies of his comrades, dropped his rifle, and ran back down the trail, making little high-pitched screams that fortunately didn't travel far through the jungle. The panic sounds he made didn't last long because in only a few paces he ran headlong into Pao's little surprise. The panicked soldier ran to his left along a dogleg in the trail just as Pao, with exquisite timing, popped the sharpened tree loose from its bent position and impaled him.

Pao came out of the underbrush and looked at the gurgling young man with obvious pleasure. His eyes were bulging, mouth open, blood spurting from the place in his midsection where he'd been cruelly pierced by the tree. Pao stared at him until his lights went out. Except for some little bubbling sounds, there had been no noise. The team was safe.

As Pao started up the trail to join the team, he murmured happily, "That's number 46!"

All was well. They had four kills to their credit, the clearing was about 200 meters away, and all they had to do was wait about half an hour and they'd be going home.

Quick math, counting water bottles less four, told them there were six other NVA soldiers somewhere up the hill. They would be looking for their buddies soon. Probably not before the pickup time, but soon after that.

Christian had to make a decision. Find the enemy and take out the rest of the squad or just go to the pickup point and hope they wouldn't draw enemy fire. He went over the choices in his mind because he, along with everyone else, was well aware of the Grunt Air Commander's inflexible policy. If there was any chance of being shot down and captured during the extraction, pilots had to break off the attempt and leave the recon team in the jungle, possibly for days. Christian and his men would have to evade the NVA, who would be looking for them, and make it to an alternate pickup point. It was eight kilometers away as the crow flies, and they weren't crows. They'd have to hump through steep hilly jungle with the enemy on their ass and survive for as much as 48 hours. Not a pleasant thought.

The SOP directive had been initiated by Lieutenant Colonel Whaley, Grunt Air's Commanding Officer, who was scared to death of anything that would compromise their mission, which was good, but the result was a policy that put his recon teams in enormous danger, which was not. Christian found it hard to have respect for an officer who would do that to his men. If you asked the Grunt Air pilots, they'd have told you Whaley would have been better qualified for counting paper clips in some far outer ring of the Pentagon. He was that kind of officer.

"If it ain't one goddamn thing it's another," murmured Christian, looking around the jungle, peering into the brush, trying to decide whether fight or flight was the preferred alternative. He pointed at Pao, who scurried up the hill at an angle to the line of march, trying to scope out the remaining NVA soldiers. He hoped there were only six. With any luck they would be at the other end of the hilltop and no problem for the incoming helicopter.

The clearing was on the edge of a cliff overlooking the valley. Anderson looked over the edge from his concealed position in the woods on the north side. He could see the POW camp in his mind, bounded by a marsh on one side and wide open rice fields to the south and west. It wouldn't be easy to invade the place. Whoever put the camp in that spot knew exactly what he was doing. Any approach would be spotted in plenty of time. Worse yet, the road that ended at the front gate went straight down the valley to Ban Lak Xao, then through the mountain pass into Vinh, North Vietnam. The road was a major part of the Ho Chi Minh route system used to move men and equipment to the south. The Ho Chi Minh Trail was actually a complete system of paths through the jungle, flooded with busy little men, like columns of ants, bringing supplies and equipment south in an unending, unsleeping line.

Bupbupbup … the first sounds of the chopper came to them from the distance. Stibbens picked up the radio. It was Grunt Air Five Five with Hetler at the controls. He and Stibbens were drinking buddies back at Udorn, where they were based. Anderson heard the call at the same time. Christian nodded so Stibbens could respond.

"Grunt Air Five Five, this is Echo. We're green for pickup. The wind is light from the east. Recommend approach from the southwest."

Out of the corner of his eye, Christian got a glimpse of Pao, off in the jungle, frantically holding up six fingers. Visitors, and just the number Christian had feared. Great. His dream of steak, potatoes and a hot shower started to evaporate. While Pao melted off again into the jungle, everyone else froze. Pao reappeared briefly and held five fingers up, and one down. Anderson whispered to Christian, "Well, our little buddy's got number 47. That'll help."

"Excellent," Christian said. "Now we just have to worry about the other five."

Christian motioned to Pao, questioning where the other five NVA soldiers might be. Pao just shrugged.

The radio crackled again, "Echo, this is Five Five on short final for pickup."

"Roger, Five Five. Be advised that we have bad guys in the area, but they have not fired at us. They may be anywhere, but the LZ is still green."

"Roger, Echo." Hetler responded.

As soon as the radio went silent, the other noises began. Automatic rifle fire, and plenty of it, from the tree line to Pao's right. The Huey came into sight and was instantly peppered with gunfire, holes appearing in the forward door panel on the right side. More holes along the tail boom. Hetler pushed the nose down, added power, and tried to pull the wounded machine out of the line of fire, dropping the chopper down below the lip of the cliff.

"Echo, Echo, this is Five Five. We have taken hits but seem to be okay. What's your status?"

"Five Five, this is Echo. We're trying to silence those AK's. We have a 'positive' to report. Pass it on. I repeat. We have a 'positive' to report."

Hetler sounded excited. "Okay. I'll go over to the west for a couple of mikes. Take care of those guys. I'm getting low on fuel and I'm not sure about the battle damage. If you don't wax those clowns pretty soon, I'll have to abort. Sorry, but it's SOP."

"Roger that. Hang in there for awhile. We'll get them. Nobody wants to spend two more days in the jungle."

Christian sat up from his position, signaled Stibbens to move left, pointed at Pao to move right. He was trying to get the NVA in a two-way fire fight. Once they were eliminated, the team could go home.

Pao and Stibbens circled around toward each other and met up in the middle with no sign of the NVA. The chopper reappeared, Hetler rising up from below the lip of the cliff, moving forward toward the small flat space in front of the tree line. No good. The firing started again. Where the hell was it coming from?

"Echo, Echo, taking fire. Executing abort. Follow SOP for pickup at LZ Bravo. Sorry guys. You know the old man and his fucking rules. This is Five Five on the go. Archangel, do you copy?"

While Hetler waited for a response from the command and control aircraft somewhere above, he felt the anger rising inside him. Again! Once more he would have to avoid the enemy and leave troops in the middle of the goddamn jungle. Once more he'd have to cut and run when what he really wanted to do was put the chopper's nose down, charge in there and give them a healthy does of fire from the M-60 machine guns mounted in the cargo bay doors. But no. He was under orders.

Archangel's radio response was almost immediate, "Archangel copies. Will advise Grunt Ops."

Archangel was the orbiting command post sitting at 10,000 feet, 22 klicks to the west. They were the eyes and ears for the low flying helicopters and ground recon units. Flying high above the combat operations area they could monitor and assist any Grunt Air helicopter in case of trouble. They maintained radio contact with both Headquarters and the helicopters at all times. Archangel could direct rescue operations should the vulnerable low flying helicopters be shot down. Pilots and recon teams always felt better when they knew that Archangel was up there, just in case.

That was small comfort to Christian and the rest of Echo Team. They were alone in the jungle. Help was two days away. The enemy was near. And it would be dark soon.

2

Laotian Musical Chairs

Tan Son Nhut Air Force Base, Saigon
November 8, 1971
0800 Hours

Propelled by a vicious kick, a leather executive chair careened across the gray linoleum floor of the commander's battle cab inside Blue Chip, hit a desk, and fell over on its side like the guy on the tricycle on *Laugh-In*. It got everybody's attention.

Blue Chip, the 7th Air Force Tactical Air Control Center, was a huge, dark, high-ceilinged room located at Tan Sun Nhut Air Base in Saigon. Inside it, fifty or so troops sat monitoring the flight status of all their aircraft. Other troops milled around the room using bright grease pencils to mark aircraft positions and status on huge clear Plexiglas panels, overprinted with maps of Southeast Asia.

In the approximate center of the tables and troops, there was a clear glass room, about 10 feet on a side, up on a platform. Inside were a small conference table, a wrap-around desk and a few brown leather executive chairs on wheels, one of which had just met its fate.

The chair's attacker, Major General Al Mattix, was called "Bulldog," and he'd done much to earn the distinction. His low jaw and ever-so-subtle underbite did their share, but so did his resolve and tenacity. He was, at that moment, being tenacious.

"Calm down, Al," insisted the Commanding General of 7th Air Force, a four star general named P.P. "Pistol Pete" Coroneos.

"Calm down, hell," said Mattix, setting the chair upright. "We've got a recon team stuck in the jungle in the middle of Laos, surrounded by enemy, and we fly away and leave them there? For forty-eight hours?"

"But Al ..." offered Lieutenant General Ike Hamilton, the Vice Commander. "You know the reason for Whaley's rules. He is only trying to maintain the secrecy of Grunt Air's real mission."

"Yeah, I do. We have word of an American held prisoner at the Homestead along with who knows how many others, and the information we need is spending two days—and nights—in the jungle, waiting for a ride home. This has gotta stop."

"Colonel Whaley runs Grunt Air by the book, Al," said Coroneos. "He's got his own Rules of Engagement and he's the commander of the unit. He is trying to keep our collective asses out of Leavenworth Stockade. You can't fault him for that."

They all knew Whaley's Rules of Engagement ... the Standard Operating Procedure and the US Ambassador to Laos capricious and tough prohibition on POW recovery missions. But Colonel Whaley's SOP said that if you were flying an insertion or extraction, which regular helicopter units did, and you came under enemy fire, which happened with depressing regularity, you were to break off and retreat. But Grunt Air was no regular helicopter unit. Its true clandestine mission had to remain a secret from all outsiders and especially the bowels of the government in Washington and the Ambassador to Laos. It is said with conviction by the men in uniform that in any war they always have three separate enemies to fight; the enemy, the climate and the bureaucrats in Washington. The latter is always the most formidable and most harmful to their survival.

"Shit, I don't want to fault him," said Mattix, shoving the chair back under the table. "He's a great officer. Got Grunt Air up and running from scratch in no time. Don't misunderstand me. I've got a lot of respect for him."

"What do you think we should do?" asked General Coroneos.

"Bring in somebody who has the good sense to know when you follow the rules and when you break them. Unconventional warfare requires unconventional methods."

"Okay," said Coroneos. "We'll transfer Whaley to that Assistant G3 Air slot over in Creighton Abrams' staff. He wanted an aviator, so he just got one. Give Whaley a strong unclassified letter of commendation from me, praising his outstanding work with the 7th Air Force. Al, you write him a maximum Officer Efficiency Report. He deserves it and I don't want anybody to think he was relieved for cause."

"Who do we replace him with?" asked Ike Hamilton. His first name was Isaac, so the nickname was probably inevitable, but he was fortunate enough to remind people of Dwight Eisenhower. Not resemble him, exactly, but put people in mind of him. "Far as I'm concerned, Colonel Herbert here fits the bill pretty well. And he wants the job."

"I sure do, sir." Colonel Morton J. Herbert responded enthusiastically.

Herbert, a six-footer with thinning black hair, had a thin, prominent nose, slightly stooped shoulders and eyes like black marbles. He paid attention to everything, knew every detail, could almost see into the future.

"Thanks, Mo," the Commanding General said, "but you're moving up to the Joint Chiefs Staff in a couple of months. Besides, we need some young guy who's got sparks flying out of him. Anybody have any suggestions?"

"Sir," offered Captain Mansen, aide de camp to Major General Mattix.

"Yes, Captain Mansen, do you have somebody in mind?"

"General Mattix was telling me about a pilot he served with some years ago in South America," Mansen offered. "You know General, that Army pilot that you talk about from time to time? Well sir, he's currently assigned as Operations Officer to a helicopter company in the Delta."

Mattix's head snapped toward Mansen so quickly that it startled Mansen and Herbert. "Dan Roman?" Mattix asked.

"Yes, sir. I saw his name on the morning strike report covering a Combat Assault in the U Minh Forrest. He really broke the bastards back down there. Confirmed 177 VC dead and he got a very large ammo dump."

"General Coroneos, we may have our answer. Let me tell you about this man," Mattix said. He filled the Commanding General in on Roman's actions while serving with him in South America, along with some of Roman's other career achievements, most of which were unorthodox.

As Mattix spoke, the Commanding General became more and more attentive. Finally Mattix finished with, "Roman is not only a combat savvy officer, he's politically savvy as well. He'd fall on his sword before he'd dishonor his commander. Besides, he gets things done. Period!"

"Are you out of your mind?" Coroneos turned his head from one side to another. "This kid is Army," he pointed out. "And he's a captain. You want an Army captain replacing an Air Force colonel? They'll eat him alive."

"That'll be the day", exclaimed Mattix. "Sir, he hates staff officers. When it comes to politicians, staff officers and prima donnas, he is more vicious that a mongoose," Mattix continued. "He'll be fine, sir. Just let me bring him up here and you can decide for yourself," Mattix assured. "General, I knew this kid when he was flying covert missions for me in Colombia five years or so ago. He is exactly what we want"

"Al's wonder boy is a captain," Hamilton was being wry. "And Army no less."

"Ike," said Coroneos, "you make 'Army' sound like some kind of crotch rot. Okay, Al. Since you're directly in charge of the Grunt Air project, maybe you're not crazy. Mansen, find this guy and get him up here at 2000 hours for a briefing. Also, bring Whaley and his XO Major Fitzmorris here by 1800 hours so I can explain the situation personally. Tell them to bring their toothbrush as this is a change of assignment. They can fly down in that old C-47 of theirs, and it can take—what's his name?—Roman back to Udorn. Assuming, of course, he volunteers for this assignment after Al explains what he's up against."

Lieutenant Colonel Whaley, the outgoing commander of Grunt Air, was actually a good officer. He kick-started the unit, getting it up and running soon after General Coroneos smuggled it into its unauthorized existence. His Executive Officer, Major C. R. "Fitz" Fitzmorris, was drafted and went to Infantry Officer Candidate School. He was then selected for service in Military Intelligence. He later went through Army Flight training before assignment to an Assault Helicopter Company at Soc Trang, Vietnam in 1968. It was there he met Dan Roman who was flying with the 7th Squadron 1st Air Calvary Regiment (Blackhawks) out of Vinh Long. Whaley and Fitzmorris had set up Grunt Air Operations at Udorn Royal Thai Air Force base in Thailand while carefully guarding the secrecy of the unit and its true mission.

General Hamilton set about having orders cut to send Whaley all the way up to the staff of General Creighton Abrams, and Fitzmorris to the TACC desk in Saigon as Army Aviation liaison. Hamilton crafted brilliant unclassified letters of commendation over Coroneos' signature, following General Coroneos' instructions exactly.

Maximum Officer Efficiency Reports all around, so nobody who read them would think they'd been relieved of their posts for any negative reason whatsoever. As soon as the Generals found a replacement, the papers would go through. At the same time, the wheels turned to bring Dan Roman over to Udorn, Thailand from Vietnam immediately, and to summon the key personnel from Grunt Air on deck to meet him … assuming, of course, that he "volunteered" for the position. When he did, he'd be thrown into the job feet first. To complicate matters, Grunt Air's operations and maintenance officers had fatally flown a Huey into a hill a few days before while navigating in dense fog and trying to extract a Recon Team. Roman would have to find qualified replacements which would be difficult at best. To make matters worse, they were still waiting on the delivery of two Hueys that were undergoing major refurbishing at the Bell Helicopter facility in Vung Tau. Grunt Air had a "positive" in Laos—identification of an American prisoner of war who had to be rescued. But, for political reasons, the President of the United States—the unit's Commander in Chief—didn't want anybody rescued behind enemy lines at that particular moment. Neither did the Secretary of State, who was in Paris trying to stare down the implacable negotiators from North Vietnam. But General Coroneos would rescue them anyway. That's the kind of man Coroneos was and that is why he formed Grunt Air. He always kept the faith with his men.

3

Carol Cody and the Puzzle Palace

Alexandria, Virginia
Early evening

There's one thing you can say about chain motels. They are not only the same everywhere you go, but they're so exactly the same, so painfully the same, that, in your room, you are apt to lose not only your sense of place, but your sense of self. When you're in a room that looks like everywhere, it's easy to be nowhere. The longer you stay there, the more nowhere you are. This particular quality, along with reasonable rates, is what made the Motel 6 in Alexandria, Virginia such a magnet for those who came to do business with the government.

But, the anonymity of the motel room had not sucked any sense of self out of Carol Cody, nor had the atmosphere diminished her determination and outrage. She was a compact, trim, athletic 36-year-old, a shade under five five, with a tiny waist and square shoulders who carried herself with the agility of the varsity swimmer she had been in college. Her hair was tightly curled and frosted, cut close to her head, and shot through with tiny fingers of gray. A bit premature, to be certain, but that's what happens when your husband is a POW somewhere in Southeast Asia, you haven't heard from him for months, you know he's being subjected to physically demanding questioning, and the government doesn't know anything, or worse yet, does and won't tell.

Charlotte Hansen, Carol's best friend, who everybody called Charlie, had gray in her hair, too. It was blonde, long and softly curled, her face young but lined with months of living on the edge of the pit, her husband also a captive, dreading every knock on the door, and the sound of every car that stopped in front of her house.

Charlie was flattened on the bed, blouse, skirt, stockings and no shoes. Carol laid a new damp washcloth over her eyes.

"I can't take this any more," said Charlie. "I just can't."

"It's a migraine, sweetie," said Carol. "They haven't killed you, yet."

"Forget about dinner."

"You don't mean it. We've come this far. It's too late to stop. Don't you want to know where your husband is? I sure would like mine back."

It had been a rough flight to DC from Fort Bliss, where Major Willard "Wild Bill" Cody and Major James Robert Hansen had been stationed with their wives and children, living in a simple row of officers' housing on Rossiter Street. The dwellings were smallish, low and neat with lawns the size of thumbnails. A happy street until the two men had disappeared into the jungle, missing at least, or worse. Cody had gone first. Just as Charlie had gotten the hysterical Carol back to approximate adjustment, Jim was shot down and the two women shared a new round of tearful embraces.

They had come to Washington to lobby on behalf of the POWs and MIAs. The failure of the military to deal properly with the situation angered and energized the immediate families of MIAs and POWs. Across the country, there were angry ranks of women whose husbands and brothers and sons were over there, augmented by the concern and fear of any man who had the least chance of being sent.

Charlie and Carol had spent three days in Room 109. There was a lovely view of the Motel 6-style landscaping that framed the modest pool, but they'd seen it before. This was their sixth trip. Their first was soon after they'd received the telegrams informing them, horrifying black blotchy words against a screaming yellow background, that their husbands were listed as missing in action in Southeast Asia.

Charlie's husband, an Air Force captain, was an F-105 Wild Weasel pilot, missing over Vinh, in North Vietnam. It left Charlie on Rossiter Street with her three-year-old daughter Ann, who continued to inquire about the whereabouts of her Daddy as only a three-year-old can.

The original telegrams both women received requested that they keep their husbands' MIA status confidential. They had no idea why. Other telegrams came, reinforcing the initial "request." Later, some officers from the Department of Defense came to call, sitting awkwardly on the edge of their respective sofas, underlining how important it was that they keep silent.

"It's for your husband's safety," said one small, balding DOD visitor. "His welfare is at stake."

The women did what they were told for months, but their conversation kept circling back to one central question. Why? What possible reason was there for anyone to keep secret the dire condition of the imprisoned and missing? They talked the matter to death, back to life, and killed it several

times, assisted by many bottles of the cheap Chianti Carol loved and had started buying by the case since Bill had disappeared.

The first time they came to Washington, the absolute enormity of the
government and its bureaucracy virtually deprived them of the power of vocal
communication. They would start talking to congressmen, senators, family
assistance officers, even the fogbound Department of State. They encountered
the most brilliant techniques of buck-passing and evasion, they heard the most
jaw-dropping excuses, they listened to the most mind-numbing explanations,
and were so completely stunned by the ineptness of it all that they literally
could not speak.

Everybody was doing *everything possible. Everything they could.* Except
nobody was actually doing anything.

"When all is said and done," quoted Carol one afternoon, "more is said
than done."

"Those words should be engraved on every government building," said
Charlie. "Better yet, let's put them on the dollar bill."

It galled the two of them, and their ever-widening circle of POW/MIA
friends, that so many people in Congress were so blithely unaware of the missing servicemen in Southeast Asia. "If we're in the dark," Carol had said, "those
guys are completely blind."

It was Charlie who first came to the conclusion that the "keep silent"
policy was designed to prevent them from embarrassing the government,
which had been unable to make Hanoi budge even an inch on the issue.

In fact, that same morning, one of the State Department "weenies" (as
Carol called them) had insisted that he had reason to believe the POWs were
being "*well treated* by the NVA."

Carol wanted to reach down his throat and pull his guts out, hand over
hand.

"What's this 'reason to believe' shit?" she screamed directly into the
man's three-piece suit. "The North Vietnamese won't even tell us if they have
anybody. What are you doing *right now* to find out if we're wives or widows?"

He stuttered, he mumbled, but at the end came up with the same
answer she'd heard so many times before: *We're doing everything we can.*

"Well, you keep doing it," Charlie said, "because we're going public."
The two women stalked out of the Casualty Assistance Office and headed back
to the motel.

"We really ought to join AAPOW," she told Carol in the cab back to
Alexandria. They'd been looking forward to a nice dinner in Georgetown, but
the weenie had spoiled her appetite. It would probably be Kentucky Fried
Chicken in the room that night. Again.

AAPOW. The Association of American POWs was a political action group that had just started up. Its goal was to bring the POW issue in front of the American public in the strongest possible terms. Carol indulged in a sarcastic chuckle.

"If our fearless leaders were doing their job, we wouldn't need a lobbying group."

"True," said Charlie. "But they're not. And we do. We should go back and see Colonel Hurd."

Jim Hurd had the unenviable task of being Chief of POW/MIA Family Coordination at the Department of Defense. His office at the Pentagon was a gathering place for women like Charlie and Carol. Women who wanted to know where the hell their husbands were and why the hell the DOD wouldn't tell them.

AAPOW had been getting a lot of face time with Hurd—more than most of the other wives' groups formed for the same purpose. The organization's president, Margo Stone, seemed to have a particularly close relationship with the tall Colonel who bore more than a passing resemblance to Steve McQueen.

Carol was suspicious. She had met Hurd several times, had seen him in meetings with Margo Stone, and the two of them made her antennae quiver.

"He's a little too slick for me," she told Charlie. "But I like his aide, Major Dorsey. I trust him."

"We'll go see Hurd tomorrow," decided Charlie. "And we'll get to know Margo a little better, as distasteful as that might be. If we're going to make noise about this, that's the outfit we need."

The two women knew that Americans captured by the North Vietnamese were being considered war criminals instead of prisoners of war as defined by the Geneva Conventions. That meant that their captors didn't have to account for them, report on their condition, allow visits by the Red Cross, nothing. Major Dorsey had confided to Carol, "They can just shoot them and get rid of the bodies any time they want."

"In the war in Vietnam today ..." began the announcer on the network news. The women kept the television on constantly in the room. It helped remind them of the real world outside the predictable furnishings and inevitable wallpaper. Carol sat on the end of the bed. Charlie took the washcloth off her eyes and struggled to sit up.

The report started, as it always did, with the casualty reports. Hundreds of Viet Cong killed or captured. Very few Americans lost. Every night the same one-sided report, and every night Carol wondered why we couldn't win the war when we were killing so many enemy troops and they were killing so few of us. According to the numbers on CBS, everybody in North Vietnam should be dead by now.

"The East German news service has released a filmed report about American war criminals being held in Vietnam."

"War criminals, my ass," laughed Charlie. She squirmed closer to the screen, cuddling up to Carol.

The picture cut to a black-and-white film clip of several skinny Americans opening mail. They seemed to be all right except they weren't smiling. Most of them simply turned their bearded faces away from the camera.

Carol and Charlie put their noses right up to the screen, eyes crossing, scanning the grainy picture for a faint sign of their husbands, but no.

"Goddamn it!" Carol burst out. "We'll get ourselves on television, radio, newspapers—we'll speak to Rotary Clubs, Lion's Clubs, Veterans of Foreign Wars, even the Ladies' Garden Club. By God in heaven, we'll get the whole damned world to know what's going on. I want to tell everybody that the monsters in North Vietnam have to give us a list of the prisoners in their control. I'm telling Margo Stone that we're going to mount some kind of media blitz, and if she and the Colonel don't like it ... well, we'll do it anyway!"

The next morning brought bright rays of warm sun through the drapes of Room 109. The women were up early, dressed, and on their way to the DOD Family Coordination Office hoping to get better acquainted with Margo Stone. When they arrived, she was in Colonel Hurd's office. Major Dorsey gave them a warm, smiling welcome and admitted them quickly.

Margo Stone was the 42 year-old wife of an Air Force colonel whose F-105 had been shot down in June 1966, so he'd been missing or dead for almost five years. Nobody saw Colonel Stone's parachute, but his voice had been briefly heard on his UHF emergency radio. Margo had been pretty once, but was now carrying an excess thirty pounds in the most obvious and unattractive places. Her hair had become a frosty gray, but that was a family trait, and in her case it accented her arctic bearing, gaze, and manner of expressing herself. Her eyes were the color of the sky at the top of Mount Everest, her lips were tight, she kept her arms close to her body when she talked. Her very presence seemed to suck the warmth out of the air around her. Nevertheless, she had managed to become national president of a well funded organization that was gaining dozens of new members every day, and making its presence known in the seemingly endless corridors of the Pentagon.

Carol and Charlie shook hands with Margo, not surprised that her grip was both strong and cold. She was wearing a dark gray suit, tailored skirt, severe jacket, white blouse with the inevitable bow at the throat, and an antique brooch surrounded by small diamonds. The lack of color reinforced the frigid impression.

"Nice to see you, again," Margo greeted Carol in a throaty, intimate, surprisingly sexy voice.

"A pleasure," Carol said, not meaning it. She looked Margo up and down hardly noticing Hurd, who stood behind his desk smiling. He always smiled when his office was full of POW wives. They were so alone, so vulnerable, so deliciously determined. And they smelled good.

Charlie shook Margo's cold, dry hand in turn, wondering as she did so how the woman always seemed to have money to travel around the country visiting the chapters of the organization. It was rumored that she stayed in the best hotels wherever she went. Who was giving that kind of money to the organization?

They'd actually met the icy Margo Stone a few months before on another of their futile journeys to Washington. In the meantime, she had appointed Carol president of the POW/MIA wives' group at Fort Bliss. Since then Carol, always accompanied by Charlie, had made several uncomfortable visits to Colonel Hurd, who always seemed to be looking at her chest or the hemline of her skirt, giving her an oily smile and a few unwelcome dinner invitations.

The organizational work Carol had done at Fort Bliss had not gotten past Margo. She knew about both women and was especially concerned about Charlie, who was smart, dedicated, and never the least bit reluctant to express her point of view in the most emphatic terms.

After the Colonel had invited them to sit, Margo, her knees primly pressed together, swiveled in her chair to face the two women.

"Colonel Hurd tells me you've expressed an interest in our organization," she began, that voice still amazing Carol. "I'm familiar with your fine work in Texas, and very impressed."

"Thank you," said Carol, in spite of herself.

"As it happens, we have a seat available on the National Steering Committee for Public Awareness. I was hoping that Charlie would be interested in serving with us."

Charlie and Carol were dumbfounded.

The idea had come from Hurd, whose growing lechery had left his remarkable political instincts completely intact. In one of his many moments alone with Margo in her suite at the Willard, he had reminded her about keeping her friends close, and her enemies closer.

4

Shanghaied Again!

Seventeen kilometers south of Vinh Long
November 8, 1971
Afternoon

Captain Dan Roman ran over the day's assault on the U Minh forest in his mind and then ran over it again. He was a stocky 5'8" in his GI socks, thick through the chest from his addiction to any exercise that had the word "up" in the description. Chin-ups, pull-ups, push-ups. He did them obsessively because it helped him shut out all the smoke, fire and carnage he saw on his missions during the day and in his dreams at night. In spite of the "up" exercises, he teetered on the edge of the maximum weight authorized for his height as an Army Aviator. He had the kind of dark brown hair that made people think he was some sort of Indian—which he wasn't—and penetrating hazel eyes. Within a few months of his 27th birthday, he was an old man compared to most of the pilots in the 175th Assault Helicopter Company in South Vietnam.

Roman recalled the unit's impressive history in Vietnam. The 175th had deployed to Vietnam as the 502nd but was redesignated as the 175th "OUTLAWS" and sent to Vinh Long in the very hostile Mekong Delta. The 175th had always been a real load carrier when it came to the tough missions and Combat Assaults often called "Rat Fucks." Its ongoing successes were a direct reflection on its long line of good people. It distinguished itself during the catastrophic Easter Sunday missions of '67 and then again during the 1968 Tet Offensive that took so many good men home in body bags. Those days valor in combat became as commonplace as C-Rations. Roman thought of the units legends and got a real warm feeling. There was George Williams who left the Outlaws and became a key figure in the famous 1970 Son Tay Prison Raid in North Vietnam. The Outlaws had a long list of great and heroic combat pilots. Some of those "heroes" were as much off-the-wall characters in the air as well as on the ground. There is the story of The Great Waldo who was always making jokes to ease the tension on a very nasty combat assault. It is rumored that The Great Waldo and one of his buddies were wrestling in the platoon bunker to let off steam after a real tough mission. Another pilot entered and thought it was a real fight and tried to break it up. Waldo reportedly bit the pilot so hard on the leg that it required shots at the dispensary. He was not by far the only outstanding pilot in a tough situation.

There were stories about The Bear, Mike Nord, Bob "NoDoz" Smith, Simmons, Mac McCarty, Tominey "The Chick Magnet" Eastman, Spiers "The Spiderman" and many others in the history of the 175th.

Squinting into the late afternoon sun, he was at the controls of his Huey, last in a line of eight, returning to their home base at Vinh Long. As Air Mission Commander, he'd normally be flying the lead in the trail formation but today he was bringing up the rear so he could keep an eye on two choppers that had emerged from the mission a bit worse for the experience. Just like the day before, they'd come under heavy fire on the second insertion of a company-size South Vietnamese Army operation into the Ca Mau area. And like the day before, he had one copilot wounded, two pilots flying with a 90-mile-an-hour breeze in their faces due to the sudden holes in their windscreens, and one Huey bleeding hydraulic fluid as if from a mortal wound.

The air was cool at 3,500 feet above the hot, steamy rice paddies and he enjoyed it. But the atmosphere couldn't take his mind off Tom Futch, who had been badly wounded the day before, his leg shredded, or the young copilot who'd caught a piece of shrapnel that morning, not to mention the damaged Huey he was watching just in front of him. Outlaw Two Two, piloted by Eldon Barnes, was having an interesting assortment of hydraulic and electrical problems. Barnes was some kind of bullet magnet and was always getting shot up. He'd already managed to survive one tour and was on his second but Roman couldn't figure out how the hell he did it. This day, Barnes would need more than an average measure of luck to get his mangled machine on the ground in Vinh Long, if he could keep it flying that long.

Outlaw Two One had another set of problems. Flown by a Vermont boy by the name of Bob Manchester, the bird had intermittent radio contact, a severely mangled instrument panel, and curious puffs of smoke coming out of the engine compartment at unpredictable intervals. With no engine instruments, Manchester could have no idea what was causing the smoke.

Roman's thoughts went back to Tom Futch. He was probably in Saigon, maybe even en route to the big military hospital in Hawaii. All the guy had ever wanted to do was fly in the military but that dream was gone, as were so many others. Badly wounded, he was already nine-tenths of the way toward becoming a civilian; they just hadn't finished his paperwork yet. Maybe he'd spend the rest of his life as a flying instructor at some potato-patch airfield in the middle of Vermont. It was probably the best the poor bastard could hope for.

"Outlaw Three, this is Two One." Manchester's voice crackled in Roman's headset. "I'm starting to see some slight fluctuations in my DC voltage."

Another voice joined the radio conversation.

"I get his helmet."

Then another, "I want his electric fan. Mine doesn't work." Graveyard humor that came along on every mission.

"All right, guys, can it," Roman said. "Do you think you're losing it, Two One? Do you want to make a precautionary landing?"

"Not yet, Three. But, it can only get worse if the wiring is burning out."

"Keep me posted. Bushwhacker Six?"

"Roger, Outlaw." It was the voice of the lead Cobra pilot from the gunship platoon assigned to the 175th. "We're ready to make a run for the hot water." The showers at Vinh Long didn't produce much of the precious hot liquid and those who came home early from their missions got some. Those who came back late didn't.

"I need you to hang on. Let's see what happens to Two One."

"Band-Aid, Band-Aid, this is Paddy Control for all aircraft in the vicinity of Vinh Long." The call came from the guard channel, always tuned 121.5, the universal emergency frequency.

"Vinh Long airfield is under mortar attack. Request any available gunships in the area divert for assistance. Any assets diverting, contact Paddy Control. Out."

"Paddy Control, Knight Two Six, a flight of eight slicks over Binh Minh inbound Vinh Long, no gunships."

"Roger Knight Two Six, Paddy will advise if you're needed. Paddy out."

"Paddy Control this is Outlaw Three," Roman called. "Bushwhacker Six, Three, and Five diverting. ETA 7 mikes." He switched back to the Outlaw Company FM frequency, "Okay Six, leave Bushwhacker Two back to cover us. Looks like you'll get to the hot water first."

"Roman, you just don't live right. We're outta here!" Bushwhacker Six called back.

Roman glanced to his right and saw a flight of eight Hueys from the 114th Assault Helicopter Company, the Knights, which was also based at Vinh Long. The aviators in this particular unit, many of whom were on their second or third tours, prided themselves on flying in extra-tight formations, their rotor blades almost overlapping, seeming to be only inches apart. The pucker factor was high, but they sure did look impressive.

"Hey, Three," Eldon Barnes called from Outlaw Two Two, "the hydraulics are gone. I'm totally manual. Looks like a running landing for us."

"Okay Two Two, I'll let Vinh Long know to expect you on the active runway. Do you want to declare an emergency for the crash trucks?"

"Naw. I can make a hydraulics-off landing in my sleep."

"Paddy Control, Outlaw Three. We have the field in sight. Request frequency change to Vinh Long Tower."

"Outlaw Three, Paddy Control closing out your flight plan at 1405 hours. Frequency change approved. Adios."

"Outlaw Six, this is Outlaw Three," Roman called over the operations frequency.

"Three, this is Six," the Commanding Officer responded. Major Mac Chaney was always standing by when the birds came home to roost. Midway through his third tour in the Delta, Chaney had never learned not to take casualties personally. He'd come over with the first deployment of Cobra gunships as a member of the first class that learned to fly them at Hunter Army Airfield outside Savannah.

"Roger, Six. How bad were the mortars?" Roman inquired.

"Not bad, about six harassment rounds, small stuff. Your usual bullshit mortar fire. Two hit the ramp in front of the 611th Trans hanger, two on the side of the runway, one hit our paint locker, and one hit the second platoon billets."

"Our billets? Who got hit?"

"You did. The round hit in the hallway right in front of your room. Kiss your locker, fan and bunk goodbye."

"Great."

"Give me a report on Two Two and Two One," Chaney asked.

Roman did, running down the list of damage that could force Barnes to make an involuntary landing well short of the field. He told Chaney about Manchester's chopper which had mysteriously stopped expelling puffs of white smoke. He still wasn't sure if they'd have to pull Manchester and his crew out of the jungle south of the base.

"Here's one for you, Dan," said Major Chaney. "You'll land at the Hot Pad. Bring your gear and report. There's a plane waiting to take you out of here."

"Say again?"

"They're not telling me anything. But you got an Air Force escort and a U-21 waiting. Don't worry about Barnes. The boys'll fish him out of the bush if he goes down. Just get your ass in here on the double. You've got brass waiting." Roman was dazed by the order.

Thinking, *What the hell is going on this time?* Roman humped his flight gear across the tarmac. He'd stayed on the flight line long enough to watch Barnes miraculously make it as far as the approach end of the runway and skid his chopper onto the ground with a picture-perfect hydraulics-off landing. The more immediate concern was who was waiting for him, where was he going, and what the hell was up. Suddenly he was afraid of the unknown. Not the ever present fear of combat but fear of a different kind. *It's the fear that keeps me alive,* he thought. Roman never strapped himself into a Huey without a pang of it. His Nomex flight gloves were so wet at the end of the day he would wring them out, hoping nobody noticed. Certainly, he was afraid of all the things normal people feared. Death for one. Or worse—being shot to shit and coming home with legs that didn't work or no legs at all. And he'd learned a healthy respect for his enemy, an essential trait for those who wished to survive any armed conflict.

"If you're not afraid, you're crazy," Jan Toothman would say. Toothman, a fellow pilot and his roommate, had dozens of little homilies on subjects relating to war. That was one of them.

To Roman, and to those who didn't even realize it on the level he did, fear was a preservative. It kept him alert and it kept him just enough on the edge of his seat to make him stay ahead of his aircraft and his situation. It gave him a chance to live.

Major Chaney caught up with him almost at once, puffing a little. Roman always walked faster than anyone else.

"This comes from the Commanding General himself," Chaney told Roman. "And I'm not happy about it, I want you to know. This is Captain Mansen from Headquarters Seventh Air Force," Chaney said with little ceremony.

Roman just looked at him, switching his helmet from one hand to the other.

"Nice job on that ammo dump yesterday," the crew-cut Captain Mansen gushed. He was a shade under six feet, thin, with a mustache that looked like he'd been growing it for years with only moderate success. Old eyes, young face. "I understand Colonel Dinh called to congratulate you. The ARVN are kicking butt down there right now."

"How does he know this?" Roman asked Major Chaney.

"He seems to know a lot of things."

"I know that we'd better get into that U-21A over there and get the wheels up. General Mattix is waiting," Mansen said.

"Not 'Bull Dog' Mattix?" Roman asked.

"Well, I wouldn't recommend you call him that to his face," Mansen responded.

"I've done it before. Who else is waiting?" Roman wanted to know.

"I'm not at liberty to say."

"Mac?" Roman looked at Chaney as if to say, *Throw me a lifeline here*.

"I have no idea what the deal is. Major General Cannon personally called Delta 6 and said that you were being assigned immediately to Headquarters 7th Air Force. Why and for what, I don't know. Maybe the Captain here can tell you."

"Unfortunately, I'm not at liberty to say."

Roman paused for a moment. "'Bull Dog' Mattix. Damn. He was a bird colonel the last time I worked for him. Looks like he's been on the fast track since those off-the-wall missions we flew in Colombia."

"It was those off-the-wall missions that got him his first star and you assigned to Headquarters 7th," said Mansen.

"My respects to the General," Roman told Mansen. "But I'm happy here and I'm doing something constructive towards the war effort. You and the Bull Dog don't need someone like me on your staff. I'd be a lousy staff officer. He should know that."

"Captain Roman, I'm not authorized to divulge your job or anything else that you'll be doing. What I can say is that you were hand-selected by General Coroneos, the Commanding General of 7th Air Force, based on the personal recommendation of Major General Mattix. Also what you'll be doing is vitally important and not necessarily in a staff position. Now, what I'd really like is for you to join me on that plane. There are four general officers waiting for you."

"What's up?" Roman's roommate, Jansen "The Fang" Toothman, had walked up to join them along with the company's maintenance officer, Captain Tom Ryker. Roman had been so intent on digging some information out of Mansen that he'd hardly seen his two friends approach.

"You know the bastards blew up my bunk," Toothman said casually, like his bunk blew up three or four times a week. "Going somewhere?"

"You're Toothman?" observed Captain Mansen. "And that would make you Ryker."

"And you are …?" Toothman asked.

"I've heard of you both," Mansen said, still not identifying himself. "You and Roman have been following each other around through just about all your assignments."

"Who the hell are you and where are you taking this man?" Ryker asked, putting on his best indignation. "I can't let this little fat son of a bitch go without me. I promised him that I would be there to kill him before he ever gets captured."

"Enough of this 'humor,'" said Major Chaney. "Dan, Sergeant Morgan will clear you and forward everything. Since the mortar got most of your stuff, you'll be traveling light. Here's your duffle bag with what's left." Chaney sheepishly handed Roman a duffel bag about half full of gear, then stuck out his hand.

"Well … good luck, Dan," he said quietly, then raised his voice over the sound of some inbound choppers. "Thanks for your help. We'll miss you around here."

"Well, knowing General Mattix, I imagine I'll be missing you, too. He's hell to work for."

Chaney glanced at Mansen and then fixed a gaze on Roman. "I don't know what the deal is, Dan, but I hope they don't assign you to a staff position. You'd be lousy at it and everybody knows how much you hate staff officers. Somehow, I don't think they're that dumb up at the 7th. Just watch your mouth and behave yourself. Now get outta here, you bum."

Roman rendered a snappy salute, shook hands with Ryker, pounded Toothman on the back a few times, and started toward the waiting aircraft. He was halfway up the stairs before he turned around to look at his friends one last time, flash them a smile, and give them a halfhearted thumbs up.

෴

5

Let's Go Public and Watch the Political Rats Hide

Alexandria, Virginia
8:30 P.M.

Another day in the anonymous confines of Alexandria's famed Motel 6. After their brief meeting at the Pentagon, Carol and Charlie had been half packed to catch a flight back to Texas, but then they started talking.

"Let's do this," Carol said. "Put together a plan to take this whole POW issue national, then go back to Hurd's office and tell him to stick it where it fits."

"What kind of plan?" Charlie asked.

"I don't know. But that's why we're not going back home. You and I are going to sit in that damn room and work on this until we have something so detailed and so airtight that he'll have to support us or go hide somewhere."

"I'm not sure," Charlie said between mouthfuls of spaghetti. They'd been eating at the same Italian restaurant down the road from the motel every night for almost a week. "We both know what kind of guy our good friend Gentleman Jim Hurd is."

They knew. Everybody knew. His official title was Chief of the Casualty Branch and Family Information Coordinaton and he worked closely (Carol thought too closely) with the formidable Margo Stone. He did, in fact, bear more than a passing resemblance to Steve McQueen, but he was taller, in his late thirties, and his ego was as big as his office, which is saying quite a bit. His sandy brown hair, every strand in place, smooth skin, smooth talk, and carefully tailored uniforms earned him the title of "The Pentagon Prima Donna," but he didn't mind. He still found ways to insinuate himself into all the important photo ops with the general officers and distinguished members of Congress. He also found ways to stay out from under any failures or staff disasters. A master politician and inveterate lecher, he'd had affairs with more of his colleagues' wives and office secretaries than anyone could dream of. His wife either didn't know or care because she was the most successful interior

40

designer in Philadelphia, with clients that included the largest, wealthiest law firms in the city. She made three times as much money as her husband, who commuted to Philadelphia on those few weekends when he wasn't philandering, and she was very much her own woman.

Three days later, Carol dragged herself out of bed and into the shower just before 6:30. She felt old, certainly much older than her 36 years, and it wasn't because of the two carafes of Chianti they'd put away the night before. It was thanks to the constant pressure of being a POW wife with two teenage kids. She hadn't had a good night's sleep in months because when she closed her eyes, she saw in the darkness a feverish jungle, her husband wandering through it, wounded and lost, followed by evil-looking men, all of whom were eight feet tall, wearing black pajamas and carrying huge guns.

Wiping the steam from the bathroom mirror, she peered through the droplets of water at her still pretty face, searching for (and finding) the deepening creases around her eyes, the corner of her mouth and upper lip. Look at me, she thought. I'm 36 years old, I have a 15-year-old son in high school, a 13-year-old daughter who's developing a chest, and a husband who's missing in action in Vietnam or wherever. I deserve these wrinkles. I've earned them.

Her musings were interrupted by the rattling of the doorknob just before the bathroom door burst open, allowing Charlie to fly through.

"You done, yet? Gotta go!" She was bright, alive, cheerful, and always optimistic even though she, too, had a missing husband and a young child. Helps to be young, Carol thought.

"It's all yours. I'll dry my hair in the room."

As she styled her frosted hair with the ease of long practice, she couldn't keep the thoughts away. With a birthday coming up in just a few months, it was hard not to reflect back on who she was and how she came to be a regular guest of the Motel 6 in Alexandria, Virginia.

She was the former Carol Durden, daughter of Command Sergeant Major Gene Durden, United States Army, and she was used to the problems and challenges of military life, moving from one base to another, having a father who was always off in some other country. She had developed the inner strength and composure to deal with it and had sworn to herself as a girl that she'd never marry a man in the military. That oath went right out the window about thirty seconds after she'd met Bill Cody. She was a third year nursing student near Fort Bliss when Bill had appeared in the emergency room with a badly sprained wrist. He was coaching little league football when he was tackled by two of his fun-loving players and landed badly. They were married three months later.

Charlie bustled out of the bathroom, stood in back of Carol and looked at her in the mirror.

"Why the long face, dearie?" Charlie asked in a bright voice over the roar of the hair dryer.

"I'm starting to look like an old lady."

"Get real," Charlie said. She'd heard that edge of weariness in Carol's voice before. "You have a face like Joey Heatherton and a body like Ann Margaret. It doesn't get any better than that. Those men at the Pentagon eyeball you every time you walk down the hall. I'll bet Gentleman Jim pictures you naked every time he looks at you."

"Charlie!" Carol had never been comfortable with her friend's often unladylike manner of expression.

"Seriously. You look a damn sight better than I do and you're eight years up on me. Must be all that swimming you do."

"You should try it."

"Chlorine is hell on blonde hair. You know that."

"Fine. Let's get checked out and over to the puzzle palace. We have a 4:30 flight to catch today. You do remember we have a home and children to take care of."

"Oh, right. I almost forgot because of this life of luxury here at Motel 6 and all the parties we go to at the embassies, and all that."

"Get dressed," Carol commanded. "Let's go rattle the prima donna's cage."

Precisely at 10:00 a.m. Carol Cody and Charlie Hanson arrived at the office of the Chief of POW/MIA Family Coordination. Major Dorsey was in the front office talking to several POW/MIA wives and Margo Stone. The women greeted each other as politely as they could manage.

"Margo, can we have a few minutes of your time?" Carol asked. "We have an idea, or should I say a concept, to run by you."

"Of course," Margo condescended. "I'm due to meet with Colonel Hurd, but I'm sure he wouldn't mind if you joined us for a few minutes. Come with me," Margo said, gesturing toward the door to Colonel Hurd's office.

Colonel Hurd's face illuminated as the women entered his office, but he always lit up when women came in. As he ushered them into his small conference room, he ran his usual "to what do I owe the pleasure" spiel on them, but they'd heard it all before.

"Jim, you'd flatter Mammy Yokum," Margo responded, "but I love it anyway. The girls just asked for a few minutes of our time to present an idea or two."

"Very well, I'm always ready for new and innovative ideas," he said as he stared directly at Carol. She could almost believe he had x-ray vision. He pulled out a chair for her, but she remained standing.

"Colonel, I don't want to waste any of your valuable time," she said, knowing that he'd be delighted if she spent the entire day in his office. "Frankly, it's obvious to me that our efforts to get a list of American prisoners from the North Vietnamese over the past few months have been somewhat less than successful."

"You can say that again," muttered Charlie, under her breath. Margo gave her a brief and frigid glance.

"We believe we should shift our focus to mounting a public awareness campaign that would inform not only the American people but other nations about North Vietnam's inexcusable failure to comply with the terms of the Geneva Convention. Let's bring the pressure of the entire world down on them to acknowledge our troops as prisoners of war instead of war criminals, give all POWs proper treatment, and let the Red Cross see if they're being treated humanely. I suspect they're not."

"Well, now Carol," began Colonel Hurd, steepling his fingers in front of his face.

"And most important of all," she persisted, "they should provide a full and complete list of prisoners. We can hit the rubber chicken circuit, give speeches, get people angry, call them to action. We should give media interviews. You don't think there's human interest in a bunch of lonely American wives who are trying to get along and raise their children while they're worried sick about their husbands? We can send our members to the countries that have relations with North Vietnam and ask them to help. We all know how badly public opinion has turned against the war and we know what a powerful force it is. But we can make it work for us. We have to start now."

She stopped and sat down, looking from Margo's face to the Colonel's. They were both obviously stunned by the force of her emotion. Neither one spoke for several seconds.

"Well, Mrs. Cody, I—" the Colonel began, but Charlie wasted no time.

"We've developed a detailed media and public relations campaign," she said, placing two copies on the table. She and Carol had rented an electric typewriter and spent the last two days writing, rewriting, and making it letter perfect. It was sixteen pages long, complete in every detail and handsomely bound in folders they'd bought from an office supply store. They'd wanted it to look official and impressive, and it did.

Colonel Hurd picked it up they way you'd pick up a rotten banana. He leafed through it trying his hardest to look interested.

"Well, there's obviously quite a bit here," he said in the most considered tone he could summon. "We'll need some time to go over it. Certainly very impressive. Not exactly what the government policy has been, of course …"

Carol wanted to choke him. "The government policy, if there is one, isn't working. This will."

"I'd estimate it will take Major Dorsey, Mrs. Stone and me a couple of weeks to get on top of this before we can sit down with you to hammer out the details. Would it be possible for you to return in, say two or three weeks, to do the detail work?"

Charlie and Carol were astounded. They never expected him to roll over that easily.

"Yes, of course," Carol stammered. Hurd smiled and turned to Margo Stone.

"Can your organization cover their expenses for another trip?"

"Yes, Colonel. I'm sure something can be worked out for such an exciting opportunity," Margo said.

Her polite but patronizing tone didn't escape Carol's notice. *Bitch*, she thought. Margo smiled.

"Well then," said the Colonel, "we'll adjourn this meeting until we're ready to proceed with the details in a couple of weeks. My office will make the appropriate arrangements with Mrs. Stone." He stood up, treated Charlie and Carol to warm handshakes, smiles, and overly polite goodbye noises, and guided them to the door, his hand lingering a few seconds too long on Carol's upper arm.

The second the door closed, he turned toward Margo and pounced.

"How *dare* you let these women into my office!" He picked up Carol's carefully bound presentation and threw it across the room. "Do you have any idea how dangerous those two bitches can be? You're the one who's supposed to be controlling crap like this. Kissinger's negotiating his ass off in Paris, and if this issue hits the front pages the goddamn President himself will hang me out to dry. Now, we can bring them back in a couple weeks for show, but you've got to squash these two, and right now. Isn't that why we secretly give your outfit so much money?"

Margo stood up to the tirade fairly well. She was used to his temper. She picked the presentation up off the floor and rifled through the pages.

"They do seem to know quite a bit. I'd like to know where they're getting all this information."

"So would I."

Margo stared at the pages for a second, reading more carefully.

"Okay, Jim, here's what we'll do. You can work from your end to see if anybody in your outfit is leaking. I'm in good shape to get friendly with them, do my little 'just between us girls' act and see what I can find out from my end. I can put a stop to this in a hurry, but let me do it my way. There's nothing they can do to hurt us."

∽∾

6

Congratulations, You Just Volunteered ... For Laos

Commanding General's Office
7th Air Force Headquarters, Saigon
November 8, 1971

Across the hall from the security checkpoint and the Tactical Air Combat Center, better known as Blue Chip, was a secure room drably furnished with a typical conference room table and ten typical executive chairs. The room was guarded around the clock by Air Force Air Police.

Around the table were General Coroneos, the Commanding General of the 7th, his Vice Commander General Hamilton, plus Generals Mattix and Geiger. Behind them, seated along the wall, were their aides, Captain Mansen, Colonel Herbert, and five field grade Air Force officers, each with briefcases full of information and charts, ready to start the briefing of one bewildered and extremely tired Army Captain who Mansen had flown in from the field.

After the introductions and a brief long-time-no-see greeting from General Mattix, Roman was seated with his back toward the aides, scanning the array of heavy brass seated across from him. Tentatively, he folded his hands on the table, not sure whether military protocol specified that they should be in his lap, or where. He'd never been in front of a four-star general, much less four generals at one time. Crazily he wondered whether one four-star general was worth four one-star generals or how did that whole thing work? He took a few deep breaths. He was very tired.

Coroneos was silent, working his way deliberately through Roman's DA 201 personnel file page by page, examining the 10-year career of Daniel James Roman, serial number 05429934.

He reached up, took off his glasses and looked over at Roman. "I see you're on the promotion list for major. Congratulations. I've read your 201 file. You've had a lot of command time and not much staff time. Why is that, Captain? I'd like to know a bit more about your staff experience."

"Well, sir, I've been a battalion S-2 or Intelligence Officer, then an S-3 Operations Officer with the Hawk Battalion, also a Brigade Level Operational Readiness Evaluator Team Chief in Korea and Germany, and I've even had some time as an Assistant Adjutant. Not a lot of staff time, but some."

"This is your second tour, right?"

"Yes, sir, I was here three years ago."

"Says here you made the big Tet in '68."

"Yes, sir."

"You've commanded four Hawk Missile batteries, one group aviation detachment, and were an aviation platoon leader in the 7th of the 1st Air Calvary Squadron over here. Most captains your age don't get that much command time. Doesn't the Army rotate people in and out of command slots?"

"I think I just got lucky, sir. My commanders often put me in charge of ... let's say, the more ... challenging units."

"So, you clean up problem units. That right?" Coroneos put his glasses back on and looked over the rims. Roman shifted in his seat. "I get the feeling you may not get along so well with staff officers."

"I get along with most of them, sir. Except the ones who don't do their job or let their egos get in the way of their job to support the troops in the field. Then there's the ones with bad attitudes and the ones ..."

"I get the idea, Captain." Coroneos held up his hand. He glanced over at General Mattix. "Well, at least he's honest about it." He turned back to Roman.

"Captain, have you ever heard of project Bright Light?"

"I think so, sir. It has something to do with rescuing prisoners of war."

"That's correct. It's the code name for a unit organized a couple of years ago by Heinie Aderholt. It was a combination of Air Force Air Commandos and Army Special Operations people out of Vietnam. How about the Green Hornets—ever heard of them?"

"I guess everybody has."

"That's the problem. Everybody knows who they are ... all the way up to the White House. They're always being watched and the higher-ups have put some pretty strict limits on the kind of missions they can take on. They've proposed a lot of missions to rescue our boys across the border but they keep getting delayed or cancelled." He tapped his pencil on the table. "Price of fame, I suppose."

"Then there's the goddamn Rules of Engagement," Coroneos continued. "I'm absolutely convinced the NVA wrote them for us. You know why it takes two pilots to operate an F-4?"

"Uh, no sir." Please, Roman thought, please tell me what's going on here.

"One to fly the airplane and the other to carry the briefcase full of Rules of Engagement! Captain, here's the situation. This war is a political experiment conducted by the insane and the inept."

Roman sat back in his chair. He'd never heard a high ranking officer openly criticize command policy. But General Coroneos was just getting warmed up. He soliloquized for several minutes outlining the problems the 7th was facing, all of which directly affected Roman and the new operation. When he slammed his fist down on the table, Roman jerked up straight.

"The trucks going south on the Trail look like the Pentagon at five o'clock!"

There was a polite cough from Colonel Herbert. It usually helped get the General back on track.

"Sorry, son. I just don't like losing men and I don't like losing this damned war. Anyway, here's the point. The troop levels are being drawn down which means we don't have a lot of people going out in the bush hunting for our downed airmen and soldiers. We know they're out there. We just don't know exactly where." The General abruptly shifted gears. "Mattix here tells me you're some sort of a Heinie Aderholt." Roman almost couldn't answer. Aderholt's name was a legend in Special Operations.

"Beg your pardon, sir. I'm not even worthy to carry that man's briefcase."

"Doesn't matter. He's not available anyway, and even if he were, he attracts too damned much attention from the wrong people. Look, son, this awful war's almost over and we're going to lose it. Bright Light is pretty much out of business, we can't go into Laos or Cambodia without written permission from two dozen agencies and the White House janitor. It's a mess. The enemy knows all this and that's why they keep our boys over there. Even if we had a green light, we don't have ground forces available. The only people really doing anything about the POWs are the diplomats and we all know what they're worth."

"I've still got air crews down in Laos and more going down all the time. Washington's no help because Kissinger doesn't want any rescue missions gone wrong to interfere with his negotiations in Paris. I'm sure he's got a good heart and means well, but the POWs in North Vietnam are at the top of his negotiating list. They guys in Laos are being forgotten. Every time we've mounted a raid to get some of our boys out of Laos, somebody shuts us down with the comment, 'we're negotiating.' Well, I'm tired of negotiations. My hands are tied and I don't know what to do ... at least I didn't, until recently. Captain Mansen, will you read that directive to Captain Roman?"

Mansen pulled out a thin folder, laid it on the table and cleared his throat. The directive was from Ambassador Godley in Laos. Mercifully, Mansen summarized the several pages of turgid diplomatic prose into a few sentences. The Special Operations Group of MACV was standing down. However, certain missions called "crash site evaluations" were still authorized as long as they didn't result in the recovery of personnel and provided there would be no hostile contact and no risk of casualties. Coroneos couldn't suppress a sarcastic chuckle. Mansen looked up from the paper, directly at Roman.

"Basically, the idea is to study crash sites and develop information to be used in future escape and evasion training. That's it, sir."

Coroneos leaned his bulk back in his chair, peeled his glasses off his face, and stared past Roman at the opposite wall. "We figure there are at least 200, maybe as many as 350, of our boys still in Laos in the hands of the enemy. Somebody put the number at 228, but that's still a guess. These guys are mistreated and tortured and abused, but that happens in every war. Problem is the powers that be are writing them off as expendable. But that directive from Godley gave us an opportunity. Along with my buddy General Cannon over at the 1st Aviation Brigade, and a couple of Army and Marine general officers whom I could trust, we formed a crash site reconnaissance and evaluation team, just like the directive says. Al?"

General Mattix sat up straight, leaned forward and stared at Roman. *Here it comes.*

"Dan, I recommended you for this job, so the General is letting me tell you the good part because of the history we have together. Officially, the unit is named U.S. Army Aviation Tactical Recon Team - Lima. The Air Force boys have nicknamed it Grunt Air. Understand that this is Top Secret/Sensitive Information. If any of this comes out, a lot of very senior officers—me, for example, and the rest of the officers at this table—will probably wind up as guests of the US military at Leavenworth. You get my drift?"

Roman nodded. General Mattix plunged ahead.

"If you can keep a secret and want to help those poor bastards in the cages, you can volunteer for this operation right now. It's over the border, it's dangerous, and if you get shot down or captured, you're screwed. Did I make this sound attractive enough for you?"

"General, I volunteered as soon as I found out you were involved. I told you back in South America that if you ever needed me, I'd be there."

"Thank you, Captain," said General Coroneos. "We have a company-size Aviation Intelligence Unit up at Udorn and a small Recon force that looks for the camps and prisoners. It's completely independent and it's under the direct control of General Mattix. You answer directly to him. He writes your Officer's Efficiency Report, General Hamilton endorses it, and I review it. As long as we can stay out of the stockade."

"Our 'job' is to locate, identify and recover all U.S. and Allied prisoners of war," said Mattix. "When time permits, we actually go to crash sites to pick up information about the downed pilots, just like the directive explained. Since August '71, we've gotten organized, equipped, and we've established a good cover story up at Udorn. The original commander for the unit was Lieutenant Colonel Whaley. He's been reassigned to Headquarters MACV with a great Officer Efficiency Report. Unfortunately, as it turns out, he's just not the man for this job. But we think you are."

"Excuse me, sir," said Roman.

"You'll remember his executive officer, Major Fitzmorris, from when you were in the Delta. Since he outranks you, we're pulling him in here to Blue

Chip. He'll be your direct communication with Headquarters on a day-to-day basis. We'll give you all the support you need but you absolutely cannot blow your cover."

Coroneos looked once again at Mattix, who sat up even straighter and put a formal tone in his voice.

"Captain Roman, your mission is to assume command of Grunt Air. You will locate, identify, and recover all U.S. and allied prisoners of war in Northern Laos and not get caught doing it. Bring them home, Dan. Do it any way you see fit, but bring them home."

Roman responded in an equally formal manner.

"General Coroneos. If we can find them, we'll bring them home. If we're ever compromised or discovered, I understand that you will hold me personally responsible for not following the Ambassador's published guidelines. Obviously I would have exceeded my authority entirely on my own and would be held responsible for the unfortunate breach of your directions." He paused for a second. "All I ask is one thing. No staff officers on my court-martial board."

The assembled brass burst into laughter.

"Let's hope that never happens," said General Coroneos, pushing himself up to his feet. He held out his hand across the dull brown table. "Good luck, son. You'll surely need it."

"Very well," General Mattix said, "let's get down to details."

For the next hour and a half, the exhausted Roman listened to the details of the unit he was to command ... an Army captain replacing an Air Force lieutenant colonel. He wondered what kind of greeting he would get. He was startled at the size of the unit. According to Mattix, Grunt Air consisted of 21 officers, 41 enlisted and 9 foreign nationals. They all had at least one combat tour in Vietnam and Intelligence experience as well. There were even some officers who Roman knew from his previous assignments, and that made him a little more comfortable.

Of course there were problems, and Mattix wasted no time in detailing them. Grunt Air was authorized eight Hueys for their "crash site assessment" mission but had only six, which had been stolen from the Army. Two were on order and would be delivered when Bell had finished the refurbishing. The unit's maintenance and operations officers had been killed the previous week trying to extract a reconnaissance team when their Huey slammed into a fog-covered hilltop, which have a habit of appearing out of nowhere in Laos. Laos is mountainous and littered with limestone karsts that stick out of nowhere in the area. They had claimed many an aircraft over the years.

One more problem—a big one called Lieutenant Colonel Sweeney, the head of Supply and Logistics. A stickler for the rule book, he routinely denies all equipment requests that are not completely and properly filled out. Roman rolled his eyes. He knew all about supply officers.

As an aside, Mattix confided, "There's some kind of situation there," he said. "Something between Sweeney and the Grunt Air supply officer, a guy named Gedeon. I'm not sure Sweeney is completely on our side. You'll have to deal with it."

Mattix went on, filling Roman in on the backgrounds of most of the important Grunt Air personnel. As tired as he was, Roman tried to take it all in, then decided he'd just have to deal with it when he got there.

"I have a question, sir," said Roman. "You said there are 21 officers, all these enlisted men, reconnaissance teams, a ton of equipment. How have you kept this secret for so long?"

"First of all, everybody in the unit is hand picked. Nobody blabs. Then there's a kid named Duncan. They call him Mr. Touchdown. He prepares the crash site reports that go up the line to support the illusion of the official mission. He goes out when there's no other mission scheduled and takes a few quick photographs of old crash sites, rewrites the old reports and throws in new pictures and a bunch of new bullshit. Keeps the boys in Washington very happy. In fact, we get a lot of compliments on his work. No real value in what he's doing, and it's all shit, but it makes the unit look like it's really doing the job. He's key to our cover story."

Mattix went on, telling Roman about the overall commander at Udorn, a Major General Dodge, who was in the dark and had to stay that way. He was a friend of a previous Commanding General who was at odds with Coroneos. There was the base commander, Colonel "Jumping Jack" Odom, also not cleared for this very sensitive knowledge.

As Mattix spoke, Roman found himself answering his own question about how Grunt Air managed to keep itself secret. The unit was assigned to ramp space at the far end of the Air America ramp, next to the puke ditch. They were getting the worst of everything since they were Army personnel on an Air Force base. Whether it was supplies, maintenance, support, Grunt Air was at the ass end.

"I don't need an American body count up there, Dan," said Mattix. "No screwing over staff officers. No body count. And you will not leave some stupid Air Force pilot in a Laotian LZ as a joke. It may not seem like it, but we're on the same side."

"Yes, sir."

"There are Air America and Air Force personnel all around and they're all nosy. Watch out for Eastwood, the Air America Operations Officer, and Caldwell, the CIA station chief. They're big buddies and they're suspicious. They tell me there's a control tower officer who shows an unhealthy interest in where those Grunt Air Hueys take off to. If he gives you any trouble, let me know. I have a spot for him."

"Someplace chilly?"

"You do know me pretty well, Dan."

One by one, the staff officers played their parts in Roman's intensive briefing. He found out that the unit stages its operations out of a place called Long Tieng (LS 20A), also known as "Spook Haven" if it was known at all, because it was operated by the CIA. A base that "didn't exist," Long Tieng was also the home of General Vang Pao, the commander of the Laotian troops who worked with the Americans. There was an Air Force Operations Coordinator at 20A named Major Weir, another person to watch out for. "Good man," said Mattix, "but he'll try to trick you into saying something by letting on he already knows the score, but he doesn't. Never leaves the base. Just stays up there like a hermit."

Captain Mansen reviewed operations procedures, including cautions like refueling away from the main parking area and staying away from the Air Operations Center and its café, peopled by Air America pilots and support personnel. Fortunately, Air America and the Ravens had their own secrets to hide and generally avoided contact with the Grunt Air "survey crews."

Colonel Herbert reviewed other security and secret-keeping details, like the necessity of being back at Udorn by the end of the day because there was no reason for a crash site survey operation to be out overnight in Laos.

General Geiger took over, and gestured to one of his aides, who positioned himself next to a huge map of Southeast Asia on the opposite wall. Major General Francis W. Geiger, better known simply as Frank, was an honor graduate at West Point who decided to take an Air Force commission and go into the high altitude Air Reconnaissance assignments and, later, into the Intelligence field. His straight black hair constantly fell down across his forehead, especially when he stalked the hallways of Blue Chip, walking with his characteristic hunched over gait. A native of New Jersey and the son of a Civil Service employee, he was a quiet man, bordering on overweight by Air Force standards, wearing uniforms that always had a rumpled, slept-in look. He was a fingernail-chewer with a quick wit and methodical mind. Nobody disturbed him when he paced the hallways because they knew the analytical engine was in high gear, getting into his enemy's mind and taking actions to trick him into field operations that would result in disaster. Some thought he did this as much for fun as for a military strategy. He'd had countless offers from major corporations, security firms, think tanks and, of course, the Central Intelligence Agency, to come work for them after retirement. Frank thought this was fine and would eventually get around to considering which one to accept, but not now. Not for a long time in the future, he hoped.

Compared to previous wars, Intelligence gathering in Southeast Asia was a massive operation. The National Security Agency was the overall coordinator of all electronic activities on foreign sources, referred to as Signal Intelligence, or SIGINT, which was analyzed and distributed as Communications Intelligence, or COMINT. The mainstay of SIGINT collection methods was special aircraft used as collection platforms, such as the Army P2V and RU21A Fullerbrush aircraft, the Air Force EC-135 Combat Apple, the EC-130 Comfy Gator, and the very sophisticated U-2 Olympic Torch. On the ground, intercept operations like Songbird focused on all electronic communications regarding prisoners of war and downed airmen.

Geiger cued the Major who quickly looked over the map, cleared his throat, picked up a pointer, and started to speak. Roman, who had already soaked up massive amounts of information, tried his best to concentrate.

Basically, the Major pointed out Grunt Air's prime areas of responsibility: the very central and eastern part of Northern Laos, where the CIA believed over 200 POW camps were located, 30 or so of which were active on a regular basis.

He reviewed some of the reports received from villagers who wanted to sell information for money, and showed Roman the cluster of camps around the Plain of Jars, which were the main holding areas for POWS on their way to the north.

"Prisoners considered especially important to the NVA, or the Russians, are transferred to the main camps next to the Pathet Lao and NVA headquarters in Sam Neua. Prisoners are also held in the cave complex at Ban Nakay Neua and the cave at Ban Na Eune, just east of Sam Neua. We've had sightings at camps at Ban Puem, Muong Soui, Muong Liet, and Nong Het. There are probably fourteen or fifteen 're-education camps' in the area as well, but they're for criminals and political prisoners. We don't think there are any Americans there."

There were many more camps, the Major said, and many more American prisoners that were unaccounted for. Nobody really knew how many.

The big news, and the real revelation to Roman, concerned a camp called the Big Casino. Most of the smaller camps were guarded by police or by soldiers too old to fight. But the Big Casino was much more modern, with concrete cells, solid walls, double barbed wire fences, and was located well to the rear, away from any front lines.

"Unfortunately," said the Major, "it's a little too far for your Hueys to reach, and they know it. Someday, I would just love to bust it to show them we can do it." Geiger heaved his bulk forward in his seat and stared at Roman.

"I don't have to describe the treatment our boys are getting. It's abominable. Besides the unhealthy living conditions, there's the torture. In all fairness, however, I'm not sure our interrogation methods are any better. We do provide better living conditions for them, though."

The Major pointed out landing sites and landing strips operated by Air America in Laos, where Grunt Air helicopters could get fuel. The main one was at Long Tieng, known as Lima Site Two Zero Alpha. They also used several other designators for it just to keep things confusing. He informed Roman that he would have access to all Intelligence information, including radio intercepts.

"With Bright Light and the Green Hornets all but shut down, there's not much coming out of southern Laos and Cambodia. We've just about stopped all activities down there."

Roman interrupted the Major and said, "Sir, would you have any objection if I set up an unofficial contact with a couple of spooks working in the Dak To and Nui Ba Dinh area? They won't be told about our mission, just the kind of info I'll need."

Geiger looked surprised. "I'm not familiar with any major Intel Ops in these areas. Who are they?"

"The Kingfish out of Dak To is running Recon along the Ho Chi Minh Trail along with a Vietnamese interrogator known as the Dragon Lady. Down at Nui Ba Dinh there's the Fiddler. They're both junior captains, but good at what they do."

"How do you know about these people?" Geiger asked, then added, "Never mind. That's your business. Besides, I've heard about the Dragon Lady and her spike heels. Okay, if you really trust them and need them, you can use them as long as you keep the secret."

The Major had more to say, about an expected NVA dry season offensive and the buildup that U-2 flyovers had detected around Sam Neua and Muong Soui. It was going to be big, and Roman wouldn't have much time to get the job done.

"We estimate over 6,400 NVA regulars, including artillery, with a dozen 130mm long range field guns. These are strong, dedicated troops that Vang Pao's boys are just not going to be able to fight off."

There was more, much more. The 312th Division, with the 141st and 165th Regiments attached, was part of the movement along with the notorious 335th Independent Regiment. There were unconfirmed reports that the 19th, 27th, and 41st DAC Cong Battalions were moving in to the area west of Muong Soui toward Sam Neua. The arrival of the 226th Regiment of the 365th Anti-Aircraft Division was another concern because they would station Surface to Air Missiles along Route 6 and Route 65. Their anti-aircraft guns were scattered everywhere, including 32mm and 23mm weapons, and the ever-present 12.7 anti-aircraft guns on every hillside.

More worries—the 866th Independent Regiment, scattered around the Plain of Jars and southward toward Muong Pot. Control of Skyline Ridge and the pass going from the staging area at Long Tieng to Sam Thong was always in question. Sappers sneaking into the area were always a threat. Gun emplacements high on the hills would fire downward on low-flying choppers navigating through the pass.

"Don't believe what you read about the NVA soldiers. They're very smart, well-trained, and have excellent leadership. The little buggers actually hit Vang Pao's house at Long Tieng with a B-40 around last February. No injuries other than his pride, but I can assure you, there was hell to pay for that security breach."

General Mattix said, "One other thing. There's a CIA Deputy Station Chief here in Saigon named John Henry Holbrook. He doesn't know your mission, but he'll want all your raw Intelligence. That's okay, but just be careful not to let him know what the mission is. He's a real horse's ass. He demands everything and gives you back nothing useful. I can't stand the son of a bitch. We give him good raw Intelligence and we get back a bunch of bullshit in the

CIA Intelligence summary, with none of our own hard info in the report. He says it's because we give him flawed information. Horseshit.

"Well, it's late," Mattix said, standing up. *You can say that again*, thought Roman. "Let's break this up so you can get to Udorn. We've got a C-47 waiting for you. Some of the Grunt Air crew flew down so they could fill you in on the way back. You've got a team that's in contact and evading the enemy, and trying to make it to an alternate pickup point. Any questions or requests?"

"Actually, sir, I would request the assignment of Captain Thomas Ryker and Captain Jan Toothman to Grunt Air. They were with me in the Delta and I can see I'll need them. Ryker is Aviation Maintenance and Tooth-man is Operations. I don't need an XO. Ryker can handle that for me as well as maintenance."

"All right. You've got it. Captain Mansen here had already figured that you'd be asking for them."

"Are there any last questions or requests, Captain?"

"Yes, sir. A blindfold and a cigarette."

∞◦∞

7

We're Not In Kansas Anymore

Commanding General's Office
7th Air Force Headquarters, Saigon
November 8, 1971

Roman, Mansen and General Mattix left Blue Chip, passing the armed guard outside. The tactical nerve center had been attacked by Vietcong on at least two occasions.

In another wing of the building, Mattix led them to a ready room. The officers seated inside immediately jumped to their feet when the General walked in.

"Captain Roman," General Mattix said, "let me introduce you to Archangel himself, Chief Alberts. Major Fitzmorris, Captain Best and Chief Abeel, I think you already know."

Chief Warrant Officer 4, Douglas Stanton Alberts, was young for a CW4. Heavy set and slightly over 5'10", he had sandy brown hair and eyes to match. While in school back in Oklahoma, he always appeared to be bored because he was. Even though he always tested several levels above his assigned grade, his teachers wouldn't let him skip. He wanted to fly so desperately that he quit college after three years and entered the Army flight training program because only the Army would let you fly without a college degree. He racked up more than a few exceptional job performance ratings, became a talented pilot, earned two promotions and got himself recruited by the Intelligence community. After C-47 training, he was assigned to flying radio intercept duty over Cuba, Haiti and the Dominican Republic just before the Cuban missile crisis. He flew the OV1 Mohawk reconnaissance aircraft for a time, then went to Phu Bai, South Vietnam, again impressing his superiors with his perform-ance under fire. Between his first and second tours in Vietnam, he spent 13 months with the Korean Military Assistance Group (KMAG) Intelligence section. Later, Roman would find out that Alberts was on his third tour in

Vietnam. He had been flying reconnaissance missions across the border into Laos and Cambodia when his CO "volunteered" him for Grunt Air in hopes that the assignment would be less dangerous and would save him from himself.

"He was afraid I'd kind of got out of touch with myself," Alberts would tell Roman later on. "I used to schedule myself for all the really nasty missions, so everybody thought I had some kind of death wish. Wasn't true. I knew what the risks were and I knew that what I was doing was important."

As Archangel, he flew an aging but dependable C-47 at 10,000 feet above the danger, controlling the aircraft and recon teams in Laos. His every command had life-and-death consequences, and he knew it.

"You guys are going to have to take care of Roman," Mattix said. "He's a little overloaded after that briefing."

"I'll take care of him, all right," said Best. "The way he took care of me in college."

Glances shifted to Roman, then back to Best. "I'd like to hear that story," said Mattix.

"No, you wouldn't, General," Best said sheepishly.

Captain Jackson "Jake" Cornwall Best III had left the Cheese State for the somewhat warmer climate of Oklahoma after high school. Although he was bright in class, he wasn't the most worldly boy you'd ever meet. Not much for the school social life, he found more pleasure in solitary pursuits, and loved to hunt, fish and cross country ski alone.

His shyness was a disappointment to the girls because, by the time he left for college, he was 6'6" with blonde hair and deep blue eyes. It was a disappointment for him, too, because he could never bring himself to accept the invitations, no matter how boldly stated, to lose his virginity. Even so, he managed to get himself accepted to the most degenerate party fraternity on campus, which is where he first met Dan Roman, who, incidentally, led the fraternity in sexual home runs and the fewest strikeouts.

Once he became comfortable around Dan and his friend Cort Fraley, he admitted that he just couldn't seem to get himself laid. It was all Roman needed to hear.

One of the fraternity's favorite party guests was a young lady named Mary Ann, who, much like Will Rogers, never met a man she didn't like. Roman arranged a date, but he briefed Mary Ann first.

When Best picked up Mary Ann on the agreed-upon evening, he had to white-knuckle the steering wheel to keep from shaking. They drove to an oil field miles from the campus and Jake, seeing the words "sure thing" swimming before his eyes, sneaked his arm up along the seat back and slid his hips closer to hers. All was quiet.

Suddenly, out of the underbrush, a screaming voice splits the night.

"You son of a bitch, I'll teach you to screw my wife." It was Fraley, but his voice was disguised. Exactly on cue, Roman fired both barrels of a twelve gauge shotgun over the top of the car from right behind the trunk. Barely opening the door, Best soared out of the car and bolted into the darkness, scrambling through the thick scrub brush and thorny vines. He jumped over a five-foot high barbed wire fence like it was a low hurdle at a track meet and disappeared into the night. Fraley and Roman called for him to come back until they both lost their voices, but he never did. He ran the two miles back to the fraternity house through brush, brambles, undergrowth and who knows what else. When he dragged himself up the front stairs of the house, his clothes were in ribbons, he was bleeding from a mass of scratches, and he demanded Scotch.

A few shots later, Roman and Fraley drove up and filled him in on the little joke. He wasn't amused, stalked out of the house and disappeared completely until late the next day. When he returned, it was obvious that he had changed. Whatever emotional transformation took place, it allowed Jake Best to take his rightful place in the party animal pantheon, and he never had a problem around women again.

After graduation, Best joined the Marines, which was the same as volunteering for Vietnam. He pulled duty with the Force Recon Team at DaNang, and accomplished some things behind enemy lines that became the standard for other recon teams. He earned two Bronze Stars, one Silver Star and the Navy Cross for heroism. When Roman's path crossed his for the second time in their lives, he was the commander of the Recon platoon for Grunt Air, and Dan was glad of it.

"Well, Jake, it looks like you're still running through the underbrush," Roman chortled.

"This ain't Oklahoma and I'm not a virgin," Best responded.

"Okay," said Mattix. "You need to get this guy up to Udorn right now. Dan, you're getting another briefing on the flight, so you'd better get in the air."

"Let me run to the PX first," Roman said. "I've got to pick up some stuff since most of my gear was destroyed in a mortar attack. I also need to pick up some lady's makeup."

"Some what?" Best said.

"It's hard to explain."

The group moved toward the door heading to the flight line to preflight the C-47, but just as they turned the corner, Roman collided with a tall thin man with slightly graying hair.

"Ooops … sorry," said John Henry Holbrook. "I just wanted to meet the new ringleader of Grunt Air before he charges off to the life of luxury."

Roman looked at the man through narrowed eyes, then over at Alberts. "Who's this?"

"This," said the Chief, "is John Henry Holbrook, the CIA Deputy Chief of Station here in Saigon."

"I'm the man you must ultimately satisfy," Holbrook said ungraciously. Roman just stared at him, thinking, Jesus, I've had this job for 20 minutes and this guy knows all about it. How does that happen?

"It's nice to meet you, Mr. Holbrook," said Roman, shaking his hand, and holding on. "An unidentified civilian who tells me he's replacing a Major General in my chain of command."

Holbrook tried to get loose from the grip but Roman wouldn't give him his hand back.

"I'm sorry that General Mattix here was under the impression he had command authority over me. Certainly was a mistake on his part." Holbrook squirmed in Roman's now painful grip.

"For the record, sir, I work for the General and I don't see your name anywhere on the Table of Organization. He's the only one I need to keep happy. Are we clear?"

Holbrook managed to wriggle his hand free. He took a step back, startled at Roman's barely concealed anger, and addressed himself to the General.

"Excuse me, General, I meant no offense. Just wanted to introduce myself …"

"No problem, Mr. Holbrook. I took no offense." Mattix was used to Holbrook's officiousness and overwhelming self-importance, but it had caught Roman very much by surprise.

"Look, Captain Roman, what your unit is doing out there is important, not so much for the war but for the future of our air crews. You might even get lucky and find an important piece of information that could lead to existing POWs. It's important that you send all of your raw intelligence up through channels to us so the professionals can put the pieces together and form a clear picture of the entire situation. Your unit has been productive so far, and some of the Intel they've sent up has led us to at least three possible POW camps. We're grateful for that. Grunt Air is making an outstanding contribution." Holbrook was trying as hard as he could to regain the ground he'd lost in the confrontation, trying very hard to keep the customary patronizing tone out of his voice.

Roman and the group moved away from the building. Holbrook hurried to keep up.

"That's good to know, Mr. Holbrook. But what do we get from you in return? Our crews are heading into Indian country every day, putting their lives on the line, and we need to know what's going on before we get out there. I hear that the crash sites are cold and they're not supposed to be dangerous, but Laos is still Laos."

In spite of himself, Holbrook stiffened. "Captain, we analyze every bit of data we receive. The Intelligence summaries we send to units like yours give you all the information we think is important for you to know. We're on the same team, right? We just want to help."

Roman reflected for a second on the phrase, "the information we feel is important for you to know," because, obviously, there was other Intelligence that wasn't reaching them if civilians like Holbrook thought it wasn't important. How could they judge what would be important to a recon team spending the night in the jungle behind enemy lines?

"First, Mr. Holbrook," said Roman, "this is not my first tour over here. Second, I'm a graduate of your CIA "Charm School," and I know the system. Third, I know that hard intelligence gets sent up by our units and what comes back is watered-down bullshit that has no value except maybe at the latrine."

"Now wait a minute, Captain. There's no way you can possibly understand the big picture the way we do." The patronizing tone crept back into Holbrook's voice.

"Thank you, Mr. Holbrook," interrupted General Mattix. "The Captain has a flight to catch. After he buys his makeup."

Holbrook peered at Roman. Makeup? He'd let it pass this time. He excused himself and stopped, letting the group move past him while massaging his bruised hand.

"Give me a minute with Dan," said Mattix to the group. Alberts and the rest headed off to the flight line, leaving Roman and Mattix alone on the tarmac outside the building.

"I told General Geiger we have the right man for the job," said the General.

"Thank you, sir."

"Now you see what we told you in the briefing about the whole CIA situation. You know the mushroom treatment? Keep them in the dark and feed them bullshit. Good luck, Dan."

Roman saluted, hurried to the PX to buy the personal items he'd lost in the attack, along with the cosmetics he needed, and then made his way to the base transit parking area.

A very old C-47, possibly a veteran of the Berlin airlift, squatted on the ramp. It was painted black, olive drab green and gray with a few barely visible markings. Alberts walked around from the other side of the aircraft, looked it over and said, "She's older than any of us, sir, but we always get a round trip out of her."

"That's good enough for me," said Roman, handing the Crew Chief his duffel and the bags he'd brought from the PX. "Let's kick the tire and light the fire."

Affixed to the side of the aircraft was a small metal rack that normally held a metal placard identifying the rank of the general officer on board.

"This is going to look great with captain's bars in it," Alberts said sarcastically.

"You can paint CW4 bars in it, Chief."

"Maybe later." Alberts looked at Roman, turning the remark over in his mind. He liked his new CO's healthy disrespect for rank. This Army Captain was replacing an Air Force Lieutenant Colonel as commander of Grunt Air. Maybe it would be okay, after all.

"You can do it tomorrow, Chief," Roman said as he climbed the stairs. "It's your aircraft."

Once they'd been cleared and were in the air, Best and Abeel pulled a couple of mail pouches and boxes over to where Roman was sitting on the web jumpseats.

"Dan, are you really ready for this?" Best asked. "You look beat, and this is a tough mission for a senior officer, much less a captain. Nothing against your ability or your qualifications, okay? Just a fact."

"Jake, if I had the slightest question, I would have said no. If the brass had any doubts, Mattix wouldn't have pulled me in to this."

"That's another question," said Abeel, "if you don't mind my asking. How do you know Mattix? And why did he pick you?"

"We go way back to 1965 in Colombia. He was just a colonel then, on his way up like a rocket. After I got my commercial multi-engine license, I got hired as a civilian contract pilot and sent down there. When he couldn't get certain things done officially, I did them. Hope I can do the same now."

"So, that's how you got the job instead of Colonel Herbert."

"You mean General Coroneos' senior aide?"

"Yep," said Abeel. "He's a good pilot with Military Intelligence background. Knows the mission, too."

"Sorry, but I'm what you got," said Roman, leaning back into the dubious comfort of the web jumpseat. "Now, since we have a little time, why don't you tell me what I'm in for? I can't back out now. We're at eight thousand feet."

Best and Abeel talked nonstop for the whole flight to Udorn. Roman's head ached. Too much information. Too many things to do. And Best had spent most of the time talking about nothing but problems. Aircraft down for maintenance. Requisitions for material and supplies that never got filled. Men lost in combat and crashes. Roman started to think that everyone had been right. Herbert would have been a better fit for the job.

Flying wasn't the problem. Roman knew how to fly. But all these administrative and logistical issues made him dizzy. It was almost like the vertigo you feel when you fly in fog and can't see the horizon. You literally don't know which end is up. How to get a handle on the endless litany of problems Best and Abeel had poured out to him? Everything he'd heard about Lieutenant Colonel Whaley said he was a damn good man. Maybe too organized and too bureaucratic, but a good man. Mattix was making Roman fill a very big pair of shoes.

Roman closed his eyes and listened to the drone of the C-47's two huge engines. Almost everyone who pursues a military career has his own personal heroes, people whose achievements they want to emulate. For Roman, it was Heinie Aderholt, who they had mentioned in the briefing a few hours before. He'd come to Vietnam in the early sixties with no infrastructure, no Lima sites to work out of, no effective Forward Area Controllers, endless political and petty bullshit from above, and all of it shrouded in secrecy. He and General Secord got the job done anyway. *I'm no Aderholt*, he thought. *I'm in way over my head, but this isn't the first time.*

He opened his eyes, stood up, stretched, and made his way up to the cockpit, squeezing between the two radiomen monitoring the air waves on either side of the aisle.

He stuck his head in the cockpit and asked CW4 Alberts, "Archangel, how long to Udorn?"

"Well, Captain, the winds are starting to die down so we should be there in about 55 mikes."

Archangel introduced his copilot, CW2 Mike Jenner, and then told Jenner to go back and get a cup of coffee. Jenner got up clumsily and slid past Roman.

Alberts pointed to the copilot seat and said, "Welcome to the front office."

Roman squirmed into the seat and put on a safety belt. The guys who flew these things in World War II must have been a lot shorter.

"So, Captain. You feeling like the world just fell on you?"

"The name is Dan, and the answer is yes."

"From what I hear, you're a quick learner. Good thing, too, because there ain't going to be any on-the-job training. It's life-and-death from the get-go. We listen to it all day long."

"Thanks for the encouragement. Now fill me in on how you operate."

Another briefing and more tightly packed information for Roman to squeeze into his head. Archangel had two missions. First, the aircraft and its configuration of radio and weather radar equipment were the Command and Control Center for Grunt Air, acting like any other air traffic or mission control center. Off the ground at first light, they flew north to check the en route weather for the helicopters, reporting back to Operations, which would then launch the missions or stand them down for weather.

"There's a lot of fog covering these hills in Laos most of the time," said Alberts. "That's how we lost our Ops and Maintenance Officers last week. Just one of those things. They turned into what they thought was just a little puff of fog and went square into a karst that sat right out in the middle of a valley."

Archangel also kept track of the flight plans for the day, mission objectives, intel summaries, and just about everything else. After the unit's aircraft were released by the Udorn tower, they would check in with Archangel and receive flight following services. Archangel's only responsibility was Grunt Air, and the C-47 operated day and night, whenever required. The aircraft's radios had double and triple redundancy, monitoring other air control facilities—the airborne ones, and ground-based operations like Air America—Long Tieng tower, and the private frequencies of some of America's allies, like the troops under the command of General Vang Pao.

"Just in case he gets some information or Intelligence he forgets to pass on," observed Alberts.

Equipped with two bilingual radio operators and a half ton of broadcasting and receiving equipment, Archangel was the first aircraft off the ground in the morning and the last to land at night, after orbiting most of the day at 10,000 to 15,000 feet for the widest area of radio reception. They flew far enough North to pick up transmissions from South China, and would venture even farther north except for Albert's regular copilot, Captain Muang, a Laotian who couldn't risk getting killed in an American aircraft.

As if they didn't have enough to do, Archangel's other mission was to provide logistical support to Grunt Air, flying to Saigon or Binh Hoa a few times a week to take classified reports to the head shed and pick up parts and supplies.

"This thing was built in 1942," Alberts said with pride. "But it's in great shape and you'd have to be a genius to make it screw up. You can count on us for reliability and flexibility when you plan your missions."

Roman thanked Alberts and sat for a moment looking out the front windscreen into the black void before him. Little spasms of doubt and fear scurried along his nerves. Could he pull this off for Mattix without getting him and the other generals court-martialed? He sure was going to miss that cushy operations job back at the 175th.

⊂∽⊂∽

8

Welcome to Udorn

Udorn Air Force Base, Thailand
November 9, 1971
Early morning

A knock on the door woke Roman. His eyelids flipped up, he looked for a moment at the stained ceiling above his cot, then his eyelids closed. Briefly, he couldn't remember where he was. He opened his eyes again, carefully, and turned his head to the side. The room was an even bigger shithole than he thought when he collapsed on the cot at 0200, just three hours before. He'd had vague glimpses of the Grunt Air quarters, but it was dark, he couldn't see much, and he was too dazed and tired from the events of the day for any of it to register. It was registering now.

A second knock would remind him what had awakened him in the first place.

"Come in," he mumbled as he struggled to sit up. Every joint, every muscle, ached from fatigue. Fortunately, the face he saw was cheerful. It belonged to Chief Abeel.

"What makes you so damn happy at this hour of the morning, Bill?"

"I have the pleasure of getting you up so you can handle the first problem of the day."

"Nice of you." He swung his legs over the edge of the cot and put his bare feet down on the cold, rough floor. "What exactly is the first problem of the day?"

"Actually, it hasn't happened, yet, but it will. I wanted to give you a heads-up so you'd have some time to think about it." Abeel grabbed a rickety wooden chair, turned it around backwards and straddled it. "We're extracting Echo Team today at 1600 hours, but there's only one operational Huey here for that mission. It's Steve Dorsey's Grunt Air Six Six. Dorsey's copilot, Brad Carter, is grounded for maybe 48 hours with some medical thing."

"So? We've got plenty of crews to pull a copilot from."

"The problem is Steve Dorsey is black. So is Carter. Both of them are great pilots, good combat history, multiple tours, all that stuff. But some of the Southern boys are—how can I say this—a little reluctant about being a copilot to a black man. If you ask me, I think this is a kind of test. They've pulled shit like this before. They want to see how you handle it."

Just what I need this morning, Roman thought.

"Okay, Bill, let's see if I can pass the test. You might let those white prima donnas know there will be a white copilot on that mission. Thanks." Abeel heaved himself up out of the chair and let himself out of the dingy room. Roman sat for a minute on the edge of the cot and shook his head in disgust. He'd never understood the whole black and white thing and, after the civil rights upheaval of the mid 1960s, had thought people were more or less getting over their petty racial prejudices. Now it was his first problem of the day in a place where being on the same side and fighting for the man next to you was a matter of life and death.

Promptly at 0800 hours, still aching from fatigue, Captain Roman marched professionally to within 30 inches of Colonel "Jumping Jack" Odom's desk and saluted smartly. His voice was clear and confident.

"Sir, Captain Daniel J. Roman reports to the Base Commander."

Odom, a combat ace in Korea with two credited kills in Southeast Asia, returned his salute and then came around the desk and offered his hand. "Glad to have you aboard, Captain Roman. Take a seat here at the table." Roman did. Odom had a map of the entire Southeast Asia operating area under the table glass.

"Coffee?"

"Thanks, sir. That would be great."

The Colonel leaned back in his chair, opened the door and told the airman outside to bring in three cups of coffee, and to call in Lieutenant Colonel Skinner, the Base Operations Officer.

"They pulled you up here from the Delta pretty quick," Odom observed.

"It was kind of a surprise, sir," said Roman. "I was an Assault Helicopter Company Operations Officer at lunch and, by supper, I was a Special Operations Unit Commanding Officer on my way to Thailand."

Odom laughed just as Skinner entered the office. "This is our Base Operations Officer." The two shook hands as an airman came in and set three white mugs of steaming coffee on the glass tabletop.

"It damn sure came as a shock to us here, didn't it, Dave? The Commanding General himself called me and told me that the Grunt Air Commander and XO were being bumped upstairs. Would you happen to know why? Was it because of the Grunt Air crash last week, or something else?"

Roman wasn't stupid and he recognized at once that he was being sandbagged. He had his story all figured out.

"Well, sir, as I understand it, there were two reasons. First, General Abrams at MACV made a levy on the 7th Air Force for a critical aviator slot on his planning staff. It was a short fuse requirement so they naturally wanted a lieutenant colonel with combat experience. Colonel Whaley certainly fits the requirement. Also, the drawdown has created a severe shortage of good field grade officers. They're assigning a lot of slots to company grade officers like me, out of pure necessity. They tell me I'm on the major's list, so I'm hoping for a promotion in a few months. Besides, Grunt Air is not really a combat command. We're just a survey team."

Colonel Odom looked at Roman without comment, then at Skinner. Some kind of understanding passed between them.

"What you say is true, Captain. But, your unit has taken some combat losses." The words hung in the air.

"Six so far. I was told that four of the casualties were the result of weather-related accidents. The other two were just lucky shots at a passing helicopter. We've had no problems in the crash sites up to now but that could always change. That's why we have a small security force with each team."

Skinner leaned forward, his arms on the glass. He pushed his coffee cup out of the way.

"Captain, have you seen any of these security personnel or read their records?"

"I've known Captain Best for over ten years. We went to college together back in Oklahoma. As far as their records are concerned, sir, I just got here."

"Of course," said Odom. "We know you just got shanghaied last night, but these guys aren't exactly from the safety patrol at the elementary school. They're big, they're tough and their combat records read like a combination of Chesty Puller and Audie Murphy. You might say they're a bit ... overqualified for this mission. Any ideas about that?"

"Well, sir, I'm sure the drawdown has created some unusual assignments, but why higher command picked these particular people, I have no idea. They could be warehousing them for future assignments."

Odom had to agree that it did make sense. Roman took a few deep breaths.

"Just for your information, sir, our program is about half done. We should be out of your hair by June or July if the weather holds."

"And," said Colonel Odom, "if there's no significant dry season offensive by Hanoi. Our CIA boys don't think it will be much of an operation, if there's one at all. I assume you've met the Station Chief in Saigon?"

"No, sir. But I did meet his deputy, John Henry Holbrook."

"That asshole?" said Skinner, "Sorry. That was out of line. But we send him good Intel and he sends us totally worthless shit back."

"Yes, sir, I'm aware of the problem. Speaking of problems, could you spare me a moment to discuss the quarters, maintenance facilities and supply situation?" Odom stiffened a bit and sat up a little straighter.

"We're working on it. Lieutenant Colonel Sweeney in Saigon tells me they're filling all of your valid requisitions as quickly as the items become available. I understand you have an experienced supply warrant officer who has signed on with Grunt Air to deal with these problems. Give Sweeney a little time and I'm sure it will all work out. About the billets, though … we're full on the Air Force side. Air America has told me they're full, so I'm not sure what can be done. I'd tell you to go see Mr. Yamato, the K&S Facilities Coordinator, because he's responsible for housing, but it would be a waste of time. All he tells me is no. No money, no space, and no personnel. Nothing I can do about it because he reports to the Pacific Air Force Headquarters as a civilian contractor. Sorry."

Roman thought the interview was over and was expecting to jump to his feet, but Odom continued.

"Before you go, maybe you could explain to me why crash site surveys are so sensitive … and so secret. Your unit seems to have an unusually high priority with the Commanding General. You can't be detailed for anything on the airbase or interfered with except by his personal authority. Very unusual. What's your read on it?" Odom stared and waited. Roman put on his best aw-shucks Oklahoma smile.

"Well, sir, I'm just a captain, you know, but this seems to be a big political football with Washington. The reports from Grunt Air are getting some attention at the White House and in Congress."

"Well, maybe that makes some sense. Anyway, let me welcome you once again to Udorn. There's not much I can do in the areas you need help with, but call me if there's anything."

Roman stood and saluted, then hiked back across the base to his own office, such as it was. He got lost only twice on the way.

It was a long walk and Roman had time to think about all the problems and situations he would be dealing with in a matter of hours. But he didn't. Instead, he thought about his two children, a million miles away, living with his parents in Oklahoma. They'd been there since Cindy's death. He missed them terribly, but not her, of course. He closed his eyes and shook his head, trying to shake the awful thoughts from his mind. There was nothing he could do about any of it where he was. Besides, in a few minutes he'd be struggling with other problems, like Steve Dorsey and the missing copilot.

The Grunt Air orderly room was, like the rest of the quarters, a shithole, but at least everybody stood at attention when he walked in. He immediately put them at ease and looked over the new faces. He wondered what was going on in those minds, but knew they were wondering the same about him.

"Specialist Seacrest, please round up all the pilots, the First Sergeant, Captain Best, Mr. Gedeon, Mr. Abeel, and Sergeant Major Panfil for a meeting in 15 mikes."

Roman went back into his office and just sat there for a minute looking at the drab walls, trying to put everything in order in his head. He waited fifteen minutes, and paced back into the briefing room.

"Ten HUT!" called First Sergeant Woods.

"At ease. Take your seats. For those of you who haven't met me yet, which is almost everybody, my name is Roman. I hope to be with you for the next few months. Who's the Operations Sergeant?"

"SFC Hardy, sir," said a man in the rear as he stood up.

"What's the unit status today?"

"We have six Hueys assigned, one operational and five down for maintenance, and we have two replacements on order. There's only one Recon Team out at present and that would be Echo Team. They're scheduled for extraction at 1600 hours today. Sir, I believe Mr. Dorsey is up for that mission."

Someone at the back of the room commented, "Mr. Dorsey doesn't have a copilot."

Roman looked at him. "Your name, soldier?"

"Hetler, sir." Roman looked at Hetler with an expression that needed no interpretation. The room became silent. Roman looked around and picked out Dorsey. He was the only black man in the place.

"Mr. Dorsey, you'll plan all aspects of the extraction. You can brief me just before you depart at 1300 hours. You'll have a qualified copilot at that time. He'll report to you at the flight line prior to takeoff. Any questions?"

"No, sir," Dorsey responded.

Roman looked down at the podium and noticed two, thick three-ring notebooks with red "Secret" covers.

"What in the hell are these?" he asked nobody in particular.

"Sir," replied Alberts, "that's our unit Standard Operating Procedures and Rules of Engagement."

"SOPs and ROEs, huh?" Roman looked at the two monster books, then brushed them off the podium and into the trash can just below the table where they landed with a clang. "Gentlemen, my Operating Procedures are as follows: From now on, Aircraft Commanders are restricted only by their own best judgment. You'll evaluate all situations carefully and make decisions based on your experience and your best judgment. We have a mission here and we're going to accomplish it."

There was shock throughout the room and incredulity on every face. Nobody had spoken to them like that since they'd found their way to this secret unit.

"Mr. Duncan, I want you and First Sergeant Woods and Sergeant Major Panfil to look through the books for any material that might actually be useable. Keep it short and let me know by tomorrow what you come up with. I'm talking about call signs and other specific information, not any limitations on the Aircraft Commanders. There will be none!

"Now, let's move on to the housing situation. Who's got something to offer on that?"

"Sir," said a pilot named Ditton, "we've been fighting this battle ever since we got to Udorn. Actually the BOQ and BEQ are full, except for a few spaces reserved for transit fighter aircrews. We wanted to build our own building, or take over that old warehouse down by the lake, but the Facilities Engineer just laughed at us. Anyway, nothing ever happened. We still don't have his decision on the warehouse conversion plan."

"What's the story on this warehouse?"

"It's an old Thai Air Force supply center, large enough to provide quarters for all of us plus the office and mess hall space. We could be completely on our own if they'd let us. What gripes me, sir, is that the place is totally abandoned. No reason we shouldn't be able to use it. Mr. Yamato said maybe, but we never heard a word from anybody. I guess we're screwed again."

Roman made some notes on his pad and said, "Don't bet on that. I'll have a talk with our illustrious Facilities Engineer. Commo," he said.

"Here I am, sir, Sergeant Nelson." The Communications Sergeant raised his hand.

"I need two secure lines, one to Dak To and the other to Tay Ninh. Get with me on this later. I believe it's already being coordinated out of General Geiger's office in Saigon. Now the big problem," Roman said, looking around the room for CW4 Gedeon, "Ah, there you are. Mr. Gedeon what's the problem with all these requisitions?"

The Senior Warrant Officer brought himself slowly to his feet. He acted like a man who had bad news, and he did.

"Two problems, sir. First, the Udorn base supply doesn't want to give the Army anything the Air Force boys may need later. The main guy is Chief Master Sergeant Dickson, and he's a pretty reasonable sort who takes a lot of heat. He has to give whatever he gets from Saigon to his boys first, and I can live with that. Second problem is a major one, or should I say, a lieutenant colonel problem. Lieutenant Colonel Sweeney is the Tan Son Nhut Supply and Logistics Officer. For some reason, he hates this unit. He tells us our requisitions ain't filled out right and cancels them the second they hit his desk. Captain, I been in supply for over 25 years and there's nothing I don't know about Army and Air Force supply reqs. He's full of it. He even cancels mission-essential repair parts for our birds, which is why most of 'em are down right now. Lieutenant Colonel Whaley went to his boss at 7th Air Force, Brigadier General Kelso. Kelso got told a bunch of lies from Sweeney, backed him up all the way, and Whaley came away with nothing.

"Is there a bright side to all this?" Roman asked.

"Well, sir, I think Kelso's a little more up on what's happening now, but the situation is pretty grim and getting worse. Before he left, Colonel Whaley talked to General Hamilton and asked for some help. We can't carry on our mission without some cooperation from the supply people. General Hamilton said he'd look into it and get back. I hope he does.

"The NCOIC at supply is Rex Rogers and he's a good man, but he can't sneeze without permission from Colonel Sweeney. Rogers is a real wheeler dealer. Seems to have a soft spot for stuff like Lao and Meo crossbows and spears and he's willing to trade. My kind of supply sergeant. Could be a help to us.

"Okay, but where are we on all these requisitions?"

"As of 0830 hours today, I've checked all 236 outstanding requisitions, including 14 Blue Streak reqs for aircraft. Sir, every one of them more than meets all DOD, Air Force and 7th Air Force policy and procedure requirements. We just can't get them filled."

Disgusted, Roman shook his head. "Goddamn staff! Are you sure all your paperwork is completely in order?"

"Yes, sir, absolutely!" Gedeon responded.

"Okay. Get a complete list of those requisitions ready to go to Saigon with me tomorrow morning. Have Sergeant Campbell ready to go with us. Chief Alberts, have the C-47 ready to take off for Saigon at 0430 hours. Don't file your flight plan until 0400 hours. I don't really want them to know we're coming."

Roman started pacing the room, his mind stirring with new plans of action. He was determined to break this bottleneck and get his men what they needed to perform their mission safely.

"Captain Best, I need to borrow eight very big volunteers to go with me and help load our grocery basket."

"Consider it done, sir."

Everyone in the room started shuffling in their seats. Roman could feel their excitement. This new guy was going to get things done. They could feel it.

"Sergeant Campbell, do we have any trading material?" Roman asked.

"Yes, sir, a few choice items."

"Bring 'em."

SP5 Seacrest appeared at the door.

"Sorry to disturb you, but Mr. Caldwell and Mr. Eastwood are heading this way. They're obviously on another snoop mission."

"Thanks. Chief?" Roman pointed at Abeel, who turned and nodded to SP5 Duncan.

"Duncan, could we please have your famous lecture on site investigation techniques?"

SP5 Duncan hurried to the front of the room, picked up a pointer, stationed himself in front of a map and started talking. He was about 30 seconds in to a nearly incomprehensible discussion when Caldwell and Eastwood, the CIA and Air America snoops, came in and strolled to the back of the briefing room, hoping to hear some interesting information. No luck. They listened for a few minutes, became convinced that Duncan was holding an actual class, and wandered out.

"Good show, Mr. Touchdown," said Roman. "That ought to take care of them for a few days. Is there anything else that's real pressing? Okay, let's go to work."

Some of the men drifted toward the base cafeteria for lunch. Lieutenant Dorsey headed for the flight line with his crew to start their preflight for the 1300 mission. As he came through the door, Roman stopped him.

"I'll catch up with you in a few minutes to go over your extraction plan."

Dorsey looked at him, obviously uncomfortable. He wanted to ask about his copilot but decided not to say anything. He knew whoever flew with him would be the man who pulled the short straw. Dorsey pushed through the door followed to the flight line by Alberts and Captain Muang. Alberts had to have Archangel in the air by 1200 hours for weather and route check before becoming the airborne command post.

Roman stopped Gedeon in the hallway.

"Mr. Gedeon, just be damn sure we're in the right before we go shopping tomorrow."

"Not to worry, boss."

At precisely 1245 hours Roman walked out to the flight line. As he approached Dorsey and his crew, he watched them completing their preflight checks, moving with practiced confidence around the Huey. Roman arrived just as they settled down in the shade to wait for crank time. Everyone got to their feet when Roman came up.

"Get back in the shade before you melt," he told them.

They smiled and retreated into the somewhat less broiling shade offered by the Huey, but sat up instead of lying back. They wanted to see what was going on and hear what was going to be said. Nobody else had walked out with the new captain. Where was the copilot?

"All right, Steve," said Roman, sitting down next to Dorsey. "Give me your plan in detail from the start."

"Sir, I've never done this before. No one has ever asked me to do this, but I'll give you what I've got."

"Good enough."

"Okay, sir, here it is. First off, we obviously have to fly to Nakhon Phanom for refuel." Dorsey got his tactical map out. He pointed to the POW camp called the Homestead and made a little grease-pencil mark on the first extraction point to the north and the alternate extraction point they would be going to on the south side. Dorsey explained the camp and how they had to abort the extraction mission two days before.

"They're going to be right here on a little cliff at the top of this long hill next to a river. We have to get in there without being discovered so we don't attract fire. I assume we don't have to abort the mission at the first sign of hostilities."

"That's correct. You have to use your judgment as to whether you think you can get in and out safely."

"Okay, sir. Here at the camp, it's flat and open until you get to the slight hill mass in front of it about a kilometer away. I think the NVA will set up a flak trap on this hillside and over here at the original extraction point. They'll think we're going to come in over the hills because it's more direct. Looks to me there's a better way to do it, coming east until we cross over this first line of hills." Dorsey indicated the large chain of hills that ran northwest by southeast, followed by a low flat area. "There's this little valley that has a small river going through it. It's very narrow and there are no roads, just the river. They're not likely to put any type of anti-aircraft in there or have infantry units. Maybe a few along the main road running from the POW camp south and east into the main route structure going to Vinh, but not here. This whole area is a major part of the Ho Chi Minh trail and we're awful close to it. That's why these POW camps are here." The black point of his grease pencil pointed to five camps in the general vicinity and then to the Homestead.

"If we fly up very low through this valley and then up to the ridge line, I think we can get in and behind the flak trap, grab the guys, and come back out quickly. We'll go back down the same canyon a few klicks then cut back west. We'll be fuel critical when we come out so we'll have to go as direct as we can."

Roman looked at the plan. His face didn't show it, but he was impressed.

"Okay. Fly it."

"Yes, sir. We're ready to go as soon as the copilot gets here."

"You're looking at him."

Dorsey's eyes went wide. His mouth opened, then quickly closed again.

"That's right, Lieutenant. I'm your Peter Pilot. Let's crank this sucker."

Dorsey looked at him strangely.

"Come on. I want you to show me how this is done. Let's see how well your plan works out. You can also give me an area orientation at the same time."

"Well ... okay, sir."

The two pilots climbed into the helicopter. The Crew Chief released the blade, swung it to the 90-degree position, fireguard set, ready for crank up.

Roman grabbed the preflight checklist and started going down it item by item just like in flight school, just like it's supposed to be done, by the book. Dorsey did the same. When all the items were ticked off, he cranked the turbine engine, scanned the instruments to be sure all systems were operational, looked over at the Crew Chief, got the nod.

"Are you ready?" he asked Roman.

"I'm ready." Dorsey squeezed his microphone switch.

"Udorn Tower, this is Grunt Air Six Six at the Air America "Back Forty" ramp ready for hover taxi instructions, eastbound departure."

"Roger, Grave Robber." The controller's voice was tinny in their headsets. "You're cleared across the active runway. Depart heading zero one zero for three miles before right-hand turn back to departure course. Wind one three five degrees at one zero knots, gusts to one five, altimeter two niner niner five. Report frequency change to Archangel. Grave Robber Six Six, expedite your departure, inbound F-4, five mile final."

Unexpectedly, Roman grabbed the controls from Dorsey, startling him just before he lifted off.

"I have the aircraft." Dorsey put his hands in his lap as Roman manhandled the Huey into the air, flying over the tops of the Air America buildings straight to the tower about 1400 meters away. Pulling up on the collective, he lifted the helicopter up about 40 feet to the level of the tower. The tips of the rotor blades whirled within just a few feet of the structure, dangerously close. He was eye to eye with the tower controller, who stood horrified behind the glass.

"Excuse me," Roman said into his mike. "Grave Robber is not the call sign of this unit. You can call us Ferret. You can call us Grunt Air. But you'll never call us Grave Robber, again. Do I make myself clear?"

The Lieutenant standing behind the controller reached around to grab his mike just as Roman nudged the cyclic forward, bringing the madly whirling edge of the rotor blades maybe eighteen inches from the tower. The glass rattled. The whole tower started to shake.

"I'm going to tell you this for the last time. You call us Grave Robber again and I'll blow this Tower right off its mountings. Do I make myself clear?" He watched through his windscreen as the Lieutenant snatched the mike from the shaking hands of the controller.

"We understand, but I'm going to report your actions to the Base Commander as a flight violation."

"Please do. Tell the Base Commander you want me on the carpet. While we're there, we'll discuss your violation of communications security, ignoring DOD Standard Operating Procedures and a half dozen major security violations. You can talk about that with him at the same time. If you or your men call us Grave Robber again, this tower is history. Now, do you understand me, Lieutenant?"

"Yes, sir, I do."

"Good. Let's try this, again. Udorn Tower, Grunt Air Six Six, we're ready for takeoff request eastbound departure."

"Roger, *Grunt Air*. You're clear for immediate takeoff on course eastbound, winds one three five degrees at one zero knots, altimeter two niner niner five. Report frequency change to Archangel."

"Grunt Air Six Six, Roger. Grunt Air Six Six on the go. Okay, Mr. Dorsey, take the aircraft and let's go flying."

Dorsey was still staring at him when he took back the controls and pulled the Huey around toward the east. He couldn't believe it. The Air Force controllers had been calling them weird names since they got to Udorn and nobody had ever stood up to them. Dorsey was reasonably certain they weren't going to be called Grave Robber again.

As the chopper gained altitude, clearing the outer limits of the Control Tower's airspace, Dorsey radioed once again.

"Grunt Air Six Six request frequency change to Archangel for flight following.

"Roger, Grunt Air. Good day," replied the Tower operator.

Dorsey got busy with the radios, switching frequencies from the control tower to Archangel. Once contact was established, Albert's crew gave them a weather report, suggested some adjustments to their route of flight and recommended an altitude. Dorsey added power climbing en route to 6,500 feet.

The flight to Nakhon Phanom Royal Thai airbase was smooth and uneventful. The base was in a strategic position adjoining the slender panhandle border with Laos. The US forces used it for air strikes and clandestine special operations in the northern part of Laos and North Vietnam. Dorsey flew the approach smoothly, landed, and began to supervise the refueling while Roman headed for the Base Operations to check for any information that might be helpful on the mission. There were no known fast-movers or fighter aircraft operating in the area, an important piece of information to know in case they ran into trouble.

Once they were airborne with full tanks, they crossed the first mountain ridge to the northeast. Roman could tell Dorsey was a bit uneasy flying with his commanding officer, but he was still very much in control, confident and competent. At the river, they turned northeast and descended to fly through the narrow canyon, no more than ten to fifteen feet above the river.

"Archangel, this is Six Six. Can you confirm that Echo is ready for pickup?"

"Roger, Echo has reported in. No hostile fire so far today. There are known hostiles in the area. You have a cold LZ at this time."

"Roger, Archangel."

They flew through the deep and narrow canyon only a few feet above the water, roiling the surface and kicking up spray. Once in a while, they'd see a local fisherman trying to get something out of the little river, but there were no troops, no anti-aircraft fire. Maybe Dorsey's plan would actually work. About halfway down the canyon, Dorsey engaged his deadman setting on his cyclic. If he were wounded or killed, at least the aircraft wouldn't fly out of control. Not right away.

Dorsey knew what he was doing. He brought the aircraft lower and lower to make sure they weren't discovered prematurely and to make it harder for enemy forces to shoot at them. The larger caliber anti-aircraft weapons, except the 12.7mm, had a minimum elevation limit, so they couldn't depress the barrels downward to shoot at them at this altitude. They were designed to shoot at fast-moving jet aircraft and not low-flying helicopters.

Dorsey felt he had gotten the most out of his airspeed and power settings without excessive fuel consumption. When he got approximately five klicks out, he dialed up on the Recon tactical frequency and called Echo Team.

"Echo, this is Six Six. Are you ready?"

"We're ready and there are NVA in the area. No fire yet, but we've seen them and there's nothing we can do about it. We're on the ledge ready for pickup."

"Roger. This will be a quick extraction," Dorsey replied.

He was getting ready to start lifting up to the ledge as he came out of the very narrow valley when Roman stopped him.

"Leave it on the deck. Right here till the very last second. See that sheer wall? Let's use it to block the fire and noise of the chopper. When you get to that little canyon over there, pop it up hard and get us up on top of that ledge. Use a combination of collective pitch and cyclic climb." Roman kicked up the power from 6600 to 6700 rpm by using the "beep" switch on the collective handle.

"You sure?"

"It'll work. Just keep us on the deck. When I tell you, pull up and head towards the ledge. Trade off some of that airspeed for altitude."

As the sheer cliff wall got bigger and bigger in their windscreen, Dorsey kept waiting for Roman's cue, but it didn't come. Dorsey was convinced that they would overshoot, and if they had to come back around, they'd be spotted for sure. It seemed like forever but finally Roman spoke up.

"Now! Back on the cyclic! Pull! Get everything you can get out of that pitch. Come on! Hard! Bring her back. More!"

The low rotor rpm warning light came on, sounding the tone in their headsets.

"We're losing rotor rpm," Dorsey yelled with obvious concern in his voice.

"No problem. You've got plenty to lose. Keep pulling back. Harder. Harder," Roman calmly reassured him.

They soared almost straight up the ledge, topping out right at the lip. Frantic, Dorsey nosed it back over again, reduced power, and moved the helicopter toward the lip of the cliff, watching the men of Echo Team appear out of the woods, run toward the Huey, and clamber aboard. Just as they did, the NVA opened fire from all directions except behind them, which was thin air.

"I've got a better view," Roman shouted. "I've got the aircraft." He instantly pulled the collective upward, lifting the shuddering machine off the ledge, moving it backward and dropping down into the valley. Two of the Echo Team members in the back had no time to grab on to anything in the cargo bay and floated up toward the overhead. It looked like Roman was going to dive the falling chopper right into the ground, but he smoothly pulled it back to five feet above the bottom of the canyon, leveled off, and headed southwest as planned.

"Damn," said Dorsey. From the rear, a few riper words were heard.

After about 20 seconds, they were out of range of small arms fire and Dorsey started to breathe a little easier.

"Okay, you've got the aircraft, Mr. Dorsey. Let's go home."

Dorsey took the controls in his hands and said, "I've got the aircraft."

Once they were stabilized, Christian poked his head between the seats.

"Well now, Dorsey. Looks like you came in and got us under fire. When the old man finds out, you're gonna be looking for a new job."

"My job is just fine, thanks. The old man ain't going to say a word. He's gone. Reassigned to MACV Headquarters."

"Oh, Jesus. That means the new guy is gonna be worse. What kind of ring-knocking Pentagon warrior did they send us this time?"

"Never been in the Pentagon," Roman observed. "Hope that doesn't matter."

"Who the hell are you?"

"I'm Dan Roman. Don't have a ring, either, but I'm running this operation now."

"You must be," said Christian. "Otherwise, nobody would have come in under fire to get us."

"Times do change. What can you tell me about the positive you saw?"

"Well, sir, he's definitely an American. He's a tall man, pretty thin, even skinnier now since he's been a POW. There's also an Australian Air Force major, along with a Vietnamese full colonel from the Vietnamese Air Force. We call it VNAF."

"We called it VNAF in the Delta, too," Roman replied.

"Sure. Sorry. The camp is in a bad location. It's gonna be a bitch to get in."

"Any chance the prisoners will get moved?"

"Yes, sir. Most of these are transit camps in this area so I assume they'll move them somewhere pretty soon."

"How long have we got?"

"No way to tell. It's not predictable, at all. Leastwise we've never seen a pattern. But from this location they'll move them by truck, up the main highway that follows along the Thai-Laotian border to a place we call the Tollbooth. The road forks and they could go northeast towards either Hanoi or Sam Neua, or they could go into the Plain of Jars. Lots of camps in the PDJ. They'll probably go there first."

Christian talked all the way back to the refueling stop at Nakhon Phanom. There were a bunch of other Vietnamese in the camp, he said, but not of any consequence. When Grunt Air busted the camp, they'd release the Vietnamese and help them make their way back to Thailand. He told Roman the NVA was keeping the Vietnamese colonel alive for some reason and that the American and the Aussie were huge prizes. He was puzzled, though, that the Army Major was Air Defense. What's an Air Defense officer doing in Laos?

Roman looked over his shoulder at Christian and said, "I'm Air Defense. What in the hell am I doing here?"

"The only units I know that Air Defense has over here in Southeast Asia are a Chaparral-Vulcan unit and some 40mm anti-aircraft on track vehicles, and they're all around Saigon."

"Well," Roman said, "the Chaparral-Vulcan unit has already been pulled out. They used the Vulcan a little bit, but the Chaparral is not working to specs so they moved it back to the United States. They're using the 40mm's as convoy support. Could be the Air Defense Major was caught with a convoy that got ambushed."

"There's something here we're not seeing yet," Christian said. "Why is it so important to the NVA to keep these guys alive and move them this far north?"

"Who the hell knows? All we can do is report it and see what we can come up with."

When they finally landed at Udorn and shut down the aircraft, Roman climbed out of his seat and waited for Dorsey on the tarmac.

"Lieutenant Dorsey, you're now in charge of all hot LZ extractions. Your plan was fine. Your execution was even better. You and Mr. Carter can plan on taking the lead on future extractions when we know they're hot. That is, assuming you want the job."

"Yes, sir, I'd love the job. Hope my stomach can take the excitement."

"I just wish the NVA hadn't started shooting at me again, so soon," Roman said quietly. They shook hands and parted company, Dorsey to the Officers Club for a drink, or two, or three, and Roman back to his office. He'd be drinking black coffee for a while.

When Roman arrived at his office, he called Sergeant Hardy aside.

"Write this down. I want you to send a classified coded message to Commanding General 7th Air Force with a copy to General Geiger and General Mattix, operational priority, at exactly 0700 hours tomorrow. Message over my signature, to read as follows:

'Grunt Air has four Hueys down for lack of repair parts. One Huey down for hostile damage. With only one operational helicopter, Grunt Air is not combat ready and is now in a 48-hour stand-down for maintenance, subject to availability of repair parts. Will give a progress report in 24 hours, signed Roman.'

"My God, Captain," said Hardy, looking the message over. "The shit is going to hit the fan when the Commanding General gets this."

"I'm counting on it."

9

Attila the Hun Goes Shopping

Udorn Air Force Base, Thailand
November 10, 1971
Early morning

Next morning, at a time pilots usually refer to as "zero dark thirty," Roman arrived at Udorn Base Operations where Chief Alberts was just turning in his flight plan for the mission to Tan Son Nhut. In answer to the desk sergeant's question, Alberts told him they wouldn't require any ground transportation or other services except fuel.

"Just a regular old milk run, is all," Alberts said. "Routine. Right, Captain?"

"Oh, but of course it is. Are you ready to go?"

"That we are. Everybody on board is trying to figure out what you've got up your sleeve. After that control tower incident yesterday, they're kind of curious."

"I hope we don't disappoint them. Let's kick the tire and light the fire."

When they arrived at the C-47 parked in the darkness at the end of the flight line, Alberts produced a small metal placard with captain's bars painted on it. He tapped the aluminum rack that held the placard and pointed to the newly painted CW4 bar in it. Then he slid the placard with the captain's bars over it.

"Got it done last night," Alberts stated proudly. "Let's go to Saigon."

On the way, Roman briefed Gedeon, Best and Campbell. "Here's the deal. We're going to taxi right up to the cargo access point at Tan Son Nhut. Then, we go inside with everybody and give Sergeant Rogers all 236 of our requisitions. Jake, we'll need one of the bigger guys to stand behind his chair ... Intimidation factor."

"I've got just the guy," Best said.

"Mr. Gedeon, you will present the requisitions and, as each one is ticked off, Campbell will go through the facility and pick up the item. Give the supplies to the recon boys to take and put on the plane. As you pick up each piece, come back to Rogers' desk and verify the requisition. We take just what we're entitled to, not a single stick of gum that's not on the list. Clear?"

"Crystal, sir," Sgt. Campbell replied.

When Grunt Air entered the supply office in force, Sergeant Rogers almost choked on his first cup of coffee. He looked up at the men surrounding his desk, staring into one set of eyes after another. When he tried to get up, one of the recon troops with hands the size of house pets gently eased him back to his original seated position. He tried to speak but Roman beat him to it.

"Sergeant Rogers, you don't know me but my name is Captain Dan Roman. I'm the new commander of Grunt Air. We're here to get our requisitions filled." Rogers could hardly get the words out.

"But … Colonel Sweeney has not authorized release of any requisitions to Grunt Air. You need his permission."

"Sergeant, you and Mr. Gedeon here are going to be left to negotiate the transfer of certain items you may be interested in. While you do that, Sergeant Campbell and his crew will go on a little shopping trip in your warehouse for the parts and equipment we've been requisitioning for months. You may rest assured we'll not take anything that has not been properly requisitioned, and we will not take any item we're not entitled to."

"You know how much trouble this is going to cause? Sir?"

"Oh, I'd be surprised if it didn't cause a ripple or two, but we're taking what we need to get our unit operational. Mr. Gedeon, I think Sergeant Rogers needs to be convinced that our mission here is being done according to proper procedure."

With that, Gedeon heaved a wooden box onto Rogers' desk and opened the lid. Rogers almost stopped breathing. Inside was the finest collection of tribal bows, arrows, crossbows and other primitive munitions he'd ever seen, all acquired by the recon teams during their forays into Northern Laos.

"Gentlemen," Rogers said smiling, his mood suddenly elevated. "Welcome to the Saigon super store. We are open for business. May I offer you a cup of coffee? A whole coffee pot?"

The recon team, headed by Sergeant Campbell, descended on the aisles and shelves of the warehouse like 21-year locusts, bringing each item back to the desk, matching it with the requisition and crossing it off. For half an hour, a continuous line of men, much like a bucket brigade, transferred the logistical riches of the Air Force to the C-47 with the captain's bars on the side.

On the way back to Udorn, the C-47 bouncing gently in the early morning air, the recon team and supply troops couldn't stop talking among themselves. Had they finally got a commander who would stand up for them? Were they really going to be able to accomplish their mission this time?

Meanwhile, Roman and Gedeon evaluated the results of the little trading session with Rogers.

"How did we do?" asked Roman.

"Not too bad," Gedeon replied, "but I wanted Rogers to get the best of the deal … just a little. That way he'll help us out next time we need him. If we're not in jail over this."

"Nobody's going to jail." Roman exuded confidence. "He's already called Colonel Sweeney about what happened and Sweeney has no doubt talked to General Kelso. I may have some messages waiting when we land at Udorn."

He did. Ten minutes after he got to his office, Seacrest handed him the phone.

"It's your favorite colonel from Saigon."

Roman had never met Lieutenant Colonel John Jacob "Jack" Sweeney, but could picture him from his voice on the phone, bad as the connection was. He visualized this tall, skinny staff officer. To Roman, all staff officers looked and sounded the same. In reality, Sweeney had a narrow face with eyes like a snake and a classic Boston Blackie pencil-thin moustache.

He didn't mince words. Roman made himself as comfortable as possible in his desk chair, held the receiver away from his ear and continued to picture Colonel Sweeney.

Pale face, unhealthy color, certainly he would look older than he was. Pompous, using language more bitter than it had to be. Got his commission through his university's ROTC program, his time in college not being without unpleasant incident. One night during a summer ROTC training camp, his fellow cadets threw a blanket over his head and pounded the crap out of him. Days later, when he got out of the base infirmary, he'd adjusted his attitude as best he could, but his bitter vengefulness never left him.

Once in the Air Force, Sweeney handled his staff assignments with enormous confidence and miniscule leadership. He had become officious, which nobody likes, and condescending on top of it, the classic recipe for unpleasant interpersonal relationships. It kept him off every list for recommendation to a command position and, without a command position, he could not make full Colonel. This sorry, thankless assignment running the supply depot at the world's largest, busiest aviation facility was the key to his promotion. If he doesn't make it, it's forced retirement after twenty years and some depressing golden years fishing on a lonely lake in New Hampshire.

"You come in here and help yourself to everything I denied you. There are other units in this war, CAPTAIN, a lot more worthy of those supplies than you. And you want to know what's worse? Your little stunt today upset THE ENTIRE SUPPLY CHAIN!"

"All due respect, sir, we had to have those items. We were non-operational, and crash site assessment is extremely important to a lot of people. We live for it. Without those parts, we can't conduct our mission."

"Don't play me, Captain. You're not even a combat unit."

"That may be true, Colonel, but we do fly in hostile territory. All those parts and supplies have been authorized. Every requisition was correct in every detail."

"Even so. These items are critical to the war effort. I release them when I see fit and not until I verify that you really need them. You, Captain Roman, are at the bottom of my list of priorities. I'm taking this to the Commanding General and I'm telling him you ought to be court-martialed."

"Very good, sir. But, would you also talk to General Coroneos and tell him why you've denied our requisitions when everything was in stock."

"You're really cute. Next time you come down, it won't be for supplies. They'll be throwing your ass in Long Binh jail."

"Thank you, sir. Is there anything else?" A click and a crackle. Sweeney had slammed down the phone.

Seacrest stood just inside the door, his eyes wide. Sweeney had been yelling so loudly the First Sergeant had heard every word.

"What are you going to do, Captain?"

"Wait and see. This won't get very far. General Coroneos has already read my early morning note about the unit being non-operational for parts. I'd love to be there when Sweeney tells him. Meanwhile, I'm going to see a man about a warehouse."

Roman rose from his desk and picked up the bag of makeup he'd bought at the PX in Saigon.

"You buy that for Mr. Yamato?" asked the First Sergeant. "I don't think he'll wear it."

"No Top, but I know someone who will."

The secretary at the Facilities Engineer's office told Roman that Mr. Yamato was at his quarters. Roman drove his jeep across the base to a living area reserved for high ranking, civilian personnel. This section of the base was partially wooded, with nice, civilian-type houses, and Roman parked in front of Number 17. Not bad for a civilian contractor, he thought.

When the door opened, Roman was greeted with a rare, beautiful sight. Han Bok Soon, Sam Yamato's long time live-in girlfriend. She became more beautiful when she smiled, which she immediately did when she saw Dan Roman.

"Oh, my God! What are you doing here?"

"You are more beautiful than ever, Miss Han."

"Not Miss Han any more! I finally got Sam off his ass and he married me. I'm an honest woman, now. Come in."

"This is for you, MISSUS Yamato." He handed her the bag of cosmetics that he'd bought … was it only two days ago?

"Real makeup! I'm delighted." Her face lit up again.

Roman wasn't surprised that Sam Yamato would be at home instead of in his extremely busy office at 11:30 in the morning. Back in Korea, he'd always made his own hours, war or no war.

Sam put his coffee down the second he saw Dan. The two men hugged and pounded each other like the close friends they were. There were pleasantries, catching up about the old days in Chunchong, Korea, and everything that led Sam to his little empire at Udorn. Colonel Odom might be in command, but Sam Yamato was in control. He made the electricity happen, the water, everything.

"Do people bow when they come to your office?" Roman wanted to know.

"If they don't, we take them outside and shoot them."

Yamato was curious, too, about his old friend. Dan told him he was running the crash site survey operation for the Air Force, but Yamato knew Dan never had such simple assignments. He also knew not to pry.

"Sam, I need quarters for my troops."

"I figured that's why you were here. Haven't got anything. Sorry. We've tried to solve this problem every way we can. Right now, there's nothing we can do."

"Well, what about that warehouse back over by the lake?"

"Oh, my god!. The place is infested with mosquitoes so big they show up on radar."

"I don't care. Can we get the building? Can we rehab it and move in?"

"You got authorization from Headquarters 7th to move in there? You got money?"

"Authorization's no problem. Money could be a problem."

"Maybe I can make it work. One week I'll put some wiring in, few days later, do some plumbing. Keep it small and nobody'll notice. Now the inevitable question. What's in it for me?"

Dan smiled. He and Sam had been swapping favors back and forth ever since they'd met.

"I don't need anything right this minute," Yamato continued, "but I'm always in the market for something new and unusual."

"Such as what?"

"You guys ever fly up near the Plain of Jars?"

"All the time." Then, Dan realized what Sam was asking. "Now, hold on. Wait a minute."

The Plain of Jars was perfectly named because the land was strewn with huge earthen jars, the smallest of them weighing around two to three hundred pounds. Perfect size for the cargo bay of a Huey.

"You want me to steal a treasured cultural artifact of the Laotian people? That's probably punishable by death. And right out of the enemy's backyard?"

"Brand new spacious quarters, comfortable beds, plenty of hot water …"

"It's out of the question."

"Rooms for all your men, officers, enlisted …"

"Air conditioning?"

That stopped Sam for a minute. "Done."

"And self-contained. If we had a mess hall, we could be out of everybody's hair. Nobody would even know we were there."

"Get me a really good jar and we'll talk again." Dan stood up.

"Miss Han—uh, Mrs. Yamato," he called. "Come say goodbye. I'm leaving while I still have my wallet."

∞∞

10

Flying Pirates 2, Headquarters 0

Tan Son Nhut Air Force Base, Saigon
November 10, 1971
1100 Hours

It was late morning by the time General Coroneos tore into the pile of overnight dispatches that appeared on his desk every day. Everything seemed routine until he read the priority message from Grunt Air. Then he read it again.

He could actually feel his face turning warm colors as he slammed the paper down on his desk and stabbed at the toggle switch of his intercom, asking Colonel Herbert and General Mattix to come to his office.

Herbert was barely through the door when General Coroneos shoved the message at him.

"Have you seen this dispatch from Grunt Air?"

"Yes, sir, I have."

"I want to see General Kelso and Colonel Sweeney right now, and I mean now."

"No problem, sir. They happen to be in my office as we speak, wanting to see you about court-martial charges against Captain Roman." It took the General a second to regain his breath.

"Court-martial charges? What for?"

"They're making it sound like he spearheaded some kind of predawn commando raid on Colonel Sweeney's supply warehouse and had themselves a little shopping spree." He clenched his jaw, holding back the laughter.

"Roman will be sitting at my desk some day, if he doesn't get tried and executed first. Okay, we'll listen to what Sweeney has to say. But, when they come in, you don't know anything about this message, right?"

"Oh, no, sir."

"I want to see what kind of angle Sweeney will play. If I know him, we'll get everything but the facts. A noncombat unit raids a supply depot in the middle of the world's most active military installation."

Suddenly, the General's doorway was filled with people. Colonel Herbert admitted General Mattix and General Kelso along with Sweeney and Captain Mansen. They all saluted and shuffled into position, Sweeney looking like he was ready to turn purple and explode. He had plenty to say about Roman and he'd rehearsed it.

"General Kelso," Coroneos said firmly, "I understand that Colonel Sweeney wants to court-martial our new Grunt Air commander. Can you tell me the charges?"

"Sir, perhaps I should let Colonel Sweeney explain."

"Okay, Sweeney, what's your beef?"

"General, Captain Roman and his gang of flying pirates forced their way into my warehouse and I'm sure they were all armed. They brutally assaulted my supply sergeant and stole a large number of critical items. They just loaded them up in that old wreck of a cargo plane of theirs and took off like a bunch of thieves. No authorization, no permission, nothing. If that doesn't deserve a court-martial, General, I don't know what does."

The Commanding General caught General Kelso's eye. They both knew how the matter would work out and Kelso didn't want to go down in flames with Sweeney. "General Kelso," asked the Commanding General, "were you at the warehouse during this ... invasion, or have you talked to anyone who was there?"

"No, sir. This all happened so fast and Colonel Sweeney was so adamant about reporting it to you, I didn't have time to fully investigate."

Sweeney stood there waiting for his next opportunity to turn up the heat. His twisted reasoning told him this was a big chance to show the Commanding General what a take-charge kind of officer he really was. His supply system was the shiniest, smoothest operation on the base, and no damn captain was going make a mockery of it.

"Colonel Sweeney," said the Commanding General, "help me clear up a few points. According to your report, these so-called airborne pirates swooped out of the sky from Udorn just as your NCOIC opened up for the day. Then Roman and his men 'brutally assaulted' your supply sergeant."

"Yes, sir."

"Was he injured? Beaten? Tied up?"

"Well, not actually, sir. But they had these combat troops with them and Sergeant Rogers told me he was very afraid. In fear of his life, is what he said. They actually forced him to inventory every item they took."

"Then, there's a record?"

"Oh, yes, sir. Right here, sir. I have it right here."

The Commanding General took the paperwork from Sweeney's nearly-shaking hands, leaned back in his chair and riffled through them.

"This looks to me like a printout of Grunt Air's outstanding requisition list. Most of the 236 items listed on this sheet have been check-marked. Are these the stolen items?"

"Yes, sir, they are."

"Everything they took was on requisition with your supply facility. Isn't that right?" Coroneos was setting the hook. Soon, Sweeney would be reeled in. Colonel Herbert had to hold his breath to keep from laughing out loud.

"Yes, sir. But I had no opportunity to verify the correctness or the validity of those requisitions. As far as I'm concerned, they weren't valid and the parts were stolen." Sweeney tried to make his voice ring with authority and confidence. The Commanding General pondered for a moment.

"Looks like many of these items have been on requisition for over 30 days, even some Blue Streak items are listed here for their aircraft."

"Well, that's true, sir. We're a little behind in our paperwork due to the drawdown, and the volume of requisitions submitted each week is tremendous."

"They took quite a few spare parts for their Hueys. You had them in stock. Why didn't you hand them over?"

"Sir, we have other Hueys in very important missions. I took the responsibility of prioritizing how the mission aircraft would be supplied and supported."

"Colonel Sweeney, how many Hueys do we have in Headquarters 7th Air Force, besides those in Grunt Air?"

"Sir, we have two. Your's and the Vice Commander's." Kelso started inching away from his place next to Sweeney.

"They took two starter generators that are on Blue Streak requisition. How many did you have on hand?"

"Well sir, I—I believe we had three, sir."

"So they took items they'd requisitioned to keep their unit operational. And they didn't take anything that wasn't on requisition?"

"No sir, but—"

"Colonel, have you ever had command of a unit, either here in Vietnam or back in the States?"

"No, sir, I've not had the opportunity to command. I had hoped to get a combat command while here in Vietnam."

The Commanding General looked around the room, then fixed Sweeney with the cold look that had helped make him a General Officer in the first place.

"Explain to me why in hell you would place a higher priority on two administrative helicopters here at the Headquarters, birds that fly less than twenty hours a month, over aircraft that fly behind enemy lines in Northern Laos every single day?"

"Sir, the aircraft here at the base must be ready at any time to support your travel needs. Besides, Grunt Air's Hueys are only survey aircraft. They don't have a combat mission. As far as priority is concerned, they're at the bottom of my list."

"And you're at the bottom of mine," Coroneos said quietly to himself. The only person in the room who remained unprepared for the General's imminent detonation was Sweeney.

"Colonel," he began, in a voice that was as ominous as it was quiet, "I don't think the White House, Members of Congress, Chairman of the Joint Chiefs of Staff, the Chief of Staff of the Air Force, the Commander in Chief Pacific, and many others in high places share your priorities. I make a daily report to those people. If I don't, they get mad as hell and call me personally. The President himself considers Grunt Air a very important mission. He told me that himself. So, your priorities don't seem to be consistent with those of higher command. The Grunt Air aircraft and crews fly important missions every day of the week right into the most dangerous combat area in all of Southeast Asia. And your 'priorities' keep them on the ground. If you like, I'll make sure the Air Force Chief of Staff knows your position on this when I report to him later today. He might agree with you, but I know the President won't. It's no wonder Captain Roman's favorite expression is 'goddamn staff.' If you're an example, I don't blame him.

"General Kelso, I want you to give Colonel Sweeney some one-on-one training in the nature of combat mission support. It would be nice if he understood how to prioritize military missions especially those of Grunt Air." He gave the Colonel another of his frosty stares.

"Sweeney, I'm going to give you a chance to pull your career out of the dumper. Start helping those boys at Udorn. You screw those guys up one more time and your next assignment will have snow in July."

Colonel Sweeney was so petrified he could barely snap a salute, but he did manage to execute an about-face without falling down and race through the door as fast as he could while maintaining a shred of dignity. Coroneos motioned General Kelso to stay behind.

"Think he got the message?"

"Yes, sir. Five by five. If this is all sir, I'll go give my first lesson on combat support priorities."

"Go," said Coroneos, in good humor once again. "And keep that sorry-ass son of a bitch out of my headquarters. Al, stay here a minute."

Just as Kelso left, Colonel Herbert cleared his throat in a manner that Coroneos recognized. More bad news.

"Sir, we also had a call from Lieutenant Colonel Skinner at Udorn about Roman."

"What now?"

"It seems our flying pirate took offense at the Tower Operator referring to Grunt Air's call sign as 'Grave Robber.' Roman flew a Huey so close to the tower that it almost blew the windows out. And he told them he'd blow it up if they ever called his unit Grave Robber, again."

Mattix laughed out loud for the first time that morning.

"He'd probably do it, too. Mo, I think it would be a good idea if you personally called Skinner and gave him a polite warning. I don't want to rebuild the Udorn Tower. Roman's been there only two days and the staff body count is starting to rise. I hope he starts turning that killer instinct towards the NVA. It would make Kissinger's job a lot easier."

"And," said Coroneos, "you can call Roman tonight and tell him no more raids, no more attacks on the control tower. No more battles with the staff. Let him know he can expect the support he needs from here, but he has to calm down. I'll ask General Hamilton to get the word to the other staff members to give those boys a little more attention and help."

"Yes, sir."

"Okay. Let's get back to the war against the North Vietnamese. Maybe we can win against them. We've already lost two battles today to a bunch of flying pirates."

It was almost 1800 hours when Roman got up from his desk, stretched, and headed for the Officer's Club. His body was catching up with everything that had happened in the last two days and he finally had an appetite—and a taste for a couple of scotches before dinner.

He had barely made it to the door when his secure phone rang. It was Captain Mansen with an update about Colonel Sweeney's fateful meeting with the Commanding General, and it was a good laugh. As instructed, Mansen read Roman a mild version of the riot act.

"Don't put the Commanding General in another compromising position like you did today," Mansen warned. "He doesn't like being used as your pawn."

"Well, I had to get some support and I figured that would be a pretty good trap for Sweeney."

"It worked. You got your parts and Sweeney's been ordered to give you the support you need. But you need to know this. After the meeting, I talked to Sergeant Rogers to get his side of the story. Apparently, Sweeney came back from the meeting and said he was going to get you court-martialed even if it cost him his career. You've got a big enemy there, Dan. He's a slimeball and he'll get you for something, no matter what. Heads up. General Mattix can't afford to lose you."

"I appreciate it. But, it's not the first time I've had staff officers come after my ass. Maybe one of them'll get me sooner or later, but until that happens, I'm going to do my job."

"Take care. We'll be back in touch tomorrow."

The phone rang again the second Roman put it down. It was the Kingfish, the Intelligence officer from Dak To.

"Roman, the Dragon Lady was having a pleasant but somewhat stressful conversation with an NVA major today, and he decided to tell her about some Army major who was captured. The only one we know about is that Air Defense guy picked up on the convoy duty near An Loc. Do you know anything about it?"

"One of our teams says they spotted him at a camp, but we were kind of hoping you could tell us something."

"Whoever he is, he's drawing some high-level interest around here. I'll ask the Dragon Lady to be a little more convincing in her interrogation techniques. We'll try and get back to you tomorrow."

"Okay. Thanks for the call."

Meanwhile, a C-130 carrying Captains Toothman and Ryker, fresh out of their assignments in the Delta, pulled up in front of Udorn tower at the south end of the north ramp. Chief Abeel waited at the base of the ramp.

"You dinosaur," said Toothman. "I guess old soldiers really never die."

"I'm here to provide you children with a little culture and professional help."

"Great. Help us to the Officer's Club. That was a shitty ride and I need a drink."

Roman had just finished his conversation with the Kingfish when Toothman called. He hadn't expected his two reinforcements to show up for another two days but the generals had pulled them out fast, just like they had Roman. He made it to the club in record time.

Over dinner, Roman tried to bring the two up to date on the mission of Grunt Air and more recent happenings.

"The C-130 crew that brought us up here told us about your raid," said Ryker, between bites of hamburger steak. "They called you the *Flying Pirates*."

"That's Colonel Sweeney's problem. I don't think the Commanding General was very sympathetic to his position. Guy's running his own little kingdom here and, if he doesn't watch out, he'll be looking at the whitest Fourth of July he's ever seen."

Loud voices from the bar. Roman looked around and spotted Hetler and Lieutenant Davis having a small but heated confrontation with a few of the Air Force fighter pilots. He took one quick swallow of his drink, strolled over and placed himself in the middle of the group. It was the perpetual stand-off between the Army and the Air Force.

"Gentlemen, it's been a long day. You're going to buy me a drink and go sit down. You Air Force guys need to learn some manners." Before the pilots could think of a response, he was back at his table, huddled with his newly arrived friends.

All the talk at the Grunt Air table that night was held in hushed voices. It was all about the missions to be flown in hostile territory, the gunfire, the twinkling streaming tracers that arched up from the ground reaching for them with fiery fingers. Roman wasn't a fan of gunfire either, but he'd rather fear death than some mundane boring assignment at Fort Something or Other in the middle of Bungfuck, Egypt.

Their conversation was interrupted, but not rudely, buy the arrival at their table of an Air Force Lieutenant Colonel and a Major who seemed to be joined to him at the hip.

"Captain, I understand you were a little bit harsh with my young fighter pilots over there." Roman heaved himself to his feet. He'd started the day with a pre-dawn raid on an American military facility in a war zone and now had to end it straightening out some officer with his nose out of joint.

"Colonel, we don't need a fight in the Officer's Club. It doesn't matter who said what or who started what. The thing of it is, it needed to be broken up and that's what I did. If anybody got their feelings hurt, it's too bad. I wasn't going to let them knock heads."

"Well, you need to keep these Army animals away from my guys. They just don't mix well."

"Yes, sir, they're certainly not housebroken, are they? But one thing's for sure, they're good at what they do and, all due respect, sir, they'd mop the floor with your boys."

"You're talking about men who fly in combat, Captain. All you guys have to do is flutter around crash sites and inventory them."

"You've got your job and we've got ours. We're all on the same side, after all. Aren't we?"

The Colonel turned, bumping into his Major and strode away from the table. Roman had made a new friend and he'd been at Udorn what? Maybe 48 hours?

After the briefings, the mission, the raid, and the problems he'd faced since he arrived, Roman thought he had a handle on what awaited him at Grunt Air. He didn't, of course. But, as he considered what the days ahead would throw at him, he watched his friend Jan Toothman get shit faced as he downed his Scotches with progressively less water.

It was inevitable that, with a name like Toothman, Jan would be called The Fang. He would be the new Grunt Air Three, a Southern boy who loved country music. He loved it so much, in fact, that he'd play his favorite song of the week over and over until he received a quota of death threats from his roommates. Slightly over 5'10," he sported sandy blonde hair, hazel eyes and a perpetual smile in a cherubic face. His trademark was "Toothman's Axioms of Combat," a series of cynical observations about how to lose your life in a war. Even though he never exercised and hated sports, he was in excellent shape. Roman had never quite figured that one out. He was an extraordinarily talented pilot, and Roman was always awed when they flew together because The Fang became part of the machine in a way Roman would never accomplish. Toothman had decided to stay in Army Aviation as a career instead of going back to the dead end of the family farm. After all, he doubted that his degree in History from Georgia Tech would open any real occupational doors.

Tom Ryker lived for one thing: aviation maintenance. An excellent pilot under fire, his true calling was elsewhere. He had grown up in an aircraft hanger watching his father work on private aircraft and the passenger planes of Trans Texas Airlines. He'd absorbed everything he could about how to keep inert metal in the air. Six feet tall, reddish brown hair, persistent grease stains on his arms and in his hair because he refused to wear a hat when he was working.

Ryker was on his second tour and was headed straight for civilian life when this hitch was up, joining his wife and their three children. Last fall, he had married a woman named Carrie Blackburn, the widow of Larry Blackburn, a pilot who had bought the farm in a combat assault up in I Corps three years before. Carrie was a dedicated camp follower but Ryker knew she deserved to have a husband who stood at least a chance of coming home at night.

Ryker wanted to tell Roman he was leaving the service and had, in fact, wrestled for months with how to break the news. He'd put it off four or five times. He knew Dan would be happy for him because he'd once had his own wife and children, a family life that had ended tragically.

Recently, Ryker had worried more and more about Roman. Maybe the shock of what had happed was getting to him. One of Ryker's tasks back in the Delta was to patch the bullet holes in Roman's chopper. Lately, their number had increased. If he was taking too many hits, he was taking too many chances. Now that they were together at Grunt Air, Ryker could keep an eye on him. There were eight months left to his tour and he wouldn't let his good friend down.

∽∾

11

Roman's Ghosts

Ryker's concerns were not unjustified. Like many military pilots, especially chopper jocks, Roman was driven by forces he barely understood and could never put into words. Down low where the tracers reached up for him and his machine, above the trees where the fear really kicked in until you could pull your straining helicopter up above the kill zone, the fear kept him going. But afterwards, when he was safely back on the ramp at Udorn or Tan Son Nhut, or wherever his service took him, the fear was replaced by ... something else.

Aviation pretty much ran in Dan Roman's family. His father was a Navy aviator during World War II, and didn't bother to look for a flying job in the States like his fellow veterans did. Instead, he found work flying DC-4's and 6's for an airline in South America. After a tragic crash in bad weather, he moved to another airline flying between San Francisco and Hawaii, and made the long trip over open water until a problem with his vision put him out of the flying business. That took him back to Oklahoma where an old family friend got him into the oil business. The timing was perfect since the post war boom put at least one car in every garage. He became quite wealthy.

Roman had two older brothers and a younger sister. The oldest brother died in the South American plane crash and none of the other family members had any interest in or aptitude for the oil business. His father's long absences and the death of his oldest brother made him a bit hard to handle in his early teens, so his mother shipped him off to St. John's Military School in Salina, Kansas. His father wasn't too happy about it but the tight discipline and high academic standards did turn him around. He loved the military environment and showed a real aptitude for the structure and regimentation. After completing his high school years at St. John's, Roman went to college and did another complete turnaround. The lack of discipline was disastrous and, when

a few seemingly innocent fraternity pranks went awry, the Dean of Men reported him to the draft board for "poor scholastic attitude."

They drafted him in a heartbeat and sent him to the infantry. From
there, he volunteered for drill sergeant school hoping to stay out of Vietnam,
but the plan backfired.

It didn't take long for Roman to realize that he'd be better off as a commissioned officer, and his military school background got him into Officer
Candidate School fairly quickly. He had a natural ability to play the system,
and he maneuvered into the Air Defense Branch and then to flight school.
Somehow, he was picked up by Military Intelligence and sent to Intelligence
school, but they left him in the Air Defense branch as a cover. His skills caught
the attention of the resident CIA instructor, who recruited him for advanced
training with the Company.

He did so well learning his tradecraft at the CIA "Charm School" in
Virginia that he was sent to Germany for an advanced tradecraft course, and
was turned into a European specialist. It didn't take long for the CIA to come
calling with all sorts of recruitment offers, but he was more at home in the military life. And besides, while he was taking his advanced courses in Germany,
he met Cindy, an administrative assistant in one of the base offices, and they
were married in practically no time at all. Instead of going to Vietnam, he
accepted a CIA offer to fly "The Courier Run" for the U.S. Embassy from
Bogota, Colombia to Caracas, Venezuela. His boss there was Colonel Mattix,
the Air Attache. These dangerous, clandestine missions excited Roman but,
after six months, he elected not to continue in favor of a more normal family
life. After all, he was a husband and a father. His decision was rewarded by
immediate assignment to Vietnam.

Back in the States after his first tour in Vietnam, things started taking several turns for the worse. By the time he was assigned to the Southeast
Asia Tactics Development Department at Fort Rucker, he and Cindy had two
small children, a boy and a girl. It was there that Cindy met Vic, a smooth-
talking, good-looking Italian from Brooklyn. Somehow, she managed to take
a quick trip with him to a beachfront motel in Panama City, Florida, a favorite
resort for the Ft. Rucker pilots, and not that long a drive from the base. She
knew that her husband, as Air Field Duty Officer, was not allowed to leave the
airfield and so she thought she'd be safe for the day.

The maid found the couple the next morning, Cindy and Vic, lying
in a bloody bed with their throats cut. The police said there were no signs of
a struggle or break-in. The detectives bore down hard on Dan because Vic's
testicles had somehow become detached from his body and placed in Cindy's
mouth. It was definitely a job done by a military professional. The kind of cul-

tural thing that would have been done in Vietnam. Given the military connection, Dan Roman was the first person they questioned. The first session lasted over fourteen hours but that was a stroll in the park to someone who had survived The Charm School. Dan was eliminated from the list of suspects when they confirmed that he was on duty at the time of the murders.

The NCO on duty swore to the police that Roman had never left the airfield that night. They checked him out in every direction. Had he stolen a Huey and flown down there, murdered his wife and her lover, then flown back? After all, Tyndall Air Force base is in Panama City, and he could have landed there. But, there was no record of any such landing or takeoff. It was decided that he could not have done it.

Cindy's father was dead and her mother was an alcoholic, which put the two children with Roman's parents and sister during his overseas tour. He wrote to them faithfully every time he had the chance. To shut out the bloody tragedy of Panama City, Roman pursued women wherever he found them. His R&R leaves from Vietnam to Bangkok were two-day blurs of drinking and womanizing. He came to know the city's notorious Patpong district like his tongue knew the inside of his mouth. On the outside, he was quiet, decorous, the very model of an officer and a gentleman. Inside, away from the base and away from people who knew him, he was just short of being a Mr. Hyde. It was frequently said that he was the man that mothers warned their daughters to stay away from.

His father, former military man that he was, tried more than once to bring his son into the oil business that he'd built so well, but, on some deep level, Roman realized that he not only loved the structure and regimentation of the military, but actually needed it. He often thought back on his days in military school and how much trouble he had when exposed to the complete freedom of college. He was smart enough, or cunning enough, to understand that the nature of the military gave him all the opportunity he needed to fly into danger and either distinguish himself in combat or be foolish and get himself killed. Otherwise, the service provided him with a barrier that kept him from diving off the deep end once and for all.

∞∞∞

12

A Friendly Chat with Captain Ho

Son Thy, North Vietnam
November 12, 1971
Late morning

Major General Thran Van Ho, Deputy Commander of the Enemy Proselytizing Department of the North Vietnamese Army, a division of the Ministry of Public Security, was reviewing the daily reports when one particular item stopped him. There was an American Army major being held at the southern end of the transit POW camps in Laos. Thran read the report again. Why would an Army major be captured and shipped towards Hanoi? After all, he wasn't Air Force or Navy, and was not serving in any technical capacity. This major was apparently part of a convoy's support team in South Vietnam. They used old World War II 40mm anti-aircraft weapons as close support for truck convoys going between Saigon and some of the more northerly bases.

Someone in the local North Vietnamese command structure must think this major would be of value to Hanoi. He'd have to look into this. He'd also have to look into the reports of Army helicopters flying frequent missions in Northern Laos. He couldn't understand why the Americans kept going to the same old crash sites and looking around. They were flying unarmed Hueys, except for the standard M-60 machine guns on either door, and they took with them two or three, possibly four, soldiers to act as security guards. Did these missions have anything to do with his prisoners? These missions did not appear to be of hostile intent or threat to his operations. They were, however, operating in his backyard and he wanted to know who they were and what they were doing.

His thoughts went back to the Army Major and, suddenly, something he hadn't understood dawned on him. This was an Air Defense Artillery Major, which meant he might know something about the Americans' surface-to-air missiles. It also meant the Russians could find some value in him. He could always count on getting additional supplies and a little cash bonus from the Russians if he found anyone who interested them. He'd never had the opportunity to interview any American Air Defense people. This might be interesting.

"Get an interrogation team down there," he told his aide de camp. "Find out who he is and why he was sent north. He should have been shot just like the rest of them. If anybody finds that this man has value, send him north as soon as possible. Bring that Australian who's with him, and the Vietnamese colonel, too."

Six hundred and fifty-two miles south of General Thran's headquarters in Son Thy was the prison camp the Americans called the Homestead where, only a few days earlier, Lieutenant Alan Christian, from his position in the underbrush, had witnessed the brutalization of Major Cody. This day, at 0430 hours, in complete darkness, Major Cody was about to be brutalized, again.

There was a clanging at the metal door of the cell he shared with Major Reginald Smythe-Gordon of the Royal Australian Air Force. Colonel Nguyen Van Nam of the South Vietnam Air Force was kept in a separate cell since he was the senior ranking prisoner of the Homestead.

The guard came into the cell and beat both prisoners with a stick to make sure they were up and ready to go to work. They were shackled together so they couldn't run once they got outside of the bamboo-and-steel cage.

Cody's first sensation when he woke was the sharp shooting pain of the guard's baton crashing into his ribs. The guard, who Cody and Smythe-Gordon called Rat Face for obvious reasons, hauled him off the wooden plank he slept on and pushed him out into the hallway. Rat Face did the same to the Australian, who could barely walk because of the infection that was eating into his legs where the rusty metal shackles had worn away his flesh.

The guards took Cody to a room just off of the camp commander's office where an NVA Captain waited for him. Cody knew at once that he was in for a bad day. The Captain had a vicious look to him, with a drawn, joyless face and eyes that were as dead as two black rocks.

"Ah, Major Cody," said the Captain in amazingly good English. He spoke with a slight New York accent. "I am Captain Ho Nguyen Bak, sent from Hanoi to greet you and to invite you to provide us with some small details about yourself and the circumstances of your capture."

Bullshit, Cody thought. This was just an excuse. The real questions would come later.

"Captain Ho," Cody said in the most formal tone he could manage given the pain of his daily wake-up call, "within reason, I'll be glad to answer your questions so long as they don't involve information that would be detrimental to my fellow soldiers in the South."

Captain Ho smiled and managed an earnest expression. "Please, Major. I would never want you to break your Code of Conduct or do anything of that nature. Have a seat and let us talk like gentlemen."

Cody sat but could feel the presence of Rat Face, who shifted nervously from one foot to the other immediately behind him.

"For you, the war is over. You're going to be counseled and consulted here at this camp and then moved to another camp. Your treatment will depend upon how cooperative you are. I would hope that you'd work with me and not force me to take a different approach to this whole matter. As soon as your countrymen understand that they have lost the war and agree to our demands, you'll be repatriated with others whom we already have in custody."

"As long as you respect what I can and cannot say. I will not betray my country."

Yes, you will, thought Ho, *by the time I'm finished with you*. But his smile remained frozen in place.

"Certainly. Now, Major, it's my understanding that you were captured in the vicinity of An Loc while on convoy duty with a 40mm Duster unit."

"That's correct. We were headed back to Long Binh when we were attacked and captured."

"Can you tell me why your weapon did not work?"

"I think your people already told you. It jammed because of the dust and small rocks we had collected during the road march."

"Well, that was their opinion, but we would like to know from you."

"They were right. The 40mm will sometimes jam when grit and dust get into the recoil assembly and that's what happened in my case."

"How long have you been in the service?"

"Twelve years."

"In all that time, have you been with the Air Defense Artillery?"

"No. I've spent most of my career in Field Artillery. I've attended some Air Defense familiarization schools and had some other short assignments in Air Defense. But primarily, in Field Artillery."

"Have you always been with Dusters?" Cody started to understand what Ho was fishing for. He wanted to find out whether his prisoner had any real value or had just been in the wrong place at the wrong time.

"Well, actually, I started off in Field Artillery and then they moved me over into the Air Defense branch. I'm just an old artillery man, at heart. The 40mm, to me, was an improvement. It was a lot easier riding around in a self-propelled 40mm vehicle than hauling cannons around. It made life a lot easier."

"Have you ever been involved with the Hawk Missile?"

"No, not really. I got a standard briefing on it when I went through the Air Defense basic course, but I really don't know much about how it works because I've always been in 40mm. Most officers going from Field Artillery to Air Defense were assigned to Duster or Chaparral-Vulcan units. We are too old for the technical aspects of the missiles."

"I don't think that's true. I want to know about your career, but if you are not honest with me, things will not go well for you. Let us try this one more time. Were you ever a part of the Hawk Missile operation?"

"No."

Captain Ho looked up at the guard who hovered over Cody's shoulder. "I am told by Colonel Nam that you call this guard Rat Face. It is well that he does not speak English, yes? However, if you fail to answer my questions honestly, I will be obliged to translate for him. He will not be happy."

"Captain Ho, I've told you, I don't know anything about the Hawk Missile System."

Captain Ho said a few sentences to Rat Face in rapid, singsong Vietnamese, and the guard instantly locked an arm around Cody's throat and pulled him to his feet. His huge, rough hands grabbed Cody's hair and slammed his face down on the table, then, with a surprisingly skillful motion, he grabbed the Major's wrists, pulled them sharply behind his back and twisted them together with a piece of rough rope. The man was ugly, fat, and noxious, but he knew what he was doing.

Here comes the rope treatment, Cody thought. They'd done it to him before and it was horribly painful. His elbows were forced behind his back and tied together with rope. Then Rat Face pulled his wrists upward, forcing his head and shoulders down toward his knees. In less than thirty seconds, Cody was completely unable to answer any questions, even if he wanted to, because he was screaming too loudly.

The other daily guard came in the room when he heard the screaming. It seemed that if you wanted to be a North Vietnamese prison guard, you were required to have some sort of obvious physical deformity. In this guard's case, it was his left eye, which didn't work with the right one. The prisoners called him Wild Eye.

Visual impairment aside, Wild Eye had no trouble forcing a foul rag into Cody's mouth, using a steel bar to help the process. The end of the bar hit one of Cody's front teeth and chipped it in half. More pain! Once the screams were silenced, Captain Ho started again

"Now, Major Cody, would you like to answer my question, again?"

His back and shoulders rioting in pain, Cody choked on the rag and shook his head, which displeased his interrogator even more. A signal to Rat

Face brought more pressure to the wrists, forcing Cody's head further down between the knees. The doubled over position made it almost impossible to breathe. In a few moments, Cody saw the drab colors in the room fade and he blacked out.

Major Smythe-Gordon had been shackled to the wall outside Ho's office and closed his eyes when he heard the screams of his friend. When the screams stopped, he was hit by a sick jolt in his stomach. Had Cody been killed? He didn't have much time to worry about the matter because his turn was next. A third guard, known as Mushmouth because he had no teeth and could barely speak, appeared before him carrying a bamboo pole that had been split at one end into six long pieces. He brought it down across the Major's back five times, and hard across the backs of his legs another five. Then he noticed the infection in the legs. He gave Reggie a horrid toothless smile and began beating him on his ankles. In seconds, his feet were covered with blood.

Adding to Smythe-Gordon's pain was the sight of the door opening and the two guards dragging the unconscious Cody out of the other room. The Australian was at least relieved to see that the American was still breathing, though just barely. Rat Face and Wild Eye chained the two of them together and forced Reggie to carry Cody back to their cell. The chain between them was very short, which made the task even more agonizing. Smythe-Gordon fell twice, hurting both of them.

Just before they went into the cell, Mushmouth hit Reggie in the back of the head with the cane, splitting his scalp open in two places. Reggie fell forward landing in the middle of the floor with Cody on top of him. The door slammed shut. Reggie couldn't move and lay there for a while with Cody moaning on top of him. He thought he'd gotten off easy because all they did was beat him. Thank God, they didn't ask him any questions. He thought this might be one of the "good" days.

Not so. A few hours later, the door opened again and Mushmouth dragged him off to his appointment with the sinister Captain Ho.

Unbelievably, the camp had a doctor. The next morning, Cody and Smythe-Gordon were given their customary wakeup beating, followed by a visit from the dark, wizened little man they called Doctor Strangelove. He cleaned Smythe-Gordon's infection with a saline solution, which was predictably painful, then sprinkled the open wounds with yellow sulfa powder. It was all they had.

Cody shuddered and watched the doctor work on his cellmate. What kind of medical practitioner could serve so cruel a purpose? What sort of doctor had he been in his country before the war? Was he a different man from the one they saw before them?

Later that day, Cody and Smythe-Gordon, along with the Vietnamese Colonel, were dragged from their cells and loaded on to a flatbed truck. The guards laid them down on the steel floorboard with their legs extended and their arms interlocked. Wild Eye provided the finishing touches, chaining them to either side of the truck. Soon, they would endure a bone-jarring ride along rutted jungle roads, bouncing on the hard cold metal.

Dr. Strangelove was apparently in charge of the transport operation, stationing Wild Eye on a pile of sandbags in the back. Rat Face drove with the doctor sitting next to him in the cab.

By the time the sun came up, the truck had made its way to the west and was heading toward the mountains to the main road just east of the Mekong River. There, they would turn north and head to the next stop, the Tollbooth.

The trip took all day, and when they got to the Tollbooth it was just getting dark. The three men in the back had wandered in and out of consciousness due to the pain of their position. A guard at the Tollbooth told Doctor Strangelove they couldn't spend the night there because General Vang Pao's troops had been causing them some problems.

"You must go to Bampho," the guard said. It was the notorious camp the Americans called Disneyland. "Turn over your prisoners to Major Quan Nui. He is the camp commander."

"How far?" asked Rat Face.

"The road is bad. Maybe one day. You will stay maybe two, three days so the Major can interrogate your prisoners and patch them up."

"This is not good," Rat Face told Dr. Strangelove. "Major Bai, our camp commander, will be very mad."

"I'm not worried," said the doctor. "If he's mad, he'll make the prisoners suffer, not us."

⊂◎∽◎⊃

13

The Inscrutable Sam Yamato

Udorn Air Force Base, Thailand
November 13, 1971
Morning

Thanks to Roman's act of "piracy," the newly arrived parts helped to get all six of Grunt Air's Hueys back into flying condition. They were now mission ready and the situation made more of a difference in the unit's morale than Roman had thought possible. Everyone was ready to get back to work.

"Good morning, gentlemen," Roman said when he arrived in the briefing room. "Your coffee break is over. We're going back to work. Later today, Captain Best, Captain Toothman and Mr. Abeel will give you details of insertion and extraction schedules. We're sending four recon teams out into the bush.

"Echo, I need you to go back out to the Homestead area and get some more information on the POW you reported. Mr. Donovan, Grunt Air Two Two will take you out. After you recon that camp, report back to Archangel. Afterwards, you'll proceed down to Valley View, then to Happy Valley and then to your pickup point. We want to see what's happening at each of these areas. Be prepared to go on to the Tollbooth area if necessary. We'll advise you on that at the time you're picked up.

"Bravo Team will stay here on reserve.

"Charlie, I'm going to send you out to the western Plain of Jars with Captain Toothman. I want you to check out the Fish Trap from the air then insert south of the Rat Terminal. Be ready to continue on order to Easy Street.

"Delta — Where's Sgt. Krumins? You're going out with Chief Hetler. He'll drop you off at the Bird Cage. You'll wind back around to the Soup Kitchen before you come back.

"And finally, Captain Best, you'll be out in the eastern PDJ. I want you to focus on Disneyland and Dogpatch. You'll go out with Lt. Ditton. It will be a full load for you, but I want you to drop Sgt. Richardson's Charlie Team off. Then, I have a special assignment for your team before you deploy to Disneyland. I'll brief you in a minute.

"Archangel will be making twice daily sitreps with all of you at the usual times. Please be ready so we can keep track of where you are and what's going on at each of these camps.

"Okay. Are there any questions?

"Captain Toothman, will go over your assignments. Captain Best, Lieutenant Ditton, could I see you for just a minute?" Outside the briefing room, Roman pulled the two men close and spoke softly.

"Lieutenant, after you've dropped off Sgt. Richardson's Charlie Team, proceed to these coordinates: Uniform Golf Zero Five Five Eight. I understand there are some small earthen jars in that area. They're just miniatures of the big ones farther North in the Plain of Jars. Some of them are turned over, according to the reports I've got. I need you to load one of those on the aircraft and bring it back. We need a good one so make sure it's in the best condition. Don't ask why and don't get caught. Just do it. If anybody sees you taking one of their national treasures, they'll have conniptions.

"Call me when you get south of the Mekong. You'll meet me and offload the jar someplace on the field where we won't be seen. Now, go ahead and get back to the meeting. Let's get this show on the road."

Toothman carried on the briefing as Roman went to use the secure phone in his office.

"This is Kingfish."

"Hey, Kingfish, Roman here. How are things down in Dak To?"

"What? They haven't shot you, yet? Our guys, I mean."

"I'm making enemies every day," Roman replied. "Listen, I'm working a special op here and I can't tell you what it is. That's why I had the secure line put in."

"I was wondering why I rated a secure phone. Our battalion commander can't even get one."

"Well, it's simple. I need real-time hard information on prisoners of war in the Ho Chi Minh route structure. If you find out anything about a POW, call here and give me the information, even if it's speculation on your part. I want to know everything I can. Now, I'm sending down some information to you. Do not pass it on. It'll help you and the Dragon Lady get the information we need real bad. We understand there's a constant stream of POWs coming up the Ho Chi Minh Trail into Eastern and Northern Laos. I want to know more about it."

"We can do that. We get a lot of information here, some good, some not so good. But we'll give it all to you and tell you what we think about it."

"That's what we need. But not a word to anybody. Don't even speculate on what I'm doing."

"You got it," Kingfish said, "we can do it. Where are you? You in Saigon?"

"Well, that's where my mail officially goes, but, obviously, I'm not there. Don't ask."

"Okay."

Roman had the same conversation with The Fiddler at Tay Nin. Then, he walked down to the maintenance area to admire the maintenance miracle Tom Ryker had pulled off.

"Tom, you think they'll hold together?"

"Some of them are a little weak, but they'll all fly and they'll all come back. Even with the new parts, we still have a lot of problems with these birds. But we'll keep them going."

"Good, because it's going to get real busy around here. We'll be moving faster than we did at the 175th. We have only about six to eight months before we're out of here. They tell me there are over 200 POWs in cages out there. I want them back."

"With these birds? We'd need a Depot Level maintenance team to do that."

"That's why you're here. I know you can do it." Roman punched Ryker on the arm, then left.

When he got back to his room, Roman received a telephone report. All teams had been inserted without compromise and the aircraft were on their way back.

"Great," he said into the phone. "Relay this to Ditton. Meet me at the ramp area across from the Triple Nickel revetments on North Ramp. Keep the package wrapped. It's top secret. What's Ditton's ETA?"

"Archangel reports he'll be at the Triple Nickel revetments at 2115 hours."

"Thanks. Get a hold of Mr. Gedeon and ask him to meet me at the K&S pad at 2100 hours."

"Yes, sir."

Roman ended the conversation, pulled out a slip of paper from his wallet and dialed another number.

"Sam, this is Roman. If you'll meet me at the helipad in front of your office at 2115 hours, I'll show you something unique from Laos."

"Is it a—"

"Stop. You know what it is. Be there at 2115 hours or I'll take it back tomorrow."

"That won't be necessary!" The phone clicked off.

Roman got in his jeep just before 2100 hours and found Gedeon coming out of the BOQ. As they drove from the Air America ramp area to the northern part of the big Air Force ramp, Roman told Gedeon about the deal he'd made with Yamato on the old warehouse.

"Captain, you should have been a warrant officer," said Gedeon. "You certainly have enough larceny in your heart."

"Thanks, Bob, I'll take that as a compliment. I want you to oversee the whole project and be a real bastard about timely performance on Yamato's part. Make sure he delivers. Just keep telling him you won't release the jar until the job is fully completed to the agreed specifications. Sam is a tough, tough businessman. He'll skin you if you let him. He's honest, but a real horse trader. He doesn't think I know what one of those jars is worth to him on the black market. My sources tell me he could sell a small one for over ten grand."

"Jesus," Gedeon said with amazement.

Yamato's car was already at the helipad when they arrived.

"Sam, I want you to meet Bob Gedeon. He'll be working with you on Grunt Air's new quarters, office, bar and mess hall."

"I assume you have the asking price for my personal services," Yamato said. Just then, Ditton's Huey came into sight at the far end of the runway.

"Sam, you see the Huey headed this way."

"Yes."

"That worthless piece of rock is in that bird, or so I'm told."

"We'll see. By the way, I can deliver everything but the mess hall. Even I have limitations."

"That's not our deal, Sam"

"I have an alternative for you. You remember the 'B Frame Bar' at the 38th ADA Brigade BOQ at OSAN AFB, Korea?"

"Yeah, nice bar with a big grill, refrigerators, beer coolers, the works."

"That's right. I can put in two of those. One in the officer's lounge downstairs and one on the second floor in the enlisted area. I doubt if the EMs will want to drink with a bunch of criminal officers who stole a Laotian treasure. You can hire locals to run the bar and cook for you like you did in Korea. I'll give you the names of some locals who can do the job and have been cleared by Air Force security. This is assuming you truly have that rock jar I want."

The noise of the landing helicopter put an end to any further conversation. As soon as Lt. Ditton throttled back the turbine engine to flight idle,

Roman climbed into the cargo bay. He pulled the canvas tent back exposing the treasure they had liberated from the Plain of Jars.

Yamato drew closer, peered into the cargo bay and his eyes opened wide.

"Ohhh. This is in better condition than I expected. We've got a deal, Dan. Can your boys load this in my car?"

"No," said Roman. "We'll deliver it personally the day you complete the project and Mr. Gedeon signs off on it."

"Dan!" Yamato acted genuinely hurt. "I'm shocked you don't trust me to deliver."

"But Sam, I do trust you. I'm just being very thorough, just like you taught me back in Korea."

"Screw you, Roman! You'll have your new palace in about two weeks."

"Then you get the jar. Until then, it will be in Grunt Air's safekeeping. And Sam, I want the new home by the end of next week, by Thanksgiving. This jar's in mint condition. You'll get a lot more than ten thousand for it. That's your incentive."

"How do you know what this thing is worth? Never mind. I shouldn't ask. Okay. I'll put up a security fence around the warehouse tonight. We won't paint the outside or clean it up. You don't want to attract attention. I don't want to explain to Colonel Odom why every asset I have is working on rehabbing an old warehouse. We'll keep this real quiet, okay?"

"Deal, Sam. See you tomorrow."

Yamato said goodnight, patted the jar lovingly and left.

"Hey, Ditton," said Roman. "This jar is Grunt Air's new home and I want you to treat it like gold. Lock it up in the commo room. It will be tight but Sergeant Nelson will just have to live with it until Thanksgiving. Mr. Gedeon, this project is yours. Squeeze everything out of Yamato you can. Meanwhile, I'm going to bed."

CRACD

14

In the Bush with Uncle Ho

A jungle in northern Laos
13 November, 1971
Early afternoon

Donovan and his copilot, Larry Lawrence, flying as Grunt Air Two Two, inserted Echo Team without incident behind a hill just east of the Homestead. The four men were moving silently down the road leading toward the POW camp when they spotted a soldier ahead of them, walking into the local village of Ban Phon Tan. Christian motioned for Sergeant Pao.

"Get into your civilian clothes, circle around ahead of this guy, and wait for him down the road. Talk him up and see what you can find out."

It took Pao a few minutes to get there but he managed to be comfortably seated by the side of the road when the soldier walked by. It was the guard from the Homestead that Cody and the other prisoners had nicknamed Mushmouth. Pao could hardly understand him when he spoke.

The conversation started with Pao telling Mushmouth he had just come from the West. He'd heard about the conflict in his country and had come back to answer the call to arms.

Mushmouth was impressed and walked along with Pao toward the village. Until, that is, the rest of Echo Team burst out of the tree line and captured him and seemingly captured Pao, as well. Fortunately, Mushmouth wasn't a strong believer in the military code of silence and had heard all kinds of stories about how the inhuman American devils tortured their captives. So when Sergeant Stibbens asked him questions, he answered. For most of the conversation, Pao had to interpret.

Just for show, Stibbens asked Pao a few easy military questions, which the Laotian answered in impressive detail. This gave Mushmouth more confidence to speak openly hoping the American devils wouldn't tear his skin off, pull his fingernails out or just plain kill him.

During the questioning, Stibbens managed to discover that the three prisoners in custody at the Homestead had been moved earlier in the day. When Christian heard the news, he swore, using every filthy word he knew and making up some original ones. Mushmouth disclosed that they'd been taken by truck to a camp near the town of Borikhan. The other South Vietnamese prisoners had been shot over by the drainage canal. The Americans knew the POW camp at Borikhan as the Tollbooth.

Pressed by Stibbens, Mushmouth said he knew the prisoners would be taken further north but did not know when or where. He and Major Bai, the Homestead camp commander, were the only two left. Captain Ho had gone with the others, but in a private car instead of the truck. Ho had gone to Sam Neua to call his report in to his superiors.

Echo Team also learned that the camp doctor had left with the prisoners to tend to the Aussie Major's leg infection and the lacerations on the American's wrists. They were starting to get infected and make the Major ill. Mushmouth expected the truck to return in two or three days.

As soon as Christian heard that Major Bai was alone in the camp, he and Anderson trotted down the hill, walked in and paid the camp commander a surprise visit. He was not immediately as talkative as Mushmouth, but when Anderson tied him to a chair and picked up the split cane that Wild Eye had used on Major Smythe-Gordon, the information started to flow.

According to Bai, Captain Ho believed that the American Army Major was more important than he seemed. It was Major General Thran Van Ho himself who ordered the prisoners transferred to the complex in the Plain of Jars.

Stibbens brought Mushmouth back to the camp, and Pao had the pleasure of watching the mumbling man's face as he locked the cell door behind him and Major Bai. They'd have no food or water but would be released from the hot cell in the middle of the camp in a few days when the truck came back. If it came back.

Since no one ever came to the camp from the village and there was no military reason for higher command to send anyone there, Echo Team felt safe in spending the night. At 1800 hours, they made a special report to Archangel that the camp had gone negative and the POWs had been moved north to the Tollbooth, but they had no confirmation as to where they would go beyond that. They passed along Mushmouth's opinion that Valley View and Happy Valley were empty.

"No use going there," Stibbens told Archangel on the radio. "Tell Udorn we need a ride home."

The night was quiet, and in the morning, Echo Team awoke, checked on the comfort of the prisoners and then moved out to the extraction point. Donovan landed Grunt Air Two Two just at sunrise and took the team to NKP to brief Abeel and Roman, who had flown in with Archangel.

Knowing that the POWs were headed toward the Tollbooth, Roman directed Grunt Air Four Four to insert Bravo Team in the vicinity.

At the same time, in the western portion of the Plain of Jars, Richardson's Charlie Team had finished their air reconnaissance of the Fish Trap and was setting up in a night defensive position just south of the Rat Terminal, so called because of the huge and perpetual infestation of rats in the area. The vermin were said to carry more diseases than the girls in Bangkok. They'd stay there until the predawn hours and then, while the local residents slept, would cross a series of streams and a major road to enter a more dangerous area. While most of the PDJ was under the control of Vang Pao, there were still isolated pockets of Communist true believers. The team had to transit the area invisibly so they were not attacked.

The Fish Trap, on the other hand, was exactly that—a series of fish traps out in the open at the confluence of eight streams coming out of the hills surrounding the western PDJ. The NVA kept prisoners in the traps, which were five-foot-square cages made of bamboo and thatch netting. Prisoners so detained could neither stand up nor sit down and usually squatted in water about three feet deep. When it rained and the water level rose, they would drown unless the camp commander got them out in time, which didn't always happen. Since the camp was so exposed, it could be reconned from the air and didn't require a team on the ground.

It always got dark fast in the jungle. Bravo team would establish a nighttime defensive position and hope to be left alone. Even though they hadn't been compromised on insertion and hadn't seen anyone close by, they would maintain a night watch on two-hour shifts starting at 2000 hours. Each man on the team would take a turn watching for possible NVA or Pathet Lao soldiers in the area.

Being off the trail in a thick, heavy jungle area gave them some security because the NVA seldom walked through the dense jungle or underbrush when they had a nice trail to walk on. The one trail the team did see looked to be little-used.

Richardson double-checked the perimeter made up by the other members of the Recon Team. He verified the deployment of the eight Claymore mines put out in case of attack. All was ready.

At one corner, Spec 5 John Schwartz pulled out his poncho to help keep the dew and the mosquitoes off. Schwartz was a very good man in the bush but something of a lunatic in camp, compelled to hunt down and seduce married women whenever he had the chance. He was good-looking enough and could probably have had any single woman he wanted, but, to him, the ring was the thing. Richardson was certain that if the NVA didn't get him, some husband would. Richardson wanted him gone, transferred, anything. But it was dark, they were in the jungle and he had other things to worry about.

At 0400 hours, Richardson quietly got his team up. They march-ordered their gear, pulled in their Claymores and prepared to move out. Richardson wanted to get across the main road in the area before the locals started moving around. Their Hmong scout, Corporal Khan, took the lead, with Sergeant Ramirez to the rear to check for trailers. The very first hint of dawn threw dim apricot colors along the hills in the east.

They crossed a large creek without any trouble except for the ever-present leeches, which sucked their breakfast and dropped off. Any that didn't would get their butts burned when they were out of the water.

The creek was easy, but the road was a different story because of the open area 15 to 20 meters on each side. There was a curve to the north and a curve to the south. If anyone came around those curves while they were crossing, it would be bad news. But it seemed safe because there were no villages or houses near the curves and it was still fairly dark.

On the other side, they headed into the jungle about 20 meters to stop and "lay dog." When a team lay dog, they set up a perimeter defensive position, remaining silent and almost motionless so they could listen for human noise. It would also provide the opportunity to rest and, in this case, put a heated knifepoint against the remaining leeches. The more common remedy was a lit cigarette, but the smell would give them away.

At 0700 hours, they made a situation report to Archangel. All was well and on schedule. The Fish Trap was empty and cold, indicating no recent activity.

About 1045 hours, they stopped and formed a quick defensive perimeter so they could lay dog until mid-afternoon when the sun would create enough shade for them to hide in. Shadows would allow them to move toward the Rat Terminal without being easily detected.

Richardson sent Khan out ahead to check for the Pathet Lao troops that often worked the area. He was gone almost an hour and reported a battalion-sized NVA unit camped alongside the main road east of the Rat Terminal. Not good. They hadn't heard about the troops in their pre-mission briefing. The info would, however, go out in the next sitrep, just before dark.

"We'll need to go to the alternate extraction point," said Richardson. "This is too close to the NVA."

After the briefing, Khan led them to their observation point not far from their planned nighttime defensive position. They arrived just before the darkness took over. There was some activity in the camp but no sign of prisoners. The team surveyed the area looking for possible approaches to the camp before dark.

"We might be able to start the close-in recon real early," Richardson told his team. "The darkness will help us move closer and get across the rice paddies."

His radio earpiece crackled, reminding him it was time to make his evening report to Archangel. The news of the NVA battalion caused some concern in Archangel's voice.

"Be careful. Out." That was all he said.

Seventy-seven miles to the southeast, Gunny Sergeant Thornhill of Bravo Team surveyed the Tollbooth through his binoculars, trying to take in as much as he could before darkness engulfed him. He could still make out the camp and its activities but, after dark, he would use his night-vision goggles, the "starlight scope."

From his position to the west of the limestone karst that ran along the side of the camp, he peered toward the fence trying to make out Sergeant Gryner, who would be checking out that area. On the north side, Spec 5 Brindle was doing the same. Their interpreter and scout, Mona Tong, had changed into his native attire and headed toward Borikhan to see if he could learn anything from the locals.

If there are prisoners here, thought Thornhill, *we'll see them*. The three prisoners coming up from the Homestead were generating a lot of interest from the top down. Thornhill looked west of the POW camp and village and saw the campfires of Vang Pao's troops operating in the area about five miles away. Probably a company-size unit on routine patrol along the border. Not much chance they would venture this far east.

The lights of an approaching truck caught Thornhill's attention. It rambled through the village without slowing down and headed for the camp. Thornhill's breath quickened. This could be it. He hoped his boys were in position to see who was inside.

The truck jerked to a stop in front of the biggest thatch and bamboo building in the compound, obviously the camp headquarters, with the tailgate facing away from Thornhill's vantage point. The headlights went out. For ten minutes, the ancient vehicle sat there ticking in the gathering dark, then drove out of the compound and turned onto the road that led into the mountains.

What the hell? Thornhill had no idea what was going on. Maybe he would find out in an hour or so when the team rejoined him. Meanwhile, he was satisfied with the position he had taken up. It would be easy to defend, and they would be able to keep the camp under constant observation through the night.

He was impatient for his men to get back with their individual reports.

Tong was the first to arrive. He started to change back into his Hmong uniform, if one could call it a uniform.

"Gunny, you're not going to believe this. They're closing the camp because of Vang Pao's troops. The village is solid Vang Pao supporters. They hate the NVA because they came in last week and beat the village elder to death with iron bars. He wouldn't give up any information on Vang Pao or the location of his troops or the names of any supporters in the village. They say it was really gruesome. They loved the old man and are ready to avenge his death. If you want them to attack the camp for us, they'd do it. But I told them not to because it would only get them killed. Did you see the truck?

"Yeah, but it was too dark to make anything out."

Sergeant Gryner came in so quietly he took both Tong and Thornhill by surprise. Brindle showed up a second later.

"I saw them," said Gryner. "Our boys. The NVA pulled them out of the truck and threw them on the ground. Someone took a flashlight and looked at the bandages on the Aussie's leg and then the wrists of the American. I guess it was a doctor or medic. The driver came back out of the headquarters and put some gas in the truck. Soon as he was done, they left. You saw which way they went."

"I did get one good piece of information," Brindle added. "They're driving the prisoners through the mountains to Bam Pho."

"That's Disneyland." Thornhill reached for his radio. "Archangel. Archangel. This is Bravo."

"Go ahead Bravo, Archangel copies."

Thornhill gave a coded message about what the team had seen and heard. It was lengthy and detailed. Archangel responded that it copied the transmission and they were to stand by. Ten minutes passed without anyone saying a word. Then Archangel came back to them.

"Bravo, this is Archangel, do you copy?"

"Roger, Archangel. Go ahead."

"Bravo, Four Four will extract at 0600 hours at primary. Do you copy?"

"Roger, Archangel. We are a go at 0600 hours. Bravo out."

"Looks like we may be back at Udorn for Thanksgiving." Gryner was being jovial.

"Don't count on it. This whole thing is too hot to sit on," Thornhill said as he lay down. "Okay, Gryner. You take the first shift, Tong the second, and I'll take graveyard. Brindle, you get the morning shift, if we have one." Then Thornhill closed his eyes to sleep.

Alpha Team, under Captain Jake Best, had initially reconned Dog Patch. It was vacant, and had been for what appeared to be several weeks. The team was moving southeast toward Disneyland when they got the call from Archangel.

"Proceed to Disneyland at best possible pace. Anticipate hotel guests to be checking in soon. What's your estimated time of arrival Disneyland?"

"Archangel, estimate Disneyland in eight hours."

"Roger. Report on site. Archangel out."

The radio went silent. Best knew he had just been given the hot potato. "Okay guys, let's boogie."

Near the Rat Terminal, Richardson had listened to the Alpha Team transmission several hours earlier. He and his team had left their nighttime defensive position a little after 0430 hours to move into their assigned observation points. The POW camp was 15 or so meters in front of him.

The sun had come up, and the North Vietnamese and Pathet Lao guards were busy making repairs, possibly in preparation for some new prisoners. Maybe Archangel was wrong. Maybe those three guys were coming to the Rat Terminal after all. It didn't matter. If they did, Charlie Team would be there to report their arrival. They could spend the day making detailed notes on the area and the camp—useful information if this was a final stop for the three POWs. To bust the camp and recover the prisoners they'd need every shred of information available.

Archangel called wanting to know if the NVA unit was still in the same place.

"That's affirmative, Archangel. We haven't seen or heard any movement."

"Roger, Charlie. Pull back to your NDP as soon as possible. There'll be a fast-mover strike in three zero mikes. You'll observe and report battle damage. Do you copy?"

"Roger, Archangel. Charlie copies and will be in position to observe. Charlie also reports an empty nest at the location. Lots of preparation for visitors, but no positive joy."

"Roger, Charlie. Stand by."

"Archangel, this is Delta."

"Go Delta."

"Delta has found no joy at the Bird Cage and we're almost to the Soup Kitchen. Will be in place by 1600 hours."

"Roger, Delta. ETA Soup Kitchen 1600 hours today. Archangel out."

"Archangel, this is Charlie. In position. Bring on the court jesters and the clowns."

"Roger, Charlie," responded Archangel. "Expect the first clown in zero two."

Sergeant Ramirez was the first to spot the two F-4s when they burst out of the sky thundering over the tree line at 200 feet. Four dark shapes dropped from beneath their wings and the jungle exploded into gouts of glorious orange fire.

The first two F-4s hadn't even got back to altitude when the second pair repeated the same move. They dropped their loads at the end of the first burning area so as to get the entire battalion under fire.

Richardson said to Ramirez, "I don't know what the body count is, but it'll be good. That unit is history."

Then, he picked up the radio mike to call Archangel just as the first two F-4s returned to rub it in a little, dropping four bombs each on the burning napalm, which spread it even further. Then they pulled up to gain altitude again.

"Archangel, this is Charlie. Best seats in town to a perfect show. The boys in blue took that unit off the active rolls."

Before he could say anything else, he heard the sickening sound of anti-aircraft fire. From a small hill east of the camp, a 32mm gun opened up on the lead F-4. The F-4 had just started his climb when it took a full burst and started smoking and breaking apart. The front ejection seat fired clear of the burning jet as it tumbled toward the earth. The second pilot had not ejected.

Come on. Eject! Richardson watched the plane cartwheel to earth and saw the first parachute float toward the jungle. Shit. One dead and one possible POW.

"Archangel, this is Charlie. We got a fast mover down. One good chute."

"Roger, Charlie. Keep an eye on the chute."

"Archangel, the wind is blowing him towards us. We'll grab him before the bad guys get here."

"Roger, Charlie. I'll advise the boss."

"See that?" Ramirez pointed to about ten NVA headed in their direction, watching to see where the chute would come down. The recon team had to get there first. The NVA wouldn't be goodwill ambassadors after the F-4 jock had just roasted their entire unit.

Sgt. Richardson nodded and got to his feet. "Okay," he said, "let's get him before they do. Khan, head straight for him. Schwartz and Ramirez, circle around to the back of his landing point." Richardson turned back to see where the NVA troops were just as the other F-4 dropped a napalm canister right on top of them.

"Well, that should stop them for now," Richardson said as he turned towards the pilot and started through the jungle.

Captain Pete Condon checked his chute to confirm it had fully deployed. Then, he looked back towards the billowing smoke that had been his plane. He looked in vain for his copilot who had not responded to the command to eject. They'd been hit too hard to save the aircraft. He was lucky to pull his handle before it broke apart. Now, he had to start planning his landing and escape to freedom.

Freedom? He was in Northern Laos over 140 miles away from the nearest air base. That situation met his definition of being completely fucked. *Maybe*, he thought, *I can work my way south to the Thailand border, then to a friendly unit.* The ejection seat had blown him high into the air and, as he floated down, he had plenty of time to think. If he survived the landing and wasn't hurt or run through by a tree limb, there would be no way to avoid the NVA. He had seen a lot of them as he made his napalm runs and he knew they would not arrive in good humor. Even before he touched down, he was preparing himself for a stay at the Hanoi Hilton. If the NVA didn't just kill him on the spot.

He pulled on his risers trying to steer his chute toward a small clearing. The last thing he wanted to do was end up in the trees. He hit the ground hard but did a tuck and roll, just like he'd learned. Alive and unhurt. So far, so good. He shucked out of his suit and looked around, running through the drill he'd learned during all those boring Escape and Evasion classes. He wrapped his helmet in his chute, buried them in a small hole, covered it with brush and stood back to admire his work. He was satisfied the NVA wouldn't spot it. Then he squinted into the jungle all around him, trying to get his bearings. He got his emergency radio out and tried to turn it on. It was broken. There was a big gash in it where part of his exploding aircraft had hit it instead of him. Once again, good luck.

The compass and escape map were next. Moving to the edge of the clearing, he kept checking his compass and trying to remember whether Air America flew over that particular region. Maybe he would get even luckier. With his head down, looking at his compass, he moved out of the clearing and into the cooler darkness of the trees. He stopped to let the compass needle settle down when a hand reached out from nowhere and clamped itself over his mouth to keep him from screaming. He felt the backside of a knife blade against his throat and instantly stopped moving.

"Need a taxi, Captain?"

He relaxed in more ways than one. His flight suit could be cleaned out later. Whoever had the knife against his carotid spoke English with a very American accent, and that was a very good sign.

The hand came off his mouth and he spun around to find himself face to face with an unusually large black man in Army camouflage fatigues.

"Don't say a word," Sergeant Richardson whispered. "Do what I say and we'll both make it to our next birthday."

Richardson tugged him toward the west and they moved through the underbrush as quietly as they could, making it to a tree line next to a small stream. There, they found the other three members of Charlie Team in a defensive position.

Condon started to greet his rescuers but Ramirez put a finger to his lips. Condon nodded to each of them and then sat down to wait.

Sergeant Richardson moved away from the group, picked up the radio mike and called Archangel. "Archangel, this is Charlie."

"Go ahead, Charlie."

"We've got the downed pilot. I think he's recognized me and our uniforms. Can we keep him or do we throw him back?"

"Good question, Charlie. This is not an easy one. I'll contact Six and get guidance. I'm launching Three out of two zero alpha to get you. Expect extraction in about 45 mikes. Stand by."

Back at Udorn, Captain Roman was walking back from the construction site when the First Sergeant ran up to him on the tarmac.

"Sir, Archangel needs you on secure Fox Mike. It's urgent."

"Thanks, Top."

"Archangel, this is Six. What's the problem?"

"Six, we have a situation. Charlie rescued an F-4 pilot that got shot down after he napalmed the NVA battalion on the east side of the Rat Terminal. Charlie says it's one of the pilots out of Udorn. He thinks the guy recognized him. Wants to know what to do with him."

"Great," exclaimed Roman. "Has Charlie finished the mission? Where are the NVA?"

Archangel came back immediately. "Both recons complete. Unit is ready for extraction. Current situation is static with the NVA disorganized and not searching too hard for the pilot. Charlie has not been compromised."

"Roger. Who's scheduled for the pick up?" The concern in his voice was clear, even on the radio.

"I've got Three cranking at two zero alpha for the mission instead of One One. I thought you might want him in on this mission for horse power."

"Damn good call, Doug. Is Three's secure mode working?"

"It's good, Six."

Roman outlined the plan to handle the Air Force pilot and their mission security, then sat down in his chair and put his face in his hands.

"Top, this could be the end. If that pilot blabs, we're finished."

"I dunno, Captain. If he blows our cover, the old man will transfer him to Alaska or Greenland."

On instructions from Archangel, the recon team moved toward their extraction point with the Air Force pilot in tow. Meanwhile, Jan Toothman, call sign Grunt Air Three, looked down at the road between Skyline Ridge One and Skyline Ridge Two just north of Long Tieng, also known as Two Zero Alfa or "Alternate." From this super-secret CIA airfield in Northern Laos, hundreds of support and combat flights originated each day. Only Chicago's O'Hare Field had more daily operations than Two Zero Alpha. It was also Grunt Air's forward operating base for its clandestine missions.

Toothman finished the lengthy call from Archangel over the secure FM radio and then nodded to his copilot, Jack Fondren, to see if he understood, which he did.

"This is a tall order," he said.

"You got that right," Fondren replied.

The copilot riveted his attention on maneuvering the Huey through the pass, a possibly deadly journey. Once clear, they turned northeast for the 24-mile flight to the extraction point.

"Archangel, this is Three. Advise Charlie to get ready for a quick extraction in one five." Toothman signed off, then signaled Fondren to begin his descent for a high speed tactical approach.

"Roger, Three, Charlie is ready to go. Be advised that the NVA is less than a klick to the east," Archangel responded.

"Mr. Fondren, let's do it."

Fondren put the helicopter down below the tops of the trees and increased the speed to one one zero knots. He jockeyed the Huey through the trees and clearings with a light touch, hands and feet working together. He stayed as low as possible because at this speed and altitude, it was very difficult for the NVA to hit the aircraft, even with small arms fire.

After about fifteen minutes of tactical flying, Fondren suddenly pulled the nose up and reduced the power to slow down, maintaining the low altitude until they were over the clearing in the trees. The space was small but the Huey could clear its rotor blades by about ten feet on each side as it lowered the 40 or so feet to the ground below. It took only about five seconds for the members of Charlie Team to shove the F-4 pilot through the cargo bay door and clamber in.

"Clear," yelled Spec 4 Prince from his position as the door gunner. The engine roared and the Huey flew straight up, dropped the nose to gain airspeed and clattered off, just clearing the treetops.

Once everyone had sorted themselves out in the cargo bay, Toothman turned around to look at Captain Condon. Then he looked again.

"Son of a bitch. Aren't you the asshole who was giving the Grunt Air guys so much shit at the Officer's Club the other night? Hey, Prince. Give that guy a headset and put him up on the private intercom channel." Toothman switched his channel so nobody in the aircraft would hear him except Condon.

"Looks like you're going to make it home alive," Toothman said.

"What the hell are you guys doing up here?" Condon demanded. "You're no damn crash site unit!"

"Well, that's true," Toothman admitted, "and the fact you know it is a pretty big problem for us. You guys have a couple hundred Air Force pilots down here in Laos, and all the units who have tried to rescue them have about disappeared from Southeast Asia due to the drawdown. Now, Kissinger's trying to negotiate for the release of all POWs here in Laos and in North Vietnam but, so far, only the boys in Hanoi are being discussed. The guys who got shot down in Laos, like you, could be abandoned. Your Commanding General at 7th Air Force thinks that's unacceptable. He's made a pledge to get all you guys out and back home and he won't go back on his word. Stuck his neck way out. Grunt Air is his way to locate and bring home our boys. If anybody finds out what he's doing, he gets fired, we get shut down, and 228 of your colleagues get to stay here and get fed a daily diet of fish heads and torture.

"We've located a bunch of Air Force POWs in the area and we'll be getting them out in the next few months. But only if we can keep our operation secret. That's where you come in, Condon.

"Everyone in the region knows you got shot down. If you tell anyone about this, your guys are fucked. Life imprisonment, torture. Execution. Your friends and classmates. Oh, and by the way, any blabbing on your part gets you transferred to someplace really cold where the sun doesn't come up for eight months a year.

"What do you say? Can you keep a secret and save your guys, or do we take this chopper up to five thousand and let you walk home from there?"

Condon was quiet for a long moment taking in the implications of Toothman's confession. He wiped away a drop of moisture that had collected in the corner of his right eye.

"We're all on the same side," he said. "And I'm pissed that you think I won't keep something this important to myself. I'm an American military officer, and a pilot, just like you."

"Right answer. Welcome aboard, Pete. It is Pete, isn't it?"

While Fondren flew, Toothman fed Condon his Big Lie. When they landed at Long Tieng to refuel, Condon would wander into the Air Force Liaison's office and tell Major Weir he got picked up by an Air America helicopter and dropped off.

"If he starts asking any questions, look sick or battle shocked. He'll leave you alone and put you on an aircraft back to Udorn. Hell, you'll probably get home before we do. Remember, it was some unidentified Air America crew that rescued you, not a bunch of Army weenies. Deal?"

"On my word as an officer."

"That's good enough for me."

At Udorn, Roman was back on the air to Archangel asking about the status of the crews and recon teams. Alpha Team was at the NDP at Disneyland. Bravo had been back at Udorn for a while, Charlie was inbound, Delta Team was waiting at the NDP at the Soup Kitchen, and Grunt Three was also on the way with its unexpected passenger. Everybody safe and coming home to roost.

"Good show," Roman said. "I want all birds and teams, except Alpha, home by 1200 hours tomorrow. It's Thanksgiving and I have a treat for Grunt Air, after we go to the obligatory rubber turkey meal with the Air Force."

"Roger. I'll get home in time," Alberts said. "Archangel, out."

Roman picked up the phone and dialed a number at K&S. Sam Yamato was not there. He was at the warehouse with Gedeon. Roman got the number. He dialed 4085, and after five rings, somebody picked up.

"Gedeon here."

"Bob, how close is Sam to finishing?"

"Hell, boss, he's done. We're just discussing the turnover date."

"Great! How many corners did he cut?"

"Why boss, you underestimate me. We got everything we asked for. All of it. We're going to deliver the jar to him at 2200 hours to some warehouse just off base. Good thing Yamato and his missus like you so much. That went a long way on this job."

"That's good to hear. I thought he was sick when you said he hadn't tried to cut corners or skin us. Meet me at the club. I'll buy you a drink or three and we'll figure out how to handle the turnover tomorrow. I assume the guys still don't know about the place, yet?"

"I think we still have a surprise for Thanksgiving."

"Great! See you at the club."

When Roman walked in to the Air Force O Club to meet Gedeon and the rest of his team, the noise from the bar almost knocked him back out the door. The fighter jocks were celebrating the miraculous return of Captain Condon by Air America. The whole group was two sheets to the wind, well on its way to three.

A thought raced through Roman's head. In wine, there is truth, the ancient Romans used to say. Would alcohol turn Condon into an honest man? He tried not to think about it as he pulled out a chair and joined his group at their table.

"Quite a day. Let's just hope that Captain what's-his-name over there keeps his mouth shut or our surprise tomorrow won't mean a hell of a lot."

"Surprise?" Ryker was justifiably puzzled.

Gedeon told him the whole story, all about the air conditioning, the bars, the hot griddle on each floor, one for the enlisted men and one for the officers. He enjoyed the expressions on Ryker's face as he revealed each delicious detail, every unexpected amenity.

"We'll assemble the company after lunch tomorrow and tell them the good news. Things are slow for the next two days, so we can move and get organized. I cleared it."

Just then, a roar of laughter came rolling out of the bar. Roman looked up just in time to see Condon turn toward his table, raise his glass and wink.

"Well, there you go," said Roman. "He's just the kind of lying bastard we need. Drunk on his ass and he sticks to his story. Now, what's good on the menu tonight?"

Gedeon responded dryly, "C-rations."

᳕᳕᳕

15

Texas Turkey and the Udorn Hilton

"Archangel, Archangel, this is Alpha."

A call from the four-man recon team that had previously been inserted by Grunt Air into the jungle of Northern Laos near Disneyland. They were monitoring the arrival and departure of POWs, especially the Big Three, as they'd named the prisoners who had been moved from the Homestead camp.

"Go ahead, Alpha." Archangel responded.

"Our visitors checked into Disneyland at 0245 hours. They got here by truck with a driver, officer and one guard. They don't look too good from the trip. So far today, they've been left alone in the cages. The truck is still here so they may be transferred again. We think we should stay here another day or two to keep an eye on them. Alpha will move to the alternate southern extraction point. Request water and rations be dropped off there just before sunset. We'll relocate to the hill 1.2 klicks southwest of current position to monitor. If they move, we can see them for miles."

"Roger, Alpha. I'll clear it with Six. Out."

Roman agreed with Jake Best that Alpha Team should keep an eye on the Big Three from a distance. It was too bad they would miss the Thanksgiving Day turkey, such as it was.

When it came to cooking turkey, military cooks, no matter their branch of service, could never get the hang of it, turning out unfortunate birds that tasted like the worst kind of hospital food. It may not have been the cooks' fault, since the military provided them with fowl more closely related to Texas

121

buzzards than the big-breasted gobblers consumed back in the States. *But,* thought Roman, *it's the tradition that counts.*

Thanksgiving dawned beautifully with comfortably low humidity, which helped to minimize the normal steam bath atmosphere. Everyone at Grunt Air was in good spirits, and they hadn't even been told of the big surprise yet to come.

After the unremarkable but good-spirited Thanksgiving lunch, Grunt Air personnel slowly walked back to the briefing room for some mysterious announcement by Captain Roman. Precisely at 1500 hours, the First Sergeant called the room to attention as Roman and Gedeon entered. Mr. Gedeon carried a big cardboard poster covered with a sheet. Everyone assumed it was an operational map.

"At ease. Take your seats, gentlemen," Roman said. To build a little suspense, he regarded the assembled faces carefully. "Gentlemen, Grunt Air is moving."

The men looked at each other. Everyone knew there was no other space at Udorn.

"While you were out having fun and games in Laos, Mr. Gedeon has been supervising the rehabilitation of that old Thai Air Force warehouse as our new home."

A stir went through the room. There were murmurs of "Yeah" and "All *right!*"

"As you may have noticed, a high-security fence has been installed around the warehouse. It's for us. Today and tomorrow, we'll be moving into our new home. I'm going to turn this over to Mr. Gedeon who has worked damn hard to make this happen."

"Thanks, Captain Roman," he said. "The building is divided into three main areas. First, there's the downstairs front area which will be the Headquarters and briefing room." He pulled the sheet off of the first chart and pointed to the Headquarters area, the offices and communications room.

"Behind the offices and briefing room will be the officers' rooms and a small bar with griddle and assorted coolers and refrigerators. You'll note that the B-Frame, as I've named it, is at the end of the building for security reasons. There's a cyber lock security door here at the end of the briefing room so no one that's not a part of our operation, or cleared by Grunt Air, is permitted into the office area. That's another reason for the high-security fence and gate. The Commanding General, 7th Air Force, has made this building off limits to all unauthorized personnel. That means no more snoops.

"Now, let's go upstairs. This is the enlisted area. E7s and 8s have their own rooms. Everyone else will be two men to a room."

There were cheers of excitement. Specialist Shack asked if there were any new screens for the windows so they could get cross-ventilation.

"Sorry. No screens, gentlemen," Gedeon said. The room quieted. He could see the disappointment on all the faces. "Because screens would let out our air conditioning."

Cheers. High fives. The men almost stood up and cheered. Air conditioning! In Southeast Asia, only Generals had air conditioning, and only if they were lucky. Gedeon started to smile but thought better of it. He didn't want the men to start thinking he was human after all. He continued with the good news.

"Quiet down, please. Also at the far end of the second floor is a bar set up exactly like the one downstairs. It, too, has a high-security door at the stairwell that leads down into the Headquarters area. This configuration will allow security-approved housemaids to keep the place clean and get the laundry done. We do have our own washer and dryer in the supply room. Everyone will chip in each payday to cover the service of the housemaids. Everyone will use the doors at the back of the building as the normal entrance. That will keep the congestion and noise down in the Headquarters area. Are there any questions?"

"When do we move?" asked Sergeant Teddy Priest. Gedeon looked at Captain Roman.

"Well," Roman said, "I thought we might need to work off all that turkey. So, how about now?"

A roar filled the room. Roman held up his hand for quiet and then continued. "We'll move the Headquarters first, then supply and other mission-essential equipment and services, then we move individually. The First Sergeant has the sequence of the move. Sergeant Nelson, your commo lines have already been installed. Now, I expect everyone, and I do mean everyone, to follow the First Sergeant's plan. We need to complete the move and be fully operational by 1700 hours tomorrow."

The move went smoother than expected. By 1700 hours the next day, when the First Sergeant called a halt, everything and everyone was moved, except some large items in supply. Even Alpha Team, who was still out in the bush, had been moved to their new rooms. They were going to be very surprised when they returned.

About 2000 hours, Roman picked up CW4 Alberts and Specialist Burke, the Crew Chief, went to the flight line and took off in the C-47. As they climbed to altitude to get a good communications signal from Alpha Team, Roman had a rare brief moment to look out the window and appreciate the calm beauty of the night.

A few miles north of the Mekong River, they made contact with Alpha on the FM tactical radio.

"Alpha, we need a sitrep," said Roman.

"Is that you, boss?" asked Best.

"Yeah, I drew the short straw," Roman replied.

"The truck left about noon with only the driver, guard, and doctor onboard. They went back south along the same road they came in on. I assume back to the Homestead. No other activity all afternoon. They've left the Big Three alone all day. Looks like they're letting them rest and heal before another move north."

"Roger, Alpha. We'll extract tomorrow morning after the fog burns off. Delta will relieve you on watch." Delta was the four-member recon team led by SFC Krumins. It was one of Grunt Air's five Recon Teams commanded by Captain Jake Best. "What do they need to bring?"

"Have them bring food, extra water and sleeping bags. The nights are cold at this elevation. More batteries for the radio and a good set of binoculars or a telescope. A second starlight scope would be a help."

"Any NVA around you?"

"Nope, we're too high for those lazy bastards to patrol up here. We're well hidden and haven't been compromised. We're in good shape and have a good view."

"Roger. Sleep tight. Archangel, out."

The next day, with the move completed, the unit went back to mission-oriented duties. Maintenance became the main priority, especially since the weather had turned damp and foggy. This gave Roman an excuse to keep his birds on the ground. Once they had a handle on what was happening to the Big Three, things would start getting busy.

Delta replaced Alpha on the camp watch detail. Back at the base, Alpha Team reported that they'd seen a lot of vehicle traffic at night in the area. They couldn't see what was being moved but assumed it to be personnel. Some of the trucks were straining, like they were pulling artillery.

That got Abeel's attention. He sent a request for information to 7th Air Force Intelligence. After he received a rather lengthy response from the Intel boys in Saigon, he went to see Roman, who was in his office working through the unit's many maintenance problems with Tom Ryker.

"Sphinx," Ryker said, "you're starting to look like Gedeon. You never smile. I don't think you appreciate the wonders and beauty of Thailand anymore."

"Like there's so much to smile about," Abeel retorted. "You didn't smile for weeks after you got here."

"Okay, Bill," Roman said. "What have you got?"

"I'm worried about these reports of movement in the Ban Ban Valley and the eastern Plain of Jars," Abeel reflected. "There's a lot of traffic and it's probably the reason they haven't moved the Big Three on to Sam Neua or Hanoi. The Intel boys at 7th gave me some good info, and they're sending me some U-2 photos on the courier flight tomorrow. But, there's something else."

"What's your gut feeling?" Roman asked.

"I wish I had one. I'm not sure about anything. Remember back in late '67, early '68, when you got the hunch that the VC were about to attack in strength?"

"Yes." Roman's face twisted at the unpleasant, frustrating memory. "Everyone wanted to send me to the shrink until the gooks were in the fence and running across the Vinh Long runway."

"It's kind of like that," Abeel observed. "Look, the CIA Intel summary says the dry season offensive may not be too big, and might even be delayed, but there's way too much movement in the northern and eastern portions of the PDJ. And it's too early for any build-up for Tet. I think the offensive is about to begin. Remember your Intel briefing by General Geiger?" he asked. "He spent all that time talking about a big increase in troop strength and the NVA's prepositioning of supplies and ammunition. He didn't come right out and say so, but he wanted you to know the NVA was preparing for a big dry season offensive. Now that I have some answers from the Intel boys at 7th, I think he's right. All hell is about to break loose up there, maybe in the next two or three weeks, but for sure before Christmas. And it'll be worse than anybody thinks. When it happens, we'll be in deep kimchi right along with Vang Pao's troops."

Roman thought for a second. "What do you think we should do in the meantime, Chief?"

"First, you can call and get an update on the situation, the POW info, troop movements, and the gut feelings of Fiddler and Kingfish."

"Okay, I'll do that in a few mikes. Can you give me an EEI for them to work on? I don't want it to be too general." An EEI report stood for Essential Elements of Information, a kind of boiled-down briefing document hitting only the high points.

"You'll have it in an hour, sir."

"What else?" Roman questioned.

"I think we need to get teams up tomorrow and check out all of the PDJ and see if we can figure out where they'll take the Big Three next," Abeel observed. "I'm thinking it'll either be the Rock House or the Museum, and soon."

Not good. The Rock House and the Museum were POW camps located further north of the Disneyland camp in the Ban Ban Valley of Northern

Laos, farther into enemy territory and harder to reach. But Abeel wasn't finished with his bad news.

"The PDJ is too strongly controlled by Vang Pao's troops for the NVA to take a chance on the camp getting busted and losing what Hanoi considers important prisoners. They may even take them to the caves over at Sam Neua or that new camp, number L711. Frankly, that's where I would take them, but the roads are jammed at night with priority truck traffic. I suggest we do some reconnaissance in and around Sam Neua and west towards Site Eight Five. We need a good look at Eight Five as well as that landing strip to the west at Lima Site Five Niner and Lima Site One Eight Five. You might want to use them as forward supply points. You'll want to hide some fuel and ammunition there next week while things are still calm." Roman was quiet for another long moment, looking at Abeel through narrowed eyes.

"Chief," Roman said, "I do believe you're thinking about a possible extraction of the Big Three around Sam Neua."

"Well, sir, if we miss the opportunity at the PDJ, that will be our last chance. I know the NVA Headquarters is in that area, but they'll never expect us to hit there. If they find out how important the Big Three are to us, Hanoi will move them in a heartbeat. Then we'll be under the gun to get them out."

"Or kill them," Roman observed.

"Well, that would keep them from spilling classified info under torture, for sure," Ryker said sarcastically. "Pretty tall order, Bill."

Roman didn't speak. The idea of killing Americans didn't sit well with him even though he knew that, at some point, he might be faced with that possibility. He picked up the phone and summoned Best and Toothman to his office. When they arrived, Roman brought them up to speed on all of Abeel's feelings, hunches and intuitions. They sat for a second, taking it all in. Toothman was the first to break the silence.

"Tom, what shape are the birds in for extended operations?"

"There's not one circled red X in the fleet." Aircraft down for maintenance had a sign posted in the windscreen–a big X inside a red circle. "You can fly the crap out of them," Ryker continued. "We've done all the 100-hour inspections, hot end inspections, even the TACANS and glide slopes are up and calibrated for instrument operations."

"Okay, Jake," Roman said to Captain Best. "Tomorrow, you'll bring Delta Team back in for rest and refitting. Doug, take Archangel up to Lima Site Five Niner with 15 barrels of fuel for the Hueys, 20 barrels of Avgas for the C-47, and 12 cases of M-60 ammunition. The airfield commander is one of Vang Pao's wives, and she's as tough as he is. Make a deal with her to come through there on your crash site surveys. If you can, use her fuel, but leave six barrels of JP4 and the Avgas with her for our use later. You might take some trading material to soften her up. I hear she likes Jim Beam. A couple of quarts should do it. Jan, send two birds with Jake and Christian up there to meet Archangel. The C-47 stays on the ground to monitor Ops frequency while you and the other bird fly up to Site Eight Five and hide the rest of the fuel and ammo.

"It's real tight out there, I understand. But we can get eight or so birds in there if we have to. Jan, who do you want as your second bird?"

"Dorsey. I think he should go on this one."

"Good choice. Now, what about the Rock House and Museum?"

"We can send Thornhill and Bravo Team to the Rock House with Grunt Air Five Five," Toothman said. "And insert Charlie into the Museum area with Davis in Four Four. Then, we'll have the two aircraft recover to Long Tieng and wait for orders from Archangel. If one of these camps is the next stop for the Big Three, it could get hot and we may need to extract in a hurry. Donovan in Grunt One One can recover Delta Team and bring them back here to stay on stand-by."

"That should cover it," Roman said. "After you do that, fly to the old F-4 crash site at UH9447 and circle in plain sight. Land and conduct one of Mr. Touchdown's famous surveys. Be obvious so the enemy can see you. On your way in and out, look at the area around Sam Neua if they'll let you. Keep an eye out for a new camp four klicks northeast of town on the north side of the road. Maybe you can get one of our interpreters to make some kind of casual contact with the locals. Tell 'em we're conducting crash site surveys, we're non-combatants, our Hueys only have the two machine guns on them. No threat. After you do that, go back to Lima Site Five Niner and refuel. Then come home."

Roman looked long and hard at Toothman and Best to impress on them the importance of what they were about to do.

"Before you go north, get teams into the Rock House and Museum area for detailed, and I mean detailed, recon. Those two teams will be the primary if we have to go in, which, according to Mr. Abeel here, is pretty likely.

"Jake, tell Krumins that he may only have one day, possibly two, down before he has to take Delta back to Disneyland."

"Yes, sir."

"Tom, has Gedeon told you when those two replacement Hueys will be ready?"

"Nothing new, but I'll ask him to push," Ryker replied.

"Abeel, you and I are going to start squeezing every bit of raw Intelligence out of our sources, especially who these three guys really are, okay?"

"Right."

Roman stood up. "Okay, guys. Let's hit it."

Ryker, Toothman, and Best hurried away, but Abeel stayed behind.

"Dan," he said. "I think if you and I went over to Tan Son Nhut it'd be worth the trip. We could get more info if we met with General Geiger's boys face to face."

"You're right. I'll call General Mattix and see if he can arrange the briefing. Find Alberts and warn him that we may be taking off for Tan Son Nhut either today or tomorrow."

"Consider it done, sir. Back in one five."

Roman picked up his secure line to Blue Chip and connected with the jovial Major Fitzmorris.

"Party Palace. Jester speaking."

"Good god," Roman said, laughing, "I knew the staff was a bunch of clowns, but you just confirmed it."

"That's us. Better than Ringling Brothers around here. Now, what the hell can this clown do for the flying pirate?"

"I need to come in with Abeel to see General Geiger and his key Intel people. We need every shred of intelligence on northern Laos and on who the Big Three really are. We can be there in four hours or tomorrow morning."

"It so happens that General Mattix and General Geiger are right here with the Commanding General. Wait one."

The phone went silent as the push-to-talk secure function activated. This was to prevent other secret conversations from being heard over the phone. After a couple of minutes, Major Fitzmorris came back on the line.

"Make it 1600 hours in the Commanding General's conference room. You're to stop by and see the CG before you go back. Mattix also wants to see you. You need to pick him up on the way to the CG's office."

"Thanks. I'll see you for supper. We'll go to that Mexican restaurant over by Hotel Six helipad."

"Great. You're buying. You owe me and Mansen big time for keeping your ass out of the stockade." Roman laughed. The trip would cost him some money since Fitzmorris could really put away the beer and Mexican food, but it would be worth it.

∽∽

16

It's Great Being a Single Mother

Cody residence
Fort Bliss, Texas
Morning

Carol Cody sat at her small desk next to the breakfast room with her forehead resting in the palms of her hands. Tired, frustrated and spending the Thanksgiving weekend without her husband, she felt that she didn't have much to be thankful for. The trips to Washington had worn her out. She and Charlie hadn't accomplished a thing, and worse, her attempts to help her husband and other POWs had cost much more than she was prepared to spend. In front of her, a pile of bills that seemed to get taller every day remained unpaid. She was the head of her family for now and there seemed to be no end to her responsibilities.

Next to the bills, something even worse sat on the gray Formica table-top: an official "Dear Mrs. Cody" letter from the high school principal. She'd read it twice and gotten angrier each time.

Chris, her fifteen-year-old son, had been caught cutting class with three other boys who were smoking pot. Chris hadn't been smoking, according to the letter, but his actions were still unacceptable. "Please call me at your earliest convenience," said the letter, "so that we may discuss this problem." Well, there was no time like the present.

"Chris!" she screamed at the top of her lungs. "Get in here, now!"

He came into the room, a tall, thin boy who was starting to look heartbreakingly like his missing father. Carol could tell he knew what was coming.

"I have the principal's side. What's yours?"

"It was no big deal, Mom. I just cut one class and had a beer with my friends."

"Beer! The letter doesn't say anything about beer."

129

"Well, actually, I ditched it before we got caught."

"Great! What about the pot?"

"Mom, I know better. I had a beer, instead. I haven't been smoking dope. I swear! I just wanted to be with my friends and I didn't want to be totally square, so I had a beer instead of a joint."

Carol closed her eyes and counted to five. She knew she'd never make it all the way to ten.

"Chris, how many classes have you cut this semester?"

"Two, Mom" he responded.

"You were supposed to start driver's education next week. Now, you'll wait until the next cycle in three weeks. If you pull this shit on me again, I won't let you start driver's ed until you're 16. If you do start in the next cycle and get into trouble, I'll pull you out of class so fast you won't know what hit you. You can wait another year while all your friends start driving without you. Do you understand?"

"Yes, Mom."

"You're underage and you shouldn't be drinking, but I'm proud of you for not using pot. If you ever mess with that stuff, it'll be the end of the world for you. Now, get out of here before I change my mind."

"Thanks, Mom . . . and Mom," Chris said, "you can trust me on the important stuff. I do know the difference between right and wrong. Besides, my grades are A's except in chemistry. I'm having a little trouble in that class."

"How bad is it, Chris?"

"If I get a C, I'll be happy. It's really tough for me."

"I wish I could help, but I don't know a thing about it. Your dad is a whiz in chemistry. Too bad he isn't here to help you."

"Don't worry, Mom. He'll be back." Chris lowered his head and left the room.

Once again she shook her head and thought to herself, it could have been much worse.

Just as Carol started to sort through the pile of bills, the back kitchen door slammed open and Stella Dalton charged into the room talking a mile a minute in that throaty voice of hers. Surprised, Carol couldn't catch the drift of Stella's one-sided conversation, but she knew enough to sit quietly until Stella helped herself to a piece of coffee cake and leaned her wide, attractive hips against the counter.

Stella was the very young wife of one of the Hawk Missile Unit's executive officers, 24 years old and a complete knockout. One of the most desirable women at Fort Bliss, she had been spreading her charms around the base ever since she and her husband had arrived. She tried to be discreet, but Carol was convinced she'd be caught sooner or later.

"Well, how are those trips to Washington, Carol?" Stella asked. Then, without waiting for an answer, she went on, "Do you ever run into any cute studs?"

"Jesus, Stella. Don't you ever think about anything else besides sex?"

"No. I'm not a chaplain or a saint, and I get lonely, so please don't be so condescending."

"You amaze me, Stella. You have a great looking and loving husband and you run around like a bitch in heat. Hell, you've gone down on everything but the Titanic."

"Titanic? What's his phone number and I'll take care of that oversight," Stella said with a mocking laugh. "Just dropped by to say hello. I've got an … appointment in fifteen minutes. Are you going to be around for a while?"

"Yes, I'll be here for a couple of weeks."

"See ya, dear," Stella said. She disappeared as quickly as she'd come in.

Carol spent the next two hours paying bills and struggling to balance her checkbook. There was practically no money left over. She was just about to pack up all the paperwork when the phone rang.

"Major Cody's quarters," she said in a proper military fashion.

"Hi, Carol, this is Brad Morris. Got a minute?"

Brad Morris was an intelligent young Captain who worked in the Commanding General's office at Fort Bliss. His position gave him access to a lot of information coming back from Vietnam and he used it as an excuse to see Carol Cody as often as possible. Ever since her husband had been reported missing, Morris had driven himself to distraction over Carol's green eyes, frosted hair and athletic body. He had persistent dreams and fantasies and wild imaginings with her as the leading lady. He was sure that if he could get her to spend enough time with him, he'd get her into his bed.

"Hi, Brad, how are things at the 'Head Shed'?" she asked.

"There's a new panic every hour. How are things going in Washington?"

"Pretty uneventful. We may get a chance to start a program and go public next month. Keeping our mouths shut sure hasn't helped."

"You want to go public? That ought to frost the White House and State Department. Did they give you any good info?"

"Not really, you got anything?"

"I think so. How about meeting me at the O Club Annex later for a drink and we can compare notes."

"Brad, I'm beat. But if you think its good stuff, I'll be there in … let's say 30 minutes."

"That'll be fine," he said, then hung up. He felt a sudden rush of blood to several parts of his body.

The O Club Annex was crowded with junior officers as usual. The more senior officers stayed in the main club, while the younger officers pre-ferred the Annex because it was considerably less formal and out of the sight of the big brass. When Morris arrived, Carol was already there having a drink with Stella Dalton and her husband, David.

Introductions were performed and Morris dragged a chair over from another table and waited for Carol to speak. She'd let him know if it was safe to discuss her husband or Vietnam in front of these people.

"Brad has been an absolute godsend the past few months," Carol explained. "He keeps me unofficially informed about rumors and scuttlebutt about the POW/MIA situation. I wish he could give me the real goodies, but they're classified."

"Well, I try," Captain Morris acknowledged. "I know how hard it must be to have a loved one in limbo." He got the hint. No classified information on this visit. "The only news I've heard is that the drawdown is affecting the number of units available for the long-range reconnaissance patrols working on POW location or extraction. About the only unit left is the Green Hor-nets, and they're highly restricted on POW missions. The Secretary of State makes all these statements about accountability for our prisoners but he won't let units go into Cambodia or Laos to get them."

"Great," Carol said sarcastically.

"Sorry, but there's more bad news. He advised the Pentagon not to execute any POW recovery operations without his personal approval. That means if any POWs are located, commanders on the ground won't be able to launch immediate recovery missions. That pretty much blows any chances for …"

He stuttered and stopped talking when he suddenly felt a foot work-ing up and down his left leg. Carol was across the table, so it had to be Stella. He took a quick sip of his drink.

"… effective rescue missions." He took another sip, looked over the rim of his glass at Stella and was met with a warm, attentive smile.

"Damn," Captain Dalton said with both women chiming in. "If we don't get those guys out now, the gooks'll move 'em north and we'll never recover them."

Brad barely heard him. He was still interested in Carol but now there was this gorgeous feminine foot working him up under the table. He felt like it was bonus time.

"I gotta go," said Stella after the two couples had finished a second round. "Want to come with me, Carol?"

Carol politely declined. She'd never been much for sharing bathroom trips with other women. Brad Morris sat for a moment, appreciating the sight of Stella's spectacular backside. He forced himself to wait for all of thirty seconds before making a lame excuse about the work that was waiting for him at his office. He walked out of the lounge leaving Carol and Dalton at the table.

Stella was standing alone next to the restroom door as Morris passed.

"I'm so interested in this POW situation," she breathed. "Why don't you come by the house and give me a private briefing?" She slipped a cocktail napkin with her address and phone number into his hand.

"How about tomorrow around 1000?" he asked with a mischievous smile.

"David gets off duty at noon. So make it 9:30, if you can. I hate being rushed."

∞∞

17

Who Are These Masked Men?

Tan Son Nhut Air Force Base, Saigon
27 November, 1971
Late afternoon

As CW4 Alberts brought the aging C-47 to a stop at the Tan Son Nhut transit parking area, two blue staff cars drove up alongside. The door of the lead car opened and Captain Mansen got out to meet the Grunt Air commander.

He loaded up Roman and Toothman, along with Best, Chief Abeel and Alberts, and drove straight to the Headquarters building. They signed in with the Air Force Air Police at the security desk and were escorted to the secure conference room adjoining the Commanding General's office. General Geiger and the Commanding General's senior Intelligence staff, loaded with file folders ready to provide any information the Grunt Air team needed. entered the room just as Roman started to sit.

"Regarding the identity of the three officers currently being held prisoners at the Disneyland POW camp," began the senior staff officer, "they are Colonel Nguyen Van Nam, the Vietnam Air Force Deputy Chief of Staff for Operations Plans and Deployment Directorate. In short, he knows every operational plan in effect now and those to be initiated upon our withdrawal. We don't believe the NVA have discovered his identity so far. If they do, they will subject him to some physically demanding interrogation."

Nice way to say it, Roman thought. *But torture is torture, no matter how many pretty words you use.*

"There is Major Reginald Smythe-Gordon, Colonel Nam's counterpart at MACV Headquarters. Lastly is Major Willard W. Cody, US Army Air Defense. He's the real wildcard. Cody was the Executive Officer of the 40mm Duster Battalion operating out of III Corps. They're being used as mobile

134

direct fire weapons in support of our logistical supply trains going south to Can Tho in IV Corps and as far north as Loc Ninh, east to Nha Trang, and west to Chau Duc on the Cambodian border. He doesn't sound like a valuable individual but, unfortunately, he is.

"Major Cody has been very active in his 12-year career in both the Nike Hercules surface-to-air missile, which has a nuclear capability, and the Hawk Missile System deployed in both Korea and Germany. His last assignment is the one that has Washington excited. A top secret development project called SAM-D. This is the follow-up system for both Hawk and Hercules. His head is crammed with some of our nation's most important electronic and nuclear technology. We must get him out if we possibly can."

"If we can't get him out," General Geiger interrupted, "the Commanding General's orders are to put an Arclight Strike on him and the other two, but that should be our last option."

Damn, Roman thought. *They want to call in a B-52 strike on this guy?* His musings were interrupted by General Geiger asking about Cody's status.

"Sir, as of 0730 hours today, Cody and the other two were caged at Disneyland. We don't think they've been mistreated since they got there. The doctor who escorted them from the Homestead left yesterday. We're thinking that they are getting better, so the doctor was able to leave."

"Any indication they're going to move them?" the General asked.

"No, sir, not at this time. But one of the recon teams reported three days ago that there was a lot of cleanup and preparation at the Rat Terminal, like they were expecting prisoners soon. We think Cody and the others won't be moved into the PDJ because it's mostly controlled by Vang Pao.

"Mr. Abeel recommended that we should insert teams at the Rock House and the Museum tomorrow morning," Roman said as he pointed out the positions on the wall map. "We're doing that. These camps are in the Ban Ban Valley and along the main road to Sam Neua and Muong Soui. Just to be safe, we're doing a site recon of the old abandoned Heavy Green Installation at Site Eight Five and Lima Site Five Niner. The two-ship recon mission will make a highly visible trip to the F-4 crash site here," he said as he again pointed to the site on the wall map, "at UH9447. We want the NVA to see us and think our mission is non-threatening, like always."

"Captain," remarked an officer at the end of the table, "I assume you're aware that site is less than four klicks from the NVA Headquarters for all of Laos. That's deep in their backyard."

"Yes, sir, we are. But they know if they take any action, it would call attention to their buildup. We're sure they think their buildup is still secret since they've been moving men and equipment forward at night."

"Captain Roman, who's flying this suicide mission?"

"I am, sir," responded Captain Toothman. "And I agree with Captain Roman and Chief Abeel that it's a relatively low-danger mission. It's not likely they'll expose their strength and true objectives over a couple of small Hueys that they know are just surveying crash sites. I'm not worried, sir."

"We're very interested in getting a good look at the area," Chief Abeel explained. "Especially to the northeast of Sam Neua where they just built a new POW camp we're calling Big Casino. If the NVA does try to move the Big Three to Hanoi or out of the combat area, that's where they'll hold them. The Sam Neua caves are getting full and our Laotian Intelligence teams report there are a few diseases cropping up in the caves. They wouldn't want their new prizes getting sick and dying."

Colonel Felter of General Mattix's staff got up and made his way around the table to the wall map.

"Wait a second," he said. "Let me get this straight. They're here at Disneyland now, and you expect them to go there." He pointed to the Rock House and Museum. "But, we're planning for a strike here, at the Big Casino, from an abandoned Air Force radar site over there." His fingers stabbed at locations all over the map. "And all these places are deep in enemy country. Is this correct, Captain?"

"Essentially correct, sir," Roman replied. Colonel Felter shook his head and looked at General Geiger in amazement.

"What percentage of aircraft and casualties are you anticipating, Captain?"

"Colonel, I haven't made that type of estimate. I do expect to have casualties in such an operation. My staff and I unanimously agree that our losses will not be significant or impede the ongoing mission of Grunt Air, sir."

"Frankly, Captain, I think you're being overly optimistic. I've flown air strikes in that area and it's bad—damned bad. I hope you can get the Big Three out down near the PDJ so this last-ditch mission, as you call it, won't be necessary."

General Geiger muttered impatiently. "Let's move on. We've covered this subject."

It took Roman almost an hour to get the intelligence he needed from the senior staff. He got the impression that everyone in the room, including the General, was encouraged by the raw data brought down from Grunt Air. They were up-to-date and confident, and they all agreed that the NVA dry season offensive was imminent and that it would be massive.

The room went to attention as General Geiger left. He waved to Roman to follow him.

Roman looked at Alberts and said, "Meet me at the plane at 2200 hours and we'll head back."

"I understand the Commanding General wants to see you," General Geiger told him in the hallway. "Let's go. We'll pick up Mattix on the way."

Captain Roman formally reported to the Commanding General as the other two general officers came in quietly and sat down at a small conference table.

"Well, Captain Roman," said the CG as he returned Roman's salute. "No court-martial charges this week. I haven't had to send a single one of your problems to the Distant Early Warning Radar Site in Alaska." Roman tried not to laugh.

"Good to know I haven't inconvenienced the Commanding General again, sir."

"Have a seat Dan," he said with a big grin. "Now give me a five-minute synopsis of your meeting with our Ops and Intel boys."

Roman made it as brief as he could. The Commanding General exhaled loudly and looked up at the ceiling in thought for a few moments.

"You bust a camp and the cover for Grunt Air is history. At least as far as the NVA are concerned. You handled that F-4 pilot recovery very well. Good thinking. I understand he hasn't said anything." Roman was about to answer when Coroneos started speaking again.

"Dan, I agree with your plan so far, but I reserve the right to make the final decision on your Big Casino mission. Don't execute it without my permission. Before we let you get slaughtered at Big Casino, I want to make sure of the situation and all the details. We still have the B-52 Arclight option in our hip pocket. That would save you a lot of casualties, wouldn't it? Neat, clean, and we protect vital information. You agree?" The CG looked at Roman closely to see how he would react.

"Actually, no, sir," Roman said. "My reasoning is based upon target identification and confirmation. If we try to get them out before they arrive at the Big Casino, we'd have to insert recon teams everyplace we think they'd stop on the way ... because we'd need to know everything about their exact location. That means teams at Sam Neua, Muong Soui, all over the place. That's more dangerous than what I propose, sir."

General Mattix shifted in his chair. It wasn't often that someone openly disagreed with General Coroneos. And it wasn't usually very wise.

"Any other reasons, Captain?" The Commanding General didn't take his eyes off Roman for a second.

"Frankly, sir, I have a hard time accepting the idea of calling in an air strike and wasting our own guys. My men and I would rather save their lives, danger or no danger."

"Captain Roman, very few officers ever openly disagree with me, but you just did."

"Sir, the last thing you need in this kind of sensitive situation is a 'yes man.' I know General Mattix has always demanded honest input on critical areas. This is an important matter. I assume you want honest opinions."

"Good enough. Now, how is your maintenance and supply situation?"

"Actually, it's quite good, sir. We still need the two replacement Hueys but that's about all, sir."

"You haven't got those yet?"

"No, sir," replied Roman.

"Al, check with Kelso and find out what the trouble is, as if I don't already know. We'll look into that and get back to you, son."

Captain Roman stood, saluted and left the room. Major Fitzmorris and Captain Mansen were waiting for him outside. Mansen looked him up and down.

"Still in one piece. It must have gone well in there. Did you tell him about your suicide mission?"

"Yeah, he approved everything but he wants to make the final decision about letting Grunt Air go in or hitting those poor bastards with a couple hundred five-hundred-pounders from a B-52. I hate that idea and don't want to think about it. However, I do want to think about a couple of double margaritas and some tacos. What do you say?"

"You're still buying, right?" asked Fitzmorris. "Step right this way."

☜☞

18

Standing Guard on the Home Front

Cody residence
Fort Bliss, Texas
Mid-afternoon

It had been over three weeks since Carol and Charlie had returned from Washington. They'd spent the time working together three or four days a week perfecting their "going public" plan. As they worked, they talked for hours about the worms in Washington, especially those who wanted them quiet for some obscure political and personal benefit and not for the best interests of the nation's prisoners in a hostile land, suffering under inhumane conditions and treatment.

They had drawn up time lines for the entire campaign, along with pages of special interest groups that would be sympathetic and prone to take an active part in the POW/MIA efforts. They also had commitments from daytime talk shows on television stations around the country and abroad.

They had lists of "talking points" for each type of group they'd targeted. They'd made a list of civic and professional organizations that were known to be vocal and active in good humanitarian causes. They were ready, itchy and axnious for their next meeting with Colonel Hurd, but they hadn't heard a thing from the Pentagon or from frosty Margo.

"That's great, Charlie," Carol said as she handed back a draft speech for the Alamogordo VFW. "Let's hope we can present it real soon." She poured herself a third cup of coffee resisting the temptation to put a shot of brandy in it, and then sat down across the kitchen table from Charlie.

"You know, Stella hasn't been over here for coffee lately. I wonder what she's doing in the mornings?"

"You mean who she's doing, don't you?" Charlie smiled.

"You're probably right. I feel sorry for her when David finds out. This is a pretty big base, but it's not that big. Tell you what I care a lot more about, what Margo is up to."

"We haven't heard from her in weeks," observed Charlie. "And she won't return our calls. Bitch!"

"Be nice," Carol counseled. "If we don't get some action soon, we'll make our own. I think we've been patient enough." The phone rang and Carol got up to answer it.

"That's the provost martial wanting you to come and identify Stella's body," Charlie said.

"Major Cody's residence," Carol said in her official voice. She pulled the receiver away from her ear and put her palm over the mouthpiece.

"I'll be damned," she said to Charlie. "It's Margo." She put the phone back up to her face.

"Margo, dear, I'm delighted to hear from you." Charlie listened to some very polite and very forced chit-chat for as long as she could stand it, then got up to pace.

"We've just completed the last of our proposal points," Carol said into the phone. "When can we present them to Colonel Hurd?"

"That's why I'm calling," replied Margo. "He wants to know if a week from Wednesday would be okay."

"Sure, my kids are used to being orphans. Charlie, you okay with a week from Wednesday?"

"Sure!"

"Then it's set." Margo confirmed. "We'll meet late afternoon to go over the schedule and program. We have a meeting with some congressmen Thursday morning and a stop at State in the early afternoon. Our meeting with Hurd is at 3:30. You can catch the early flight back home on Friday."

"Sounds great, Margo. Looks like we could do some good for a change."

"Oh, it certainly does," Margo enthused. "Now, Carol, I want to touch on another sensitive subject with you. Jim Hurd is a very influential and powerful ally for us. We must keep him on our side at all costs. He likes you, Carol, he likes you very much, understand? So don't do or say anything to hurt or offend him, okay dear? He's always given us his best advice and information, much more than what he gives to the League. We must keep that going, if you get my drift."

"Oh, I get your drift, Margo, but I'm not going to bed with him just for information. Besides, he used that same ploy with a couple of girls at the League and it didn't get them anything. I think any woman who would sleep with a man like that is out of her mind." Margo was silent for many long moments.

"I'm sure you're entitled to your opinion, Carol, but you know what they say in Washington. If you want to get along, you have to go along. Perhaps you may want to rethink your position on this matter. Probably do you some good, too. I mean, how long has it been, dear? Anyway, I'll send your tickets by registered mail today. See you in Washington. Bye-bye."

"Bye-bye to you, too," Carol said as she hung the phone up. A warm flush of anger reddened her cheeks.

"If you want to get along, you have to go along," she whined, mocking Margo's sniffy tone of voice. "I'm about done going along and I'm not going to screw Jim Hurd for the good of our cause. Hell, even if I was a widow I wouldn't sleep with him. Besides, he's married." Charlie drained her coffee and tilted her head to one side.

"Don't you think something's fishy, here?" she observed. "Margo breaks her butt for him. She actually does more for him than she does for us. You ask me, she's been boinking him all along."

"Yuk," said Carol. "I guess I put my foot in it. Well, if I didn't have any respect for her before, I have even less now. Why don't you call a couple of the girls at the League and see what you can find out?"

Carol was saying goodbye to Charlie at the front door when Chris arrived with his friend, Jimmy Phelps, who everybody called Jethro because he looked just like the character on *The Beverly Hillbillies*. Jethro was the first-string offensive guard on the high school football team, but Carol thought he could be the whole front line. He was over six-four, around 265 pounds and as solid as he could be. He'd been All-State right guard the previous year and was a sure bet for a football scholarship at the University of Texas.

"Hi, guys," she said. "I suppose you're here to give me a head fake, rush downfield and tackle the refrigerator."

"Jethro hasn't had anything to eat for over an hour," said Chris.

"Well, he's in luck. I went to the commissary today and the fridge is full."

The phone rang and Chris ran to answer it, expecting a call from one of his many girlfriends.

"Mom, it's that Captain Morris again." He sounded irritated.

"Thanks, I've got it," she said. She took the phone and watched the boys jostle down the hall heading straight for the food supply.

"Hi, Brad, what's up?"

"I've got some news for you. Mind if I come over?"

"That's fine. I'll be here fixing supper for the kids." After hanging up the phone, she called to her son, "Chris, would you mind straightening up the living room for me? Brad Morris is coming over."

"Sure, Mom," Chris said as he rolled his eyes at Jethro.

It took the overeager Brad Morris less than ten minutes to pull up in front of the Cody house. As he walked up to the front door, Chris came out. Morris struggled to conceal his disappointment. Carol was not alone in the house.

"Hi, Chris," Morris said brightly. "How's school?"

"I'm getting pretty smart," Chris blurted.

"Really? That's ... uh, great."

"Want to know how smart I am?" Chris challenged. "I know why you're here. It's not to give us information. You're trying to make it with my Mom. I've seen you sneaking into Captain Dalton's place in the mornings, nine-thirty like clockwork."

"Wait just a second, son," Morris put on his best indignation. "You're just a kid. First of all, you don't know what you're talking about. Second, it's none of your business where I go in the morning, and third, you damn sure don't talk to adults and officers with a mouth like that. I have a good mind to slap you silly."

Jethro appeared over Chris' shoulder right on cue. Morris took a surprised step back.

"My dad's alive and he's coming home," whispered Chris. "And Mom has enough to worry about without you. Don't call her, again. Don't come around here, again, or I'll whip your ass."

Morris stood on the bottom step with his mouth open. Chris, on the top step, towered over him. Jethro cast a wide shadow in the doorway.

"Mrs. Cody isn't like Mrs. Dalton," said Jethro. "If you want to get laid go see her, but stay away from Mrs. Cody or I'll get what's left of your sorry ass after Chris is finished."

"We'll talk about this again with your mother," Morris said, trying his best to sound defiant. He squared his shoulders, turned and walked back to his car.

Chris watched Morris drive off, shouldered past Jethro to go back into the house and ran directly into his mother, who stood in the middle of the hallway with a proud look on her face.

"Mom! Uh ... I ... he ..."

"Well, I can see that I will not need to get someone to watch after you and your sister while I'm gone. It seems you can handle things around here quite nicely. Anybody hungry?"

19

Need a Lift to Udorn, GI?

Grunt Air Headquarters
Udorn Air Force Base, Thailand
17 December, 1971
Mid-morning

The morning missions launched as scheduled, except Archangel. A copilot controversy delayed their departure. Chief Alberts and Lieutenant Jenner were halfway up the stairs of the C-47 when Captain U. Muang came up to them. The look on his face told Alberts he wasn't happy.

"Why is Jenner taking my place today?" Captain Muang demanded.

Alberts looked at Jenner, then at Muang, pausing to measure his words.

"Because we're going above 18 degrees latitude to the far northern part of Laos. We're prohibited from going beyond 18 degrees with you onboard."

Muang gave them a half smile.

"I have to admit something. A … confession. There is no such rule. I told Whaley there was such an order because I wasn't ready to risk my life for that spineless shit. Roman is different. The rule is no more. I'm going and this is final. Jenner, you must come, too."

"This sounds like a bunch of bullshit to me," said Alberts.

"I swear Doug. I made the rule, and I told you why. Now, let's get this bird in the air. The war is waiting."

"You know, fat boy, I still have that 45 tracer just waiting to shoot your ass in case you're captured," Tom Ryker said to Dan Roman over lunch. Ryker was treating at the Officer's Club instead of dining on sandwiches and hamburgers at the B Frame, which was the mess hall at their new quarters.

"That's great, Tom, my future is assured." Roman made a face.

"Roman!" The voice came from behind him. Roman spun around in his chair to see Lieutenant Colonel Skinner come through the door in an hurry. Roman and Ryker stood up, still chewing.

"Dan, we've got a big problem and I need your help. The old man just got shot down by the NVA in the vicinity of UF368685. They were flying from Two Zero Alpha to NKP in a C-7 Caribou when it came under mortar attack from Skyline Two." Obviously shaken, Skinner lowered himself into one of the chairs.

Two Zero Alpha was the super-secret Long Tieng airfield used by the CIA to support its Northern Laos operations. It could be found only on maps used by pilots who flew in the area as an "Alternate" airfield. There was another airstrip just to the north called Sam Thong, or Lima Site Two Zero, the headquarters for the USAID mission to Laos.

Long Tieng lay just south of a long mountain ridge designated as Skyline Ridge. Unfortunately, it was well within mortar range of the North Vietnamese who had occasionally occupied such mountaintop positions in southern Laos, giving them an unrestricted, panoramic view of the surrounding countryside. NKP was the identifier for Nakhon Phanom, the Royal Thailand Air Base, where the C-7 was headed. The air base was located on the border of central Laos, more than a hundred and fifty miles to the south of Two Zero Alpha on the Thailand-Laos border.

"They were climbing to altitude when some anti-aircraft artillery got them," Skinner continued. "They couldn't go back to Two Zero Alpha so they tried to get to NKP but had to go down because of onboard fire. They crash landed okay and are in contact with Cricket."

"What about your joint rescue helicopters, or Air America? That's combat territory, sir, and we're not equipped for it. Besides, we're not even a combat unit."

"All of our assets are part of that big downed pilot recovery effort at the DMZ," Skinner informed them. "Air America has everything up in Laos preparing for any efforts the NVA might make during the dry season. It would take them hours to get here and we can't wait that long. You're all we've got."

"Fine," said Roman. "If you'll get your signal operating instructions, authentication tables and any other frequencies we may need, we'll pick you up at the Hot Pad in 15 minutes or so."

"I'll be ready." Skinner pushed his chair back and disappeared as quickly as he'd come. Ryker waited until he was gone before speaking.

"Do you think he has any idea what he's getting into by going into that area?"

"Not a chance. He's still thinking about his Officer Efficiency Report. That will change in about an hour. Think you can still fly a Huey in combat?"

"No, but I'll try. Why me, anyway? You've got pilots available."

"Because if I go down I need you there to shoot me with that hot pink tipped 45 bullet before I'm captured," he responded, laughing.

From the phone in the Officer's Club, Roman called his Operations office and told them to scramble the crews for Grunt Air's helicopters One One and Two Two for an immediate recovery mission. Ditton and Donovan, the regular pilots for birds One One and Two Two, would stand down allowing Ryker and him to take the mission. He also wanted Delta Team, headed by SFC Krumins, back in the saddle and out to the flight line ready for the hot mission.

"Let's roll," he said as they left the Officer's Club and hopped into a jeep.

Ryker and Roman were surprised to see both helicopter aircrews and SFC Krumins and his Recon Team already on the aircraft waiting.

"Okay, gather around," Roman said. "The Base CO and the Air America Operations Officer just got their C-7 Caribou shot out from under them. They went down in that river valley just northwest of the Tollbooth.

"It's a bad area. I expect they'll be under fire by the time we get there. I'll take One One and Captain Ryker, call sign Grunt Air Five, will take Two Two. Sergeant Krumins, you and your team will go in Two Two. We'll crank and reposition to the Hot Pad to pick up the Air Force. Then direct to UF368685, where they're supposed to be. Okay, crank in zero three.

"No time for preflight. Sergeant England, is this bird ready to fly?" The crew chief assured him that there were no squaks.

Both Hueys cranked up and were ready to go in less than five minutes. Ryker gave a thumbs up signal to Roman who nodded, then hit the radio switch.

"Udorn Ground Control, Grunt Air Six, a flight of two requests hover taxi instructions to the Base Hot Pad for passenger pick up."

"Grunt Air Six is cleared for an immediate hover taxi to the Hot Pad direct. There's no traffic on final, you're cleared across the active." No more "Grave Robber" from the boys in the tower.

Roman lifted off and Ryker pulled his Huey to a hover alongside. The two machines skimmed across the ramp faster than usual to the Hot Pad where Skinner was waiting with a briefcase in one hand, and a .38 caliber pistol in the other. Roman settled his chopper to the ground so Skinner could board, then pulled back up again and radioed for takeoff clearance.

"Grunt Air," said the tower controller, "all inbound traffic is holding at or above eight thousand feet until you're clear control zone. Good luck. Frequency change to Cricket approved."

"That's a first," said Ryker to his copilot, CW2 Larry Lawrence. "They stacked the fast movers for us. The Tower must know their boss is in the shitter."

The two aircraft climbed on course to seventy-five hundred feet and put their noses down to gain airspeed. Roman made contact with Cricket control, who advised him about the reinforcements they'd summoned to assist.

"We have four Sandies orbiting at flight level one four zero waiting for your call on Victor one two eight decimal five. Call sign Nomad One Six." Sandies were the Air Force A-1 Sky Raiders, propeller-driven fighters operating in the area and equipped with bombs and napalm tanks, called "gas cans," for close ground support.

"Roger. Keep them high until we can size up the situation on the ground. Do you have contact with the Caribou?"

"Roger. He's up Victor on one two one decimal five, call sign Blazer Five Seven."

Roman set up his radios to talk to the Caribou on the universal emergency frequency and to the fighters on a separate band. He also had Ryker dialed in on the Grunt Air company operations frequency.

"Blazer Five Seven, this is Grunt Air Six on Guard. How do you read?" Roman called.

"This is Five Seven. We hear you loud and clear, Lima Charlie."

"Roger, Five Seven. Can you give me a sitrep?"

"We're in the bend of the river just west of Hill Five Zero Four Six. The fire on the plane is out, but we have intermittent heavy hostile fire from a tree line to the east and from the high ground to the south. We think there's just a few NVA to the south, firing AK-47s. The stuff coming from the east sounds like AK-47s and heavy automatics. They're protected by a bunch of fallen trees. We have six souls on board. Two dead and one with minor wounds. The weather is fine, come join us."

"Casualties." Roman wasn't happy to hear this, but tried to keep his tone light. "Thanks for the invitation, but we'll wait until you get the pool and O Club built. Stand by, I'll get back to you," Roman switched to the other frequency.

"Nomad One Six, this is Grunt Air Six, a flight of two is with you one five south at 7500 feet."

"Roger, Grunt Air. Welcome. What's the plan?"

"It sounds like the NVA is using the C-7 for bait. I'll go down and see how mad they are. Keep out of sight. You'll be the Sunday punch. Confirm armament."

"Nomad One Six and a party of four. Each have a full load of 50 cal., four gas cans and four 250's. Good on fuel. They can't see us. The smoke and haze are so bad we can hardly see you."

"Sounds great. Keep me in sight. I'm going to break now," Roman said as he switched over to the Grunt Air company frequency. "Okay, Grunt Air Five, hold position and watch the pass. Let's see what the bad guys have to offer."

"Roger Six," Ryker came back. "Doesn't Toothman have an axiom for this situation?"

"That's affirmative," Roman answered. "'If the enemy is in range, so are you.'"

"Glad I brought my hot-tip 45 to shoot you if you go down, but I don't want to get that close to the NVA."

Roman rolled the Huey on its side and dropped it to slightly above the river, a mile north of the downed aircraft. He kept his speed up to 120 knots as he headed over the top of the tree line where most of the fire was coming from. Even before he got there he could see the bright twinkle of tracers reaching up for him. An occasional sickening *plunk* sound announced the arrival of a bullet piercing the aircraft. Skinner, holding on in the back, was yelling about the hostile fire, but Roman ignored him and flew right through it. The over-flight took less than 18 seconds, but when you're under fire it seems longer. Roman asked CW2 Redings, who was flying copilot, what the area around the C-7 looked like.

"Flat, no problems, sir," Redings reported. "But I am worried about the guys on the hilltop to the south. The Sandies can take care of the tree line, but the bastards up high are hard to see. There's all these big rocks and fallen trees."

"Okay. Take the aircraft and put us back up with Five," Roman ordered. "You have the aircraft, Mr. Redings."

"I have the aircraft," reported Redings, following procedure. Redings took over as Roman busied himself with the radios.

"Nomad One Six, did you see the bad guys?"

"Roger, Six. How do you want to handle it?"

"We'll approach in trail formation on a long final to land on the north side of the C-7. That's ninety degrees to the tree line and broadside to the hill on the right. The C-7 will block fire from the NVA on the hillside and the ones in the tree line will have to come out if they want to shoot at us when we land. When they do, you surprise them from south to north with a bunch of that napalm. I think you can catch them in the open and turn them into crispy critters. We can deal with the ones on the hill for now. What do you think?"

"Okay, Six, that works. But I don't like you taking fire from the hill on short final. If you go down, we got even more problems."

"Nomad, I don't see any other way, unless we lose the element of surprise."

"Roger, Six, let us show you Army types what TAC Air is all about. We'll go with your plan and take care of the hill later."

"Roger, One Six, we'll start into the LZ in zero two mikes." With Redings still jockeying the Huey, Roman switched frequencies and called the crew huddled inside the hull of their crashed Caribou.

"Blazer Five Seven, this is Six. We're about ready to come in for a pick up. What's you status?"

"Grunt Air Six, this is Blazer Five Seven. Heavy fire, here. I don't think you want to come in. The Colonel doesn't think you can make it."

"You Air Force types just don't understand Army Aviation. Be ready to run for the choppers when we touch down. Anybody alive and walking goes to the lead chopper. My ground troops are in the second. Have your dead in a forward position so they can pick them up fast."

"Forget the dead for now. We're taking heavy fire, here."

"Five Seven, when you call the Green Taxi you get full service. Grunt Air on the way."

"Okay, Five," Roman said to Ryker on the radio, "follow me. Put Krumins' team on the right side to shoot up the hilltop as we go in. Two of them can get the dead out of the Caribou while the other two keep the hill under fire. Got it?"

"Krumins is nodding okay. Let's go!" Ryker responded.

"Roger, Six on the break."

The two Hueys started the long descent from over two miles away. The NVA in the tree line had stopped firing, trying to lure the choppers in closer. Roman knew the bastards would pop up out of the brush and shoot the crap out of them as soon as they got in range.

Ryker kept his machine right behind Roman on the descent, hoping to limit the number of rounds hitting his helicopter. He was sitting high in the front of the chopper behind that too, too thin Plexiglas windscreen. He started to realize how nice that maintenance job back at Udorn was. Nobody shot at him when he was tearing down a turbine. It was a lot better than this craziness.

When the two helicopters got to 300 feet and 500 yards from the crash site, the NVA opened up just like Roman knew they would. Tracers went zinging past Roman's window, some rounds popping through the lower nose and upper pilot windshield. Low and slow, nosing up for the approach, the two Hueys were just like the proverbial stationery waterfowl.

Not so bad, Roman thought, but I hope those Sandies show up right damn now.

Meanwhile, the only official representative of the US Air Force, Lieutenant Colonel Skinner, had a death grip on his seat behind Roman's, screaming "Abort! Abort! Enemy fire!" with every ounce of his strength.

A flash to Roman's right … the Sandies swooping in from altitude, whizzing past the Huey. A brilliant orange light of the napalm explosion, a roil of greasy gray smoke and the entire tree line incandesced and disappeared. The firing from the ground stopped at once, but there were still the troops up the hill to worry about.

"Hey, Army, watch the NVA on the hill." The Sandy pilot's voice crackled in Roman's earpiece just as the entire top of the ridge exploded under the weight of four Air Force 250 pound bombs. They came from the two aircraft that had stayed at higher altitude.

"So much for the bad guys," reported the Sandy.

"Damn good shooting," Ryker called out. "The only thing left of those sons of bitches is hair, teeth and eyeballs."

The two Hueys flared out and the recon team jumped out just before touchdown, racing to their defensive positions to lay down suppressing fire, but there was nobody to shoot at. Two troops stayed at the ready while the other two ran to the Caribou to retrieve the two men lost in the crash.

Colonel Odom, Mr. Eastwood, the Crew Chief and the Caribou pilot scrambled aboard Roman's aircraft without any encouragement. Roman hauled up on the collective, and in seconds they were airborne. Mission accomplished.

"Six on the go," called Roman.

"Five on the go," responded Ryker. Roman called the Sandies.

"Nomad lead, we're off with our passengers. You guys did a great job. Thanks."

"No problem, Six. We like our jobs. Call us if you need your ass saved again!"

"You can count on it. See you back at the club. Ryker is buying. Six out."

"Hey, Six, Nomad One Six, one question. When you were transmitting on short final under all that fire, somebody was screaming 'abort, abort'. Please tell me that wasn't an Air Force dude."

"Like George Washington, Nomad One Six, I cannot tell a lie. He's one of yours. Grunt Air Six is clear to the southwest going up Cricket."

Roman turned the flying over to Redings and savored the sunset and the success of the mission. He looked back to see how Colonel Odom and Mr. Eastwood were doing. They were a little shaken, but unhurt. Skinner, however, was almost paralyzed with shock. His face was white, and if the phrase "green around the gills" meant anything, it could be applied to him. Colonel Odom was talking to him in a low voice, but Skinner had gotten as close to death as he ever wanted that afternoon and he didn't like it. Odom saw Roman looking back.

"He'll be okay after a stiff drink or two and a good night's sleep," the Base Commander said. Roman turned back to his radios and dialed up Archangel.

"Where have you been, Six? We've been trying to reach you."

"We had to go get Ryker some combat time. The Air Force needed a hot pick up north of the Tollbooth."

"You weren't the only one with a hot pick up. Grunt Air Four Four made a hot extraction of Charlie after they were spotted by an NVA patrol near the Museum. They're on the way back to Udorn with three wounded. No KIA but one could go either way. Ryker's gonna have a good time getting the bird repaired for tomorrow. It's in bad shape. No details from Four Four. They're limping back. I've got them in sight below me. We're crossing the Mekong now. ETA Udorn, one eight mikes."

"Roger, Archangel. This bird has a few new zits, too, but no injuries. I'll call for ambulances. Tell Four Four to park next to us at the Base Hot Pad. We'll off-load the wounded and dead before repositioning. Who got hurt?"

"Sgt. Keller on Four Four was hit in the butt with small arms," Archangel responded. "Probably an AK-47. Hurt his pride more than anything, but he'll be sleeping on his stomach for a while. Kahn took one in the left arm. Don't know how bad. Schwartz took two in the chest and one in the face. He's losing a lot of blood and may not make it. I thought you said you didn't have any injuries?"

"We didn't. Air Force did. Two dead, one wounded. Any problem up north?" Roman asked.

"No, everything went well. The NVA didn't fire a shot at Three and Six Six. They flew high enough to attract attention and ground fire but nobody took a shot at them, just like you thought. Sergeant Pao said they were spotted as soon as they landed by a bunch of NVA who tried to hide. The smoke and haze was a bitch. We almost had to abort two or three times."

"Thank God," Roman said, relieved. "Any problems with Bravo or Five Five?"

"We're keeping Five Five at Two Zero Alpha tonight. It seems there are some maintenance problems, know what I mean?"

Roman did. The "maintenance problems" on Hetler's bird would give them an excuse for Grunt Air to be in Laos at night. Archangel had more to say.

"I've got a lot of info for you and the Sphinx. Things are getting serious up here."

"Right! Grab the Sphinx and meet me at the Air Force O Club. Ryker is buying."

Ryker reached for his mike from the other Huey, then pulled his hand back. He really didn't mind that Roman just loved to invite all of Grunt Air's biggest alcoholics to drink on his tab. It had been a long day.

Roman called Udorn Approach, got the altimeter setting, winds and the rest of the information an inbound chopper needs. He requested clearance to Hot Pad for a Code Six drop off, and two ambulances for one wounded and two dead in this flight and three wounded in Grunt Air Four Four, about one five mikes out with two critical on board.

It hurt him to recite the details about all the dead and wounded they were transporting.

They cleared him direct to the Hot Pad and held off the other inbound traffic to clear his way.

"How's the old man?" asked the approach controller.

"Mean enough to eat your ass out for just existing," Roman said laughing.

After Roman landed, Ryker and Davis dropped off their passengers and wounded, then repositioned to the Grunt Air parking area, where they stood around for several long minutes counting the bullet holes and other damage to the choppers that had flown the mission.

"Not good," Ryker reported to Roman in his office.

"What's not good is writing up these damn reports," Roman said from behind his desk.

"Well, this is worse. The birds are grounded for tomorrow, at least. We got at least 30 holes and who knows what other damage. Gotta pull off the inspection plates. I can't believe Four Four even made it back here."

"Well," reflected Roman, "we don't need them for morning launch."

"Let me try this again," said Ryker. "We may not have them for anything, ever again. I know we'll find some structural problems so, if you're gonna put pressure on 7th for those two replacements, now would be a good time. They've been promising them since we got here."

"Hard to believe it's just been six weeks," Roman said looking around the room. He couldn't believe it, but he had to admit the unit had come a long way, at least in creature comfort.

"Let's go get a drink."

Roman had told Archangel and Sphinx to meet them at the O Club. He wanted to know how the wounded crew chief was doing and if Skinner had recovered from the excitement of the afternoon.

The club was in high gear when they arrived. Roman got swept toward the bar where the F-4 and Sandy pilots were congratulating themselves and others on the success of the recovery mission. Ryker dragged him toward a table in the back where Alberts and Abeel were waiting with over a dozen scotch and waters lined up on the table. If it had been a long afternoon, it was going to be an even longer night.

"Good, god," Ryker said "are you guys serious?"

"Compliments of the Air Force," said Abeel. "Hand delivered, too. You must have put on a hell of a show."

"Are you kidding? The Sandies hit one bunch in the tree line, and the others smacked a couple of 250s on their ass from altitude. Surprised the hell out of them. Us, too."

"That's probably all the good news for the day," CW4 Alberts said with a sigh. "The NVA is moving all over the place. I think they're going to hit us either tomorrow or the next day. From ten thousand feet I could see them crawling all over the place."

"Did Toothman and Dorsey get it done up there?"

"Yes, but we've got to get the teams back here tomorrow afternoon at the latest. I'll go up early and tell them to get what they can and be at the extraction points by 1600 hours. Sorry boss, but the war is about to start." Alberts paused for a moment, then asked "What's the date?"

"17 December," replied the Sphinx. "Is it your birthday?"

"No, just remember the date. It's the beginning of the end in Laos."

"That's pretty glum," Roman observed, then stood as he saw Colonel Odom approach the table trailed by about a dozen fighter pilots and Mr. Eastwood, the Air America Operations Officer. Odom held out his hand.

"Great work today! My personal thanks."

"Mine, too," said the almost unseen Eastwood. "Could I buy you a drink or two at our Rendezvous Club some night?"

"That'd be great. Just not tonight. We have a big mission ahead of us." Roman indicated the dozen drinks on the table, each in its own little circle of moisture.

"Stop by my office tomorrow morning about 1000 hours, if you would," Colonel Odom said.

"Yes, sir, I'll be there. How is Colonel Skinner?"

"He'll be fine as soon as he stops throwing up. Just kidding. You sure showed him what kind of flying you guys do. He had no idea until today."

When Odom and his entourage had left, Abeel leaned forward over the table. The intensity in his voice was obvious.

"You had better get whatever you can from those two spooks of yours. We'll know more tomorrow when our guys get back in." Roman's wheels started turning. Abeel's warning was clear. Things were going to get nasty.

"We'll get everyone in the briefing room tomorrow about 2000 hours, after they've had a shower and some chow. Now, if you'll excuse me," Roman said as he stood and downed a scotch, "I'm going to make a call about those two birds we're supposed to get."

"Major Fitzmorris, this is Dan Roman at Grunt Air."

"Dan, how's it—" That's all he was able to say before Roman jumped on the receiver.

"Choppers. Aircraft. I need aircraft. The Commanding General promised me two of 'em, and I know it's almost Christmas but I can't wait that long."

"Well, he's—"

"If that shithead Sweeney won't give them to us we'll steal them from the 1st Brigade until he does." There was silence.

"Why, I'm very fine," said Fitzmorris. "Thank you for asking. And how are you, Dan?" Roman couldn't help it. He cracked up. He needed to. Nothing he hated more than transporting dead Americans.

"The old man knows about your hot extraction this afternoon, and he knows about the other bird getting shot to hell. He's already told Kelso to be in his office at 0800 hours with a hard delivery date. I heard they've been ready for two weeks."

Fitzmorris sighed, "Dan, Sweeney is digging his heels in again. If Coroneos or Mattix find out he's holding out on you, they'll send him straight to Alaska. Hell, Mattix might even shoot him. And they'll can Kelso's ass, too. Especially after what you guys pulled off this afternoon. Rescuing the base commander under enemy fire? Shit. You'll get the new birds soon. Can you do with what you've got for a few days?"

"I guess. As long as Ryker keeps performing miracles."

"Geiger wants everything you can get on where the NVA is and where they're going. He doesn't trust the CIA or MACV. Anything new on the Big Three?"

"Still at Disneyland as of 1700 hours. But there's a lot of movement in the camp. Might be because of the offensive or they may be moving."

"Okay, Dan. Get some sleep. You've had a day."

"Right. Tell the old man we're fine up here and will deliver the goods."

"He knows that, Dan. Good night."

Roman didn't put down the phone. Instead, he called the Fiddler and Kingfish to get their latest information. Then, he made time for his most important task: writing to his two kids back in Oklahoma City. Even though he tried to write them twice a week, he was two days behind and he had a lot to catch up on.

He barely finished the letter, then fell asleep at his desk, still in his flight suit, with the desk light on.

20

Can You Spell "Tact" and "Diplomacy"?

The Willard Hotel
Washington, DC.
Morning

Carol Cody pulled the draperies apart on the full-length picture window in her hotel room and looked out at the dome of the Capitol. The view alone was enough to tell her that she and Charlie had come a long way from that hapless Motel 6 over in Arlington. It was a view she'd never seen before in spite of all the trips she'd made to Washington. She stood there, squinting at the sun gleaming off snow. She thought how amazing it was that every single one of the 435 men and women of Congress could be so blind to what was happening to their sons and fathers and brothers in Vietnam.

President Johnson had been an absolute bastard, keeping them in the dark with his bloody hand over their mouths. Then, there was Jane Fonda, and Ramsey Clark. She tried to be as fair as she could, weighing their freedom of speech against what her husband must be going through. *Ah, democracy,* she reflected. Somebody had once told her that democracy was the worst form of government on the planet, except for all the others.

She turned her thoughts to the promise of the day. With the quiet help of Major Dorsey, she had arranged a meeting with the well-known Senator John Warga. Dorsey had been a huge help all along, putting a wry perspective on the escapades and incapabilities of Colonel Hurd and trying to insulate her from him.

She had been thinking about her meeting with the Senator all morning. He sat on several prestigious committees and had, on more than one occasion, spoken of his dismay over the POW/MIA situation in the most public possible terms. He had even taken the time to come to Fort Bliss to counsel their chapter of the National Association of POW/MIA families. When John

Warga, Democratic Senator from Illinois, spoke, people listened. The media listened. But, so far, not hard enough.

After his speech in Fort Bliss, he'd met with Carol, Charlie and Margo Stone, trying to encourage them about the POW situation.

"We're really trying hard to move Hanoi," he said. "But, so far, they won't budge. We aren't giving up, I promise."

Now, it was time to meet the Senator in Washington and lay their campaign plans on the table.

Margo opened the connecting door and let herself in. Carol hadn't wanted adjoining room, but Margo had insisted, and she was paying.

"That was the front desk. Senator Warga is waiting for us in the Sky Terrace Restaurant."

John Warga was a tall, angular man, with the lean physique and prominent features of a long distance runner. He was dark, with a handsome head of hair, and his bearing was Presidential. In fact, there were rumors around the capital about just that possibility. His reputation helped his ambitions. The Senate knew him as an honest, dedicated, Intelligent lawmaker who led a clean and vigorous life. He was a devoted family man in spite of his extreme good looks.

He greeted Margo, Carol and Charlie with a cordial handshake. Carol found it warm, dry, encouraging, and even a bit exciting.

"It's good to see you ladies, again," he said warmly. "I'm glad you asked for a luncheon meeting since it will be my only chance to eat today. I have a committee meeting in forty-five minutes ... and since the meeting concerns the POW issue, I'm glad we could get together first."

Carol was determined to put her femininity aside and get down to business. The facts were cold, they were very hard, and she was aching to lay them all on the table. She hoped she could give him some ammunition for his committee meeting.

"Well, Margo," the Senator said as he sat down, "what's the latest?" Carol and Charlie watched Margo puff up, and exchanged a glance.

"Actually, Senator, we have some good news for a change. We have a meeting at 3:30 with Colonel Hurd to discuss the possibility of conducting a carefully orchestrated public information program on the POW/MIA issue."

Charlie's head snapped toward Margo. What the hell does she mean "possibility?" What was her definition of "carefully orchestrated?" *Damn,* Charlie thought. *The bitch has sold us out again.* Alarmed, she looked over at Carol, then sat back to watch the show. Carol had that look in her eyes.

"Actually Senator," Margo went on, "it's these two lovely ladies who came up with the idea and have developed a program for presentation today." She smiled at the two as though they were her daughters at their first recital.

"Every good PR program needs a hook," the Senator said. "What's yours?"

"Sir," Carol began, "we all know that there are several hundred American military men missing or taken prisoner in Southeast Asia. But the public doesn't know. Hanoi won't identify them and they're crapping—pardon me—all over the Geneva Convention. The public doesn't know that, either. We want to force Hanoi to admit they have our men, publish a complete list of names, and allow inspections that will assure the families and the world that they're being treated properly. If we can shine a light on this, maybe Hanoi will give in."

The Senator sat back in his chair, steepled his fingers and looked out the window.

"If .... If it rained single malt Scotch, I'd be a happy man. Turning on the spotlight is the problem, but we have to address this issue and we have to get some attention. But like I said, you need a hook."

"Well, Senator," Margo began in a tone she believed was ingratiating but bordered simpering. "We still aren't certain what we'll be able to do until we meet with Colonel Hurd."

Carol smiled at Margo's leadfooted attempt to lower the Senator's expectations. As far as Hurd was concerned, this was just another half-assed scheme by a bunch of grief-stricken wives, and he'd water it down to the customary stack of gray, bureaucratic drivel. Carol was determined not to let that happen.

"Senator," she began, leaning forward, getting closer. "The drawdown has almost eliminated all dedicated MACV/SOG and Green Hornet forces that *were* rescuing prisoners. They won't let the teams mount a rescue mission until days after they find a camp. And then CINCPAC has to clear the mission. This is lunacy." She glanced over at Margo, who was turning red and trying hard to swallow.

"There is *no* official program to locate and recover the two hundred or so MIAs in Laos, thanks to the Ambassador. We hear that Secretary Kissinger stopped rescue attempts because he didn't want them to screw up the peace talks. And you know what else?" She didn't give Warga a second to respond. "After July 1972, there won't be any special ops people there to go in after our boys even if we did know where they are."

Silence. Only the sound of Margo hyperventilating. The Senator stared at Carol, searching her eyes.

"How do you know all this?"

"It doesn't matter. It's all factual. Now, can you help us or not?"

A few choking sounds indicated that Margo was attempting speech. "Senator, please accept my deepest apologies. I've never heard this information before and can't vouch for its accuracy."

"Never mind," the Senator said. "You've done your homework, Mrs. Cody. I'll bring this out in committee because I believe you, but remember this. Even though I'm a Democrat and Henry Kissinger is a Republican, I have no question about his dedication to this country and our military personnel. At least *some* of us in Congress know he's not the enemy. Not many, but some.

"Okay," he said, standing up and reaching for a very heavy briefcase. The women hurried to stand, smoothing their skirts.

"I'm going to think about what you said and about your admirable desire to stick a needle in Hanoi. You're a remarkable woman. Your husband has a lot to be proud of when he comes home. But, think about this. If you want to do effective PR, if you want to attract attention and make the front page, this has to be about people, not issues. You need a theme, a central event, a defining moment. Trust me, after six terms in the Senate, I'm a pro at this. Think about it and so will I. Maybe if we put all these great minds together we'll come up with an idea. Good luck this afternoon." And he was gone.

Charlie stared after the Senator as he left.

"He didn't even buy us lunch."

Colonel Hurd rumbled into the conference room with Margo Stone on his heels and Major Calvin Dorsey a respectful third. Hurd was steamed and made no secret of it.

"Ladies," he said as he motioned for them to be seated, "you sure as hell caused a big flap on the Hill today. I don't know yet how much damage you did, but it's not good. Not good. Carol, Charlie, you're in over your heads, trust me. This issue is complicated and confidential, which is why the Secretary of State's office incinerated my telephone just now, ordering me to put a leash and a muzzle on you two."

Carol wanted to reach right across the table and dig her nails into his throat.

"Put a sock in it, Colonel," Carol barked. "Or throw a towel over it, or whatever you guys say. We did the right thing and you'll never convince me otherwise. From now on, the fate of our POWs is a public issue and, if I can make it happen, it's front page news. Are you in or out? Stop being part of the problem and become part of the solution. You'll feel a lot better."

She locked eyes with Hurd, staring him down, then glanced directly behind the Colonel and caught Calvin Dorsey rupturing himself to keep from laughing. He winked at her.

"I'm going to let your outburst pass, Mrs. Cody. I understand how women in a frail emotional condition can become … overwrought. Now it's my turn. Since the cat, so to speak, has been released from his bag, we're going to work out a plan and policy statements right here, right now. We'll develop rules for your public appearances, lists of what you can and cannot say, and how you are to conduct yourself." Carol's urge to choke had become a compulsion to kill and disembowel. "We will not work against the government's efforts and we will consistently confirm our support for the encouraging progress Secretary Kissinger is making.

"Now, I have a very important meeting with the Deputy Assistant Under Secretary in a little while. So, let's get started."

They actually worked together, covering six or seven legal pages with notes by the time Hurd left for his meeting. When the door slammed shut behind him, Carol and Charlie belatedly turned their attention to Margo, who looked like winter had suddenly come and frozen her to her chair. But inside, she was thinking of ways to get even. Margo spent most of her life getting even, and knew it would have to wait. For now, she'd work with the two loose cannons until she could figure a way to crush them.

"I feel like a break," said Major Dorsey. "How about some coffee?"

"I have calls to make," said Margo. "You go."

He ushered them to a table in the cafeteria and sat across from them. As he slowly stirred cream into his coffee, he looked back and forth between the women. His face was round, and Charlie thought it a little pudgy, but cute. In the service, they called him "Catfish."

"I have to tell you this," he started. "I'm kind of a wallflower around the office, let the boss take the spotlight, that kind of thing. But I can't stand the way he treats women. Just because I keep quiet, doesn't mean I'm okay with it. I've got a wife and three kids, been married forever, and the way he acts just isn't right. Just so you know."

"Thanks, Major," said Carol. "That means a lot to us." Dorsey relaxed, and blew into his coffee cup.

"That was quite a show you put on today with the Senator. Do you know he mentioned your names in committee? The word went through the Hill like a dose of salts. You did good. Don't let anyone tell you differently." He stopped talking, shifting a bit in his seat. Carol guessed there was something he couldn't say in front of Charlie.

"Charlie, would you mind taking some coffee up to Margo as a peace offering?" Carol suggested.

Charlie picked up on the hint, "Sure. If I'm not back in fifteen minutes, call in an air strike."

"Carol," Dorsey started, "you're doing the right thing, but you have to be careful. There's going to be a lot of people trying to shut you up. Don't let them. Okay?" She was silent for a moment, moved by his support.

"You can count on it, Cal," she said in earnest.

"I'm going to tell you something now. If there's anything more secret than top secret, this is it. I need to know that you'll never tell anyone. Not even Charlie. If you do, a lot of good men are going to spend a long time in Leavenworth."

"Cal ... what is it?"

"Your word, Carol, as sacred as you can make it."

"You have it. You know that."

"It's about your husband."

Carol knocked over her coffee cup, then, with shaking hands, tried to dab it up with the tiny napkin she'd been given.

"What! Is he alive? Is he okay? Is he ..."

"Yes, he's alive. But the NVA have him. Now, listen to me. There's a small Air Mobile Recon Unit that's secretly searching out prisoners in Northern and Eastern Laos. Maybe ten people know about it, outside the unit itself. The guy running the OP is a real hard charger ... the kind of guy who'll take the necessary chances to complete his mission and tell the brass to pound salt."

"What do you know? What can you tell me?" She could barely get the words out.

"Not much. They're running very secret, high-risk missions in Laos under some kind of wild cover story. Your husband might be there. They're trying to get him and all the rest out."

Carol laughed and cried at the same time.

"But they told me he was captured in South Vietnam."

"They moved them into Cambodia and Laos on their way north. I think your husband is on his way to North Vietnam via Laos. That's honestly all I know. They say no news is good news, but in this case, it's different."

"Thank you. But, you're saying Bill is alive in Laos and nobody on this side of the Pacific knows it."

"Less than a hundred people on the planet know it, and I'm the only one in the Western Hemisphere. Do what you're going to do. And do it loud, in front of everybody."

"Cal, how good is your information?" she asked in a whisper.

"I'd bet my career on it," he said, leaving no room for argument.

"Why are you telling me this?"

"You deserve to have any information I can find. You're working awfully hard on all this, fighting the system, taking on the Pentagon and all."

"You're taking an awful risk."

"I got less than 16 months to retirement and I'll never make Lieutenant Colonel."

"Why not?"

"Black man in this army? It's better than it was, but I've gone about as far as I can go. I have a son in the Army, did you know that? First lieutenant. Flies choppers over in Vietnam right now. Maybe he'll be the first black general. I got hopes."

"I'm proud of you and your son, Cal, and grateful for your help."

"Just keep your own counsel," Dorsey warned.

"You can count on it," she said with a big smile. "Now, let's go rescue Charlie from Margo."

When Dorsey escorted Carol back upstairs he left her at the elevator. Everyone in town would be watching to see who was feeding her information. Dorsey didn't like being looked at in that light, either.

As she turned the corner, Carol almost ran over two full colonels standing in the alcove leading to the main corridor and the conference room down the hall. As she excused herself and walked down the hallway, she could almost feel the heat of their eyes on her back. And lower. She opened the conference room door and bumped straight into Colonel Hurd, who was on his way out. She cringed backward.

"Oh! Excuse me, Colonel. I wasn't watching where I was going," she apologized.

"Not a problem, Carol," he said in his best soft-toned voice. He would have told her how much he enjoyed her closeness, but wisely stopped himself.

"Before the others get back, I'd like to say I'm sorry for the way I spoke earlier. I was a bit harsh. I apologize." He sounded like he had just swallowed a quart of motor oil. He moved in closer.

"I would very much like to make it up to you. If we had dinner tonight, you'd see a different side of me. After all, we're both trapped in this marble mausoleum and it's kind of cold out, if you know what I mean."

"Oh, I read you loud and clear," said Carol, taking another step back. "But, I'm married. Very married. And so, may I point out, are you, even though it doesn't seem to get in your way. Just show your 'better side' to the other POW wives. The ones who are dumb enough to want to see it." She pushed past him into the conference room. Hurd just stood in the doorway.

Am I losing my touch? he thought. *And those two colonels who were eyeballing Carol just now, why are they staring at me? What the hell do they want?*

21

The Biomatter Has Impacted the Oscillator

Grunt Air Headquarters
Udorn Air Force Base, Thailand
18 December, 1971

Morning came early on 18 December, 1971. The phone on the desk next to Roman's sleeping head started ringing in the dark. He jolted himself awake, fumbled for the phone with his eyes half open and looked at his watch. It was 0115 hours.

"Sir, this is Staff Sergeant Nelson. You have a call holding on secure, and two other calls in the last ten mikes. You're popular tonight."

"Okay. I'll be right in there. Who's holding?"

"It's the Kingfish. He insisted I wake you." Hot news, Roman thought. He'd never haul me out of the rack at one in the morning if it weren't important. He sprinted down the hall to the com room and grabbed the phone.

"This is Roman; go Kingfish!"

"Dan, you were right about the offensive. We've got high radio traffic levels up your way starting about six hours ago. About 1835 hours, the NVA started pounding the artillery emplacements in the eastern PDJ. They followed up with tanks and infantry. Most of our artillery positions and bases have already fallen. The others will most likely be gone by this time tomorrow.

Songbird reports that Major General Thran Van Ho, Deputy CO over the POWs, called the local area commander and had him move a bunch of prisoners around to various camps. I'll send the details to the Sphinx later, but he mentioned over two hundred prisoners in Laos." He didn't even give Roman time to make a grunt or comment, but pushed on, spilling a torrent of bad news. "More specifically, he said your Big Three were getting sent to Camp L911 before dawn. They're going to be real secret about it because they're concerned about the spy planes. The boys at MACV don't know which camp is

L911, but the Dragon Lady thinks it's the one you call the Rock House. Not real sure, though.

"We also think that after the Rock House, they'll get moved to a new camp, L711, at Sam Neua, maybe in late January. There's a special interrogation team going to the Rock House in a couple of weeks to prepare them for detailed debriefing. They're bringing some Cuban officer with them, God knows why."

"Maybe an observer?" Roman asked.

"Maybe. At least the NVA hasn't figured out who your boys are yet, but they sure don't want them getting lost. If they knew who they really were, their asses would already be on the road to Hanoi. The offensive has these guys low priority on the transportation list for now, but they'll be moved.

"Sorry I can't help you on the new camp at Sam Neua. Give the Dragon Lady a few days with some new prisoners and she'll deliver."

Kingfish still wasn't finished. Like previously, but without the sinister intent, he poured evil tidings into Roman's ear for at least fifteen minutes. The radio traffic to the PDJ and east is five times higher than normal. Other POWs are being sent north on a faster schedule than usual. A bunch will be going to Muong Soui in late December or early January, maybe to tie in with Kissinger's peace talk plans." Finally, he ran out of steam, and Roman stopped scribbling on his note pad.

"Thanks, Kingfish. Believe it or not, this is good news. Don't pass it on, but L911 is the Rock House and we have an asset watching it right now. I'll get you visual confirmation on some of the actual units in the PDJ so you'll look better than those CIA weenies."

"Actually, Dan, I think they already know. They just won't share the intel. Those guys are actually hot shit in my book. They're good at their job. You should give them another chance. If you haven't forgotten, they did train you," Kingfish added.

"Sure I will, if they ever give me some intel I can use. Talk to you later tonight," Roman said as he hung up the phone and thought about what he'd just said to Kingfish about the CIA personnel. He himself had been selected and trained for Intelligence work by the CIA, but that was in a different time and place. They were all over him to join up, but he decided he'd rather fly than snoop around in the shadowy back alleys of some east European shithole or jungle capital in South America. The CIA men he knew back then were first team, but he couldn't shake his belief that the clowns in Saigon weren't worth shit, no matter how much the Kingfish and the Fiddler liked them.

"Maybe I should think about the CIA gig one more time," he muttered to himself. "At least I wouldn't be a professional clay pigeon for the NVA."

"Sergeant Nelson, get the First Sergeant up and roll out the staff and pilots. Hell, get everyone up and into the briefing room in one hour, except Archangel. I want him scrambled and in the air in 30 mikes. Have him call me on secure after takeoff. I need Chief Abeel, Mr. Gedeon and Captains Toothman, Ryker and Best in here ASAP or faster," Roman ordered.

"Yes, sir. You also had a call from the Fiddler and Major Fitzmorris at Blue Chip."

Roman reached for the phone again and dialed. The Fiddler answered on the first ring.

"Hi, Dan. Hanoi surrendered an hour ago. Just kidding."

"Bastard. That's not funny."

"Okay, here it is. One of the Big Red One Recon boys caught a courier out of Saigon headed up to the NVA command center at Cu Chi. We have him now. He had copies of the Big Three's personnel records. God knows how he got them, but there's an opportunity here. If you agree, we can doctor the personnel records, putting in the info we want them to have. Then we let the little bastard escape. It might work and it might take some heat off your boys for a while. What do you think?"

"I think if you were here, I'd kiss you," Roman answered.

"No tongues," said the Fiddler. "That'd get us kicked out under AR635-212."

"Get this done right away. Consider this Top Secret as of now. I'll let General Geiger know, but no one else. This could really help."

"Right. This guy will be on the road to Cu Chi within a couple of hours. It will take that long to doctor the records and make them look real."

"Got to go, Warren. Thanks," Roman said as he hung up.

Best, Ryker, Chief Abeel and Gedeon stumbled into the office, followed by Toothman. They looked like Sleepy, Dopey, Grumpy, and all the rest. It was 0145 hours.

Once they'd found seats and opened their eyes a little wider, Roman gave them the news.

"Gentlemen, the bio-matter has hit the oscillator. I mean the NVA offensive has started. Naturally, the CIA and MACV boys in Saigon are completely surprised." He looked at his notes and talked them through all the information from Kingfish and Fiddler.

"Sounds like bad news," said Best.

"No, it's good news. I've already scrambled Archangel. He should be calling in shortly. Based upon his enroute weather report, we'll launch the four teams that are still here.

"Bravo stays in position, if possible, to watch for the arrival of the Big Three. If Kingfish is right, they'll be there today—or they may already be there, if they followed Hanoi's orders. We need to know what's really going on in the PDJ. Use the hell out of your scouts. Get me units, plans, time tables, etc. Don't be afraid to get rough if necessary.

"Toothman, Best—You'll need to insert or relocate teams in the area of Easy Street, the Museum, Fish Trap and Dog Patch. Check the camps when you can, but first get me intel on the NVA movements. Keep a constant watch on the road junctions.

"Note the high ground here—here—and here," Roman said as he jabbed his finger at the wall map. "From those points we can observe the critical areas of vehicle movement as well as movement in and out of the camps. Be prepared to be out seven to ten days. Stay high and out of sight. Intel is first priority. Grab a few bad guys and pick their brains. Get rough, if necessary."

"Tom, what's the status of those two birds we brought in yesterday?"

"I can get One One back up in a couple of hours, but the ADF is inop," said Ryker. "The antenna was shot up. The holes won't hurt anything. We'll put 100 knot tape on them. Davis's Four Four is down hard. I won't know for how long until we finish an inspection later today. Everything else is up and ready."

"Fine," Roman said. His mind was racing, trying to think of all the details that had to be covered. "Mr. Gedeon, after you get the critical parts list from maintenance, call down to Sgt. Rogers and see if he has them in stock. If he does, get him to fill the requisitions by phone and put the parts on the base courier bird. If he gives you any shit, tell him I'll personally come and get them tonight. Also, see what you can find out about the two birds we have coming. Have Jenner and Kellogg ready to go after Archangel recovers and refuels. We'll do daily maintenance when we get back.

"Mr. Abeel, come up with an EEI for these teams," Roman said. The Essential Elements of Information (EEI) had to be specific, or it would be worthless.

"Charlie Team is short-handed with Schwartz in the hospital and Khan wounded," Best put in. "I assume he's on a medical hold."

"Okay, put Mr. Touchdown with Charlie Team. He's been bugging me for field duty and he can have it. I can't help on the scout, but Ramirez speaks a little Laotian. Best I can do, Jake."

First Sergeant Woods put his head in the door with the weather report from Archangel. Fair, with a little early morning fog that should burn off by 0900. But there was heavier weather north of Two Zero Alpha, their staging base. Overcast and rain but clearing. Maybe! Reports from other areas were bleak. Bravo Team, spending the night in the jungle, reported heavy traffic on Route 61 and Route 7. There was Infantry from 316th Division's 174th Regiment moving through riding in Chinese armored personnel carriers. Bravo reported T-34 tanks from the 195th Armor Battalion along with the 27th DAC Cong Battalion.

It was one long night of bad news. The firebases in the boonies were getting pounded by artillery fire, some were being overrun. The only good news was that the Big Three had arrived at the Rock House. Bravo would continue their recon when things calmed down.

"Son of a bitch," Roman said. "Thanks, Top. Tell Archangel to keep Bravo in place. Have Five Five stay at Two Zero Alpha. Then you come back after you brief Archangel. Mr. Abeel, get this worked up and get it to General Geiger ASAP."

"Okay. The weather will slow the fixed wings but not us. Launch at 0745 hours. Let's meet for a quick update at 0715 hours. Let me and Archangel know the aircraft and team assignments. Let's go!" The men got to their feet, sliding the chairs back with a series of squeaks. They weren't sleepy any more.

Roman leaned back in his chair and rubbed his eyes. When he opened them, the First Sergeant was standing in front of him with a steaming cup of coffee.

"Looks like a long day ahead. By the way, Khan insists he's ready to go and was cleared by the dispensary for duty. I think he's full of it but the dispensary is closed until 0800 hours. He'll be airborne before I can check it out, sir."

"Forget it. If he wants to go, let him. We need him up there."

In the operations office, Best and Toothman worked out team and aircraft assignments, insertion points and three extraction points for each team. Abeel came in with the EEI. Nelson gave each of them new copies of the current Signal Operating Instructions, codes, frequencies and authentication tables that would be valid for the next ten days. They all spoke fast, but quietly, intense, and in low tones.

Toothman ran through all the critical items they needed to accomplish before launch, ticking them off on his fingers.

"And last," he said to himself and Best, who was distracted with his own checklist, "we need to drop off C-rations and commo packs with Hetler so he can get them to Thornhill at the Rock House."

Best and Toothman looked up at each other and nodded at the exact same instant as though they'd rehearsed the move.

"I'm good," Best said.

"I will be after I clean out my pants," Toothman quipped. "Remember my fifth axiom of combat," he said pausing. "If you're short of everything but enemy, you're in combat."

They laughed and started back to Roman's office to review the plan before sending it up to Archangel. Jake Best looked at his watch. It was 0620 hours.

"My, god," he said to Toothman, "we made up a full Ops Plan in less than 45 mikes! That's a record." Roman blessed the plan and handed it off to Hardy for transmission to Archangel.

The launch went off without any problems or delays. With all his birds in the air, Roman, who'd already put in a full day, headed toward the Air Force area to have a quiet breakfast. All he could do for the rest of the morning was wait. There was a bustle over on the Air Force north ramp and Air America south ramp. The war was getting closer.

He finished breakfast and headed over to maintenance. He had a 1000 meeting with Colonel Odom and wanted to check on Ryker first.

The crews were busy under the maintenance tents. Ryker and Sergeant Nolan were crawling around on top of the badly shot up Four Four bird looking at the rotor pitch change links and blade grips. Roman climbed up the foot holes in the side of the Huey to join them.

"How bad?" Roman asked.

"Looks worse than it is," Ryker said. "Bell Helicopter makes one hell of a good aircraft. It sure takes a licking and keeps on ticking. If we can get the parts, we'll be back up late tomorrow or the next day. Davis must be a great pilot besides being damned lucky to get this one back in one piece. You ought to write him up a commendation for this mission. Look at that mast and rotor head. Scary. No hydraulics, fuel flow had to be erratic and in manual .... Ah hell, Dan, the list is too long."

"Great work, fellas. Thanks!" Roman said as he climbed down. He had ten minutes to get to Colonel Odom's office.

"Dan, sit down," invited Colonel Odom. "Let's make this informal. Coffee?" he asked.

"Yes, sir, it's going to be a long day." What's he up to?

"Yes, it is," Odom agreed. "I've got every flyable fighter up in support of General Vang Pao in the PDJ. They caught us with our pants down. Mr. Caldwell was just here trying to explain why the CIA missed this one.

"Listen, Dan, I wanted to personally thank you for picking us up yesterday. It was real gutsy flying across that tree line to draw them out. Sandy lead told me the whole plan was yours. Very impressive!" Roman could hear the respect in his voice.

"Tell the Sandies they did a great job with that pinpoint bombing on the hilltop. I wasn't expecting that," Roman responded.

"You really shouldn't have come in for us with that much ground fire, but I'm glad you did. It made me start thinking about your unit.

"For instance, the ground security force was real professional. Crack troops and they don't just get that way on the spur of the moment. And your plan. You didn't just come up with that plan and execute it so well by inspecting crash sites. Mr. Eastwood from the CIA thinks your team is not what you appear to be, and I'm starting to agree with him. You guys are just too good.

"Now, I don't know what you're actually doing out there, but it isn't crash site inspection. Look, I've been in this man's Air Force long enough to know not to ask questions, especially when a captain reports to a two-star general at command headquarters. But I want you to know this. If I can be of any *real* help, let me know." Odom stood up.

"And once again, thanks for saving my ass." He shook Roman's hand.

"Thank you, sir. I appreciate the offer. Now, I've got a lot of crash sites to inspect."

Colonel Odom smiled as he returned Roman's crisp salute.

"Archangel, this is Six," Roman said slowly into the mike in the comm. room. He asked for the status of all the insertions. Archangel read them off.

"All in process. Delta is already complete. Lots of reports of ground fire and troops on the move. They don't love us any more. I'm glad we did that recon yesterday up by Site Eight Five. We wouldn't be able to do it today. One of my radio operators just informed me Alpha is in place overlooking the Museum and the road going west toward Easy Street. They're safe and not compromised. Okay, another message, Charlie is inserted and is setting up housekeeping and planting their spring garden."

"The way this thing is going, they may be there long enough to harvest the crop," Roman said jokingly.

"We had a report of small arms fire off Skyline Two at some of Air America's birds. Not a factor so far. Vang Pao is really moving his troops out smartly. Man's got his hands full."

"Okay, have all birds stand by at Two Zero Alpha until late afternoon before heading back here. Just in case," Roman said.

"The NVA is everywhere up here," Alberts responded. "They're using the bad weather to move in the open knowing we can't use Tactical Air. It's clearing out, so the fighters can get in after 1200 hours or so. I'll get you an update in an hour. Archangel out."

Roman wandered to the B Frame at the back of the building to grab a quick sandwich and coke. By the time he got back to his desk, the secure phone was ringing. It was General Geiger, and he got right to the point.

"I just got this intel summary on the troop activity reported by Bravo."

"Yes, sir."

"Is he sure of the troop designations and confirmed the T-34s?"

"No question. They saw the troops and tanks up close to confirm," Roman was sure of his information.

"Good work, Roman, keep it coming. This is real intelligence. Screw those bastards at the CIA."

"One other thing, General," Roman said quickly. "Bravo team also confirmed the Big Three arrived at the Rock House at 0545 hours, this date."

"Humph!" Geiger snorted. "That's what you predicted. Okay, son, keep it up."

Roman hated to wait. He would much rather be up in the air flying missions with Toothman. Mr. Gedeon passed by.

"I just got off the phone with Sgt. Rogers at TSN Supply. He has all the parts but one and he's sending a jeep over to Long Binh to pick it up. He can't get them on the C-130 courier in time, so we'll need to send our aircraft. At least they're available."

"Good. Coordinate with Sergeant Hardy and let both the Sphinx and the First Sergeant know in case we need to pick up or deliver anything else on this run. I'll let maintenance know so they can schedule their time and be ready to pull maintenance on the C-47 when it gets back from Saigon. We need it in the air by 0700 hours tomorrow. Not much down time for maintenance," Roman commented.

After a second report from Archangel, Roman made a secure call to General Mattix giving him the latest on the insertions and problems of the offensive. At least the Big Three were in a safe place for a while. Roman also told him about the Fiddler, the courier and the fake personnel files. Mattix loved the idea. He was also pleased to hear that TSN Supply would give them the parts they needed.

Archangel reported at 1500 hours that all teams were in good shape and very busy. The next Intel report from the teams would be a big one.

"They're catching a mortar or two every hour from different points on Skyline Two." Even on the radio, Roman could hear the concern in his voice. "I think we should bring all the birds home before dark."

"Okay, Doug. Bring them home when you're ready," Roman answered. "They're just targets sitting out there at Two Zero Alpha. Besides, if they're here, it won't look so suspicious."

Roman felt like things were under control after his update from Alberts. Then Ryker came in with Gedeon and spoiled the afternoon.

"Looks like we have a parts problem after all," Ryker said.

"Rogers just called back and said he couldn't give us the parts without valid requisitions," Gedeon chimed in. "Orders from Colonel Sweeney."

"Didn't he tell that jackass these parts are for a combat aircraft engaged in active combat operations?" Roman felt his face get warm.

"Yes, sir. He said that didn't exempt us from Air Force supply regulations. Sweeney said when our plane gets there, he'll come down to examine our requisitions and make sure they're filled out 'according to the appropriate regulations.'"

"Jesus Herbert Christ. Okay, Bob, you fly down and hand-carry the requisitions. You can defend them if he rejects them, which he will. I'll call and see if Major Fitzmorris can soften him up in the meantime. Sorry Bob, but looks like you're going to qualify for flight pay if you keep taking these flights to Saigon." Gedeon laughed.

"Are you kidding? I wouldn't miss this show for anything. How's he going to reject these requisitions with Fitzmorris standing right there as a witness?"

"Well, the good news is Archangel will be on the ground in less than an hour. A quick refuel and you can get there before the Mexican restaurant closes." Roman joked, reaching for the radio to call Archangel.

"Archangel, this is Six. We want your bird to make a quick turn around for fuel. Jenner and Kellogg are standing by. What's your ETA?"

"The flight of five is already south of the river. I'm ten out now," Alberts reported.

"Good. Before you change frequency, let the pilots and copilots know that we'll have a quick debriefing at 2000 hours."

"Roger. Archangel, out."

Roman went over to the O Club for supper with Ryker and found Colonel Odom at the bar. The man looked like he'd been taken for a ride by the Mob.

"We have three F-4s down up north," he began, taking a pull of his straight Scotch, then a second. "The first one went down in the eastern PDJ at the hand of a hotshot MIG-21 pilot. After he flamed the F-4, he broke for home. Two of my real sharp pilots went after him but forgot to look at the gas gauge. They're down, too. We've got a big search and rescue going on, but no luck so far and now it's dark. You wouldn't just happen to have any assets in the area to show those idiots how it's done?"

"No, sir. All my birds are sleeping outside. But I can be up there early if you want."

"No. Well, maybe later. Let's see if these SAR boys can do the job." The Colonel wandered off, taking a drink in each hand.

The debriefing at 2000 hours was anything but quick because all the pilots had plenty to say about the dangers in the PDJ. *They're scared*, Roman thought. He could hear it in their voices. *Good thing, because fear keeps you alert and alert keeps you alive.*

"Okay, tomorrow we'll reposition to Two Zero Alpha as soon as Archangel gives us the word. We'll shoot for a 0700 hours launch, if possible. Aircraft commanders listen up real good. From here on out, you'll be in combat conditions. Real combat conditions. There's no standard operating procedure for what you're going to run into. So here are your orders. Consider the situation, evaluate it, make the best decision you can under the circumstances and execute your plan. You're getting flight pay and combat pay, so get the job done and come back alive."

A few hours later, Gedeon got off the C-47 at Tan Son Nhut, marched in to the supply office, saluted Colonel Sweeney and presented Sergeant Rogers with a whole handful of Blue Streak requisitions.

"Let me see those," Sweeney said, snatching them out of the Sergeant's hands. "I doubt they'll be acceptable."

"Colonel, those are right by the regulations, sir," Gedeon assured him.

"Humph," uttered Sweeney contemptuously.

"Ten-HUT!" Sergeant Rogers yelled, jumping to his feet. Two General Officers had just entered the room, Lieutenant General Hamilton, Vice Commander of the 7th Air Force, and Major General Mattix, the Deputy Chief of Staff – Operations.

"At ease, gentlemen," said Hamilton. "Colonel Sweeney, have you seen any improper requisitions in the Grunt Air submission?"

"Sir, they just got here. I haven't had a chance to review them. It's quite unusual for this type of submission."

"Combat is always unusual, Colonel," General Hamilton said as if he were talking to a six-year old.

"The General is certainly correct. But supply procedures and Air Force regulations still must be followed. Especially in this case."

"Colonel Sweeney, you may use your authority to reject any of those requisitions you wish. But you'll explain each decision to the Commanding General and me tomorrow at 0800 hours. Do you understand me?" Hamilton said, using his general's voice.

"Yes, sir, I do. I'm sure Mr. Gedeon has properly followed the regulations and we'll fill the requisitions right away, sir."

"I sincerely hope so," said Hamilton as he turned to go.

On the way out, General Mattix brushed past Gedeon and leaned close.

"Have a safe flight back, Chief."

22

The Opposing Team Lineup—In this Corner ...

Grunt Air Headquarters
Udorn Air Force Base, Thailand
19 December, 1971

The morning of 19 December, 1971 started just like the morning of the day before. A million miles an hour.

During the night, the Recon teams had worked themselves down the mountain from their observation positions to "snoop and poop," assembling important information about the massive troop movements and the situation around their assigned POW camps. Before daylight, they would return to their mountain positions to prepare their sitreps for transmission to Archangel. The volume of information was staggering. Archangel had Alpha, Bravo and Charlie make their reports on the primary Grunt Air frequency to Sergeant Do Ka Boung, the radio operator seated directly behind Alberts in the port radio position. Delta and Echo Teams made their situation reports to Sergeant Ray Blanton in the starboard radio position on the secondary operations frequency. The Archangel's radio operators started taking team reports at 0600 hour,s and were still taking them at 0645 hours. That had never happened before. Alberts flew the C-47 but couldn't help wonder what was taking so long. Were his radio operators and interpreters that slow, or was the volume of data that massive? If there was so much of it, General Geiger and his people would enjoy an intelligence bonanza just in time for Christmas. *Ho, Ho Fucking Ho*, Alberts thought. He was sure the CIA already knew what was going on but wouldn't give the information to the field.

Strange thing, thought Alberts. *If you give the teams in the field the intel they need, they know what to look for when they're running around behind the lines.* Someone in Saigon had forgotten that and kept them in the dark on the important things.

Archangel was orbiting at 12,500 feet over Control Point Peter just southwest of Long Tieng. It was an approach fix where inbound aircraft landing at Long Tieng would report to the tower. Long Tieng was an unusual airfield. Most fixed wing aircraft could only land uphill to the north heading of 320 degrees, and take off downhill in the opposite direction. There was a huge limestone karst at the northwest end of the runway that had claimed more than one unlucky aircraft. Pilots called it "the vertical speed brake." In spite of the marginal weather, the morning light revealed to Alberts the Plain of Jars to the northeast just 25 nautical miles away. The air was hazy, and that was bad because it concealed the patchy fog that surrounded the mountaintops. It was hard on the fixed-wing aircraft, but the helicopters could stay low and then inch into the fog to get to the landing sites on the mountains.

The Ravens, Forward Area Controllers, would start bringing in the fighters by 0900 hours. Judging from the length of reports Archangel was receiving, there would be no shortage of things for the fighters to shoot at. It was, in military parlance, a "target-rich environment." Sergeant Boung put his microphone down and gave Alberts a thumbs up. He had copied all the Alpha, Bravo and Charlie reports. Alberts pointed to Blanton and gave Boung a questioning look. Boung looked over to Blanton's little radio console, turned to Alberts and held his hands wide apart. Blanton was scribbling furiously. The volume of data was enormous today.

Alberts took another look at the weather. The helicopters would be safe to launch in another 30 to 45 minutes. "Make that a 0745 hour release time," he reported to Grunt Air Operations.

"It took us fifty-five minutes to copy the morning report," Alberts told Sergeant Hardy on the radio. "Lots of intel."

The Hueys launched for Long Tieng precisely at 0745 hours. If a team needed emergency extraction, a bird could be launched in five minutes or less to pull them out.

"Archangel, this is Grunt Air Six," Roman called.

"Roger, Six, go."

"Launch was at 0745 hours. I need you to return to base and bring the reports in. The boys can get to Two Zero Alpha without you this morning. Refuel while we go over the reports with the Sphinx. You'll return to orbit later."

"Roger, Six, out." Alberts radioed Toothman in his Huey to tell him that Archangel was going off-station and to assume control of the mission until Archangel was in position once again. Toothman acknowledged the call.

Roman and Abeel were waiting in a jeep for Alberts as he taxied up to park and shut down.

At headquarters, Roman and Abeel went over every piece of paper two and three times before sitting back to absorb all the information.

"My, god," said Abeel after a moment. "We're up against Major General Le Trong Tan himself. And to make matters worse, Vu Lap is his deputy."

"Who's this General Tan?" Roman asked. "I don't know him. He wasn't in the Delta."

"This guy is on the same level as Giap or Ho Chi Minh himself, but he's the best-kept secret Hanoi has. He keeps himself out of the limelight. Brilliant. Very aggressive. Mid-fifties and some kind of strategic genius. He was a Deputy Chief of Staff under Giap back in 1961. In 1964, he became the Assistant Commander of the Vietcong. Later in 1964, he led the first corps-size operation against our Lam Son 719. He designed the counterattack in early 1971.

"His deputy general, Vu Lap, is an old Laos veteran, the tactical mastermind behind Campaign 139. And now Tan is overall commander of this multi-division operation they call Campaign Z. Oh, yeah. One more thing. He was the commander of the 312th Division that went up against the French at Dien Bien Phu with Giap. Quite a guy."

"The reports say this force is too big for General Vang Pao's Hmong forces to hold back," Roman observed. "Even the Thais working with the Hmong forces can't do it. This could be the end if they can't be held at Skyline or before. We may wind up thinking about Long Tieng with sad memories. Hell. Let's go over the deployment plan that the teams reported."

Abeel picked up another stack of reports. "Okay, sir. It seems the thrust units, as they call them, are following the same plan as they used to sweep the PDJ in their Campaign 139. Charlie interrogated an NVA captain who said they're using the 316th Division for that. Their heavy artillery has already pretty well wiped out those 'indestructible' Thai firebases. Most are gone, and the rest can't survive under this heavy an attack. They'll probably evacuate to Ban Na. They plan to use the Dac Cong to attack Phou Seu here in the south central PDJ near the Fish Trap. Delta reported heavy traffic in the area and has repositioned to the high ground overlooking the roads, river and camp. The one prisoner captured confirmed he was a part of Dac Cong. They didn't get too much out of him so they're looking to snag somebody else. Charlie reports the 335th Independent Regiment is headed to Phou Keng in the west-central part of the PDJ. That's only a temporary stop before they'll turn south along with 174th and 148th Regiments. Echo confirms this info from a senior sergeant assigned to the Regimental Operations Directorate. They wanted to get more but the sergeant didn't make the late show. The targets are Sam Thong and Skyline Ridge. Echo confirmed it was the 141st Regiment that overran the Unity forces at Finger Ridge. The forward division headquarters is planned to locate near Phou Phasai. The prisoner did not know when it would be activated. They had this artillery major as a prisoner, and he said the 130mm long range artillery would be concentrated in the Xieng Nua area, but didn't know exactly where. This tells us a lot and not enough. Maybe we'll have more tonight or tomorrow."

"Tells us plenty," Roman said. "The offensive is only 14 hours old and our teams have come up with the whole order of battle and planned objectives. Maybe I'm just a lowly and inexperienced captain, but I know a major intelligence coup when I see it. Stand by. I'm getting you a ride so you can report to Mattix and Geiger."

Roman had to beg and plead with Colonel Odom on the phone to get an aircraft to take Abeel to Saigon. In the end, he had to promise the Udorn Base Commander that no, they weren't going to the BX to buy shaving cream and the latest issue of *Playboy*, and yes, Roman would tell him what the briefing was all about because if it helped the 7th Air Force, it would help at Udorn, too.

Finally, Odom gave in and told Roman an F-4 would take Abeel to Saigon. Two hours ground time, max. Roman returned to the briefing room where Abeel was waiting.

"Okay, Chief, pull all that stuff together. You're going to TSN," Roman said smiling at Abeel. "I want you to brief Mattix and Geiger ASAP. Colonel Odom has an F-4 ready to take you there. But first, I want to give him a short briefing, off the record, on information he can use for targeting. Maybe his boys can slow the NVA offensive down a little bit. Meet me at the jeep in five. I'll call Mattix and let him know you're on the way."

Roman gave Colonel Odom a detailed briefing on the information his team had obtained so air strikes could be coordinated.

"Jesus!" Odom wiped his sweating forehead and stared at Roman. "I figured your bunch was up to something like this, but damn! You know I'll keep quiet about your unit, and thanks for trusting me. You didn't have to do this. Like I said earlier, if I had said no, the Commanding General would have ordered me to get you the aircraft."

"That's correct, sir."

"Let's get Abeel strapped in and on his way. The Intel boys needs this info immediately. Damn sure the CIA won't be telling them any of this. I am going to get more of this from you in the future, right?"

"Every morning, sir. Just don't let Grunt Air get exposed. General Coroneos' ass is on the line," Roman said pointedly.

"Right. Now get the hell out of here so I can hit some of your targets."

"Just don't hit the mountains. My people are up there by day. At night, they play tourist in the valleys," Roman said as he turned to leave.

"One more thing," Odom said as Roman was halfway out the door. "Ever flown in an F-4?"

"No, sir," Roman said. "But I'd kill for the chance."

"Be over at the 555th Tactical Fighter Ops at 1400 hours. Don't eat first unless you're prepared to clean the cockpit after you flash your hash."

"I'll be there, sir," Roman responded with excitement.

At 1330 hours, Roman was at the Triple Nickel Ops ready to go live his dream and on an empty stomach. Before Colonel Odom arrived, two of the other pilots took him through the cockpit and emergency procedures.

He was strapped in with his parachute and was talking with one of the Triple Nickel "GIBs" (guys in back), the radar and systems operators, when Colonel Odom climbed up to the front seat of the F-4, threw his leg over the side and squirmed down into his seat.

"I assume the boys briefed you on what to do if we have to go down," Odom asked.

"Yes, sir. Take my pistol out and shoot myself."

"That's probably the best idea, but we should be okay today. I don't think we'll actually get into the shit this trip. We're on Bongo Charley, a five minute standby alert for emergency air strikes in Northern Laos. We'll fly even if we don't get the call for support," Odom promised.

All four F-4s assumed their standby position on the Udorn alert pad just in case a call came in. It wasn't ten minutes before the words "Scramble! Scramble!" came through the radio. Each of the four jet fighters started its two engines and lowered the two canopies in preparation for flight. There were no delays as the four F-4s took off in pairs. They turned left after clearing the southeasterly runway and climbed to 30,000 feet. The flight leader checked in with Cricket control, a C-130 flying high over the area, the daytime airborne command post.

"Bongo Charley," called Cricket, "fly zero three five degrees for two zero off Skyline and contact Nail Two Three on Channel one two."

Nail Two Three was the call sign for a forward air controller who directed the fighter attacks in support of ground operations.

"Roger, Cricket. Bongo is going up Channel one two for Nail Two Three. Good day."

"Nail Two Three, this is Bongo Charley Lead with you at Angels Three Zero, passing Skyline. Bongo is a flight of four with snake and nape."

"Roger, lead. We have two T-34s, trucks and troops stalled at a road junction, UG2663. Make your first run northwest to southeast, with snakes. Be advised that there's AAA in area. Report run."

"Roger, Nail. We'll report inbound."

"Colonel, can I use your 'Uniform' radio back here?" Roman asked.

"Yeah, what for?"

"I'll find out where the AAA is."

"I don't believe this shit," Odom said amazed.

Roman dialed in three five seven decimal seven on the radio then transmitted, "Archangel, this is Six."

"Go ahead, Six."

"Check quickly with Echo and find out where the active AAA is near that road junction just east of their position."

"Roger, standby." Archangel contacted Echo and radioed back to Roman the exact information he asked for.

"Roger, Archangel. Tell Echo to watch the show. Six, out. Colonel, there are two ZSUs up against the hill 250 meters south of the road junction."

"I don't want to know how you know that," Odom replied, then notified Nail Two Three who changed the mission.

"Bongo Charley, Two Seven make first run with nape. Your targets are two reported ZSUs south of the road junction against the hill."

"Roger. Check change, Bongo, Two Seven inbound pickle hot."

Bongo Two Seven got to within a half a mile when the ZSUs opened up and hit the F-4 with the first burst of anti-aircraft fire. The stricken aircraft started smoking immediately. Once it was hit, it pulled hard right to avoid more fire but it was too late. He was clearly going down. Both pilots ejected in sight of Echo Team, one kilometer west. Roman immediately called Archangel on UHF.

"Archangel, this is Six. Tell Echo to go get those two F-4 pilots and to proceed to extraction point. I want Echo out as well. It will be hot so have Six Six take the mission. Make sure he swears them to secrecy before dropping them off. Our secret isn't going to last long at the rate we're going. Six, out."

"Roger, boss. I take it you've joined the Air Force," Alberts responded sarcastically.

"Someone has to take care of these fools."

When Roman dialed back into the Air Force frequency, his headset hummed with excited chatter. The second F-4 was on a napalm attack on the ZSUs with the third F-4 coming in from the opposite direction as a decoy. Odom was positioning his F-4 behind the second F-4 as follow up.

"Colonel, don't call JRCC. Air America will pick up your boys in about 15 mikes."

"You mean a Green Taxi?"

"Let's just say Air America comes to the aid of Triple Nickel, again," Roman said.

"Again? Oh. I see. Okay." Odom hit his mike button. "Bongo flight, I just confirmed Air America has a taxi in the area and will bring those two home before supper."

"Hey, that's great, Bongo Four," came over the radio, "now let's finish off the ZSUs and take out those T-34s."

Aside from the one aircraft lost (and pilots rescued by a reconnaissance team that wasn't there), the mission went well and Roman had the ride of his life. Odom made a perfect, if heart-stopping landing, taxied to the ramp and shut down the engines. As Roman climbed down the ladder from the back seat, Odom put a hand on his shoulder.

"You saved some lives today, Captain. Again. I could say thank you, but it doesn't seem like enough."

"No problem, Colonel. I'm sure the Air America boys will be happy with your thanks. But it *is* Air America, right?" Roman asked with his eyebrows raised.

"For now—Air America." Odom agreed.

"Hell, Colonel, Air America pilots do this shit every day. It's old hat for them. They won't even know or bother to ask each other who actually pulled them out. But I'd appreciate it if you made sure those F-4 pilots remember it was Air America that got them out, not a green taxi."

"I heard that."

"Thanks for the flight of a lifetime. I owe you," Roman said as he saluted the Colonel.

"Owe me! That's a joke. Get out of here, you bum."

By the time Roman got back to his office it was 1630 hours. He was greeted by First Sergeant Woods.

"Captain Roman, General Mattix wants you to call him when you get back. He seemed a little upset, sir." Roman didn't want to make the call, but he did.

"You goddamned fool" were the first words he heard followed by more bad language. He could almost see Al Mattix jumping up and down on one foot, his face red.

"Do you have a death wish or something? You expose your ass big time in a damned F-4 over Laos right after you pull the intelligence coup of this damned war. I'm telling you the same thing I told Odom. Roman doesn't fly in fighters, FACs or anything else that goes in harm's way. He said he hated snow so he'll keep you out of his aircraft. He also said you responded extremely well under the combat situation and saved two F-4 jocks. He also said you called in Air America, who flew in green taxis. I take it he knows what's going on."

"Yes, sir, he knows a little. I had to tell him something, but I have his word he'll keep the faith."

"Okay. His word is good with me," Mattix said after a moment. "Abeel was great. He had Geiger and the Commanding General on the edge of their seats for an hour. That was absolutely a fabulous job you guys did."

"We can do better, sir. I'll have more for you tomorrow. I'm bringing Echo Team in tonight for detailed briefing. They were at the main cross-roads when those three regiments went through. I'm going to use them as a quick reaction recon team. When we get a good lead, I'll insert them in the area. Christian and his team are my best Intel types. They outdo both Captain Best and Gunny Thornhill's teams."

"That's saying an awful lot," the General offered. "Does bringing them in leave that area open?"

"Not really, sir. I have Delta near the Fish Trap covering the southern areas and main supply routes, and Charlie over at Easy Street observing the traffic going north. I have both the Museum and the Rock House covered, but I'll pull them in if it gets much worse. The NVA wouldn't shoot at us a few days ago, but they will now. It's a big push with lots of NVA in the area. It will be hard to work that far up there like we've been doing.

"Right now I can pull and insert as you and General Geiger need specific information. As far as the Rock House is concerned, I think we can resupply or replace one time without compromise. Frankly, I believe our sources when they say it will be January before they move the Big Three again. That should hold if they believe the altered personnel records. Of course, the offensive itself will affect their ability and the urgency to move them. They think they're in total control of the Ban Ban Valley and no one will disturb the camps there with the offensive going on."

"I agree. Continue as you outlined. Be careful, Dan. You and those Army misfits are the best thing the Air Force has going," Mattix said.

"Yes, sir," Roman responded as he hung up the phone. "First Sergeant, please find Mr. Abeel and Sergeant Hardy for me," Roman asked over the intercom. The two men appeared in moments, along with Ryker, who immediately started throwing Roman sarcastic questions about his ride in the jet.

"Couldn't stand it, could you? Abeel gets a ride and you don't? Got jealous?"

"Frankly, you can have those fast movers. They're dangerous to your health," Roman said. "What's new, guys?"

Ryker briefed Roman on the maintenance situation. Four Four was ready to fly. Schwartz had been evacuated to the 121st in Saigon and was going to make it.

"The bad news is his face will be disfigured pretty badly. His right leg is also in bad shape. But he's alive," Ryker said in consolation.

"Okay, Sphinx, what have you got?" Roman asked Abeel.

"Not much. But the teams are really loading Archangel with info. They're all going out tonight to get prisoners and sweat them. We'll have a lot more in the morning."

"I have Echo inbound," Roman informed Abeel. "They pulled a couple F-4 boys out and possibly compromised themselves. Anyway, I want to have them ready to insert as we need."

"Yeah. I heard from Archangel that Dorsey got them out under moderate to heavy ground fire. He apparently did one of your pop up extractions that caught the NVA by surprise. No casualties reported other than his bird took a few rounds. Anyway, we may have a better feel for what's going on by this time tomorrow."

"Sir," the First Sergeant said as he stuck his head into the office, "General Mattix for you on secure."

"Thanks Top," he said as he picked up the phone. "Captain Roman, sir."

"Dan, the shit is getting real deep up north. The Thais at the firebases are being hit hard and will not hold. We're hoping they can disable their artillery and move out to the south towards Ban Na airfield Lima Site One Five. Air America is going to airlift them and the Hmong soldiers out of the PDJ and to Ban Na. They've requested the Ambassador's permission to recruit Grunt Air for this combat mission. He agreed but told Mr. Eastwood not to expose you to hostile fire as you're not a combat unit. Eastwood said he wouldn't let you fly any mission beyond your capability. The Ambassador agreed so, starting tomorrow, the Green Taxi rides with Air America."

"That's fine, sir, if I can keep two birds back to support my teams in the field," Roman requested.

"Of course. Wait, how many birds do you have operational?" the General asked.

"All six, sir. Ryker got Four Four up overnight once we got the parts from Sgt. Rogers."

"Remind me to write Ryker up for commendation. He's a miracle worker," Mattix said.

"I couldn't agree with you more, General Mattix. Ryker is doing a real half-assed job. A real slacker!"

"He's there, I take it," the General said.

"Yes, sir. I'll pass on your reprimand to him after this call."

Ryker extended his fist and singular digit.

"You haven't changed a bit since you were a kid in South America. Good night, Dan."

Roman thought for a minute, then recounted what the General said about helping Air America as well as existing Intel missions.

"Sergeant Hardy, set up the missions for tomorrow as follows. Captain Toothman, Air Mission Commander, along with One One, Two Two and Five Five fly rescue with Air America. Four Four and Six Six will stay back and support the Intel Ops. I'll fly Four Four. Have Lieutenant Davis work with Archangel. We're going to need help there. Davis is fixed-wing rated so he can get transition to the C-47 with Alberts. We'll use Davis in both areas as we need help.

"Mr. Abeel, I'm thinking of pulling Alpha and putting them somewhere in the area of Finger Ridge to monitor the NVA progress south. The village of Lat Houmong is right in the crossroads, and the people are very pro Vang Pao. They'll be a good source. Look at the area and let me know where you want to put Alpha late tomorrow or first light on the 21st." Looking at the wall map, Roman pointed to Ban Na.

"The plan to regroup at Ban Na is okay as long as they don't stay more than one night. The NVA will be hot on their heels. That means they'll be moved again either to Two Zero Alpha or to Padong. My bet is they'll try to take a stand here at Long Tieng and start building up a counter-force over here at Padong. I figure we'll be playing bus service for two weeks. That's all I give Two Zero Alpha before they take it. That means we'll support our main mission through Padong. Sergeant Hardy, Mr. Abeel, Captain Ryker, you'll go with me to Padong after we launch in the morning to check it out for future Ops. Better get Nelson to go for commo recon.

"Sphinx, give those boys in Echo Team a good debriefing. They were in an active position last night. They may have more to add to the morning report. Keep them here as reserve or a replacement for Bravo in a couple of days. I'm not even sure if we want to resupply Bravo. I think we'll just get them out and hope the Fiddler and Kingfish can keep us informed after that. Also, look at this road area south of Ban Na and west of Lima Site One Five. This high ground could cover the northern approach to Sam Thong. You couldn't get armor through there, but it would be a good avenue for infantry. Echo could do some good in there. These are just thoughts, Chief. Let me know what you think tomorrow after you go over the morning reports. That's it. I'm going to the B Frame for a stiff scotch and water ... or three."

Roman drank the first one quickly, then nursed the second. The magnitude of what was happening slowly crept into his thoughts. Did he and his team really pull off the biggest intel coup of the war? Was a secret unit designed to rescue prisoners of war the best thing that happened to Military Intelligence? How long would he have to order those recon teams out into the jungle, spending nights behind enemy lines with every chance of getting killed? He thought of Schwartz, who would never be the same again, and what would happen if he lost any more of his people.

I'm over my head in this job, he said to himself. *I don't care if Odom or Mattix think I walk six miles on water before breakfast. If I screw this up, people are going to die.*

He decided to finish his drink and go write to his kids. It always made him feel better.

∞∞

23

Sanity, Secret War, *and* Incest *are Relative Terms*

Grunt Air Headquarters
Udorn Air Force Base, Thailand
20 December ,1971

One of Jan Toothman's axioms of war is that *no operations plan ever survives the first hostile fire.* He was willing to take credit for the insight, but it's an observation that has its roots in the earliest armed conflicts of mankind.

It was certainly the case on 20 December, 1971. The Unity Firebases Cobra, Panther and Stingray were under heavy mortar and artillery fire. The NVA were enveloping the Plain of Jars just as they had done so well in Campaign 139. Unfortunately, General Vang Pao had developed a defensive plan that counted heavily on the Thai and Lao artillery firebases, which were falling one after the other.

Dan Roman had gone to bed thinking he had a good plan for the next day, but Abeel changed that at 0235 hours when he reached through the doorway of Roman's room, flipped on the overhead light and sang a cheery "Good morning, Sunshine." Roman sat upright in his rack blinking at the brightness.

"Who said that thing about the best laid plans of mice and men?" asked Abeel.

Roman was in no mood. "Some poet. Robert Burns, maybe. What the hell is this?"

"We got a call from Eastwood over at Air America. He had some intel that was worrying him and wanted us to know just in case we had plans to 'recon' some crash sites tomorrow."

"Okay, what?"

"The NVA is moving harder and faster than predicted. Your flight to Padong needs to be scrubbed for today. I think our teams are in danger and putting Echo west of Ban Na is not such a good idea anymore. You may be right about Ban Na being a temporary point of retreat. I'd like to get Archangel in the air right away and see if our people have any current reports. We can make a new plan of action after we get the updated team reports." Abeel sounded pretty confident.

"Right," Roman said, his head gradually clearing. He sat on the side of the bed for a few seconds, pulling his hazy thoughts together. "How long's this gonna take?"

"Actually, Alberts got up when he heard the phone ring. He's already headed out to preflight. All you have to say is yes and he'll be airborne in 20 mikes. We'll have the reports back to us by … say 0400 hours," Abeel said looking at his watch.

"Do it. I'll call 7th Intel Shop and see what they've got. Then King-fish and Fiddler. Maybe they know something about the offensive or the Big Three. I'll also go over to Air America Ops and see what they have." Roman started to put on his flight suit, struggling with the zipper. "I hate these god-damned zippers almost as much as I hate the goddamned staff." The zipper suddenly went up and Roman gave his full attention to Abeel. "Have the First Sergeant get everyone up at 0400 hours, and get Toothman, Ryker, Hardy and Christian into the briefing room. We'll figure this all out then."

In his office, Roman started working the phone calling both Fiddler and Kingfish. No help. No information. Fiddler confirmed that the counterfeit personnel documents for Cody looked very real and believable. "The courier left on time and according to plan," he told Roman. "He should have reached Cu Chi yesterday. They'll want to digest the information and make sure it's all valid. Hanoi's pretty hot on these guys. I'm sure they'll report today."

"Right," Roman said, "let me know what you learn. I've got people at risk."

"Will do, Dan. Fiddler, out."

Eastwood over at Air America Ops was surprisingly cooperative and so was his staff, but Roman was sure (and not surprised) that Caldwell was holding back, as usual. After they'd spoken for a few minutes, Eastwood asked if Roman might have something to contribute. Loaded question.

"My crash site recon boys might have something for you before 0600 hours. It may not be very useful, but Grunt Air will help."

"Anything you can tell us will be very helpful," said Caldwell. "Of course, we'll keep it confidential." *You keep everything confidential, you prick,* Roman thought. *We're all on the same side, here. You either know what Grunt Air is really doing out there or you don't. At least you're playing the game about crash site recons, and that's a good thing.*

"I've got four crews ready for assignments at 0600 hours or sooner, if you need them. I've got to get over to Base Ops."

Colonel Odom was busy planning air strikes for later in the day.

"We need better weather before we can make the runs," he told Roman. "It's been a bitch ever since they took out Commando Club." This was the facility that provided the radar for bombing attacks on North Vietnam and Laos, operating out of Site Eight Five up north.

"I'm putting everything I've got in the air," Odom said. "You know anything?"

"I'll have overnight updates to you by 0600 hours. I'm pulling my teams out at first light. I don't want your boys dropping anything on them."

"How close are your boys to the NVA?"

"Close enough to smell the fish heads on their breath, sir."

"Well," Colonel Odom said in amazement, "I guess you better get them out."

At 0410 hours, Roman met his key staff members for a briefing by Archangel and Abeel. Roman added what he had learned at Air America and Base Operations. The faces were serious, the atmosphere somber. Conditions in the PDJ were getting worse by the hour.

Archangel's weather report didn't give them much encouragement, either. Conditions were foul in the northern and eastern PDJ and not a whole lot better in the south and west. "Air Force operations will be at a minimum until noon or after, and they've got over fifty Air Force and Navy aircraft committed to finding some downed F-4 pilot to the southeast. That draws off a lot of air-support assets we could use in the PDJ," Alberts told them.

"Unity forces are in trouble and Fire Support Base Panther has been taking heavy artillery barrages. King Kong Fire Base was still fighting at dawn, but it's going down. So is Phou Kong."

Thanks to Abeel's delivery of the morning reports, everyone in the room got progressively more depressed. According to Sergeant Richardson's report, it was like having 50-yard-line tickets at the Super Bowl. The enemy was less than 50 meters away at times. Sergeant Krumins at the Fish Trap had reported that he also felt like they had a 50-yard-line seat. He went on to add that Firebases Cobra and Stingray were sure to fall. Except for Bravo Team at the Rock House, all team chiefs indicated that extraction would be a very good idea, and soon. No team had been discovered or compromised, but there were far too many NVA infantry soldiers running around. Delta had to reposition to a hillside 1.5 klicks south of the Fish Trap.

"Okay," Roman said decisively, "the program is changed as follows. Toothman, you go fly taxi for Air America with Ditton, Donovan and Hetler. They're going to start evacuating Panther and Mustang as soon as you can get in there at first light. You need to crank by 0500 hours. Go up to Two Zero Alpha, refuel and report to the Ops Officer there. You should plan on relieving Phou Kong as well. It'll probably be gone by noon. You can expect to fly the survivors to their rally point at Phou Long Mat or possibly Ban Na. That's Lima Site One Five, but that won't hold for long either. If Krumins is right, the NVA will be there by tomorrow. After that, you can help move those reinforcements coming in from Kanchanabur to Two Zero Alpha by C-123 about 1200 or 1300 hours. They'll be deployed to two points. Elements of BC616 will go to Tha Tam Bleung and BC617 to Phou Long Mat. There are troops on Hill One Six Six Three southwest of Ban Na so we don't need to put Echo there. Besides, it's bound to fall in the next forty-eight hours. Air America may or may not have any work for you. If not, come home. I would plan on going back north to Cobra and Stingray, however. They can't last. They say they can, but our teams say no.

"Dorsey, you and I are going after Alpha, Charlie and Delta and then to resupply Bravo. I want you to extract Delta first, then take a roundabout route through the hills to this clearing at UG625735. You'll drop off chow, ammo and other supplies. Tell Bravo to hide the fuel for future use. Then, get your ass back to Two Zero Alpha. Forget the night restriction, if necessary. We'll make a decision at 1800 hours whether to stay at Two Zero Alpha or return to Udorn." Just as he finished laying out the plan, Seacrest handed him a message from Air America.

"This just in. Cobra and their infantry support BC604, and Stingray with their support BC610, will continue fire support until 1600 hours. That's when they'll set charges in their howitzers and evacuate to Phou Long Mat. Toothman, you'll assist. Then come home at dark. Anyone in your group that's not instrument qualified and current?"

"No, sir," Toothman responded.

"Good, I think the weather and darkness will give you and the boys a little instrument flying practice back to Udorn. Mr. Robinson and I in Four Four will go get Alpha and Charlie and bring them home. I'll reposition back to Two Zero Alpha after that."

Roman pressed on. "Archangel, when you advise Bravo about the resupply mission and location, tell them I'll try to replace them at first light on the 24th. They need to keep making night recons on the camp to verify that the Big Three are still there, then relocate to an observation point at UG524765. It's a hillside that will give them a good view of the Rock House and the two main supply routes from the north and east. From there, they can see any trucks leaving the Rock House and give us information on traffic going through the Ban Ban Valley to the PDJ." He stopped for a moment, leaned back in his chair and stared at the ceiling, trying to put the rest of his thoughts together.

"Frankly, I think our good friend Vang Pao and the Thais will hold at Long Tieng, but it will be rough. There's too much at stake for Vang Pao and Ambassador Godley to fail there. We'll start using Padong if things get bad at Two Zero Alpha. I'm going to talk to Air America and the Air Force about getting an advance team to Padong to set up commo, fuel, etc. I doubt that we'll get it, but I could be surprised. At any rate, we go back to our primary mission after tomorrow. Questions?" No one responded. Everyone clearly understood the mission.

"Okay, let's roll!" Roman said as he left the room.

Roman expected to encounter chaos and confusion when he entered the Grunt Air Headquarters, but, to his surprise, the place was very orderly and professional. He found Abeel in his Intelligence office.

"Bill, I need you to go see Mr. Eastwood and Mr. Caldwell at Air America and give them the info that we got from 7th and our teams. Just tell them Grunt Air crash teams have learned the following information. Don't admit to our mission. I think they've already figured it out but are playing along with us for some reason. Anyway, they need the information. Do the same with Colonel Odom and Lieutenant Colonel Skinner. I understand Skinner's back on the job after that extraction he went on with us."

On his way to the flight line, Roman stopped to see Dorsey.

"What's your plan for the extraction of Delta and the resupply of Bravo?"

"Well, sir," Dorsey said as he got out his map and pointed to Two Zero Alpha, "after departure, I would go west of Skyline One and hit the Ngum River. North from there until I hit this big bend in the river. Then, through this valley to the west of this hill mass west of Ban Na. We have troops on Hill Five Seven Seven Five, so ground fire should be minimal to this point." Then he pointed and described turning east, crossing another river that went north, re-intersecting the big Nam Ngum River. The Nam Ngum flows from the west side of the PDJ south, passing two miles west of Long Tieng, and empties into the Mekong River. He'd fly easterly, close to the mountain wall until he could go direct to the pickup point on the nose of the hill mass. His exfiltration route would be due south along the west side of the road going to Muong Poi, then turn south until he hit the southern extension of Route 74, then fly direct to Two Zero Alpha.

"The area going south will be filled with infantry on the move south. They'll nail you," Roman said.

"If I stay low and against the hills, they won't be able to get a good shot at me. They won't expect me coming from the north. I think I'll be fine.

Besides, I may be marginal on fuel by then. We can also get some idea on the extent of their move south," Dorsey suggested.

"Go for it," Roman said as he put his hand on Dorsey's shoulder. "Stay alive, Steve. I need you."

"Thanks, sir. I appreciate that," Dorsey said, surprised at the intensity of Roman's statement.

"Now, how about the resupply mission plan?"

"That's pretty simple, sir," Dorsey continued. "I take off to the northeast going south of Xiang Khoung to avoid the front lines moving south. Then low level through the valley by Lima Site Seven Zero, then to the west of Hill Five Seven Four One, then north to the clearing."

"Watch out crossing Route 7. It's very busy and there's lots of triple A," Roman warned.

"Sir, there's this saddle just to the east of the crossing point. I feel sure they'll have 12.7 ZSUs there and on the higher ground. That means I can go through below their minimum depression setting. They can't shoot me. Besides, I'll be going across there too fast and low for a shot either going or coming. It should be pretty easy." Roman liked the confidence in Dorsey's voice.

"Okay. I'll go with your plan," Roman said cautiously.

Roman's Huey and its crew for that day were waiting for him. They flew north to Two Zero Alpha to refuel, then on in for extraction of Teams Charlie and Alpha. Both teams were right in the path of the NVA westward thrust.

Despite the hazardous area, the extractions came off easily. They ran into small arms fire crossing Route 7, but none of the rounds hit anything critical. Roman picked up Charlie Team on the forward face of a prominent limestone hill east of Easy Street. Then they went east 16 klicks to Alpha's extraction point southwest of the Museum. The ride back to Two Zero Alpha was quiet and pleasant. Silence was abundant.

They were almost back to Two Zero Alpha when the silence was broken by an emergency call from Archangel.

"Six Six took heavy fire on the extraction," Alberts told him. "He's okay. They're at Two Zero Alpha working on his bird. I broke Three off standby, and he's making the resupply mission to Bravo. Six Six will fill in for Three if they're needed. Six Six is flyable but will need Ryker's magic fingers tonight."

Roman landed and parked with the other Grunt Air Hueys near Air America Ops. As he shut down, he saw a couple of Air America pilots standing near Six Six and strolled over to evaluate the damage to Dorsey's bird. As he got closer, he saw that the pilots were Ravens—Air Force pilots who volunteered for the Steve Canyon Program. That meant they were taken out of the Air Force units in South Vietnam and given civilian status so they could fly in Laos. They were absolute legends in the flying community. They flew the slow, high-wing Cessna 337 into the most dangerous areas of Laos to direct air strikes and artillery fire. The Cessnas were unusual-looking twin-engine aircraft with one engine in front, the other in back and a distinctive twin tail.

"Just admiring the stitching on your Huey, Captain," said one of the Ravens. He pointed to the eighteen bullet holes spaced evenly along the lower part of the tail boom and the other fifteen or twenty along the side of the copilot and cargo door. "All those holes," remarked the Raven, "and no one was even hurt. Amazing." The other one looked at Roman and said, "Welcome to Laos, where we don't exist and neither do you." The two men walked away joking about something Roman couldn't hear.

Dorsey and Ditton came out of operations at a run. Dorsey called out, "Crank em!" Roman grabbed Ditton by the arm.

"What's happening, JP?"

"We're going to extract Cobra and Stingray before we go home. We'll drop them off at Phou Long Mat. Situation pretty much as briefed," Ditton said as he gave the crank sign to Redings, his copilot.

"Who's the air mission commander?" Roman asked.

"Dorsey."

"But you're senior. Why not you?"

"Hell, he deserves it. He's flown some really tough missions lately. Let him run this one, boss. He's a good guy."

"Okay. You better get going before Redings and Dorsey leave you behind."

"See you at the B frame," Ditton said as he climbed into his Huey.

Roman stood in the swirl of dust as the rotors of the two Hueys cranked up. He was pleased at the change of attitude about Dorsey. *Maybe*, he thought, *we're growing up at last.*

CC∞CO

24

Paris. Finally.

Le Bourget air terminal
Paris, France

The American Airlines 707 touched down at Le Bourget Air Terminal in Paris exactly on time, at 7:15 in the morning. Carol Cody and Charlie Hansen, exhausted from the nine-hour flight from Dallas, shuffled off the plane, made their way to baggage claim, waited an hour for their luggage and breezed through Customs without being checked.

Waiting for them outside the international arrivals area was Sergeant David Walsh from the VFW Post in Dallas. A Medal of Honor recipient, he'd flown over a few days earlier to pave the way for what Carol and Charlie were about to do. Walsh was a Korean War veteran who had spent a great deal of time in Paris attached to the American Embassy, since soldiers who receive the CMH generally get their choice of assignments. He was meeting the plane because he knew the city blindfolded, because he was eminently capable, and because he believed in their purpose.

"Are we on schedule?" Carol asked, once the greetings were over.

"Yes," said Walsh. "Everything is arranged. Did you bring the letter?"

"You bet." Carol carried with her a letter that bore over two thousand signatures and was addressed to the Chief Negotiator of the North Vietnam Delegation to the Paris Peace Accords. The letter demanded that the NV government release a list of the POWs being held in their prisons, along with a detailed report about their condition, all in accordance with the Geneva agreements of 1954. According to the plan that Senator Warga had devised, it was Walsh's job to help them get the letter into the hands of the North Vietnamese Chief Negotiator. The Senator, of course, had kept his participation in their activities confidential, putting all his trust in the Sergeant. So had Carol and Charlie.

Walsh led them to the parking lot where their rental car was waiting, wrestled their luggage into the trunk and set off for the 45-minute ride into downtown Paris.

"Do you have a map of the city?" Charlie asked Sergeant Walsh.

"Yes, Charlie, I have a map of the city," he said patiently. "They give you one with the car. Besides, I know Paris like my own home town."

"The government buildings, are they on the map?"

"Yes. And our source at home made it very clear where the Peace Accords are being held, so stop worrying," Walsh admonished, grinning.

Gradually, Charlie started to relax and enjoy the ride, recuperating slightly from the nine cramped hours she'd spent on the plane. "We're gonna be okay, right?"

Carol and Charlie both perked up when the car left the expressway from the airport and they found themselves engulfed by the charm of Paris. It had started raining, of course, but they didn't care once they'd come upon the Seine River and saw the elegant architecture around the back of Notre Dame. They were enchanted, but Walsh didn't notice.

"We'll do our recon this morning and then work out the details at the hotel this evening," Sergeant Walsh advised. "Around here, they won't let you check in to your hotel until afternoon, anyway."

"Well, we need to be there this morning if we want to see their recess routine," Carol stated. She couldn't decide whether to be nervous or to keep looking out the window at Paris' charming tree-lined streets with their benches and kiosks. She tried not to notice the heavy, frantic rush hour traffic.

"We'll be there on time," Walsh assured them as he navigated along the narrow Paris streets.

When they reached the street in front of the building where the Provisional Revolutionary Government of the Republic of North Vietnam Peace Accord Negotiations with the United States were in progress, they were stunned at the elaborate security measures in place to protect the negotiators. The lone entry into the courtyard was manned by three French policemen and a police Captain, all armed with automatic weapons. Along the street was every car the French police owned, or so it seemed.

"My, god!" Charlie blurted, her voice full of disappointment. "Who's watching the rest of the city?"

From inside the car, Carol, Charlie and the Sergeant took careful inventory of the scene, starting at one end of the building and working their way along the sidewalk. The press corps was restricted to a cordoned-off area with a set of bleachers where the photographers and cameramen perched up high. The risers were packed with camera crews from all over the world, working the scene with telephoto lenses two feet long and dish microphones that could pick up every word from fifty feet away. In addition, a bristling bank of microphones was positioned in front of the press corps gallery where the public relations person for the negotiations would emerge from time to time and deliver a briefing. The area was crawling with every policeman in the city.

They sat in the car for over an hour, boosted a bit by the cups of dangerously strong French coffee that Sergeant Walsh brought back from a café down the street. At 10:30, both delegations emerged from the building for a smoke and a stretch. The reporters started yelling questions at a man who was obviously the Chief Negotiator for the Vietnam delegation. Every camera was pointed at him.

"I think we've seen enough," Sergeant Walsh said. "Let's get outta here."

After dinner at the hotel that evening, Charlie and Carol, jet-lagged and exhausted, were just deciding to go to bed early when Sergeant Walsh knocked on the door.

"Bad news," he said, throwing his coat over a chair. "We're going to have to postpone things a bit."

"What happened?" Carol asked.

"Late this afternoon, the Chief Negotiator was mysteriously called back to Hanoi for consultations. He just got on a plane. My sources think it's just a ploy to throw the Americans off balance and disrupt the talks, but nobody knows for sure."

"But … when's he coming back?" Charlie asked.

"Two, three days at the most. The talks will probably start up again by the end of the week."

"Damn," Carol said. "Now what do we do?"

Sergeant Walsh smiled. "Well, this is kind of a setback and it's going to cost us some time, but I think two women who've never been to Paris before can find a way to keep busy. There's the Louvre, the Eiffel Tower, the Opera—"

"Are you kidding?" Charlie interrupted. "Three days in Paris with nothing to do and you want us to go to museums? Sergeant, I don't suppose you could recommend any good department stores?"

∽∞∾

25

Can't Anyone Stay in One Place?

Grunt Air Headquarters
Udorn Air Force Base, Thailand
21 December, 1971

Anybody who understood anything about the history of human combat knew the war in Southeast Asia, and Laos in particular, was vastly different from any war the Americans had ever fought before. There were no front
lines, no FEBAs (Forward Extension of Battle Area). There were only areas or
pockets of occupation or control. Towns one or two miles apart might be on
opposing sides, and the area between the two towns was no-mans land. The
southern portion of Northern Laos was predominantly pro-government or
Vang Pao. As you traveled northeast, the support became less and less consistent. Yet, in all areas, whether pro-government or pro-communist, there were
pockets of resistance and small irregular forces striking the opposing side. In
that conflict, the communists had home field advantage as well as the greatest number of troops. The Americans had the air power, technology and a
belief in personal freedom.

Freedom is a more rare and more precious commodity than most
Americans realize. Many of the troops in Vietnam, and especially those in
Laos, had seen what the lack of freedom does to societies and individuals. In
Northern Laos in 1971, the communists were expanding their political and
economic control while the Laotians (with unofficial US help) were fighting
for their freedom.

The day started for Dan Roman exactly like the two previous days,
with the phone ringing in the middle of the night. In this case, it was 0320
hours and Roman was awake at once. He was getting used to it. It was Jim Eastwood at Air America and he sounded way too chipper.

"How can you be so goddamn cheerful at three o'clock in the morning?"

"It's my sunny nature. Listen. The 174th Regiment with the 14th Anti-Aircraft Battalion just started an assault on Hill One Six Six Three from Phou Keng, like one of your crash site survey teams predicted. And as much as I hate to admit it, you were also right about the Pathet Lao and Neutralists taking Muong Soui and moving west on Route 7. Your crystal ball is 20/20, Dan. We sure could use your help today moving those shell-shocked boys off that hill and back to Two Zero Alpha."

"The green taxis are at your disposal, sir," Roman replied, trying to sound chivalrous. "I'll have them at your place at 0500 hours for a briefing."

The First Sergeant was already awake when Roman called him. "Top," Roman said, "we need to get the crews for One One, Two Two, Three Three, and Five Five up and ready to play taxi service for the Air America boys. Briefing at 0500 in the Air America Ops room. Let all the Recon Teams sleep in and have an easy day. They're going back out on the 23rd for extended reconnaissance. You might want to round up some really good binoculars and telescopes for them. They'll be static, observing road traffic and camps. When you get everyone organized for the day, I want you to go with me and key personnel to Padong."

"Can do, sir," First Sergeant Woods said.

Roman heaved himself out of bed and wandered into the B Frame to make some coffee. To his surprise, Abeel was there with Captain Toothman and Sergeant Hardy.

"What the hell are you all doing up at this hour?" Roman demanded.

"Just trying to keep up with your ass," Toothman said. "I expect we're going out for Air America again today and we'll put the teams back out soon as well."

"Not a bad guess," Roman said smiling.

"Actually, we're trying to do a little advance planning, here, if that's at all possible. I can hear the First Sergean,t so I know we're in for an early flight."

"Yes, the green taxi hits the road at 0500 hours at their Ops shack here. The same as yesterday. And, yes, the teams will go out again day after tomorrow."

"What about the plan for the recon teams?" Abeel asked.

"Same as before, Chief, except I want to focus on road traffic. Keep track of the Big Three and give us better intel than we've been getting. I want to preposition to Two Zero Alpha, arriving at first light. Hot refuel, then insert. One team on the hillside near Lima Site One Four Zero, another team near the main road junction near Easy Street, one team will replace Bravo and another team up north near Lima Site Two Niner to monitor road traffic. When the Big Three go north, we need to know it. As always, we take a prisoner or two for intelligence purposes." Roman paused a moment, then continued, "I expect the teams to be out at least a week to ten days, maybe longer. We'll have Bravo start a rotation schedule, if necessary. Today we'll be making a site reconnaissance at Padong. I have a gut feeling we'll be operating out of there fairly soon."

Toothman smiled at Abeel and said, "Ask a simple question and you end up on a work detail."

"I want Archangel to stand down today. They've been hitting it real hard and need some rest. Jan, you guys on taxi service will be up on the Air America frequency or Cricket, anyway. Tomorrow, Grunt Air will be down for crew rest and maintenance in preparation for Operation Road Watch day after tomorrow. That will save a briefing later."

The morning briefing and launch of the four Grunt Air birds at Air America went without a problem or breakdown. Maintenance was holding, thanks to Ryker. He had established a solid maintenance program and it showed. The pilots and crew chiefs had long since stopped bitching about the completeness of the aircraft daily inspections and preventative maintenance requirements. The pilots had become part of the daily maintenance program. Instead of landing and heading to the bar, leaving the after-flight daily maintenance to the crew chief and door gunner, they were helping. Maintenance quality improved and so did morale. The exhausted crew chiefs managed to get a little more sleep.

Abeel wandered into the briefing room at 0800 hours and found Roman, First Sergeant Woods, Sergeant Major Panfil, Captain Best, Captain Ryker and Chief Alberts already there, standing around a wall map. Sergeant Hardy was telling the group what he knew about Padong.

"It's 19 klicks east of Two Zero Alpha but it's not in the line of advance as Two Zero Alpha is. While the NVA will make some attempt to neutralize it, either with infantry, snipers, or more likely artillery, it won't be the point of a major attack. If they don't neutralize Padong, it'll be their mistake because our side will have a good spot to launch a counter-attack."

"That's assuming the brass is smart enough to figure it out," Ryker interjected. His sarcasm was apparent.

"Well, yes. But Lima Site Six Five and Lima Site Niner Five are the only other landing sites in the area and they have tough runway conditions. They'll eventually decide on Lima Site Five," Hardy predicted. "Padong is Lima Site Five, located here," he continued as he pointed on the wall map. "It has a 1670 foot by 75 foot sod runway that's rough but can take a Caribou, if it isn't too heavy. It runs one niner zero degrees by zero one zero degrees. Elevation is 4500 feet. The big problem is crosswinds. Fixed wing have the main problem with winds but it could affect us, too, if they're strong. Not much parking area, but I'm told there's sort of a clearing adjoining the runway, just off the high ground. It's big enough for eight or nine Hueys next to some high trees. There's good cover and concealment, and it's far enough off the runway and main parking area to be clear from mortar and artillery attacks."

"Good job, Sergeant," said Roman. "That's all for now."

After evacuating two loads of troops from King Kong BC608 and BC606—troops escaping from the Phou Keng summit—Captain Toothman settled down for some coffee out of his all metal Uno-Vac thermos at Two Zero Alpha. As he poured out the last drops, he turned the thermos over to read the imprint on the bottom. "Union Manufacturing Company, New Britain, Conn. USA." His Uno-Vac carried serial number T270SE2. Dan Roman's thermos was one number lower. Dan's late wife, Cindy, had given the bottles to Dan and Toothman as they left for their first tour in Vietnam in late 1967. Toothman smiled as he thought about the time Dan had gotten himself shot down and was picked up by a flight of Navy Sea Wolf in the lower Delta. He had run halfway to the rescue copter when he turned around and dashed back to his burning Huey to rescue his stainless steel Uno-Vac. He wasn't going to lose it to those bastards, even though he couldn't find the cap in all the smoke and fire. Now, many years later, they both still had their Uno-Vacs.

"Hey, Grunt, 'Scramble.' We got troops in contact." It was the voice of an Air America pilot breaking into his recollection. When a soldier heard "troops in contact," there was strong motivation to take action.

"The NVA took Hill One Six Six Three," said the pilot. "There's heavy artillery up there shooting at Ban Na. We gotta pick up the stragglers and move them to Sam Thong."

Jan Toothman listened and remembered Dan Roman's prediction that Ban Na wouldn't last a day. Roman's instinct in these matters was uncanny. More often than not, Roman had foreseen the enemy activities as though he had their battle plan.

As they took off heading north, Toothman looked ahead at the terrain just over Skyline Ridge. It's thirteen very long and hilly klicks as the crow flies between Ban Na and Sam Thong. The troops escaping from the firebase were shell-shocked individuals, not much of a fighting unit any more, and they certainly were not crows. They'd need at least a day and a night to get to the rendezvous point if they could make it at all. But, between Air America and Grunt Air, most of them should get pulled out to the safety of Sam Thong before dark.

"Grunt Three, this is Banjo." Toothman's radio crackled with the incoming call.

"This is Three, go Banjo."

"Butterfly just gave us a heads up on some 12.7 and machine gun fire hitting our passengers from time to time. Make your approach and departure quick. Don't give them a target."

"Roger. Thanks," Toothman answered.

"Take two of your birds over to that group down by the creek at your 2 o'clock two klicks. Put the other birds over at your 11 o'clock two klicks and get that group. Possible casualties. Don't forget the ground fire and artillery."

Toothman directed Ditton and Donovan to take the first group. He and Hetler would take the farther group, since they were in the greater need, not to mention danger.

Hetler's Huey swam into Toothman's field of vision in a loose echelon-right formation, swaying gently in the air. Toothman pushed his cyclic to the side and headed west about a quarter mile past the pitiful group of soldiers and casualties, then turned toward them into the wind. He came in fast and low hoping to avoid, or at least reduce, the small arms and machine gun fire he knew would be attacking his vulnerable chopper. He brought the machine down, hovering just inches above the ground while the tired troops, suddenly finding new energy, ran toward the choppers and swarmed aboard.

Hetler screamed in Toothman's headset. "Go! Go! I'm taking fire on my right!" Toothman went, yanking up on the collective and shoving his cyclic forward to get some airspeed.

Both helicopters lifted off and gained about 20 feet and forward motion when the first artillery shell hit 15 meters to the right of Five Five. Even with a helmet covering his ears, Toothman heard the blast. Hetler's chopper started to jerk around in the air just above the ground. Bad sign. It probably meant that one of the pilots was wounded, or worse. Just as quickly, Five Five's movements smoothed out and the machine gained some forward speed turning to the right. Toothman took his chopper in the opposite direction trying to evade the incoming fire. Both helicopters stayed close to the ground while another shell landed well behind them. Safe. For now.

Toothman screamed over the radio, "Five Five this is Three. Are you okay?"

"This is Dodson." His voice sounded weak. "Hetler took it in the right side. He didn't make it. Fragmentation came through the window and armor plate, blew him away. We got blood everywhere. Most instruments gone. The ones that still work we can't see because they're covered with blood."

"Can you make it back to Two Zero Alpha?"

"Yeah, I guess," Dodson replied, his voice shaking. "I have no engine instruments. The instrument panel is just about gone. The controls seem to be okay. Engine sounds okay."

"You lead," Toothman told Dodson. "I'll fly on your left to watch out for fire. Go directly to Two Zero Alpha. These guys can take a truck to Sam Thong. Hell, some of them need medical attention at Two Zero Alpha, anyway."

"Okay," Dodson replied without emotion—a sign that he was in shock.

Toothman radioed Banjo and advised him of the situation. Then he switched to Archangel's frequency. No joy. He'd forgotten that Roman had Archangel stand down for the day. He couldn't call Cricket because that would relay the call all over Southeast Asia, all the way up to the Ambassador and blow their cover. There was nobody to call.

When the two choppers landed at Long Tieng, the Air America and Grunt Air pilots ran to Hetler's chopper, amazed that it could fly at all. The right side door was gone. So was the right side of the instrument panel. Hetler was lying in the back, both parts of him. His bloody body stretched out in the cargo bay with his right arm lying alongside. Toothman choked back his rage, anger and grief as a team of Hmong medics hurried to the chopper, slid Hetler and his arm into a black body bag, and carried him over to Toothman's helicopter for the last ride home.

Once they'd flushed all the blood out of the cargo bay, they had a better idea of the damage. The Bell Huey was a remarkable machine, able to take a huge beating and stay in the air. Aside from the right side door and the instrument panel, the damage was minimal. Should be no problem getting it back to Udorn and handing it off to Ryker.

Dodson was in no shape to fly. He'd just seen Hetler cut to pieces by shrapnel and he sat in the wet cargo bay staring off into space and shaking. Toothman helped him into his chopper, turned the machine over to his copilot, CW3 Fondren, and prepared to fly the damaged chopper back to Udorn. He felt like he was moving through glue as the image of Hetler lying in the cargo bay in pieces burned into his mind.

The darkness was just beginning to seep over the hilltops as Toothman and his four birds cranked up and departed. Thankfully, the ride back was quiet, giving Toothman time to call Grunt Air Ops on the company frequency. He asked Sergeant Hardy to notify Six that they were inbound with a badly shot up bird and would need an ambulance for a "wounded" passenger in Fondren's aircraft. They would go to the Hot Pad for casualty drop off. No medical emergency was called, giving Sergeant Hardy a sick empty place in his stomach. He knew the casualty wasn't wounded. Somebody had been killed. It was one of their own.

Roman swallowed hard as he stood next to Colonel Odom, watching the Grunt Air crew take Hetler's body out of the chopper and slide it gently into an ambulance. They watched until the vehicle had disappeared around a curve far from the pad. They then walked back to Headquarters. Nobody said a word.

Just as they reached the building, Colonel Odom spoke. "Dan, can you give me a minute?"

"Yes, sir. Not much else to do now." Like most unit commanders, Roman couldn't help feeling that he could have done something, somehow, to prevent the death. Odom walked him away from the building, their feet shuffling on the tarmac.

"Dan, let's put our butts on the table, here, okay? We need to get around all the secret bullshit about your unit. You're short one pilot and one Recon Team Intelligence Specialist. And as much as I hate to say it, you keep flying missions like this and you'll lose a few more before you stand down. The war's almost over. You've proven that your type of unit is effective. It works, which is great for the Army, but doesn't help the Air Force much. We don't have any experienced people for training. Yeah, there's the Green Hornets and Air Commandos, but they work completely different."

"What are you trying to say, Colonel?"

"I'd like you to replace your losses with my people. They'll learn a lot from you. I'll give you a Huey-qualified pilot who's been flying Jolly Greens in SAR Ops out of NKP. I'll give you a great Intel Specialist and swear them both to whatever kind of secrecy you want. They'll earn their keep, I promise. They'll become Army. No association with any Air Force personnel, only Grunt Air. What do you say?"

"Who's the pilot?" Roman asked.

"Captain David Tripp," Odom sounded confident.

"I know him from rotary wing transition at Rucker. Didn't know he was at NKP. How long's he been here?"

"Four months on his second SAR Tour," Odom quickly responded.

"I'll take him. He'll fit in okay. I'm surprised you Air Force types haven't run his disrespectful ass off. Now what about the Intel Specialist?"

"He has 14 years in service. Most of the time in overseas Intel assignments, including Air Commandos and some long-range patrols in the Bolovens down in the southern part of Laos. He's just back from leave, over at TSN awaiting assignment."

"Sir, my recon boys are in great physical condition. If this new guy isn't in shape, he won't survive."

"Sergeant Mason is built like a brick. At least talk to him. See if he'll fit in. Okay?" Odom asked.

"Sir, did you sell used cars before the service? Bring him over and I'll let him sit down with the others in Charlie Team. If they like him, he's in. But, it will be up to them, sir. They have to live or die as a unit. You don't know how dangerous crash site survey work can be."

"When do you want Tripp?"

"Yesterday, sir. I really need him soon."

"I'll have him here tomorrow. Looks like I owe you another big one," the Colonel said.

"Just don't get shot down any more. Actually, sir, you're helping me out. I like Tripp just fine, and I don't have to attract attention in Saigon by ripping off a pilot from some slick unit. Helps keep our cover. The boss's ass depends on it."

"I'll let you go, Dan. And thanks."

Back at the B Frame, Roman rounded up Toothman, Best, First Sergeant Woods, Sergeant Major Panfil and Abeel. Once they'd arranged themselves around the table and had full glasses in front of them, Roman told them about his deal with Colonel Odom. To his surprise, everyone thought it was a good idea. Either that or they were too depressed about Hetler to argue with him.

The replacements arrived as promised on the 22nd, flying in on the Air Force Courier run. Roman welcomed Tripp. Toothman remembered him from Fort Rucker and they started right in on the "do you remember whens." He'd fit in just fine.

"You'll be flying copilot for Jan for a while," Roman explained to the new pilot, "just until you get up to speed on what we're doing."

Meanwhile, Ryker was struggling to cast some kind of spell on Five Five to make it flyable again, and Fondren was waiting to become its new aircraft commander. Ryker made it clear that his magic act was "subject to parts availability," but then he always said that and Roman was confident there wouldn't be any interference from the hapless Colonel Sweeney. He wasn't exactly being helpful over there in Saigon, but he wasn't interfering either. Roman guessed that he wanted to keep his Air Force career and not push sled dogs in Anchorage, Alaska.

The 22nd was fairly quiet by the standards of the past week or so. The Recon Teams were resting and making ready for an extended patrol behind the NVA lines. Ryker was putting aircraft together over in the Magic Castle, and Mr. Touchdown was griping. He wasn't happy about the arrival of Sergeant Mason because it meant he wouldn't be able to go out with Charlie Team.

Best, Panfil, the team chiefs and Charlie Team had spent almost all afternoon with Mason in the briefing room. Roman was on his way back to the B Frame to get a beer when a laughing Corporal Kahn stuck his head out the door and asked him to join the group. As soon as he walked in, Roman knew that Mason was already part of the team.

"This bastard's going to get us all killed on patrol," said Captain Best. Roman was shocked.

"That's right, sir," said Sergeant Richardson. "He's killing us with his damned jokes. We'll laugh ourselves right into a POW camp."

"Yeah, he's not too bad, for an Air Force guy," Ramirez chimed in. Kahn just smiled and gave a thumbs up.

"Okay," smiled Roman, "get Mason squared away with Sergeant Major Panfil and First Sergeant Woods. You go to the boonies tomorrow, so brief him on the whole situation, especially our cover story. Mason," he said, staring the newcomer right in his gray eyes, "you violate the cover story and your next assignment, if there is one, will be Leavenworth or Adak, Alaska."

"Sir, I got the word on secrecy from Colonel Odom. He wasn't as pleasant about the subject as you. You can count on me."

"Good. Now come back alive from Easy Street. It's kind of hot out there."

Roman finally made it to the B Frame, where he poured himself a stiff scotch and put together a sandwich. The operation would begin at "zero dark thirty," right around 0300 hours when the teams would gather for a last minute briefing and nighttime pre-positioning to Two Zero Alpha.

Sure enough, the following morning at 0300, the light in Roman's room burst on and Abeel sang "rise and shine" in the most sarcastic voice he could manage.

"Screw you, Abeel!" Roman yelled as he swung his legs to the floor. He hated to admit it but getting jolted awake in the middle of the night was becoming easier.

"You need to call Fiddler," said Abeel. "He called about 2300 hours last night. I told him that you needed sleep. He said that what he had would wait till 0300 hours. Wouldn't tell me what it was."

"Don't expect anything different," Roman told him. "I'd be shocked if he told you anything. I was the S-3 and he was the S-2 in a Hawk Battalion in Germany. When I signed in, he looked at my assignment record and said it was flawed, full of discrepancies, which meant he thought I had to be a spook. He wanted to know who I really was and why a spook was being assigned to his battalion without being notified. We talked on for a while and then he said something that hit me. I suddenly realized that he was the Intel Officer I dealt with in Vinh Long in 1967-68. I called him Fiddler and he sat up real straight, and it all came back to him. 'Chickenwings?' he asked. That was my unofficial call sign. We had a great time until I got transferred to 10th ADA Group Aviation unit. He's a real pro. Gets things done. He was West Point, but you'd never know it because he works way outside the box."

When Roman finally got to the phone, what Fiddler told him lifted him right out of his chair.

"I got some news about the Big Three."

"Terrific," Roman said excitedly, "I think."

"Songbird picked up a message from Cu Chi to Major General Thran Van Ho in Hanoi. They transmitted exactly what we gave them in the fake documents."

"You must be pretty pleased with yourself."

"Oh, yeah. General Ho said the info wasn't—how did he put it?—consistent with his interrogator's basic instincts. The personnel file backed up exactly what Major Cody had told them, to the letter. Maybe we did too good a job. Cu Chi is sending the files to him for a closer look, and maybe some verification. Because they're so busy with the offensive, the interrogators haven't been able to get to the prisoners, which is a blessing. If they find out the interrogator was right and the papers are fake, they'll send him to Sam Neua in a hurry.

"We also found out it takes at least eight to ten days for documents to work their way north to Hanoi. They didn't say anything about a special courier, so you have a little more time to get them at the Rock House. I'll keep working here."

"Fiddler, you are a quality individual," Roman said. The news was good.

"I know. Now I'm going back to bed."

Roman put down the phone and sat still, staring at the wall and turning over what Fiddler had just reported. It was perfect, so why didn't he believe it? Maybe one of Toothman's little combat sayings would occur to him, something simple, like "If a situation looks too good to be true, it is."

Roman thought it through: General Thran Van Ho wouldn't accept Cu Chi's report until he personally checked out the documents, but that would take time. He already believed his interrogator, Captain Ho, was onto something big, so he'd view anything the Captain said in a favorable light. Okay, so if either the American or Australian is what Captain Ho thinks, it would be a big catch and both his superiors and the Russians would reward him. But he couldn't get his interrogators to the prisoners because his transportation network was way too thin, and he didn't dare take assets away from the offensive, not for this. That meant he had to bring the prisoners to him—closer to Hanoi. To do that, he'd need some people and a truck, and that meant an appeal to higher authority. But where would he take them? Roman rolled it around in his head for a few minutes and decided the General would have to bring them to the new camp—the Big Casino, Camp L711, the crap shooter special. But when? How long would it take to get the permission he needed and put the orders into the field? What would it take to get approval from higher command, who was very busy fighting a war in the south and planning an important dry season campaign in Laos? What would he use to justify the move? There were the inconsistencies between Captain Ho's intuitions and the bland personnel files. Not much, but it might work for him.

Roman began to calculate. We've got ten days, maybe two weeks, before General Ho gets the permission he needs. Then, another two to four days to disseminate the orders to the two camps involved and the local Binh Tram commanders. So, it would be the middle of January before they got to the Big Casino. But can we get them out of the Rock House before then? Maybe. Depends on the forces and guards at the camp, and we can get that Intel from Bravo.

Since there was no direct communication with the ground teams, he'd have to call Archangel and pass the word along. *If we can't get them at the Rock House, the second choice would be along the road to Sam Neua. But what if we got the wrong truck?* Then Hanoi and General Ho would know how important they were. No good. If they do get all the way to the Big Casino, Grunt Air would have a go for broke situation to deal with. *The Big Casino is the highest-risk target,* Roman thought, *but if we don't pull them out of there, Headquarters will send in the B-52s.* Can't let that happen.

Roman suddenly returned to life and grabbed the mike to the secure tactical FM radio. It took only a few minutes for Archangel to reach Bravo and get back to him. Rock House was a no-go. Too many NVA in the area. It would be either the Big Casino or the B-52's. Before calling General Mattix to report his conclusions, he wandered down the hall to get a cup of coffee. As he passed the operations room, he saw Sergeant Hardy making a notation on the mission status board. Something about the notation caught his eye.

"What's the deal on Four Four?" he demanded.

"What do you mean, sir?" Hardy asked.

"Who's the aircraft commander? It says Fondren."

"That's right, sir. Lieutenant Davis is working Archangel and we needed an AC, so Captain Toothman put Fondren over on Four Four for today's mission. His bird is still in maintenance, sir."

"Okay, that's fine. It just struck me strange, at first. That's a tough flight for his first combat mission as an aircraft commander in Laos."

"Yes, sir," Hardy responded, and turned his attention, and his grease pencil, back to the mission board.

Over at maintenance, Roman found Ryker sitting on the edge of the cargo bay of Five Five making notes in the aircraft logbook.

Roman looked at all the holes, the missing door and windscreen, and asked, "How long, Tom?"

"Well, if 'how long' means, when can you get the bird back, the answer is not soon. Let me show you something." Ryker got up and went over to the pilot's door on the right side. There was a very thin split in the aircraft outer skin. Roman had to squat down to see the gash in the side, then looked back at Ryker, raising his eyebrows.

"Dan, this is where a piece of the artillery shell went in. It was dark at Two Zero Alpha and they missed it before letting Toothman fly it back." Ryker took a flashlight and pointed the beam through an open inspection plate to the control tubes that went from the pilot's cyclic control in the cockpit to the rotor mast. These tubes translate the pilot's movement of the cyclic control to the rotor blades, which direct the path of the helicopter.

"That shrapnel almost totally cut the right control tube and mount. It could have broken at any time during flight and Toothman would have bought the farm. The tube is no problem, but it may take depot-level maintenance to fix the mount. I just don't know." Roman sympathized with the frustration in Ryker's voice.

"Depot level repairs mean we have to take this bird by ground, or as a sling load, back to Vung Tau," Roman said. "That's close to 400 klicks, Tom."

"Well, I can try, but I strongly recommend you put some pressure on your buddies at the 7th to get us a replacement." Roman shook his head in reaction to the bad news about Five Five. First he lost Hetler, now the bird. Hell, he could have lost Toothman, his best friend, on the flight back to Udorn.

"Okay. I'll get with General Mattix after lunch."

Roman decided he needed a good lunch, but before going to the Air Force side and the O Club, he stopped at Headquarters to get an update from Archangel. All was going well. The birds had made their insertions and were just starting back to Two Zero Alpha for refuel.

He was on the last bite of his club sandwich when Abeel and Ryker burst into the dining room, hurrying to his table.

"We just lost Four Four," said Abeel. Roman suddenly couldn't swallow. His stomach lurched. "They were on their way to Two Zero Alpha after the insertion. A 37 millimeter caught them with a full burst. Some Air America pilot saw the whole thing and said the thing just blew up in flight. He circled the crash site but there were no survivors."

Roman was speechless for a long moment. He made a conscious effort to settle his stomach. "Where did it happen? Is the recon team compromised?"

"It happened just as Fondren crossed Route 7 on the east side of the PDJ. We think he cut the corner to save time and went right in front of the 37 emplacement. The team wasn't compromised, but we can be pretty sure the enemy knows we're not just a crash site survey team," Abeel recounted.

"Now we're short two birds and a crew. Fondren, you poor bastard. This is shaping up to be a real bad day," Roman muttered as he headed out the door. Then he stopped and turned back to Abeel and Ryker.

"Any chance we can recover the bodies?"

"It's a real hot area," said Abeel. "But Archangel directed Two Two with Bravo onboard to try to get them, if possible."

As he got to the Headquarters, Hardy confirmed that Two Two and Bravo had recovered the bodies and were enroute to Udorn via a refuel stop at Two Zero Alpha.

"Thanks," Roman responded. "I better call the boss."

In his office, Roman sat down heavily at his desk chair. He felt like he weighed five hundred pounds and he could barely move his arms to pick up the phone to call Fitzmorris at Blue Chip. He told the Major everything that had happened and asked him to locate General Mattix so he could give him the news before someone else surprised him. After an eternity on hold, Fitzmorris transferred the call to the Commanding General's office, where Coroneos, Mattix and Geiger were waiting.

"I've got you on speakerphone, Dan," Mattix told him. "The Commanding General wants to hear your report."

"I wish I could say good afternoon, but it isn't, sir." Slowly and painfully, Roman told the two Generals about the death of Fondren and his crew, and how the bodies had been recovered. "All insertions were completed as planned. We should be able to start inputting to General Geiger in the morning, sir."

"Son, are you okay?" asked the Commanding General.

"It's hard to lose five men and two birds in less than 48 hours, but we'll be fine at Grunt Air, sir."

"Two birds?" the Commanding General said, "I thought the bird that came in yesterday could be repaired on site." "More bad news, sir." Roman had to fill the General in about the severed mounting. "It'll probably require depot-level maintenance," he said, "which means sending it all the way to the Bell facility onboard the Corpus Christi. Ryker's trying to save it, but we're not too sure."

"Sorry about the losses, Dan," said Coroneos. "But there's a war out there and people die in wars. Even Grunt Air pilots. Please accept my sympathy. Now, give us a rundown on your plans and the latest on the Big Three."

It took Roman over twenty minutes to detail the events that had taken place, the information from Fiddler, his personal evaluation and what plans he had made to carry out Grunt Air's mission. "Do you have any changes or additions, sir?" he concluded.

General Geiger's voice came across hollow on the speakerphone. "He makes my shop look like amateurs. Keep it up, Roman. No changes here."

"Dan, you have an excellent plan." Roman recognized the sobering voice of General Mattix. "Continue as outlined. We'll get you some U-2 and Mohawk Air Recon Photos of the Sam Neua area. The good news is that we have two Hueys here at Hotel 6 for you. They're putting in the TACAN, HF Radio and crypto as we speak. They'll be ready for pickup in three days. Do you have any requests for a replacement crew?"

Roman thought for a moment, then said, "If the 175th has stood down, I'd like to have Red Staggs, Eldon Barnes and their crews, if they're willing, sir. If they are not, I would like someone from the 114th AHC."

"I hear you let Odom con you into using some Air Force boys," the Commanding General said.

"That's correct, sir. I thought I better get Captain Tripp out of the Air Force before he gave you a bad name. I knew him back at Ft. Rucker. He acts more Army than Air Force. Sgt. Mason fit right in with Charlie Team. Let's just say we're integrating Grunt Air, sir."

In spite of the somber mood, Roman heard laughter in the speaker. Then the Commanding General closed the conversation.

"Captain Roman, you're doing fine and so is Grunt Air. Keep it up, son. Goodbye."

Roman headed once again for the B Frame, needing an impressive shot of alcohol before writing the saddest of all letters to the families of Hetler, Fondren, Robinson, Keller and Shack. Abeel was in the briefing room with Bravo Team, conducting the debriefing. Roman would get the notes later. He was in no condition to deal with anything just then.

Writing to the families is the hardest part of any commander's job, but Roman actually looked forward to telling them how honored and proud he was to have served with the men who had perished that day. It was almost 0100 hours when he finished his last letter. Just then the phone rang. When he picked up the phone, it was Eastwood at Air America.

"Dan, any chance getting your green taxis later today?"

"Sure, what's the mission?"

"We need to move BG121 and 122 off western Skyline to an area about six klicks south of Long Tieng without the NVA catching on. We're setting up a security perimeter to stop the snipers and infiltrators from getting into Two Zero Alpha. We also need to relocate some troops in the Padong area."

"Can do, sir. It will take most of the day with only four birds, but if the weather cooperates, we can do it. I'd like to use the flat area on that shallow ridge coming off helipad Charley Golf as pickup point. That will keep us below the ridgeline and hopefully out of the NVA's view."

"Great idea. We'll be ready when you are."

"Okay. If the fog and haze aren't too bad we can start about 0700 hours, if that works for you."

"We'll be ready. We appreciate the help. We're strapped to the limit lately. You're doing a great job for a bunch of crash site survey crews."

Ryker knocked on the door just as Roman hung up. "I suppose you're here to pronounce Five Five dead."

"No, you pessimistic son of a bitch," said Ryker, with the respect he usually accorded his commanding officer. "I fixed it, or should I say, a couple of the boys over at Air America maintenance did. They were able to weld the assembly back into place. Good clean job, too. It's an illegal repair at this level, but then again, we're an illegal unit that doesn't exist. Hope that's okay with you, oh Phantom Commander?"

Roman smiled back at Ryker and shrugged his shoulders. "What's that TV show back home, *Hogan's Heroes?* 'I know nutzing!' When do we get it back?"

"Late tomorrow, I think," Ryker said.

"Ryker, you bastard. You fixed Five Five! Now if anybody at 7th finds out, we won't get the two new birds I asked for. Thanks a lot. Now get the hell out of here."

Ryker laughed all the way down the hall.

☙❧

26

Who Said Counterfeiting Doesn't Pay?

Grunt Air Headquarters
Udorn Air Force Base, Thailand
24 December 1971
Early morning

Roman left the morning briefing to Toothman and Hardy. He was more interested in hearing about the overnight activity in the field. Archangel, who decided to fly back to Udorn and give the team reports in person instead of retransmitting them, had said there was some important news for Roman and Abeel. He didn't need to stay in the air because the Grunt Air Hueys were flying for Air America again and were reporting to other controllers. They were out relocating troops in the Padong area in case of attack by NVA forces coming down from the PDJ, and they were pre-positioning supplies for their own use in the future. Quiet day.

When Alberts made it to the briefing room with the team reports, everyone was already gathered around the wall map.

"We were just going over the Big Casino mission for the umpteenth time," Abeel told him. "No changes, yet, sir."

"What do you have for us?" Roman asked.

The merest trace of excitement crept into Alberts' voice. Roman paid attention because the Chief never got excited about anything.

"First of all, Echo reports three more Americans at the Rock House. Two US Air Force captains and one lieutenant. They came in early this morning in the same truck from the Tollbooth that the Big Three used. No other details available. Secondly, they got an NVA last night who confessed that he was a courier for the 866th Regiment Operations Center. General Tan is sending the 866th south to a position just north of Skyline One. The 335th Regiment is taking up a position to the east or northeast of Skyline Two. He also ordered three regiments, the 141st, 165th and 207th of the 312th Division, to areas near Tha Tam Bleung and Ban Hintang. The 361st Division is to consolidate at Ban Na."

"Holy shit," Abeel interjected. "That throws over 19,000 NVA regulars against less than 10,000 Thai, Hmong and Lao troops at Long Tieng. That's really bad. We need to get this info to 7th and Vang Pao, and damned quick."

"Agreed," Roman said, "but tell Eastwood and Colonel Odom, too."

"Wait," Alberts said, "there's more. Charlie Team bagged one last night … a captain in a 130mm battery. He told them there were 24 battalions getting into position to attack Skyline and Long Tieng as part of General Tan's final push of Campaign Z. His battery and four others are supposed to start shelling Skyline and Long Tieng at maximum effective range. After ten or twelve shots, they move to other locations to avoid air strikes. They're going to attack Padong late today."

"Hell," Abeel said, "our boys are inserting troops and supplies in there right now. I hope they don't get caught."

"Bill, let Eastwood know right away. What else, Doug?" Roman asked.

"That's it for today, sir."

"Good work. Let's get the word out. Doug, get airborne after you grab a sandwich for the road, find Toothman on the secure and let him know. I'm sure the Air Force will put some assets in there. I hope our boys have already got the tents and fuel offloaded. We've got to have that as a preposition point. Especially if Two Zero Alpha is up for grabs."

Padong was only 19 klicks east of Long Tieng, but it was a long 19 klicks because there was only one road approach from the north. The mountains on the east and west would provide some protection and also focus the enemy advance from the north.

At 1320 hours, Alberts lifted Archangel off the runway and climbed to the east to get within radio contact range of the Grunt Air birds. Toothman was jovial, but Captain U Muang, flying right seat for Alberts, wasn't in the mood.

"Hey, Muang," Toothman greeted him, "good to hear your voice. You lost or you want to hear some of my profound wisdoms of combat?"

"Not now, Jan. I just want you to know that Charlie Team found out they're going to hit Padong from the north. Six wants to know if you have our new home away from home set up. And when will you be finished with Air America?"

"Thanks for the warning. We'll get our asses out of here ASAP," Toothman said with concern. "We got the new home ready with TV and

Jacuzzi. The last flight is inbound now. We'll be on our way back in 15 or 20 mikes."

"Okay. We'll stay up until you get home. Come back up this frequency when you get released from Air America."

"Roger. Three, out."

Muang and Alberts throttled the C-47 back for maximum fuel efficiency and began the most boring part of their job, circling above the Grunt Air birds at 10,000 feet. About half an hour later, Toothman broke the boredom and silence with a loud, frantic squawk on the radio.

"Archangel, Archangel, this is Grunt Air Three. We just finished up and were preparing to lift off when the bastards attacked. Can you fly over and see what we're up against? We don't have a big force here. We're off and heading south for now."

"Roger, Three. I'm about five klicks west of you. I'll see what I can."

In seconds he called back. "Lucky you. The NVA is mainly in the open and only on the north side between the hills. Looks like a battalion-sized infantry unit."

"Gotcha, Archangel. Stand by. We're gonna go back and shoot them up a little bit. See if we can even up the odds."

"Roger, Three. Archangel standing by."

"Okay, Ditton," Toothman called to the other Grunt Air choppers, "you and Two Two do a north to south racetrack on the west side and we'll take the east side with a south to north. Execute!"

Lt. Ditton pulled his Huey to the left and flew to the north end of the NVA unit, turned south and started firing at the enemy forces on the ground. He kept a keen eye for Toothman and his wingman who were flying in the opposite direction. The NVA troops found themselves sandwiched between the two helicopters, one on either side, coming from opposite directions, unable to shoot at one while the other was shooting at them from the rear. Toothman banked hard to the left, dropped to a position barely over the tree-tops, and barreled toward the NVA on the ground, his door gunner firing his M-60 machine gun as fast as he could. The others did the same, orbiting around the scurrying men on the ground, guns chattering without a moment of silence. Around they went, four Hueys raining fire down to the ground. In minutes, it was over. Bodies littered the hillside, and the NVA who were lucky enough to live melted away into the safety of the trees.

"Archangel, this is Three. I think we evened the score. We're heading back to Udorn. We're getting marginal on fuel."

"Roger, Three. See you at the bar."

Toothman switched over to the Air America frequency, got clearance to head back to Udorn and signed off. He sat up in his seat, flushed with the feeling that he'd actually accomplished something that day, done his part to help the war effort. He reminded himself of one of his own axioms of combat, *If the enemy is in range, so are you.* Judging by the job he'd just done, he wasn't sure if that was still true.

Christmas Eve had been a long but productive day. Even Ryker was happy as the resurrection of Five Five was complete. To celebrate, Roman took Ryker, Alberts, Toothman and Abeel over to the Air Force O Club for a pleasant supper and a few dozen drinks. At about 2330, overflowing with Christmas cheer, they stumbled back to the B Frame for a nightcap. Roman was not even halfway through his first when a call came in from Kingfish.

"You didn't wake me up this time, you bastard," he told his caller.

"I can call back around 0300, if you want."

"Never mind. I know you didn't call because you're bored."

"So true. There's a lot going on over in the tri-border area. All those troops and equipment moving south makes me think they're gonna have a big Tet this year. Never seen this much activity before, not even during Tet 68. I understand that all POWs in our area have been moved north. Some are in Laos. Thought you'd want to know. Nothing specific yet, but we're working on it," Kingfish reported.

"Thanks, let me know if you pick up anything."

"Call the Fiddler. He may have more, plus any Songbird reports."

Roman immediately dialed the Fiddler, who was located on top of the massive limestone mountain called Nui Ba Den. The black mountain was over 986 meters tall and stood all alone in the middle of countless miles of rice paddies running off in all directions. The town of Tay Ninh was about five klicks to the southwest of the mountain. The strange thing about Nui Ba Den was that US and ARVN forces controlled the very top of the mountain and the bottom, but the NVA and Vietcong controlled the middle. This was an unholy situation that seldom changed. The Army maintained a significant Intelligence operation at Nui Ba Den and in the Tay Ninh area. While the area Intelligence commander was a lieutenant colonel based in Tay Ninh itself, the real all-star was the Fiddler. Dan's connection was a young Army captain stationed at the very top of Nui Ba Den, with access to the latest radio intercepts from the Army Security Agency and a highly classified operation called Songbird, which dealt with enemy radio intercepts concerning POWs. Along with several Vietnamese Intelligence officers, the Fiddler headed up a prolific and reliable operation.

The Intel Team had their own secret weapon in the intelligence-gathering busines—"the Rose," a female interrogator who absolutely blossomed whenever her subject gave up key information. The Fiddler had told Roman she made the Gestapo and Heinrich Himmler look like babes in the woods when it came to subjecting prisoners to physically demanding questioning. Her methods always succeeded, unless her hapless subject succumbed to the rigors of the process before she got what she wanted. Her commitment was total, her methods masterful. One of her favorite affectations, and the one that made her famous throughout Southeast Asia, was her pair of 4-inch stiletto heeled shoes. She kept the steel-tipped heels razor sharp and wielded them like a surgeon. Most of her prisoners did not survive the process.

Roman's call woke Fiddler up.

"Goddamn," he said. "Don't you know it's Christmas?"

"Yeah, and a merry one to you, too," Roman responded. "How's the war?"

"Well, it's about to get real shitty," Fiddler yawned. "There's a substantial buildup all along the Cambodian border, which the Intel boys in Saigon are blowing off as usual. But, it's going to be another bad Tet. You'll be glad to know that Songbird picked up a directive from General Thran Van Ho that all prisoners in the southern area are to be moved out of the conflict areas. They're going north to the Laotian transfer camp. Important prisoners are to go to Sam Neua for evaluation and then up the road to the north. They're transferring the two at the Tollbooth right away. The prisoners in the Bolovens Plateau are going to the Portholes, a camp near Vinh.

"Long story short, there's heavy shit coming down, and soon. I assume it's a Tet offensive. You know. The one Saigon says isn't going to happen."

"Kingfish tells me the same thing. Anything about the Big Three?"

"No not a thing. Personally, I think that's good news."

"Okay. Keep me informed if anything, and I do mean anything, comes up."

"You got it. Ho! Ho! Ho!"

Why hadn't General Ho done something? He may have been fooled by the fake personnel records, but Roman didn't think that was likely. Maybe he knows they're bogus but can't prove it to his superiors. Roman hoped they would not figure out the real situation until Grunt Air had the chance to bust in and pull the Big Three to safety.

Roman fought the urge to wait up for Santa. He'd reached the end of his endurance and headed for the rack, stopping on the way to tell the Charge of Quarters he wanted Captain Toothman and his crews up for a briefing at 0600 hours.

"Wake me at 0530," he said. Finally, he was getting his Christmas present. A full night's sleep.

27

A C-Ration Christmas

Grunt Air Headquarters
Udorn Air Force Base, Thailand
25 December, 1971

It wasn't beginning to look a lot like Christmas at Udorn Air Force Base in Thailand. The weather was hot and wet, and there wasn't a snowflake in sight. At Grunt Air, nobody cared much one way or the other because thoughts of Christmas were a distant second to the demands of the daily flight schedule. Wars have always reduced holidays like Christmas and Thanksgiving to just another day. Home and family were in another time and on another planet.

Toothman and the other three Grunt Air crews had the same mission with Air America as the previous day, only this time it was more of a supply mission, since the troops were already in place. After two runs carrying C-rations, equipment and ammunition, they settled their four birds to earth in the clearing at Padong, about 50 meters away from the main landing site, which was sheltered from artillery fire on two sides. They checked out the condition of their tents and pre-positioned fuel and ammo. Toothman was concerned the troops they brought in yesterday would steal everything, which was always a risk when you left supplies at a remote site, but they hadn't. Why was a mystery. People always stole things in Vietnam. His puzzlement was solved by the arrival of a Hmong Sergeant Major and his interpreter. The Sergeant Major immediately launched into an impressive speech, complete with smiles and graphic hand gestures while his interpreter struggled to keep up.

"He say thank you for saving them yesterday," the interpreter stuttered. "He say your men very brave for helicopter to fly so low close to the enemy with only two M-60 machine guns." Toothman thought *That ain't no big deal,* as the speech concluded.

213

"You need anything, Grunt Air need anything, you ask for the Sergeant Major. He is man to see."

"Well, there is one thing you can do for us," Toothman suggested. "Make sure nobody makes off with our ammo and fuel. We need it when we move in to support your guys." This triggered a new flow of elaborate oratory from the Sergeant Major.

"You can depend on Sergeant Major and his troops. No outsiders, no NVA come close to your possessions. He is proud for your trust."

A crisp salute, a snappy about-face and the two men were gone.

That's great, Toothman said to himself, *but who's gonna watch* you?

Once all the supplies were unloaded and checked, the four choppers cranked up to go back to Udorn for Christmas dinner. On the way , Toothman positioned the other choppers high and he flew low through the canyon that they'd made so deadly to the NVA the day before. He saw nothing but some fresh tire tracks where trucks had loaded up the dead and wounded, but otherwise the area looked as if nothing had ever happened there. A few miles farther north, he scouted the area for a base camp or a rally point for a counter-attack. No luck. But, what he did see were the troops that made up the edge of the enemy area of operations, all of whom grabbed their AK-47s and began shooting. They hadn't forgotten what had happened to them the day before. Toothman, eyes wide, pulled a hard cyclic climb to the left and quickly disappeared over a ridge of hills.

Soldiers have been complaining about the food in the military since armies were invented, but they would all reconsider if they'd seen the Christmas dinner at Udorn's Air Force Officer's Club. It made all other military meals throughout history seem like a five star banquet. The "turkey" was dry and borderline cold, and the gravy was a viscous fluid that deserved no name. The mashed potatoes took an instant to prepare and a lifetime to digest. Yes, there were pies and cakes, the mediocrity of which was a welcome contrast to the main course. However, Roman reminded everyone, Grunt Air had four recon teams in the field, camped in the jungle and eating C-rations that were probably cold.

Pretty good grub, after all.

Earlier that morning, Roman had taken off with Alberts in Archangel for the morning report and to personally wish the Recon Teams a Merry Christmas. He'd tried to think of a way to bring them in a hot meal, but Grunt Air didn't need the attention just then.

"Any chance of breaking those guys out of the Rock House?" Roman asked Lieutenant Christian on the radio.

"No way. Too many troops around here. Turns out the place is HQ for the 214 DAC Cong battalion. New arrivals seem to be recent captures, flight suits in good shape, good haircuts. Then there's one other poor bastard who looks like they've had his ass for months." Roman felt his jaw get tight.

He was in his office going through the details of the raid on the Big Casino for the eighty-fifth time when Seacrest, the unit clerk, brought him a message. *Merry Christmas*, Roman thought. The message was from his favorite officer, Colonel Sweeney in Saigon. Unexpectedly, it was good news. The two new Hueys and crews would be ready for pickup at 0800 hours, 28 December 1971. Sweeney's personality did manage to shine through since he required Roman to personally come to Tan Son Nhut to sign for the birds. It was the property officer's job, but Sweeney couldn't pass up the opportunity for a little ball busting.

Shows what an asshole you really are, thought Roman. *Two Hueys and crews? I'd sign for them in Hanoi if you told me to*. He grabbed the phone and started to dial Fitzmorris in Saigon.

"Mr. Seacrest, please track down Toothman, Gedeon, Alberts, Abeel, Sergeant Major Panfil and Gunny Thornhill. Hey, Fitz! You'll never guess what Sweeney is up to. Never mind, I'll tell you when I see you. Look, I need to go over the current situation and the Big Casino plan with General Mattix day after tomorrow, if possible. Could you please set it up? And we'll need eight rooms at the Transit BOQ and two at the Transit BEQ for the night of the 27th. You can? Thanks. See ya."

Everyone was waiting for Roman in the Ops room, where he made them go through the Big Casino plan in punishing detail for three and a half hours. He wanted to put on a good show for the Generals and he wanted to be ready for absolutely anything once the mission was launched. Sometime during the session, Fitzmorris called back and confirmed a full briefing for Generals Mattix and Geiger, and possibly the Commanding General himself, at 1000 hours on 27 December. Transit BOQ rooms had been laid on and the crews alerted for an initial meeting with Roman and the others at 1600 hours.

All set. Time for another Christmas drink or two or three.

28

Smile, You're Making the Pentagon Blush

Paris, France

The three days had gone quickly. In spite of the Parisian cold and rain, Carol and Charlie had managed to figure out the subway system and attack most of the good stores, even though they gasped at the prices and couldn't afford to buy much. They'd even paid a visit to the Mona Lisa and sat on the steps of Sacre Coeur at sundown. All the while, both of them were thinking the same thing but never said a word about it: We're in the world's most romantic city, without the men we love.

Sergeant Walsh's information had been correct. The Chief Negotiator flew back to Paris and the talks resumed. Late that night, the two women and the Sergeant found a quiet corner in the hotel lobby and sat down to review the details of their actions for the following day.

"You're sure the police at the entry know what to do?" Carol asked. "That's the most critical thing."

"I spoke with our source just a little while ago. They have their orders from the highest levels, very reliable people. Everyone has agreed to this and they all know what they're doing." The Sergeant leaned forward. "Have you looked at the pictures I gave you? Can you recognize the Chief Negotiator in a crowd?"

"I'm seeing him in my sleep."

"Good enough. If you have trouble spotting him, just look where all the cameras are pointed." Walsh went over the rest of the details, put his papers in a pile, stood up and pulled on his overcoat.

"I think that about covers it. *Au demain.*" They watched him push his way through the revolving door and out to the boulevard.

"It's all up to you now," said Charlie, taking Carol's hand.

"I know. I know. Let's get some sleep."

It had been a sour morning for all the delegates to the Peace Accord as they shuffled on to the sidewalk for their recess. They'd bogged down in their discussion of item two on the Peace Accord agenda that dealt with the question of power in South Vietnam. There had been bitter exchanges, and the atmosphere was tense on both sides of the negotiating table.

Charlie dropped Carol and David Walsh off at the makeshift guard shack at the entrance to the building and drove away. She was scared silly to be driving in the insane Parisian traffic, but it was the part she had to play and she was trying to be brave. Sergeant Walsh had given her painfully detailed directions.

As the pair walked up to the guard shack, both policemen stepped toward them, automatic rifles held high across their chests.

"Your credentials, please," one of guards said coldly. Carol almost froze with fear.

The police Captain who had been sitting inside the shack stepped out. "One moment, please," he said. He was holding a clipboard with a sheet of paper attached to it. He examined the paper carefully, then looked up at Carol and Walsh. "You are Mrs. Carol Cody?" he asked politely.

"Yes, sir," a terror stricken Carol responded.

"And you're Sergeant David Walsh?"

"Yes, sir." The Sergeant replied matter-of-factly.

"Ah!" The Captain exclaimed. "I see you wear the Medal of Honor!"

"Yes, sir."

"It's an honor to meet you, Sergeant." He turned to the pair of policemen. "Let them through."

The guards stepped aside. Carol and the Sergeant edged their way into the crowd of diplomats.

"There he is," Carol said, elbowing Walsh in the ribs. She pointed to a short, stocky man a few feet away, engaged in an intense conversation with one of his secretaries. Carol muscled her way through the crowd, at the same time pulling the letter out of her purse, and planted herself directly in the man's face. He was about her height so she was able to look him right in the eye. To everyone's startled amazement, she grabbed his right hand and pressed her envelope into it. He had no choice but to take it. His eyes went wide and his head jerked nervously to the right and left. Carol looked over her shoulder and saw that all the cameras in the area were swinging toward them. She took a deep breath and spoke in the strongest voice she could manage.

"Sir," she began, "this is a letter with two thousand signatures of American women who want to know where their men are. They demand a complete list of all POWs being held in your POW camps and want to know what condition they're in."

The Chief Negotiator didn't know which way to look. He glanced in one direction searching for the security guards, and then in the other, right into the cameras.

"Your government is in violation of the Geneva Agreements, and the nations of the world are witness to your gross and inhumane acts." Her voice rose another level. "We demand that you publish a list of all POWs held in your camps at once! We want to know WHERE ARE OUR MEN!"

"Your people are being treated humanely," the Negotiator stammered, terror-stricken as he looked over her shoulder. Where were the security guards? What would his government say when they saw this confrontation on television? He took a step back, stumbling over one of his aides. "Get this woman away from me!"

Finally, a flock of policemen shoved through the crowd, grabbed Carol and Walsh, handcuffed them and hustled them aside. The Captain from the guard shack forced his way into the melee, shouting "I'll take care of these maniacs!" He grabbed Carol by one arm and the Sergeant by the other. Surrounded by his officers, he hustled them toward the guard post and the waiting police van. Two policemen boosted them into the van. One got in next to them, pulled the doors shut and banged his hand on the front wall. The van lurched and Carol heard the familiar, two-tone Parisian siren. It sounded just like in the movies. She heard the Captain's voice talking to the driver.

"*Enlevez-les,*" he yelled. "Get them out of here. Take them to headquarters. I'll be along presently to press charges."

The van roared away. Carol couldn't see what she'd left behind, but the crowd outside the building looked like an anthill that had just been kicked over. The Chief Negotiator was surrounded by solicitous underlings, all of them running in every direction, trying to soothe his ruffled demeanor.

A few blocks from the Peace Accord building, the van pulled over to a curb, the driver parked, walked around to the back and opened the doors. Blinking in the morning light, Carol saw Charlie drive up and park behind the van, a big smile on her face. Apparently, she'd gotten over the terror of driving in Paris.

The armed policeman stepped down and held out a hand to help Carol and Walsh out of the van. "Turn around, please," he said. When they did, the driver unlocked their handcuffs. He tossed a set of cuffs to Walsh and the other set to Carol.

"You can keep those as a present from the Captain. A souvenir of your trip to Paris. The Captain asked me to give you his best and said it was a pleasure to meet you." He paused for a moment, then said sadly, "We Frenchmen had a go with those bastards, you know. I lost many good men in those rice paddies over there."

Walsh and Carol shook hands with the two policemen, then they got in the car with Charlie.

"Good luck!" the driver shouted as he drove away.

"I'll drive," the Sergeant said to Charlie.

"The hell you will," she retorted. "I'm starting to enjoy this."

That night, they sat in the hotel and flipped through the channels on the television. They'd scored a public relations coup. Every channel showed the footage of Carol's confrontation that morning and mentioned that the news was being broadcast around the world. Mrs. Carol Cody from Fort Bliss, Texas, was the lead story.

They could hardly sleep that night. The next morning, they were up early to wait in the lobby for the first newspapers to be delivered. Sure enough, there was Carol on the front page, pressing her letter into the hand of the startled and flustered Chief Negotiator. The caption on the photo read: "Where are our men?"

In their room, the phone didn't stop ringing all day. They had calls from the French news media, calls from the United States, invitations to appear on network talk shows, more invitations to speak before veteran's groups, clubs and civic organizations. They accepted every one, Charlie furiously writing down a list of contacts, phone numbers, dates and places.

"I think," reflected Sergeant Walsh, "that when you get home, you're going to be some kind of celebrities. Sort of champions of the POW/MIA cause in America."

He was right.

⌘⌘

29

A Favor for John Henry

By the time Christmas was over, the NVA march south had been slowed by the terrain, unseasonable rains in the higher elevations, and by the Hmong. The Hmong had been losing ground, but as the NVA neared the Hmong stronghold of the Long Tieng Valley and the super secret airbase known as Two Zero Alpha, they started to dig in and fight harder. The area was their de facto wartime capital and they could not lose it.

Archangel departed Udorn at 0430 hours and turned north to receive the morning reports. The NVA had taken the night off and all was quiet. All four teams reported seeing commander's cars and GP vehicles shuttling back to the rear, a typical sign that a new attack was about to take place.

After the reports were in, Alberts turned the C-47 toward Saigon, arriving a little after 0800 hours. Captain Ryker went off to spend the day going over the two new Hueys before accepting them. Chief Gedeon looked up Sergeant Rogers to review the property transfer documents for the aircraft and to shovel a whole sheaf of new request forms onto the pile. To expedite matters, Gedeon had brought two duffel bags full of crossbows, pipes, captured NVA articles of clothing and insignias and a rare Chi-com pistol. He would be happy to trade it all for steaks, Scotch, and similar items of great rarity and value.

Roman and his team didn't have to wait long in the Operations office. Major Fitzmorris showed up right away with cars for the trip to Headquarters and a stop at the base cafeteria for a quick breakfast.

"Ten-HUT!" Major Generals Mattix and Geiger entered the conference room at exactly 1000 hours along with Colonel Herbert, Colonel Felter from the Operations staff, and Captain Mansen, the Aide de Camp for General Mattix. To Roman's surprise, Colonel Odom was present. The briefing began with Chief Abeel recounting the current military situation from the Grunt Air perspective. It was detailed and extensively covered the order of battle information obtained by the Recon teams as well as projected NVA plans. All the while, the Intelligence representatives were feverously taking notes. Obviously, some of this information was of significant value to them. Abeel was just finishing the latest information obtained from the teams when the Commanding General came in, bringing everyone to their feet.

"Sit down, gentlemen. Keep going, Chief," Coroneos said as he sat down.

"How close have your teams actually come to the camps and NVA?" an Intel officer wanted to know.

"Sir, during the daytime, the teams sleep and take turns observing the camps and NVA movements from a hillside, one-half to two klicks away."

"That close, Chief?" the Intel officer asked.

"Yes, sir, that far," Abeel continued. "At night or during heavy rain, they go to within five or ten meters of the camp and NVA personnel. They take pictures, make notes and listen to conversations. Sometimes, they're lucky enough to snatch an NVA officer or senior sergeant for questioning. Extensive questioning. Our interpreters and Intelligence specialists know how to find out what they need."

"What do you do with them after you get the information, Chief?" asked the Intel officer.

General Geiger gave the officer a killing look. "In case you forgot, this is a war, son." Coroneos heaved a sigh. "Go on, Chief."

Abeel covered everything they knew about the POW camps and personnel in the Sam Neua area, including the information from Fiddler and Kingfish.

Captain Toothman was next to report the air operations aspect. Sergeant Major Panfil laid out the ground plan. Panfil was a three tour Vietnam veteran and it showed. He'd been a part of two major combat parachute drops during the Korean War and wore the prestigious 187th Regimental Combat Team patch on his right shoulder. Roman watched the faces of the Generals, their aides and the Intel officers. Home run. He could see that everyone was impressed.

When Panfil was finished, General Coroneos got right to the point. "What do you estimate the number of casualties will be?"

"Sir," said Panfil, "no battle plan ever survives the first shot. But if we're not compromised and we retain the element of surprise, I don't think we'll have any. We've been through this up, down, and sideways. But worst possible case, even if we run into problems and lose half our Hueys, I expect less than 20 per cent casualties max, sir."

General Coroneos looked down at the pencil and pad before him on the conference table, silent for what seemed like hours. "Well, I just said that this is a war and there are casualties in war. You lose people. Look, I don't want another San Tay. And I don't want more casualties than the number of men we bring out. But, I also want to get the Big Three out alive, if possible. If we don't grab them, the B-52s will blow them to Kingdom Come." Nodding at Alberts, he said, "You'll confirm their location through Archangel to the B-52s waiting at altitude over Thailand. Roman calls to tell you he got them or he didn't, and you pass the word. Then, it's up to the big boys to finish things off.

"Al," the General said, turning to General Mattix, "I want at least three cells of three on that mission. If we have to take those boys out I want it quick and painless. Also, get a daily U-2 flight over the area." The Commanding General looked back and forth between Toothman and Panfil. "Are you certain this is a reasonable plan that gives you a chance for survival?" Panfil took the chance and spoke first.

"Sir, I have every confidence that the Aviation Platoon will get us in and get us out," he said. "That's the big variable as far as the Recon Platoon is concerned. Under Captain Roman's supervision, we've developed an excellent plan and we're willing to trust our lives to it." He paused for a moment. "I'd hate for someone outside the unit to screw with it." Roman almost slid under the table.

The Commanding General smiled at Panfil and said, "From you, Top, there isn't a better endorsement. Okay, gentlemen, subject to whatever minor changes Captain Roman deems appropriate, this is the way we'll go, if necessary. I do reserve final approval when the time comes." The Commanding General got up to leave. "Carry on."

After another half hour of critical discussion, General Mattix stopped them on the way out of the conference room.

"You can't afford to be half right on this, gentlemen. Be totally right or abort. The old man's neck is stuck out real far on this one. Don't let him get hurt."

"That pretty well says it all," Roman muttered to the group. "Which way to the BX?"

At 1600 hours, after buying out half the Base Exchange, or so it seemed, they were back in the secure conference room. This time the Grunt Air contingent was joined by the two new crews who had volunteered for the unit. Ryker and Gedeon had also made it back from their tasks. Introductions were made, and Roman turned the meeting over to Abeel and Toothman, who gave the new crews a unit background and a briefing that should have scared them right back out the door.

Then Ryker and Alberts chimed in, telling them about Grunt Air's maintenance and communications procedures. Their expressions became even more fearful. The new aircraft commander for Seven Seven was Randolph "Red" Staggs, and he never knew his eyes could get so wide or his jaw drop so far. Roman remembered the day not so long ago that he sat in that same chair, shocked at what he was hearing about the mysterious unit.

When everyone was finished scaring the new troops, Roman went over the plan for the following day. "With any luck," he said, "we should be airborne by 0900 hours. We'll go direct Tay Ninh West, refuel and pit stop, then direct Phnom Penh, then to Xiem Riep, then Bangkok. That's about six and three-quarter hours in the air. We should be on the ground by 1830 hours, including stops. We'll stay overnight in Bangkok, then proceed to Udorn via Korat, starting at 1100 hours." He would fly Seven Seven and Toothman Eight Eight with the assigned crew, except for the copilots, who would go in Archangel with the others to learn its function and operations.

"Sir," asked the new Lieutenant Gil Gilespie, "why are we leaving Bangkok so late in the morning?" An innocent question, but one that caused Red Staggs to spit out his coffee laughing. When the hilarity had died down, Staggs came to his defense.

"He's led a sheltered life!"

Alberts chimed in, "If I know Roman, you won't be able to walk by pitch pull."

Gilespie blushed as he suddenly understood what the Bangkok stopover was really all about.

"Okay, any questions?" Roman said. "Make sure you check out of the "Q" and have your bags on Archangel by 0800 hours. We'll depart as soon as I can get the paperwork taken care of." Roman looked at his watch. Ten past seven. He was about to dismiss the group when Colonel Herbert, the Commanding General's aide, came into the room. Everyone went quiet and stood up as he handed Roman a note from General Coroneos. Colonel Herbert said, "It's up to you if you want to help him," and stood quietly as Roman opened the note.

It read: John Henry Holbrook has a big problem and it is right up Grunt Air's alley. No other viable assets available to him. Your call. It was initialed "PPC," Pistol Pete Coroneos.

Without a further word, Colonel Herbert left the room. Roman just stood there looking at the note. Toothman peered over his shoulder and grunted. The group broke up, with most headed to the O Club for a sandwich and a few brews.

They weren't shy about their alcohol consumption at the club. By 2100 hours, the new crews and the Grunt Air regulars had become old buddies. They had to quit at 2200 hours to observe the old pilot's rule, eight hours bottle to throttle, but they'd drink like hell until then.

Roman found a song on the jukebox that brought back memories, and sat by himself in a corner. Toothman had seen this before and left him alone. While Roman was dwelling on the past, his dead wife, and kids who hardly knew him, John Henry Holbrook showed up. The bartender pointed Roman out, sitting in the shadows next to the jukebox.

Holbrook never made it to the table. Toothman and Ryker came out of the dark and stopped him.

"Excuse me, is that Captain Roman?" asked Holbrook.

"Yes, but you can't disturb him right now," Ryker said in a no-nonsense voice.

"My name is Holbrook and I have a very important matter to discuss with him."

Toothman recognized the name from the CG's note and looked the thin man up and down, his glance lingering for a second on the bow tie. Nobody in Vietnam wore a bow tie, but Holbrook did. "Okay, but this isn't a good time to be asking for favors." Toothman walked over to Roman's table and said, "Dan, Holbrook is here. You want to see him?"

Roman stopped staring at his drink and looked up. "What does he want? Doesn't he like my choice of music?"

Holbrook edged around Toothman and sat down at the table. Toothman and Fitzmorris took the other two chairs. Before Holbrook could say a word, Ryker and Alberts swung two more chairs under the table and made themselves at home. Holbrook looked around at the unfriendly faces, more than a little concerned.

"I hadn't planned on talking to the whole world."

"Forget they're here. I do." Roman said sarcastically. He stared at Holbrook through half-closed eyes.

"Are you okay, Captain Roman? This is a very serious matter."

"I've had a few, but I'm okay, and that's the bad news," he said. His gaze was penetrating.

Holbrook understood that he was dealing with a professional who could hold his liquor. "I guess you're okay," he said politely.

"Mr. Holbrook, what can our band of crash site surveyors do for the Central Intelligence Agency?" Roman asked.

"I've got two agents trapped inside Cambodia southeast of Prey Vang. The Khmer Rouge and NVA know they're in the area and have them effectively surrounded. I need to extract them before they're located and captured."

"What about Army or Air America assets? The CIA can call on them any time."

"There are no Air America helicopter assets in the area, and the Army is limited to convoy protection. I've tried every possible source. Frankly, your unit is my only hope." Roman managed to open his eyes a little wider. He was interested.

"Keep talking."

Holbrook reached into his official black briefcase, pulled out two maps and spread them on the table, first carefully wiping up the moisture from Roman's drinks. The first map was a 1 over 500,000 scale area tactical that depicted everything from Saigon to Phnom Penh. The other was the more common 1 over 50,000 scale map widely used in the field. It was detailed to the 10 meters in elevation and showed virtually every feature and structure on the ground. Roman looked at Holbrook's briefcase on the floor. It was full of maps and other documents.

"This is where the two-man team was when we heard enemy reports about two CIA agents in the area." Holbrook pointed to the Cambodian town of Prey Vang, some 40 klicks east of the Cambodian capitol of Phnom Penh. "You can guess that the NVA and Khmer Rouge leadership got all worked up about the possibility of getting their hands on them. They sent orders out to units as far away as Kompong Trach, down near the South Vietnam border, and within eight hours my guys were pretty much surrounded. They had no place to go. In every direction, enemy forces were on the alert. They'd already left Prey Vang when we told them about the situation. They made it to a lake near the town of Khum Chiphoch Phum."

"That's easy for you to say," Toothman muttered. "Never heard of the place."

"They're stuck at the south end of this small lake alongside Highway 244. Here are the grid coordinates. They've got good concealment, and the nearest unit looking for them is about eight to ten klicks away. They have a radio and a few batteries and enough C-rations for another day or so." Holbrook's voice was heavy with worry and defeat. Everybody at the table sat silently, waiting to hear what Roman would say. Holbrook was smart enough not to talk.

Roman took another belt from his Scotch and looked deeply into Holbrook's eyes. "As usual, Mister Holbrook, the CIA isn't telling the truth, or, at least, not all of it." Holbrook shifted uneasily in his chair.

"You guys in the CIA have this goddamn say-nothing attitude that makes working with you extremely dangerous, if not impossible. Even in my present condition I can see that you're lying to me. You must not be a very good spook because it's all over your face. Now, you either tell me the whole truth and nothing but, or you can fuck right off."

"Okay. But if I tell you everything, will you accept the mission?"

"Are you out of your mind? I'm not that drunk. I don't agree to anything until I have the whole story. If I think Grunt Air can do it, we will. If not, not. But I can't make a decision if I don't have all the facts. Now spit it out."

Holbrook was a smallish, thin man, almost prissy in appearance, but if he didn't have a core of toughness and a cold heart when he needed it, he wouldn't have lasted long in his job. This time, it was apparent that the usual methods wouldn't work on Roman, but it went completely against all his training to give anybody all the information he had. Still, this was not a normal situation. He took a deep breath, sat back in his chair, and regarded the circle of faces set against him.

"Okay. First, your input to General Geiger about a possible full scale attack at Tet is correct. The NVA and Khmer Rouge have eight divisions across the border in Cambodia from the Parrots Beak to just north of Loc Ninh. The VC have about the same massing in the same area. The NVA is running continuous supply trains down the Ho Chi Minh Trail twenty-four hours a day, not just during the night any more. Fortunately, they don't have a lot of triple-A with them. It's scattered along the route system and around the division headquarters. The enemy has put a priority on stopping the supply convoy going up the Mekong to Phnom Penh. They'll strike it in the usual two places, but we understand they'll keep it under attack from the time it gets to Phum Sum all the way to Phnom Penh. They want to take the supplies for themselves as well as keep the siege of Phnom Pehn going. The convoy is supported by the 7th Squadron 1st Air Calvary Regiment, the Blackhawks, and if the enemy can stop it, they get both a military and a political victory.

"Bottom line—the area is as bad as it gets. You'll be under small arms fire going in and out. That's the facts. The CO of Blackhawk has already turned me down. If you want, you can do the same." With a decisive gesture, Holbrook pushed back from the table and stood up.

"Where are you going?" Roman asked. "I haven't said no, yet. But there's still something important you haven't told me. You're far too emotional about this. You have two agents stuck behind the lines? Big deal. Must happen all the time. What's so special?" Holbrook's shoulders slumped. He sat back down.

"My wife is with them," Holbrook blurted.

"What!"

"She's French. I met her when I was stationed in Paris about ten years ago. She has a sister living in Prey Vang. A week ago, before we knew how many troops had massed across the border in Cambodia, I let her go with the two agents to bring her sister to Saigon. The agents were reorganizing the resistance movement in the area and getting them ready for the upcoming offensive. At that time, we didn't think it would be anything near the size it's becoming. I'm being promoted and reassigned to the headquarters in Langley, Virginia. All she wanted to do was get her sister to safety in Saigon. Now, she's trapped with the agents. That's it. That's everything."

"How much time do we have before they're located?" Roman asked.

"Two, maybe three days at most," Holbrook responded.

"If they're really looking for them, we may only have a day," Roman thought out loud. "The NVA's a lot smarter than some people give them credit for. Did I hear you say you have communications with them?"

"Yes. They only transmit on odd hours and then for less than 15 seconds at a time. That makes it hard to find them with radio direction equipment. We generally give them numbered questions at the half hour before the odd hour. They respond with short answers by number."

"Okay," Roman said, "let's go over to Blue Chip and see if we can throw something together tonight." He pushed himself up from the table and held on to the back of his chair, swaying only slightly. The rest of the men at the table also got up to leave. Holbrook was dumbfounded.

"You'll do it? Really?"

"Sure. You should have started off by saying 'I let my wife go to Prey Vang with two agents and they got surrounded.' Would have saved all the time I spent playing 20 Questions with you. Let's go!"

With Fitzmorris in the lead and Holbrook bringing up the rear, the group straggled toward the small conference room just outside Blue Chip and started to consider what they might do. After a few minutes of discussion, Roman grabbed Abeel by the arm with one hand and motioned for Toothman to follow him with the other.

"We're going to check the situation board in Blue Chip. Back in five," Roman said. Once inside the command center, Roman pulled the two men close to him and spoke intensely.

"Jan, get all you can on that convoy going up the Mekong tomorrow. Abeel, find out what the enemy situation is in the area. Make sure our buddies in the B-52s don't have anything planned for tomorrow between Prey Vang and Tay Ninh. I'm going to get the Fiddler on the line."

Fiddler told him there were a lot of NVA and friends in the area, and that they'd picked up enemy chatter. A rescue attempt is expected, Fiddler said, but the enemy is expecting a big event, with Jolly Greens, fighter cover, the works. More bad news. The NVA was planning on doing a real number on the river convoy.

"Okay," Roman admitted, "I'm impressed with their superior forces in the area. Do me a favor and give me the best location and order of battle you can along a route from the ferry at Phum Prak Khsay to Tay Ninh, or something similar. I figure the convoy should be at the ferry by 0930 to 1000 hours, even if they get hit north of Phum Son, which is what usually happens. The CIA is hunkered down along that line. Abeel will call you back in 10 mikes for your best guess. I'll keep everyone here on sedatives until I get your input."

Toothman and Abeel recited the information they'd learned in Blue Chip. Roman quietly asked Abeel to call Fiddler. He didn't want Holbrook to know who was supplying Grunt Air with real time Intelligence information.

"Mr. Holbrook," Roman began, "can you get four of my ground security force to Chau Duc by 0700 hours tomorrow?"

"Consider it done," Holbrook said with confidence. "I'll have Air America bring them down in a Pilatus Porter at 0500 hours."

"Okay. Sergeant Major Panfil, get Bravo over to Air America by 0430 hours. Tell them to bring four M-60s with a lot of ammo. You know the scene. Bob, go get Rogers out of bed and get us an extra eight boxes for our M-60s, one or two M-79 grenade launchers and a box of ammo."

"Boss," Gedeon interrupted, "you're supposed to officially sign for the new Hueys at 0800 hours. Colonel Sweeney will be waiting."

"Colonel Sweeney can pound salt. You can disappoint him by following Air Force regulations to the letter and sign for them yourself. Wear your rain gear because Sweeney will cause a shit storm. Fitz, could I impose on you to go with Mr. Gedeon? Maybe you can keep things down to a shit shower instead of a storm.

"Jan, go wake up the Blackhawk Ops officer and ask him if he could hold his flight up at Chau Duc until 0700 hours so we can fly with him as far as the ferry. Tell him we're on a sensitive mission and we don't want to telegraph our game plan. I know him, he'll cooperate. If he doesn't want to, just tell him if I get killed, I won't be able to pay that quart of Chivas Regal I owe him. Also, get the two new crews to the flight line by 0500 hours."

"What should I tell them?"

"Tell Red I'm going to check him and his crew out for combat proficiency before they get to the big show up in Laos. I'm sure that he'll have one of his usual wiseass comments. Have his copilot and Barnes' copilot fly with Archangel. You'll take Eight Eight with Barnes to Tay Ninh West and wait for me. Once we finish playing taxi, we can go on home from there. Archangel, you'll fly C & C for me. You can confirm the crash and burn, if necessary."

Roman glanced over at Holbrook, who had turned absolutely white. It was not a good color for him. "Just kidding, Mr. Holbrook. Just my sick sense of humor."

"I know, I know. How can I help? Do you want me to get you the latest NVA troop deployment from my office?"

"Nah," Roman said, "it would only scare me. You know what us pilots say, why check the weather when you're going anyway?" Everyone laughed but Holbrook.

"Okay," Roman said, starting on the detail work, "pitch pull for Chau Duc at 0530 hours with Eight Eight heading to Tay Ninh West at 0800 hours."

Major Fitzmorris leaned forward in his chair and folded his arms on the conference table. "Dan, are you sure you want a single ship mission? Wouldn't it be better with two?"

"Just that much more for me to worry about, sir. Also, I'll be flying high speed below the trees and I need to focus on my flying and navigation. One ship will draw less NVA attention than two. Besides, they're looking for the Jolly Greens coming in from the east. I'm coming in the back door. I should be able to get in and out before they figure out what we're doing. And, of course, it'll be easier to explain away if I don't make it."

Just then, Toothman and Abeel came in. Toothman gave a thumbs up and said with a smile, "He wants two quarts for this one."

Roman grunted and glanced down at a small map Abeel slid across the table. It had peanut shaped circles drawn on it indicating the current location, identification and composition of the major units between the Mekong River in Cambodia and the border across from Tay Ninh. The concentrations along his intended route of flight were extremely heavy.

Holbrook craned his neck to read the map upside down from across the table. "How do you know about those troop concentrations?"

"This, Mr. Holbrook, is Mr. Abeel's physic predictions on the enemy situation. They come from the great beyond when he has a couple of Scotches and locks himself in the broom closet."

"But ... but I can get the very latest reports from my office. They have to be much better than this," Holbrook offered. "No offense, Chief, but my guys have all the input. They're pros at this. You guys have to be guessing."

"Since it's my ass sitting out there, I'll go with my amateur's guesses," Roman said throwing a quick glance at Abeel.

"Well, it is your ass, but only up to a point. Then it affects me," Holbrook protested. Roman choked back his overwhelming desire to grab Holbrook by the throat and tell him if he didn't like the planning he could find somebody else to rescue his wife. Instead, Roman ignored Holbrook and turned to Toothman to ask if everything was set.

"Red is a bit confused but he'll get over it. No problem with Blackhawk, at all. He was glad to be part of the plan."

"Great! Now, let's look at the route of flight," Roman said as he went to the wall map. "My thinking is, I'll fly in the initial gun run on the certain ambush at the ferry. Instead of turning around and going back as usual, I'll break east until I hit this lake. Then, I'll go north over the lake until I get almost to Highway 244, turn east staying a couple klicks south of 244 directly south of the lake at 0945 hours plus or minus five mikes. I'll make the pickup there. I'll take four 5-gallon cans of fuel to put in on the fly at the pickup point.

"Once we're out of there, I'll get north of 244 a couple three or four klicks until I cross 155, then stay well south of 244 until I get due south of Kompong Trach. From there, it's 110 degrees until I get across the border about eight or ten klicks, turning toward Tay Ninh West. I can let the VIPs and Bravo Team off and refuel for Bangkok." Abeel and Toothman nodded. Roman addressed Alberts.

"Doug," Roman said, "you'll have visual, weather permitting, and can keep me on track if I start going off course. Tom," he said to Ryker, "you might want to go with Mr. Gedeon to see Rogers. We'll probably pick up a few termite holes along the way and we'll have to repair them at Tay Ninh West before we continue on. Maybe Rogers will give you a few spare parts, just in case."

"Fat chance," said Ryker. "Thing is, I have a bunch of spare parts in Archangel already. I wasn't going to take a chance of breakdown on the way back." Roman nodded at the encouraging news, then looked at his watch. It was 0245 hours and he'd sobered up.

"Looks like we'll be able to get an hour's sleep, then check out of the Q. Let's go!"

On the way out, Roman pulled Holbrook aside. He didn't like the fidgety little spook, but he felt a surprising amount of compassion for him.

"Have your people ready for pickup at 0945 hours and you can have lunch with your wife at Tay Ninh. Before you go to sleep, make sure your team is ready and make sure they know to look for one green taxi at 0945 hours. I assume you can get a plane to take you to Tay Ninh West that will be big enough to bring you all back here."

"Sure," said Holbrook. Before he could thank Roman, he found himself alone in the hallway. His hands were shaking, and they never shook, even when he'd been in some hairy situations in the back alleys of Budapest and Prague during the Cold War. He was worried about his wife and, strangely enough, worried about Roman, a man he'd never liked. But now, Roman held the fate of many people in his hands, and Holbrook could do nothing but trust him and depend on him. He'd been around long enough to know his wife and two agents had less than a twenty per cent chance of making it out alive, what with the huge concentrations of enemy troops all along the route of flight. The map Abeel had come up with looked suspiciously like the ones that were created in the CIA Intelligence office. If he got his wife back in one piece, he'd surely rethink his opinion of Roman and his pirates. But meanwhile, where the hell *did* they get all their information?

30

A Tourist in Friendly Cambodia

Tan Son Nhut Air Force Base, Saigon
28 December, 1971
0530 Hours

Red Staggs lifted the Huey into the air and, following instructions from Tan Son Nhut Tower, contacted departure control. Red was a gifted combat pilot who kept the tension of combat down with never-ending jokes. Roman had chosen to fly the mission from the left seat instead of the pilot seat on the right. He was more comfortable there with fewer instruments in front of him, which would give him greater visibility once the low-level tactical flying started. Although Roman considered Red Staggs a very competent aircraft commander, he would take the controls for the more difficult part of the mission. As was a common practice, Dan scribbled his routing instructions on the upper left of the Plexiglas windshield above him with a grease pencil. It kept critical flight information near the pilot's line of sight. Roman contacted his controller.

"Paddy Control, Grunt Air Six is with you climbing to 6500 enroute Chau Duc direct squaking two two four zero."

"Roger, Grunt Air Six. Radar contact 12 miles southwest TSN, you're clear as filed. Maintain 6500, Paddy altimeter two niner niner four."

"Roger, Paddy, two niner niner four," Roman responded.

"Grunt Air Six, Paddy. You sound familiar. Ever work the Delta?" the operator asked.

"Roger, Paddy. I was Outlaw Three two months ago."

"Yeah, I never forget a voice. Glad to have you back in the Delta. Staying long?"

"No. Just a tourist this time."

"I was on the day you brought those two cripples back from the U Minh Forest," Paddy Control said informally.

"Yeah, that was my last day in the Delta," Roman replied.

"Roger, Grunt Air Six." The air traffic controller's voice became formal once again. "You have traffic, your 2 o'clock, four miles, an F-4 descending to 7000 on opposing course."

"Paddy Control, Grunt Air has a tally ho on the traffic."

Roman relaxed and poured himself a cup of coffee from his old beat-up stainless steel coffee jug, just like the one Toothman had reflected on not long before. He loved flying in the predawn hours, watching the sun turn the rice paddies an astonishing shade of crimson. Below and to the right, he could just barely make out some villages with thin blue-gray lines of smoke coming out of the hooches. The day was starting for the Vietcong, too.

Everyone was quiet, even Red. Roman looked back at SP5 Espinosa, the Crew Chief, who was obviously memorizing every write-up the Bell Helicopter repair facility had entered into the aircraft log book. This was essentially a new helicopter after Bell had overhauled it from the skids to the Jesus Nut atop the rotor blades. The Huey was fresh off the Corpus Christi, a modified Navy ship at Vung Tau Harbor that had been loaned to Bell to handle depot-level maintenance for the terrific number of UH-1, AH-IG and OH58A helicopters operating in Southeast Asia. They'd done a good job on the old bird, according to Red. It handled well, he said, and he should know with over 3500 hours in Hueys and 58s, most of it in combat right there in the Mekong Delta.

Roman turned in his seat and glanced back at the door gunner, Charlie Day. The young man had already been awarded the Silver Star for heroism, along with the purple heart for the wounds he received in a combat assault in the Vietcong's backyard, a part of the U Minh Forest known as Ca Mau. Day had pulled his crew chief and copilot from a burning Huey after they were shot down. He didn't let his wounds keep him from coming to the aid of his two compadres, who were wounded more seriously than he was. If he hadn't been black, they would have given him the Congressional Medal of Honor. Another example of how insidiously racism worked in the military. *Sucks*, thought Roman. *Good crew, though. Should be an interesting day.*

Gradually, the area just east of Chau Duc came into view where the Mekong River divides into two main river channels. Farther along to the east, it divides again, into six or so smaller channels before it empties into the South China Sea down by Tra Vinh. It reminded him of the Mississippi River Delta, an area rich in oil and gas reserves. Briefly, the thought crossed his mind: What if this war were all about the oil? Johnson wanted the country so his buddies could come in after the war and make a fortune. It would be just like the son of a bitch to do that. Roman did not hate his enemy because they were soldiers fighting for their country and their beliefs, just like he was. But Lyndon Johnson? He was another story. So were people like Jane Fonda and Ramsey Clark. Roman seethed with animosity toward them and what they were doing. Roman respected Nixon, though. At least he gave a damn about the troops in Vietnam. That just left the other turncoat bastards, and Roman felt that he'd sacrifice the rest of his life in jail just to be able to personally shoot the treacherous pair. His malevolent reflections were interrupted by a call on the radio. He pushed his thoughts to the back of his mind, realizing that he'd have to concentrate on the here and now.

Paddy Control was warning them to stay north of Dong Tam because there was artillery fire in the area. Roman acknowledged and sat back once again to enjoy the flight. Through the early morning haze and smoke, the 230-meter-high limestone karst southwest of Chau Duc hunched in the distance, alone in the sea of rice paddies. Thanks to the insane Rules of Engagement in force at the time, the area, which was supposed to be some kind of governmental sanatorium, was a no-fly zone for the boys working the Delta. Maybe there was a nuthouse there, but the hill was also the headquarters of the local VC Regiment, lodged in a cave on the east side. The Vietcong didn't even bother to run for cover when a plane came by because they knew the Americans were forbidden to squeeze off as much as a single round in their direction. Another circumstance that made Roman seethe, in spite of the beauty of the dawning day. The restrictions under which they were fighting the war were more complicated than a Chinese crossword puzzle, and, to his mind at least, totally without reason or logic. The politicians sitting 12,000 miles away were unaffected by the loss of blood and life in Vietnam, yet they made rules that worked against those who did fight. Instead of winning the war, lives were being lost for no reason at all.

He tried once more to put his thoughts away, stepped on his floor microphone button and called Paddy Control to request a change of frequency. Once he'd switched to the universal frequency of 123.6, he radioed "in the blind" to any other aircraft in the area of Chau Duc that he was three miles east, inbound for landing." Air America answered him right away.

"Grunt Air Six, we're waiting on you with 4 PAX and enough weapons to start a goddamned war. The wind is calm with no other reported traffic."

"Roger, Air America. I hope you have the coffee and Danish ready," Roman responded.

"Sure don't. This is a Hardship Tour."

Staggs flew the approach beautifully, making a velvet-smooth turn to line up with the runway and starting his descent. Like most airfields in the

Delta, Chau Duc was set in the middle of a rice paddy, constructed to support the war during the early years.

The place was overrun with aircraft, which was extremely unusual. As Staggs dropped the Huey toward the runway, Roman spotted an Air America Pilatus Porter, six Cobra gunships from Blackhawk, and two scout aircraft. This was to be the combat air support for the food, medicine and fuel barge convoy going up the Mekong River in an attempt to liberate the people of Phnom Penh, in Cambodia. The NVA and Khmer Rouge had besieged the capitol to get it to surrender to the communists, but the city had held out. The Cambodians hated the communists and, thanks in large part to the supplies brought in by the convoys, their spirit had not been broken.

While the Huey was being refueled by a black-toothed Vietnamese truck driver, Roman spotted a familiar face not far off. It was Captain Jack "Briz" Brizgornia, the Air Mission Commander briefing a group of Blackhawk pilots. There was an interruption in the briefing as Roman approached the group with some back pounding, a few good natured curses, and introductions all around. Roman recognized many of the faces and some names from his short time at Vinh Long. He'd been assigned to Blackhawk on his first tour in Vietnam back in 1968. He was an old Air Cav brother.

"Captain Roman here is going to fly up the river with us," Brizgornia told the Blackhawk pilots. "He wants to blend in with us until he breaks off for a scenic tour of eastern Cambodia."

"Sounds like fun," put in a young warrant officer, obviously a newbie, fresh out of flight school at Fort Rucker. Then the kid noticed that Gunny Thornhill and his team were loading up Roman's Huey with a cluster of M-60s and tons of ammo. His face changed.

"As you can see, Mr. Watson, the Captain isn't going on a social call," said Briz.

Roman smiled. "Just your average tourist."

When Briz finished the briefing, he spent a few minutes with Roman, Gunny Thornhill and Red Staggs. Briz reeled off the Air Mission Control frequency and call signs while Roman jotted them down on the windscreen with his grease pencil. After some more handshakes and back pounding, Briz turned to his troops.

"Crank in two mikes." One sarcastic, half-assed salute to Roman and he disappeared into his aircraft.

"Okay," said Staggs, putting on a bad John Kennedy accent. "Let's do this with gusto and vigah."

Roman made one last check on the bungee cords that were attached to both sides of the chopper so Bravo Team could hang on while standing on the skids. Being outside the aircraft gave them better fields of fire than if they were inside. The two M-60 machine guns and one 40-millimeter grenade launcher on each side was decent firepower for a Huey. Not like the Cobra with its rockets and miniguns, but not bad. They had one more M-60 stowed inside, just in case.

Blackhawk took off first and started up the Kinh Vinh An Canal, which led to the main channel of the Mekong River. The convoy had already started up the river into Cambodia hours ago without air cover, relatively safe thanks to the wide open waterway with rice paddies on either side. Not much cover for the VC. They would come under attack farther on where the river narrowed and the banks were lined by trees. Roman didn't crank the chopper, preferring to wait and conserve fuel. He hit the battery switch on the overhead panel, and the radios came alive. Archangel was monitoring the frequency, and he told Alberts to let him know when the Blackhawks and the convoy got to Phum Son. The call came in less than thirty minutes.

"Six, it's time to rock and roll. Judging by the high volume of tracers, I'd say the CAV has reached Phum Son and engaged the enemy."

"Roger, Archangel, Six will report off. Okay, Red, crank this beast. The war awaits."

Fifteen minutes later, Roman spotted the Cavalry in the distance, flying an all-too-familiar racetrack pattern, attacking the tree lines along the river. Roman called Archangel and said that he was joining the fray, then raised Briz in his Command and Control ship a thousand feet above the action, where he was directing the gun runs.

"See that Cobra just starting the attack?" Briz asked. "Make your low level pass right after him."

"Okay, Red," Roman commanded. "Five feet above the river and 120 knots behind the Cobra. Thornhill, would you please throw some hot lead into that tree line?"

"It would be my pleasure, sir," Thornhill said on the intercom.

Staggs pulled his armored door plate into place. Huey pilots sat on a piece of armor plate and had two other pieces for "protection," one in the seat back and a sliding piece on the outside of the seat. The heavy metal stood up pretty well to small arms fire from AK-47s, but were worthless against larger weapons like the 51-caliber machine gun and the 12.-, 2- and 3- millimeter rounds.

Roman admired Stagg's command of the aircraft as he swooped down at maximum speed and leveled off just above the water. Glossy white spray splashed up behind them as they skimmed the surface. Just as they roared past the ambush site, tracers rushed out of the tree line toward them. Instantly, all four of Thornhill's M-60 machine guns opened up on the spots where the tracers were coming from. The firing stopped at once. They raced through the ambush untouched.

Staggs let the Huey climb to about thirty feet, which brought a sharp response from Roman.

"Red, flying this high in Laos will get you killed. Keep low!" Staggs seemed surprised, but came back down to about five feet.

Over the radio, they could hear Roman's friend Briz barking commands over the tactical frequency. Roman cleared with Briz, then contacted Archangel on the VHF.

They flew on. Roman had a good view up the river, squinting into the sparkles of sun that shot up off the brown water. In the distance, he could see the ferry crossing at Khum Prek Khsay. He had a feeling the Vietcong and NVA were waiting at the crossing in strength. He wanted to go across country before they passed that dangerous point.

"I have the aircraft," he said to Staggs. Staggs looked over to confirm that Roman did have the controls in his hands and then removed his own ,hands. "You have the aircraft."

Roman pulled the Huey to the right and lifted it over the tree line on the river bank and then back down to five feet in a long clearing. "Archangel, this is Six, we're off the river, out."

Archangel acknowledged with two clicks on the radio. They were keeping radio transmissions to the absolute minimum from that point on.

"We got gooks on the left," a voice said over the intercom. Roman didn't turn his head. He was flying at 120 knots five or six feet above the ground and couldn't afford the distraction. The shallow water and paddy dikes were whizzing below them at blinding speed.

"They didn't have a chance to shoot," the door gunner said, totally surprised.

"Okay, Red, you got us on the map?" Roman asked.

"Sure do, the lake should be just over that next tree line."

"Six, lake two klicks," came over the headset from Archangel. Roman acknowledged with two clicks. The tree line in the distance came closer and closer at frightening speed. Roman stared straight ahead as the trees got bigger in the windscreen, then brought the Huey up to skim over them with not more than two feet to spare. As he brought the roaring machine back down to barely above the lake, tracers snaked toward them from the right. Instantly, the machine guns responded. Instantly, the tracers stopped. At that speed and altitude, the enemy would not hear the Huey until about three seconds before the speeding machine was out of range. Not much time to aim and fire.

Roman banked, hugging the tree line on the east side of the lake, making it even harder for the Vietcong or NVA on the east to get a shot. There were Khmer Rouge in there, too, most likely, who were also more than capable of shooting down a Huey.

Red said, "Turn east at that cove coming up."

"Right," Roman acknowledged and six seconds later he pulled the Huey up and over the trees in a turn to the east and was back above the rice paddies. In a blur, he crossed Highway 106, pulling up suddenly to avoid a telephone line. In seconds, they crossed over another highway. It had to be Highway 152.

Red looked at his map. "On course, on time," he said, then continued, "I have Highway 244 on our left. It looks a little too close; how about coming right a half a klick or so?"

Roman was becoming concerned at the lack of enemy fire. Any time there's too little fire it meant they were gathered somewhere ahead. Toothman's treatise on war would say, "The enemy diversion that you're ignoring is the main attack." Roman wasn't sure that was true, but they were well into the game with no serious enemy threat. It made him cynical and pessimistic.

He didn't have to wait long before Murphy's First Law hit them all in the face. At 120 knots things happen fast, and they were right up on the road and the NVA trucks before they knew it. The enemy had seen them coming from a distance, giving them plenty of time to aim and fire, which they did, with joyous abandon. Tracers headed right for them and Roman jerked the aircraft to the right in a frantic evasion maneuver. He hoped the NVA would think he was going south and, if they reported it, the location of the CIA agents and Mrs. Holbrook might stay secret a little longer. Roman knew they'd taken a couple of hits but his instruments didn't show anything serious. Once across another tree line, he dropped down again and edged his course back to the east.

"Okay, Red, call the CIA and tell them we're five mikes out. Move to the highway."

"Roger," Red acknowledged, then made the coded call on the frequency being used by the agents.

"Six, you need to turn 15 degrees left or you'll miss the lake," Archangel said over the radio. Roman had almost forgotten about his eyes in the sky. He turned as directed by Archangel and raised the aircraft to miss the approaching trees. He was greeted by the welcome sight of the highway, then the lake. They had arrived.

"Okay, Espinosa, get ready to fuel." Espinosa and Day shifted to the right side of the bird with the four 5-gallon fuel cans, getting ready for the tactical landing and hot refueling.

The approach was low and fast. Roman raised the nose abruptly to kill airspeed, reduced the collective pitch and brought the Huey to a dead stop three feet above the highway, then landed. The four Bravo Team members jumped out on each side and positioned themselves to repel an enemy attack, but all was quiet. From the woods on the north side of the road, the two agents appeared at a dead run, helping Mrs. Holbrook between them. Quickly, Espinosa and Day closed the cargo door on the opposite side, opened the fuel cap, drained the JP4 into the tanks, threw the cans into a ditch, muscled themselves back on board and helped their new passengers strap into the two jump seats behind the pilots. They put Mrs. Holbrook in the center of the long bench seat at the rear of the cargo cabin.

"Go! Go! GO!" Espinosa yelled as soon as everyone was secure. Bravo Team jumped back aboard as Roman lifted the Huey and pushed the nose down to gain airspeed. He watched the airspeed indicator needle climb, then pulled the bird up and over the trees that lined the highway, racing back east, then turned quickly northeast. He had no desire to fly past the enemy, again. Red Staggs ran his finger along the map to track their course, showing Roman that he was approaching his next turn just south of Kompung Trach. Roman suddenly realized he'd forgotten to tell Archangel that the pickup was a success.

"Archangel, Six has three chicks." Archangel came back with two clicks, and then reported the pickup to Holbrook and the group at Tay Ninh, where they had been clustered around the radios in the Ops center since early morning. Somebody pounded Holbrook on the back, but he knew the worst part of the trip was still to come.

Just ahead and approaching fast, Roman spotted the heavy tree line lining Highway 243, which ran south out of the old Kompung Trach airport. It was a perfect spot for the NVA to bivouac and guard the area.

"Get ready back there," he yelled into the intercom. "I think we're gonna get a little heat." But he pressed on. It was the only way home.

His instincts were, unfortunately, correct. The NVA opened fire from the tree line on his left even before he got in range. He yanked the aircraft to the right to get away from the tracers. No good. He turned back on course and crossed the treetops, taking some branches with him in his skids when big, big tracers started whistling toward him. The scary thing about tracers is that for every bullet you see, there are four that you don't. *WHAP! WHAP!* Heavy stuff hit the chopper, opening big holes in the fuselage. It was 51-caliber anti-aircraft fire, hot and heavy, jerking the Huey in the air and opening large scary holes behind Stagg's seat. Two of the instruments on Red's side nearly blew out of the panel, showering his face with a whirl of glittering glass and plastic. Red jerked upright and dropped the map.

The sequence of events slowed down, as if in a dream. Usually, when accidents or disasters occur, people say, "It all happened so fast," but this didn't. The green Plexiglas above Roman's head blew apart, as did a part of his chin bubble, shards of plastic dancing in the air that rushed through the holes at 120 knots. Hurricane force winds hit Roman in the face. In the back, Bravo Team was firing every weapon they had. The noise, enhanced by the high-pitched shrieks of Mrs. John Henry Holbrook, was intolerable.

The intercom was full of chatter, everyone talking at once, pointing out enemy positions and trying to see where the tracers were coming from. Below, muzzle flashes from the small arms glistened at them. Anyone who has ever seen it will tell you they look like Christmas tree lights, but peace on earth was a long way off at that moment.

There was a scream. Someone in back had been hit. Roman felt sick to his stomach at the CLUMP of rounds hitting his vulnerable machine. What was left of the instrument panel twinkled with red and yellow caution lights. He felt the controls start to get sluggish, which meant a hit on the hydraulic lines. The bird stayed in the air, though, and they were almost out of range of the 51-caliber fire. Almost. But not quite.

SMACK! The rounds hitting Roman's side of the bird ripped the lower door hinge and door handle out of their mounts. Only the side armor plate saved him from taking a few himself. As they raced along, the door flapped in the strong wind, held in place only by the upper hinge pin. If he didn't remove it, the door might be ripped off by the rushing wind and fly into the tail rotor, which would put an end to them for sure.

In the back, Day saw the problem and grabbed the door from the outside while Roman struggled to reach down and pull out the pin, which released the door. Day threw the twisted metal down and away from the tail rotor, watching it spin downward and slice into the dense foliage behind their route.

They were shot to shit! Mrs. Holbrook's screams had died to low-pitched moans and whimpers as Roman put the chopper back down to run a few feet above the paddies. Such damage, and they were only under fire for five or six seconds. He had the bird down on the rice paddies again, away from the tree line. How far off course could he be?

"Hey Red, pick up the map and tell me where we are, damn it," he ordered. Red didn't move. For the first time, Roman took his eyes off the rushing landscape in front of the chopper and looked over at Skaggs. What was left of him.

Archangel had seen the violent exchange of gunfire and the erratic course changes the Huey was making, so he decided to abandon radio silence just for a second.

"Six, Archangel, turn left three zero degrees to get back on course." Roman, still looking over at the bloody, lifeless body of Red Staggs, gave

Archangel two clicks and brought the Huey up to an altitude of about 20 feet so he could get a handle on the damage.

Goddamn. Red's face and flight suit were covered in blood, and the stains got larger before his eyes as more crimson fluid seeped out of the lifeless body and spread into the fabric of the suit. Roman couldn't be sure, but guessed that a 51 round had come up through the bottom of the bird through Red's seat and stopped in his head. His eyes bulged. Blood poured out of his nose, ears and mouth.

"Espinosa," cried Roman, "pull the releases and get Captain Staggs out of the seat. He's dead." Espinosa rushed forward, knelt behind the seat and got to work.

"Six, Archangel. What's your condition?"

"We're in bad damned shape but flying so don't bother me except with course correction," Roman yelled, then regretted the outburst. "Sorry, Doug. We lost Red and one of the chicks took a couple in the leg. He'll live. The hen seems to be doing okay, considering. What have we got ahead of us?"

"There's that bad area east of the border to go through. Angle north about fifteen degrees to miss the worst of it."

"Roger that." Roman needed some muscle to push the cyclic to the left. The hydraulics were totally gone. He reached across the console and turned the hydraulics switch off to prevent an unexpected surge that could cause him to crash at this speed and altitude. The instrument panel was basically gone, leaving him no idea of what worked and what didn't. The surviving instruments told him the main generator was probably gone, but he was relieved when the standby kicked in. The cyclic control was thumping, indicating that the rotor blades had been hit.

Below him there were five big holes in the bottom of the floor, the metal forced up in jagged pieces looking like a rooster's head the way they pointed up. The fuel tanks were under the floor behind the two pilots extending to the back bulkhead, and Roman prayed they'd not been hit. The tanks were self-sealing for small arms but a 51-caliber round would do them in.

As Roman looked around to count the holes in the floor, he saw Spec 5 Brindle working on the leg of one of the CIA agents. The man was semiconscious, and his blood pooled on the floor of the cargo bay.

There was a solid line of forest ahead and it required Roman's attention. He put Staggs out of his mind, forced himself not to think of everything that was wrong with the chopper, and tried not to hear Mrs. Holbrook's horrified whimpering. The border was ahead and so was the last big NVA unit, which would be on alert by now, notified by the group who had just tried to kill him.

Keeping the top of Nui Ba Den to his left, Roman headed straight for the border. He had to cross it somewhere. As he tightened himself up, the Huey was making metal to metal noises. Something was falling apart, but he didn't know what and wouldn't know until it failed. What the hell.

"Heads up," he said over the intercom. "Get ready to shoot to the front when they open up. Make them pay a price for our ass." Just then the tree line started to twinkle like Christmas. The enemy wasn't wasting any time.

All hell broke loose as the M-60s on each side opened up. Even the CIA agent on the right side started firing the M-79 grenade launcher. Tracers flew in both directions.

He muscled the helicopter up, down, right, left, trying to evade the incoming fire. With no hydraulic pressure, it was almost impossible and took all the strength he had. Straining, pushing, he wrestled with the cyclic and rudder pedals even as his windscreen gifted him with new holes and new showers of jagged plastic. The only thing saving his eyesight was his helmet visor.

Large caliber hits! They came one-two-three, inducing ominous vibrations in the cyclic control and along the fuselage. Another blade strike. He looked left and right. The instrument panel in front of him and his late copilot was nothing more than a collection of busted gauges, shattered flight instruments and ragged, sparking wires. Normally, the instruments were used to provide critical flight and systems information but, in this case, they had served their cause better by stopping bullets and keeping Roman alive.

As he flew the wounded machine his mind was racing. Thought one: This thing will never hold together long enough to get us over the border. Thought two: Pretty soon we'll all be dead or captured. Thought three: I absolutely have to keep this son of a bitch flying just a little longer.

His left foot flew up off the rudder pedal, causing his knee to almost hit him in the chest. He looked down expecting to see blood, but there was none. The round had come through the almost-nonexistent chin bubble and hit the backside of the pedal, saving his foot and probably his life. He took his foot off the pedal and saw the round dent the bullet had made. Close. Too close.

The river was two klicks away. They were in South Vietnam and there was hope. Until, that is, the three men in black pajamas jumped up in front of the chopper, appearing out of the bushes, and started to fire their AK-47s directly at Roman. Sergeant Gryner, who was still outside the Huey hanging on the skid, squeezed off an M-79 grenade and the three men disappeared in gray smoke and red fire.

"Six, Archangel. Can you talk?" Alberts asked.

"Yeah, I think we're clear, right?"

"Yes, turn to one two zero degrees to the airfield."

Roman gave Archangel a rundown of the damage and his situation. No hydraulics. The bird has some severe main rotor vibrations. The tail rotor was also vibrating, but not too bad. One dead, one wounded, and one terrified and crying.

"I'll make a hydraulics-off running landing. I can't take any chances of this thing falling apart at the end." On the very edge of his hearing, Roman sensed a small "pop" under his feet and suddenly went cold. The sound could only be the tail rotor directional control cable. He put his foot on the left pedal and slowly applied pressure. No response. He slowly reduced his throttle control, which would give him some directional control thanks to the torque of the main engine rotation. Roman remembered another of Toothman's axioms of war, which was definitely not original with him. "There are no atheists in combat." Roman knew that it was true, and silently asked for divine intervention.

The black bulk of Nui Ba Den had gotten closer. Roman looked for the road that led to Tay Ninh. Route TL13 would put him north of the runway at Tay Ninh West. With no hydraulics and no tail rotor control, he needed room to maneuver. Turning to follow the road, he made whatever prelanding checks he could, which weren't many because he didn't have much helicopter left to check. He was going to tell everyone in the back to buckle up and secure the weapons in case of a hard landing, but the intercom was dead. So was the radio. So was his voltage meter, indicating that the last rounds had taken out both electric inverters, and the standby generator was failing. He was basically flying only on battery power. He had to get this piece of shit down before his luck ran out. Too bad, he thought. It was practically a brand new bird. They'd just flown it out of the showroom a few hours earlier.

As he started to turn for his approach two klicks north of the field at AP Binh Luong, the rotor vibrations became so severe that they blurred his vision. He lined up on the runway and pushed down hard on the collective pitch to start a gentle descent to the runway. Two ambulances and several fire trucks were waiting on the west side of the runway.

He was lucky. The helicopter continued to respond to his control inputs, coming down smoothly, making headway toward the landing site. At the last moment, Roman pulled the collective pitch up slightly, allowing the helicopter to literally fly on to the asphalt. He skidded along the surface of the runway until he pushed the collective down hard and stopped the skid at the left edge of the runway.

They were down, thank God, and most of them were safe. He shut down the engine without waiting the customary two minute cool down and stabilization time suggested by Bell. The bird was worthless anyway, and he wanted out of it right now.

Before the blades had stopped rotating, the aircraft was surrounded by ambulances, fire equipment and a dozen people. Roman looked back over the bird just in time to see Archangel land. As he climbed down, he saw Toothman and the Eight Eight crew as well as the Air America bird from earlier that morning. John Henry Holbrook had no sooner approached the cargo bay door then his wife fell out of the chopper and into his arms. The CIA agent was on his way to the dispensary with his wounded partner but took a moment to turn toward Roman and give him a thumbs up. The younger man would make it.

The medics already had Red's body out of the cargo bay and in the second ambulance. Roman tightened his jaw and ground his teeth as the ambulance pulled away. Ryker and Toothman had already started counting bullet holes. There were plenty, big ones and little ones. He knew that not even another trip to the Corpus Christi would bring it back to life.

Aft of the cabin area, Bob Gedeon measured the size of the big holes with a thumb and forefinger. He looked at Roman and said, "I guess we need to decline acceptance on maintenance grounds." Then he cracked up. Roman couldn't remember ever seeing Gedeon laugh that hard, but he bottled it up as Colonel Sweeney approached, his face the color of a bullfighter's cape and his expression far beyond apoplectic. He was almost trembling.

Gedeon quickly said, "I signed for the two birds before he got there. We're in the right according to Air Force regulations."

Roman nodded, turned to Sweeney, and rendered a salute.

"Well, Captain Roman," Sweeney began without preamble, "the condition of this helicopter will be noted in the general court-martial charges I intend to file tomorrow with the Commanding General. You stole this aircraft and flew it without flight-plan authorization into a known hostile area in Cambodia, which is a restricted area. You're finished and I'm going to love watching you go to Leavenworth."

Sweeney had much more to say, rambling on with much pointing of fingers and other uncontrolled gestures, but Roman was looking over his shoulder at the Air America pilot walking toward the group.

The pilot said, "Which one of you is Captain Roman?"

"I am," Roman said raising his hand and interrupting Sweeney's hysteria.

The pilot held up a piece of paper. "I have a message for you from the Commanding General."

"Go ahead, read it," Roman said.

"Coroneos sends, 'Roman, you are another Heinie Aderholt! Great mission. Guardian Three will debrief your mission and brief next mission at Udorn, 30 December 1971 at 0900 hours, base CO office. Good hunting at the Oriental tonight. PPC.' I assume you understand the message, sir."

"Loud and clear," Roman said giving Sweeney a big smile. Toothman slapped Abeel on the back and said, "Outstanding!"

"You can get all the messages from the Commanding General you want, Roman," yelled Sweeney. "I don't give a crap. But I'm telling you one thing right now—"

"You must be Lieutenant Colonel Sweeney," the Air America pilot interrupted. "I have a message from the Commanding General for you, too."

"Well, I'm glad he knows I'm out here doing my job," Sweeney said condescendingly.

"Yes, sir, he certainly does. I'm to take you back to Tan Son Nhut immediately where you're to pack your belongings and report to Lt. General Hamilton at 1600 hours before your flight departs at 2000 hours tonight. You're being reassigned as commander at Shemya Air Force Station."

Sweeney smirked at Roman as he said, "I'm getting a command." Then he turned to the Air America pilot and asked, "Where is Shemya?"

"If I remember correctly, sir, it's at the very end of the Aleutian Islands. A combination weather station and spook monitoring point for keeping tabs on the Russians across the Bering Sea at Kamchatka. You go to the end of the earth, look over the side and you can almost see Shemya. It's 1800 miles west of Anchorage. Actually, it's closer to Japan. One might say it's a bit…remote."

Sweeney opened his mouth to say something, closed it, then opened it again. Veins stood out on his neck and forehead and he made little blubbering sounds in his throat. His face, which couldn't possibly have turned any redder, did. Roman, in a rare show of friendship, grabbed Sweeney's hand and shook it heartily.

"Ho! Ho! Ho! Colonel. Merry Christmas from everyone here."

Roman grabbed his helmet and flight bag out of the dead Huey, trying not to notice Stagg's blood all over the cockpit. He asked Toothman if he could make Bangkok all right without him.

Toothman laughed and said, "Get the hell out of here, Heinie."

With that, Roman walked to the C-47 where Doug Alberts slipped a red metal plate into the VIP identification plate holder. The plate had captain's bars painted on it. Roman smiled and hit Alberts in the shoulder as he boarded.

31

Victims of Bangkok

The Oriental Bar
Bangkok, Thailand
28 December, 1971
Late evening

By the time Jan Toothman and Eldon Barnes, the new Grunt Air Eight Eight, arrived at the Oriental Bar in Bangkok's infamous Patpong district, there was absolutely no sign of sobriety in the place. Grunt Air was totally drunk and in full control. Jan said to Barnes, "I bet I can join them faster than you can."

"Bet is on," Barnes replied as he grabbed a bottle of Johnny Walker scotch out of the bartender's hand and drank a third of it before he stopped to catch his breath. "Get your wallet out Toothman, I'm on the go."

Toothman poured himself a glass from the bottle and, looking for Roman, wandered over to Abeel.

"He's on his third mission of the evening," Abeel said, pointing to two lovely women at the far end of the club. "There was mission number one in the white dress and the one in the red was number two. Now, he's with one in a blue dress. He's very patriotic, you know," Abeel said laughing.

Suddenly, the place went quiet. Toothman looked toward the door. Two Americans in civilian clothes stood just inside the club, glanced around, then left. The noise level gradually increased.

"Who was that?" Toothman asked.

"That was Heinie Aderholt and General Manor," Abeel replied quietly under his breath.

"Holy shit." Toothman started forward to follow the two men but Abeel grabbed him by the arm. "Bill, I gotta meet those guys," Toothman said, trying to pull away.

"Sorry, Jan," Abeel said sympathetically. "Even Aderholt can't know about us."

The most unbelievable thing about the evening is that everyone survived. The party lasted until a little after three in the morning, and Grunt Air personnel gave a new meaning to the phrase "crash and burn." At 1100 hours when they assembled at the flight line for the trip back to Udorn, they were all still alive or at least showing weak signs of a pulse. Many of them looked like rejects from the Bataan Death March. They barely had eight hours bottle -to-throttle, but they managed to get the birds in the air.

By 1600 hours all aircraft were back at Udorn, even Toothman and Barnes, who had to make a fuel stop at Korat. When First Sergeant Woods asked where the second aircraft was, CW4 Gedeon replied, "We declined acceptance because of excessive bullet holes."

The next morning, 30 December, 1971, was just another day at Grunt Air. Archangel was airborne at 0500 hours as usual, collecting the reports from the preceding two days. Most were nothing special, except for the report from Echo about the arrival at the Rock House of the two Air Force captains and one lieutenant from the Tollbooth. Roman took that to mean the NVA were consolidating positions and preparing for the next phase of Campaign Z.

That day, Roman and his key staff members held a three hour briefing with Major General Mattix in the base commander's secure conference room. Abeel, Ryker, Alberts and the newly arrived Captain Best, whose team had been replaced early that morning by Bravo, went over the operation as a whole, the apparent plan of enemy action, and their strategy for the raid on the Big Casino. General Mattix sat through the briefing saying almost nothing. When everyone had said their piece, all eyes turned toward Mattix, and they waited.

"Thank you," he said. "Roman, the old man gave you a go for the mission, don't screw it up." That was it. He stood up to leave, then turned back into the room and added, "General Geiger is very proud of you boys. Very proud." And he was gone.

After a short latrine call and coffee, they went back to the secure conference room to put the meat on the operational skeleton for the Big Casino plan. During the coffee break, Colonel Odom mentioned that some of the radio navigation aids would be relocated due to incursions by sniper fire and infiltrators. Things were heating up around Long Tieng. "Let me know if there's anything I can do," he said before he left.

The five men reviewed the plan step by step, in punishing detail, for over four and a half hours before they felt confident of success. They were counting heavily on the NVA leadership following their usual procedures and habits. Roman would help them along by leaking a few pieces of intelligence.

The important factor was to get the NVA to move the Big Three to the Big Casino before 20 January, 1972, because the moon would be at its most favorable phase between 18 and 22 January. They had decided not to try to pull the prisoners out of the Rock House because there was too much troop activity in the area both day and night. Around the Big Casino, however, there were very few units within four miles, most of them being support units at Sam Neua.

"The only combat unit in the area is the 148th Regiment," Best reported. "It's deployed along the road from Sam Neua all the way to Muong Soui, 44 miles to the east and 18 miles to the southwest. They're spread way too thin to be really effective." In Sam Neua, there were too few troops to respond and, according to the U-2 photos, they were pretty much sitting still. The real battle was over 130 kilometers away, but the roads were long, treacherous and in terrible condition. That made Sam Neua truly a rear area safely controlled by the NVA. The enemy was sure to believe that the Americans and General Vang Pao weren't a credible threat.

New Year's Eve wasn't any more of a holiday than Christmas had been. The crews worked all day. Ryker's maintenance teams were getting the aircraft in shape. A big mission was pending, and the condition of the birds meant success or failure. Failure meant people would die, and that was something everyone in the unit took to heart. Over the past several months, they had become family, as men in combat will do. After flying all the rescue missions for Holbrook, Odom and the others, they were finally going to extract some POWs, which is why they were in Southeast Asia in the first place.

Caldwell, the CIA station chief at Udorn, was in the Air America offices drinking coffee when Roman dropped in. Roman was hoping that the good turn Grunt Air had done for Holbrook might be translated into a favor from Caldwell. He didn't think it was likely, but it was worth a try.

"Coffee?" asked Caldwell when Roman walked in. "Something a little stronger?"

"Coffee's just fine, thank you," Roman said, greeting Mr. Eastwood, who was also crammed into the tiny office. Suspicious of the warm greeting, Roman put his hand on his wallet to see if it was still there. It was.

"Well, Dan, how goes the crash site survey project?" Eastwood asked with a smile that would disarm an army unit.

"Just fine, sir. Thank you."

"What can we do for you?" asked Eastwood. Caldwell was silent but smiling.

"Well, sir, I was wondering if it would be possible for me to meet General Vang Pao in the near future?"

Caldwell reached over to a phone and whispered something into the receiver. He continued to talk while Eastwood said that he saw no problem with Roman meeting Van Pong. It might take a few days to arrange, but he'd try.

Caldwell put down the receiver and asked, "Would 1500 hours today be convenient?" Roman was stunned.

"Yes, sir, that would be incredible. Whatever time you say."

"May I suggest we go in an Air America aircraft so we don't attract attention," Eastwood said.

"Great. What time do we leave?"

"Be here at 1400 hours. Are you bringing anyone else?"

"My Ops and Intel officers, if that's okay."

"Done."

A few hours later, Roman found himself in the jump seat of the Air America Pilatus Porter on the way to Long Tieng. He realized that the CIA spooks knew what he'd done for Holbrook and were finally giving him the support he had always wanted, or so it seemed. When they landed at Long Tieng, a jeep took them over to the headquarters of the famous General Vang Pao.

Two of the General's senior officers met them, saluted, shook Roman's hand and then led them into the damp, dimly lit, heavily sandbagged building.

The sat for a few moments exchanging small talk and stood when the General entered the room. Vang Pao did not look well. Pale and coughing, he was obviously suffering from a serious cold, more likely the flu.

"Captain, what can I do for you?" Vang Pao was a man of few words and got right to the point. So did Roman.

"Sir, my unit is called Grunt Air. We're going to conduct a crash site survey in the north near the old Heavy Green Site Eight Five in the next two or three weeks. We need three things from you, if possible. First, I need to be able to land my C-47 at Lima Site Five Niner to drop off fuel next week. The fuel will be for our Hueys that are range-limited. Second, on the day we go into the area, I request that one of your forces clear and hold Site Eight Five for a period of 16 hours, starting at 1500 hours the afternoon we go in. Third, I need one of your cargo aircraft to go to Lima Site Five Niner at precisely 0700 hours the next morning and bring back eight or ten passengers to Long Tieng or Padong, depending on the enemy situation. I know that's a lot to ask at this time, but I assure you … it's very important." Roman stopped talking and waited.

Vang Pao had very dark eyes, almost black, but they were red and watery as he stared at Roman. He blew his nose and was about to speak when Eastwood piped up.

"Sir, we'll supply the aircraft, if necessary."

"You're going into that new camp for prisoners, aren't you?" Vang Pao asked.

"Sir," Roman said as he sat up and twisted in his chair, "My unit is not authorized by Ambassador Godley to do such operations. I'm simply conducting crash site surveys."

Vang Pao leaned back in his chair and burst out laughing. It was probably the first good laugh he'd had in a long time, considering the state of the NVA offensive.

"Captain," Vang Pao said, becoming serious once more, "Stop giving me shit. You think I don't know who you are and what you've been doing? Your reputation has preceded you. If you want to take that big of a risk, I'll support you as much as I can. What do you want us to do with the POWs when we get back here?"

"They'll have a cover story that basically says they escaped when their truck had an accident. They then evaded the enemy until they got to Lima Site Five Niner where they were found by your friendly forces. Their recovery will be your success. If Grunt Air is exposed, if higher command or the Embassy find out, we're done for." Roman knew that he'd just blown his cover in front of the CIA and Air America. He prayed that they wouldn't send the information forward to the Ambassador, or even higher. That would kill the entire operation.

"Can I count on you not to say anything about this to your people?" he asked Eastwood and Caldwell.

"Say anything about what?" Caldwell replied. "I was having a cup of coffee outside with Eastwood when you talked to the General. Far as I know, you were discussing your crash site surveys."

"The coffee was cold, too," said Eastwood. "And no sugar."

"Thanks. I mean it. The lives of those POWs depend on our success. These men are in a position to spill some very sensitive information, and if we screw this up and can't get them out, the B-52s will blow them off the planet."

Caldwell stuck his hand out, "We're with you." Eastwood nodded.

Vang Pao stood up. "I need one day notice to arrange what you need. You let Mr. Caldwell know as soon as Grunt Air has a date and time." He shook everyone's hand, blew his nose again, coughed a few times and left.

On the flight back, Roman had no choice but to outline his plan to Caldwell and Eastwood, counting on them to keep quiet. They both agreed and reassured him that the plan sounded feasible.

"Holbrook will know about this," Eastwood said, "but he owes you big time. He's behind you all the way. He won't say a word."

Roman breathed easier hearing that. He needed the secret kept just a little longer to get those boys out of the cages.

It was almost dark as the Pilatus Porter pulled up near the Air America operations office. Roman could see his birds way down at the end of the ramp. Crews were still working on them.

When he got back to his office, he suddenly realized it was New Year's Eve and that a drink or three was in order. He couldn't find Toothman or Abeel at the Air Force O Club, but the bartender gave him a note. "Join us at the Air America Rendezvous Club. We were hijacked by the spooks. Abeel."

The next day, Roman vaguely remembered arriving at the Air America club, but couldn't seem to recall what happened after that.

⬡⬡

32

What Russian? I Didn't See a Russian.

Grunt Air Headquarters
Udorn Air Force Base, Thailand
1 January, 1972

Just before midnight on New Year's Eve, the PAVN infiltrators got close enough to Long Tieng to send in four 81-millimeter mortar rounds and disrupt the already subdued celebration. Of course, the Ravens, based at Long Tieng, didn't miss a drink because they were as brave as they were crazy. Throughout the country, anybody who flew any sort of aircraft held the Blackbirds in the highest regard. The Blackbirds flew low and slow all over Laos in light observation aircraft directing artillery fire and air strikes. They were easy targets with a high mortality rate, but they never gave up on their vital mission.

The following morning, in spite of their hangovers, Grunt Air made its appointed rounds. Alpha, Delta and Echo Teams had come in for rest and recreation, not to mention a trip to "The Ville," the strip of bars just off base. Bravo was still keeping an eye on the Big Three at the Rock House. Charlie Team was watching traffic around Easy Street.

Headquarters at 7th sent word to be on the lookout for reported Russian advisors. A Hmong unit in the southeast area of the PDJ reported seeing two Russians with an NVA colonel. Both the U.S. Embassy and Washington considered the report to be very questionable, but Vang Pao vouched for the reliability of the unit commander who made the report. Vang Pao, sick as he was, considered it an insult that his unit commander's report was being questioned.

Roman directed Archangel to relay the report exactly as reported by the Hmong unit commander. He believed in Vang Pao, who was known to refer to those fools at the embassy as "paper warriors" or "girl singers." Since joining the 7th Air Force, Roman had not seen anything to indicate that Vang Pao was mistaken.

More U-2 photos of Sam Neua and the Big Casino came in on the courier flight that day and were immediately reviewed by Abeel and Roman for any sign of change. Had the perimeter wire been moved? Were there more guards? Buildings that didn't show up in previous photos? They looked for anything that could affect the mission, and continued going over the plan, again and again.

It was the last night in the bush for Charlie Team before they were to be replaced at daybreak by Echo Team. As the darkness gathered around their hiding place on the hillside, Sergeant Richardson thought he'd end this tour in the bush with some good intel for Roman. The only way to do that was to go down to the intersection of Route 7 and 71 and grab a prisoner or two. Just before 2200 hours, an NVA command car came, driving unescorted from the east on Route 7, and stopped to drag a fallen tree limb off the road.

It appeared the branch had been blown onto the road by an artillery impact, which is exactly what Richardson intended. The driver got out of the car and strolled around to the front just as Sergeant Mason stepped out of the shadows, wrapped a garrote around the man's neck and pulled as hard as he could. He was so fast and so silent that the two officers in the command car saw nothing as Mason dragged the body into the trees.

As Mason did his deadly work, Richardson and Sergeant Ramirez jerked open both vehicle doors and put the muzzles of their CAR-15 rifles into the faces of their new prisoners. Their scout, Corporal Wang Sing Khan, came up behind and barked a few words in Vietnamese. The officers scrambled out of the car and were forced to lie on the ground where Ramirez did an expert job of tying and blindfolding them. Richardson led them off into the woods while Mason drove the car down an obscure trail and out of sight. After brushing away the car tracks and footprints, he followed the team up a dry creek bed to a spot where they could climb back up to the hilltop they had occupied for the past week.

"Holy shit," said Richardson as he looked at the two captives in the dim light Ramirez played on them. "I do believe we've bagged us an NVA colonel and a Russian major. What the hell's he doing this close to the action? Too bad nobody here speaks Russian."

Khan took the colonel off into the bushes to work his magic on him, leaving Richardson to stare and puzzle at the Russian. "This SOB's a big problem," he told Ramirez. "They're gonna miss him right away, and we don't need a bunch of troops out here looking for him."

"Why don't we do that thing we learned from Captain Best?" Ramirez asked. Richardson suddenly remembered. They stripped the major of his uniform and boots, took out all the maps and other documents he was carrying, leaving only his billfold and Russian military identification card. Ramirez and Mason went back to the road, put the uniform on the dead driver, drove the car to a spot where the NVA would find it easily and rolled it over on its side.

"Now for the good part," Ramirez said. He looked around for an unexploded artillery shell, which he was sure he'd find since ordinance of that type was lying all over the area. He slipped the shell under the driver, slapped a piece of C4 on it, backed off to a safe distance, and blew the car and driver to shreds.

When the NVA found the wreckage, they would think the major had been the victim of a direct hit. There would be no way to identify the body other than uniform remnants and identification card, if any of it survived the blast. They'd report the find up the line and wouldn't bother to search.

While his men went about their assigned tasks, Richardson sat down on the ground in front of the blindfolded major, now wearing only his underwear. He struggled to recall the few words and phrases of Russian he'd learned while stationed in Fulda, Germany on the East German border.

"*Kak vas savut?*" he asked. The major broke out laughing.

"Sergeant, you speak Russian like a Spanish cow," he said. Richardson sat back on his heels, startled. The accent wasn't so great, but the grammar was perfect.

"What are you going to do with me? You can't kill me because I'll be missed shortly, and these hills will be full of troops searching for me."

"For now sir, I'm just going to wait." About thirty minutes later, there was a loud explosion down at the crossroads.

"Hear that?" asked Richardson. "As of now, you no longer exist. They'll find your shredded uniform and body parts and report you dead in hostile action." The Russian, who had been sitting up straight in spite of his bonds, slouched. The part of his face that was visible below the blindfold went so white that Richardson could see it, even in the dim light.

"So? Now you will kill me?"

"No, sir. That's not my job or intention. I'll wait for instructions from my boss. Now, I suggest you roll over on your side and sleep until dawn."

Two hours later, Corporal Kahn came out of the woods holding a handful of NVA papers and his notes from his interrogation of the NVA colonel.

"Need a few minutes to figure this out. We should be extracted to Two Zero Alpha immediately."

"Why?" asked Richardson.

"First, we must get this Russian to Vang Pao. It will be important to him, and your government won't allow us to keep him or interrogate him

properly. Vang Pao can do whatever he wants to him. Also, he'll be very grateful to you for doing him this big honor of delivering the Russian to him. Second, there is much information here about Campaign Z ... too much to send
by radio. Third, the late colonel told me about the POW camps southeast of
Sam Neua. There are some caves that we'll want to bust. There are over one
hundred U.S. prisoners being held in the Ban Nakay area caves. I have some
details on the caves and prisons. What he told me about the Big Casino we
already knew. But the prisoners in the caves are a different matter. We have
got to get this to Roman and Seventh."

"Okay, Kahn. I'll make that recommendation," Richardson said as he
looked up at the predawn sky. "I'll get the message ready for Archangel." He
knew that anything about the Russian had to be coded, but some of the report
could be in the clear over the secure FM radio for brevity.

About ten minutes after Richardson had completed his coding,
Archangel came up on the radio. He quickly gave his morning report and
asked for a response to his coded message. Archangel acknowledged with
"Wait."

After what seemed like forever, Archangel came back.

"Grunt Air Six agrees with your recommendation. Expect extraction
at 0715 hours. Go a half klick north of your reported position to a clearing on
the north side of the hill."

"Roger. Charlie out."

Just like a scheduled German commuter train, the Huey popped over
the ridge to the east of Charlie and landed quickly in the narrow clearing
where Charlie Team was waiting. All five were on board in less than five seconds and the chopper was in the air again. Roman made a hard right turn to
the northeast until he was out of sight, then turned right again to a course that
would take them east of the known anti-aircraft fire. Once south of the major
enemy concentrations, he turned to the west for Long Tieng. During the flight,
Richardson and Kahn told Roman every detail of the mission. Roman was
amazed at the amount and quality of information Khan had extracted from the
NVA colonel.

The Russian was a big deal, an absolute Intelligence coup. Bringing
him in would vindicate Vang Pao's commander and justify the General's support of his subordinate.

As usual, there were many aircraft flying in and out of 20A, so Roman
flew the standard approach over the top of Control Point Peter and called
Long Tieng Tower. Before he landed, he called Vang Pao's command frequency and had the radio operator tell the General that Grunt Air Six was going
to bring him a present.

They landed near Vang Pao's Headquarters and the usual staff came to meet them, only the General wasn't there. Inside the HQ, Roman reported to the colonel who was coordinating matters for Vang Pao, whose flu had probably turned into pneumonia by that time. When Richardson came towing the almost nude Russian, the colonel stood up in surprise, then collapsed into his chair.

"Sir," said Roman, addressing the colonel with the highest level of formality and courtesy, "would you send General Vang Pao my compliments, and tell him that Captain Dan Roman and Grunt Air are making him a present of this Russian major we captured east of the PDJ four hours ago." The colonel, his eyes wide and jaw slack, ran from the room. Ten seconds later, Vang Pao came shuffling in, a blanket wrapped over his head and shoulders. He forced a smile as he saw the Russian, then looked at Roman with an expression in his eyes that no words could capture. Roman had made a friend for life.

"Sir, for obvious political reasons, we cannot report this matter to our Headquarters. But I would appreciate it if you would share with me any important information the Russian may give you."

"Captain, you'll receive a complete report by tomorrow afternoon." Then Vang Pao said something Roman couldn't understand, and two soldiers frog marched the Russian out the back door.

"Thank you, Captain Roman," Vang Pao said between coughs and sniffles. "Best of luck on your mission. We'll be ready for you."

Back at Udorn, Roman briefed Abeel, then called both Kingfish and Fiddler. He told them about the Russian, and the vote was unanimous not to send that information up the line.

"We can mention him as another sighting reported by Hmong forces," offered the Fiddler. "That lets Vang Pao make the big announcement, if he wants to."

New Years had come and gone. Late on 3 January, 1972, Roman got a call from General Geiger on the secure line.

"Dan, I got a fragmented report, or maybe it was a rumor, that Vang Pao caught a Russian. Any truth to it, or should I ask? It does sound like one of those crazy things you'd pull. Or is it?" Here it comes, thought Roman. He decided to be "honest."

"Sir, the absolute truth is that I saw a Caucasian in T-shirt and white underwear being taken into Vang Pao's headquarters yesterday at 0830 hours. He did not have a uniform on so I couldn't swear that he was a Russian, sir." Geiger laughed, but only briefly.

"I'm glad as hell it wasn't an American unit taking him prisoner. That would make the political shit hit the fan."

"Yes, sir. I'm sure that's true."

"Dan, where did you … I mean, where did Vang Pao capture him?" the General asked.

"Sir, I wasn't there when he was captured, but I believe it was at the Route 71 and 7 junctions near Easy Street," Roman said with mock sincerity in his voice.

"Anyone else get caught that night I would want to know about?"

"Yes, sir, an NVA colonel who was being interrogated when he accidentally fell off a cliff. A full report will be forthcoming."

Geiger responded, "That'll be fine, Dan. You know this sounds a lot like something else that happened recently. One of those crazy Ravens couldn't get authorization to utilize a BLU-82 bomb on a critical bridge and road junction in the PDJ. The Embassy denied the request, so the Raven codes in a message through Cricket to the Commanding General himself requesting the use of a nuke on a set of coordinates. The Commanding General thought you had made the request, especially when they found out the coordinates were for the American Embassy in Vientiane. He said, 'Roman has finally found the right enemy target.' Of course they found out who sent it and denied the request, but we all thought it was pretty funny."

The temperature and humidity were both lower than usual the morning of 4 January 1972. Roman sat in on Lieutenant Ditton's briefing, where he was getting ready to take Delta Team to replace Bravo, who was still keeping tabs on the Big Three at the Rock House.

At breakfast with Colonel Odom, Roman found out that Caldwell and some other CIA types were on their way to see Vang Pao.

"He's sicker'n shit," Odom said. "And he's in the dumps because his troops lost the PDJ."

"I was up there with him on the second," said Roman. "He seemed okay to me, but his cold was getting the best of him."

After breakfast, Roman received the morning report from Bravo on the Rock House. There had been a good deal of activity at the camp, but it did not focus on the prisoners. Search teams were all around the camp until they discovered a blown-up car and body near Easy Street. The teams hauled the car to the Rock House compound.

At 1000 hours, Archangel took off with Roman, Toothman, Abeel and Best for a quick visit to Lima Site Five Niner. They flew at 10,000 feet on a westerly route toward Luang Prabang to avoid any anti-aircraft fire or other unwanted attention.

The four AK-47-toting Hmong soldiers who greeted them were accompanied by the scariest woman on the planet. She may have been in her thirties but she looked at least fifty. Whatever teeth remained in her head were stained black by the betel nuts she'd been chewing all her life. She recognized Toothman right away because he'd brought her two quarts of bourbon on his last visit. The strangest part was that she was one of Vang Pao's wives, put in charge of the strategically located Lima Site Five Niner because she was reliable and had a reputation of being a fearless fighter.

Captain Muang handled the communications in Hmong because it was easier than talking through interpreters. In the meantime, Spec 5 Burke unloaded the goodies including four quarts of Jack Daniels, canned ham and turkey, a pouch of Redman chewing tobacco and three cases of Fresca, which made the woman smile even more broadly. It was a sight they didn't particularly care to see.

Captain Muang and Abeel discussed the current situation with her while the others checked the seals on the cache of jet fuel they'd prepositioned earlier. Roman was relieved to see the fuel hadn't been tampered with. They spent about an hour walking around trying to decide whether the tall trees at the end of the runway would be a problem for the C-47. They decided in the affirmative, so Alberts and his crew had brought along four rolls of primacord and C-4 explosives. With two of the Hmong guards following, they hiked to the end of the runway, wrapped each of the 12 troublesome trees with primacord and C-4, then blew the trees out of existence. It would give them the clearance they needed for takeoff and landings, especially at night.

Back at the small hut that served as headquarters, Captain Muang told Roman that the woman was prepared to help them at any cost.

"She does not know our objective but knows her job," Muang said. "Vang Pao has ordered her to give us complete cooperation. Securing Site Eight Five will be no problem. There are only platoon-size and an occasional company-size patrol coming out of the west from Sam Neua. The couple of outposts to the north and northwest of Sam Neua are very lax because the American war is a long way south. They sleep at night and never patrol after dark. She'll have two of her recon teams scout out the area between Site Eight Five and the new prison camp. She said the two outposts would be neutralized the day of our mission. She asked about the camp, and I told her it would be nice to have some information for any future operations. She thought that was a good idea, just in case, as she put it. She'll send the information to Vang Pao Headquarters at Long Tieng in four days. I told her we'd come back for it and would bring her more supplies. She said she needs a couple cases of hand grenades and some beer for her troops. She's not going to share her bourbon. She asked for a few other items I can get her at the Base Exchange."

"Terrific. Now ask her about those two North Vietnamese aircraft out back."

The aircraft were partially hidden behind the operations office in some trees. One was an old Russian Antonov AN-2M "Colt," a large, single engine, bi-wing transport plane built around 1947 and licensed to several other Communist countries. It could carry 12 to 14 combat soldiers into short, unimproved airfields. North Korea used them extensively in their spy insertion missions into South Korea. It was slow, sturdy and reliable. The other aircraft was a Russian built MI-8 helicopter, a heavy-lift, multi-role machine that NATO called the "HIP." Typical of Russian brute engineering and design, it looked like a Greyhound bus with rotor blades. It was a powerful twin turbine helicopter that could easily fly on one engine if necessary, carrying 24 combat troops in either day or night operations at a cruising speed of 140 mph.

Roman looked on patiently as Muang and Vang Pao's wife carried on a lengthy singsong conversation in Laotian. Finally, he got his answers.

"The helicopter had a mechanical problem and landed here about 15 months ago," Muang said. "The people here pretended to be friendly and helpful, so they could get some information. The pilot called his base in North Vietnam for a repair part, and the Colt brought it in with a mechanic. Vang Pao's troops waited till they fixed the helicopter, then they killed everybody and hid the two aircraft.

"Since they were flying out of North Vietnam, no one from the local Pathet Lao or NVA at Sam Neua ever came looking for them. The NVA must think they were lost in combat. Vang Pao's wife thought his troops could use them, but they don't have anybody to fly them. They've been sitting out there a long time."

Roman's mind started racing with all kinds of ideas. He took Toothman and Alberts with him to look over the strange birds, impressed that the locals had kept both machines clean and ready for use. Roman and Toothman sat in the cockpit of the huge helicopter trying to figure out the strange dials and controls. Of course an airspeed indicator was the same in any language, but they felt like kids with a new toy as they pointed to one switch after another guessing what function each might have. Fortunately, Roman found the two operator's flight manuals and looked through them briefly before leaving the helicopter with the manuals tucked into his flight suit.

Alberts climbed out of the Colt. "It's in good shape," he said, "ready to fly. Ya know, I actually flew one of these in the Dominican Republic back in '62. It's the slowest damn airplane in the world. We got it down to 35 knots and it still stayed in the air. Great aircraft for Special Operations in an area like Laos or Korea."

Roman thanked Vang Pao's wife and her men and got into their vintage 1942 antique C-47 for the flight back to Udorn. The takeoff was a typical scary short-field takeoff, even with the trees knocked down. Roman was thankful that Alberts could handle the old bird so well.

First Sergeant Woods stopped the group as soon as they arrived in the hallway of Grunt Air Headquarters.

"Sir," the First Sergeant said, "the CIA just medivaced Vang Pao to the hospital here with pneumonia. Story is, he got pretty shook up at Padong when he was checking on preparations to use it as a staging base. His troops were shot up real bad, and some fourteen-year-old girl picked up her wounded father's AK-47 and told him she was ready to fight and die. The General was so sick that the sight of the girl did him in. He collapsed and started crying, so they're pumping him full of antibiotics over at the hospital. They tell me he could be back on duty in five or six days."

"Thanks, Top," Roman said.

Just after launch on 7 January, 1972, General Geiger called.

"Dan, you haven't heard about this, but there's been a civilian employee sending our personnel information to the north. The Army Criminal Investigation Detachment at Long Binh knows who he is. General Abrams wants to get him right away, but General Coroneos has talked him into holding on a few days. We might be able to use him in one of our covert ops."

"That's good, sir. I'll have a detailed reconnaissance report on the Sam Neua and Big Casino camp tomorrow. If it jives with what we already know, it might be time to get the NVA to move the prisoners to the Big Casino." Geiger was silent for a moment.

"Okay. First, tell me who's doing the report—or did you con the NVA to do it for you? Second, how do we get them to move the prisoners? You got one of your people on the NVA general staff?"

"Well, sir, I tried, but Captain Muang said he didn't like the hours. Vang Pao's wife is in charge of Lima Site Five Niner. She's got two recon teams checking out the area and the camp. I'll get her report tomorrow. I don't think it'll show much troop concentration west and north of Sam Neua. There won't be many guards at the camp because of how it's built and because it's so close to the main headquarters. If I'm right, we'll want to put a 'secret' document in Major Cody's personnel file showing that he's being reassigned to Fort Bliss because of his past work in air defense artillery design. Our spy should find out about this and get it on the road to Cu Chi overnight. Just to be sure, we'll send a second copy to the Fiddler. He can try to get it into a courier's pouch or drop it on a VC working in his compound. Either way, Hanoi will learn about it in short order. They'll transfer the Big Three and hopefully all six prisoners north to the Big Casino. With the planted info, Major General Thran

Van Ho will have the justification to move them on a priority basis. Even if they're at the Big Casino for only one night, we'll get them."

General Geiger was silent for a moment. "Jesus, Roman. I'm glad you're on our side. You're one devious son of a bitch. This all sounds good to me. I'll run it by Mattix and the Commanding General, so you'd better plan to come down here tomorrow after you get the report. We'll want to go over everything one more time. But let me ask you this. What if they get sent straight to Hanoi and not the Big Casino?"

"I don't think that's very likely. General Ho and Captain Ho have already stuck their necks out on these three, especially Cody. I doubt they'll let them get to Hanoi, and out of their direct control, without some more interrogation of their own. If they have no value, they'll just shoot them and avoid the problem. If they are valuable, they'll get lots of brownie points with the brass. I'm sure about that."

"Glad you're so confident. Okay, I'll see you tomorrow, say 1500 hours?"

"We'll be there, sir."

Roman's next call was to Fitzmorris, giving him a heads-up on his trip to Tan Son Nhut the next day. Then he briefed Abeel, Toothman, Best, Muang, Alberts and Ryker.

The First Sergeant came in just as the conference was breaking up. "Sir, we just got this Red Cross message about Mr. Carter. His parents were killed day before yesterday in a car wreck. Mr. Carter has three school-age brothers and sisters. He'll need to take emergency leave. He only has two more months on his tour. Personnel at Long Binh recommends that he be transferred to Ft. Stewart. His family lives close by. I'll need your approval for the transfer."

"Yes, of course, Top. Poor bastard. I hate to lose another copilot, especially now, but go find him and meet me in my office. I'll break the news to him there. Top, get his clearance papers started. We'll process him out from here if Long Binh agrees."

"They have, sir. I have the personnel information and transfer codes already. I knew you'd release him."

"Thanks, Top." Everyone cleared out, and Roman spent a few minutes alone in the silence preparing himself for one of those duties that unit commanders hate to do. It was never easy to write to a man's parents or wife telling them that he'd been lost. But, at least, the grief took place far away. Now he had to tell a man to his face that his parents were dead. He closed his eyes and took a few breaths. This would be a tough one.

Chief Carter knocked on the open office door waiting for Roman's nod to enter. He walked to the front of Roman's desk, saluted and said in a formal military voice, "Chief Carter reports to the Commanding Officer, sir."

Roman returned his salute and motioned him to take a chair. "Brad, you and Dorsey have done extremely well with the tough missions and increased responsibility I've given you. Now I must advise you of an even greater challenge."

"We're ready, sir," Carter said with confidence and pride in his voice.

"No Brad, this is your mission only," Roman said in a calm, authoritative voice. "You are going to assume command of your family back home."

Carter sat looking at him with utter confusion on his face. Roman went on sympathetically, "Brad, there is no way to make this easy … your parents were killed in an automobile accident yesterday."

Carter's confident and proud demeanor changed to shock and disbelief as his shoulders sagged and his eyes filled with tears. Before the stunned Chief Warrant Officer could respond, Roman continued. "You must go take care of matters at home now. Your brothers and sister need you. This will be a much tougher command position than any I could give you here," he said, feeling a lump form in this throat.

Carter was trying not to cry as a tear slipped down his left cheek.

Roman continued, "You're on the milk run to Saigon that leaves in two hours. The First Sergeant has a seat for you on the Freedom Bird that departs at 2200 hours tonight. You'll be stateside in 26 hours," Roman concluded with a smile as he stood and extended his hand.

Carter stood up and shook Roman's hand, nodding his understanding of the situation. "I'm going to miss you, Brad. We all are. You're a good pilot and a fine officer. I hope that we'll serve together again someday," Roman said with genuine sincerity as he walked Carter to the door. "Stop by before you go, okay."

Carter looked at Roman with warmth and respect, and nodded silently as he left the room.

∽✑∞

33

I Always Wanted a Wife with Her Own AK-47

Lima Site Five Niner
8 January, 1972

8 January, 1972, was another normal morning, at least by war standards. Not much on the morning report Archangel got from Delta. Toothman was making preparations to switch teams around, replacing Delta with Bravo and inserting Charlie up at Lima Site Two Niner to watch the North Vietnamese traffic coming and going along Route 61 and bagging a prisoner or two in each direction to get the latest. It was one of Corporal Khan's favorite jobs because he burned with hatred for the NVA. He never talked about it, but the rest of Charlie figured he and his family had suffered greatly at the hands of their brothers to the north.

News came that sappers had infiltrated Two Zero Alpha the night before and blew up part of the ammo dump. Long Tieng could not hold much longer.

Archangel set the C-47 gently down at Lima Site Five Niner and, along with Abeel, got a better-than-expected, detailed report from Vang Pao's wife, who wore her AK-47 like Parisian women wear a designer bag. They dropped off the personal items from the Base Exchange along with some hand grenades, and told her they'd need her help on Site Eight Five within two weeks. "No sweaty dah," she replied with a blackened smile.

They flew back to Udorn and picked up Roman and the others for the flight to Tan Son Nhut. Abeel spent the whole time in the air making an intense study of the reports. When they landed, they got a hearty greeting and crisp salute from Major Fitzmorris and Captain Mansen.

"I'm honored. I didn't expect to see you two," Roman said as he got into the lead staff car. Fitzmorris just smirked at him.

"I'm taking you to see the Commanding General. He especially wanted to talk to you before you meet with Generals Geiger and Mattix. Now, what's happening in Laos? And what about the Big Casino?"

When the Commanding General walked into the conference room, he brought everybody with him. General Geiger, General Mattix, Colonel Odom, Colonel Herbert and Lt. General Hamilton, the Vice Commanding General of 7th Air Force. None of them sat.

"Dan," started the Commanding General, "I got some orders from 1st Aviation Brigade." He unfolded the paper he was holding, squinted and read.

"Headquarters Department of the Army, General Order Number such and such," he said skipping the formalities, "does hereby promote Captain Daniel James Roman to the rank of Major, effective 2 January 1972. Congratulations, Dan. I'm honored to present this to you. Now I have to go handle some pesky Rules of Engagement crap that just came in from the Pentagon."

Handshakes all around plus a sealed letter from Colonel Odom, which he handed Roman before leaving the room. "This is from Vang Pao. I have no idea what's in it but he said you'd know."

"Thank you, sir, and thanks for coming down for this."

"Wouldn't have missed it for the world."

Odom had left him the translated report from Vang Pao's wife up at Lima Site Five Niner and the summary of the Russian major's little interview. Roman's eyes lit up. Vallory Alexander Kosigan was attached to the Foreign Assistance Directorate of the GRU, deputy commander of a support team training and assisting the NVA in Campaign Z. The report contained 30 pages of personnel breakdowns, lists of materials Russia was providing, inside Intelligence about the larger prisoner of war camps in the Ban Nakay area of Sam Neua, with details on the prisoners' physical treatment, food, medical, and specific numbers of U.S. personnel at each site. A gold mine.

"We may get our guys home, yet," Roman said, handing the papers to General Geiger. "Maybe a hundred or more."

"Holy smoke," General Geiger mumbled. "I want to get this over to the CIA. For some reason, they've been more help lately. What do you think, Major?"

Dan thought Geiger was talking to someone else. He'd never been addressed as "Major" before. Finally, he answered.

"I'd like to keep the POW report to ourselves for now, sir."

"Okay," Mattix said, "let's get down to details. Tell me every weak point of your plan." Roman did.

There were six operational Hueys, but they were short of pilots. Hetler, Fondren, Robinson and Staggs had been killed by enemy fire. Carter had emergency leave coming up.

"I could use two copilots, sir."

"Done. I know Colonel Herbert and Major Fitzmorris can locate two good ones for you. Now, let's go over all the hot stuff you got from Vang Pao's wife." It took over an hour to get through it all and review how it would affect the mission, but they generally agreed that the situation was the same as before. The camp was lightly guarded, and the nearest significant combat force was over seven klicks away.

"It's not a walk in the park," observed Mattix.

"But it's not a suicide mission, either," Roman said at once. "As long as we keep the element of surprise."

"Which you could lose at any point in the mission," Mattix said. "When you go into Site Eight Five, when you put the recon teams in, when the Teams move to the camp, when they take control ..."

Mattix had a right to be concerned. The recon teams were small, and if they ran into any real number of NVA, they were screwed. The aviation unit would be 15 minutes away.

"Gentlemen," General Mattix said, suddenly becoming even more serious. "We've been talking about this here at Headquarters for weeks, and we decided that if you want to bow out of this mission, you can do so without any questions or second thoughts. It's totally your call. Any of you want to scrub the mission?"

Roman looked around the table. "Jake?"

"Major, we've been watching those poor bastards go through living hell for months. If anybody tried to scrub this mission, my boys would revolt."

Roman purposely didn't look at Toothman. "Jan, what about your aircrews?"

"Sir, most of us are too dumb or egotistical to know when to say no. Besides, we think it'll work."

"Mr. Abeel." Roman still looked down at the wood grain tabletop in front of him. "Can you offer any reason we should back out of this mission?"

"Not from an Intelligence standpoint. Sir."

"Captain Ryker, can the birds do what we need them to?"

"Factory fresh, sir." He tried not to smile too hard.

"There's your answer, General. We're going in within the next ten to fifteen days."

"Captain Ryker," General Geiger said, "I hope you can lie that well at our collective court-martial."

General Mattix said the parting words. "If this works, we're going to ask the Ambassador for formal authorization to go after other camps, and especially those caves. We know about 200 POWs in Laos who need to come home. We'll inform the Commanding General of your positive response. Ryker, when the war's over, you should get a job selling used cars."

When the Generals were gone, Colonel Herbert raised his eyebrows at Ryker. "Why can't you be one of the pilots?" Ryker told him that he could, but only in an emergency. He would ride in one of the choppers with a tool kit and spare parts, making emergency repairs during the mission, if necessary.

"Two pilots, it is," agreed Colonel Herbert. "Roman, as a new major, you're buying dinner for these lying pirates tonight. I strongly recommend a great French restaurant downtown called La Cave."

La Cave was almost just that, located in the basement of an old French Colonial building on Tu Do Street. It seemed almost as if they'd stepped into Paris itself, except that the waiters, dressed impeccably in traditional French style, were all Vietnamese. Roman noticed that the wine list was especially impressive.

Roman pointed to a Chateau Lafite Rothschild. "No have!" the waiter responded. He went to a Chateau Latour, and got the same result.

"Well, what *do* you have?"

The waiter flipped the list to the back page, showing Roman two badly typed entries on a sheet of paper. The waiter enthusiastically recommended a 1972 vintage. Roman thought for a second. It was the evening of 8 January, 1972. Had the wine been bottled that day?

When the waiter brought the bottle, sure enough, the label, which smeared when Roman dragged a moistened thumb over it, said 1972. "Anybody got the guts to drink this?" he asked the assembled diners. They all said yes. The "wine" was total suicide, but everyone drank it except Alberts, who was the designated pilot that night.

Things at Long Tieng were getting worse. Sappers were making night raids against the perimeter and lobbing mortar rounds into the airfield and surrounding buildings. The night of 9 January, 1972, some forty commandos from the DAC Cong Battalion penetrated the substantial defenses of the Long Tieng Valley and airfield. They fired B-40 rockets at the CIA hooch and Vang Pao's house, and knocked out the ULR radio station. Two hand grenades did minor damage to two of the Birddogs flown by the Ravens.

Two days later, on 11 January, 1972, elements of the 148th Regiment, 14th Anti-Aircraft Battalion and 355th Independent Regiment struck Long Tieng from the north, northeast, and east in a well-coordinated attack. Long Tieng was in danger of falling to the NVA. To make matters worse, the NVA pushed the BC617 off Charlie Alpha, which was Air America's highest Chopper Pad on Skyline Two, and dug themselves in to hold the high ground.

Things didn't get much better the next day, with one exception. GM30 was inserted at the base of Skyline One and regained the Charlie Echo helipad and the western side of Skyline Ridge.

Two Zero Alpha had become unreliable as a staging base. Roman sent Barnes and Ditton out to Padong to make sure the pre-positioned fuel, ammo, tents and equipment were still there. The enthusiastic Sergeant Major who had guaranteed the safety of their supplies was still there, and so was all the equipment. He'd come through, and found himself rewarded with a bottle of Jim Beam and a carton of Winstons. Another friend for life.

Fiddler called Roman the morning of 13 January reporting a Songbird intercept from Hanoi. The high command was concerned that Cody and the other prisoners had made statements under strenuous questioning that were inconsistent with their personnel files. The NVA sources in MACV Headquarters were directed to check deeper into their background ASAP.

"Does that blow your plan?" Fiddler asked.

"Not at all. It's the break we've been waiting for," Roman said. "Thanks, I'll get back to you."

When Roman assembled his team in the Ops room and told them about the message, Abeel pounded the wall with his fist. "We've got them!"

"Okay, Abeel, get that "secret document" we've been working on over to the CID OIC at Long Binh. He's expecting it. We'll get that into Major Cody's file today. Alberts, fire up the C-47. I'll arrange ground transportation. Let's go."

Their plan was a long shot. The North Vietnamese knew that the resources of the Americans allowed them to attempt extremely elaborate deceptions, such as forging very official-looking paperwork. But this time, Hanoi needed answers right away. Their spy in the Long Binh personnel office took a chance, made a quick copy and hustled it out of the building without getting caught. The CID and military Intelligence filmed him every step of the way. As he left to send the precious papers on their way to Hanoi, he had no idea that when he returned, the rest of his life would be nasty and short.

Watched by the CID, the copy left Long Binh at 1805 hours carried by three separate couriers on motorcycles, and ended up at the underground command post at Cu Chi by 2140 hours. It took them over three hours to encode and transmit it. The hook was almost set.

The secure phone rang at Roman's desk less than six hours later. It was the Fiddler, in a very good mood.

"Hey, new Major, you win the prize today. Hanoi acknowledged the message at 0615 hours to Cu Chi. There was a second message to commander 148th Regiment at Sam Neua to transport POWs at the Rock House to Camp 711. All coordination and transfers to be made through Senior Captain

Nguyen Bac Ho, and to be accomplished no later than 18 January 1972. The commander at Camp 711 is to make preparations for the housing and support of four special interview personnel who will be arriving on 20 January 1972. Details to follow."

"Sensational. Thanks, Warren. Now, all we have to do is deliver." When he swiveled around in his chair, Abeel was standing in front of his desk, staring at him.

"Well, Mr. Abeel, we're gonna make a pizza delivery the night of the 19th. Better notify Vang Pao."

Back in Ops, Roman checked on the three birds Air America had requested to support the insertion of GM30 and Unity troops on Skyline after a B-52 strike on the north face of the Ridge. The troops reclaimed the Charlie Whiskey helipad, but it had cost them —35 killed and 69 wounded. Grunt Air ferried the casualties until sundown and returned to base very depressed.

As expected, earlier that morning, Delta had reported the 0500 hours departure of the POWs toward Sam Neua, which caused Roman to pull everyone into the briefing room. The place was wall to wall.

"Gentlemen," Roman said, "effective immediately this unit is on stand down for all outside assistance. We can't take any requests for help because we need to prepare to go shoot crap at the Big Casino in 24 hours. Guns and helicopters need to be ready for maximum effort. All passes off base and leaves are cancelled. Stay away from other base personnel. The success of this entire mission depends on surprise. If we lose it, we die, and so do those poor bastards we're after. Captain Toothman, you'll recover Delta as soon as this meeting is over. Captain Ryker, all birds belong to you for maintenance as of now, except the one mission to recover Delta.

"It's time to earn our combat pay. There are eight men out there who deserve our very best effort. You know what you need to do."

The room snapped to attention as the commander of Grunt Air departed. Everyone in the room could feel the energy and excitement as they left to swarm over the flight line in preparation.

Fiddler called and confirmed that the Big Three had arrived at the Big Casino at 0205 hours, 19 January, 1972. Plus the troops on Skyline had driven out the remaining NVA and now secureky held helipad Charlie Whiskey and the rest of the high ground. Once again, Skyline Ridge was firmly under control of friendly forces. That meant Grunt Air could stage through Two Zero Alpha instead of Padong. Every little break helped.

They'd leave at 1000 hours, taking the Hueys and recon teams to Two Zero Alpha two choppers at a time, so as not to attract attention. They would refuel at Long Tieng and rest until it was time to slip into Site Eight Five. Everything was go.

Roman had still not seen the two pilots Fitzmorris and Herbert had promised, and time was getting short.

"What time do you leave for Two Zero Alpha?" Fitzmorris asked him on the secure phone.

"1000 hours. Briefing at 0800 hours."

"You'll have two pilots by then, but I can't guarantee what you'll get. I can promise they'll be Huey rated with some combat experience."

Great. They were just about to launch, having lived with the planning of the mission for months and, at the last minute, he was getting two copilots who had no idea what was going on and had "some combat experience."

Roman left orders with the Charge of Quarters to wake everybody up at 0430 hours for a 0530 meeting in the Ops room. He tried to squeeze a few more minutes of sleep out of the night, but couldn't.

∽∾

34

One Cuban, but no Cigar

Bill Cody's right shoulder hit the rough, bloodstained, wooden floor first, then his cheekbone. They had his wrists in some kind of metal ratchet device, like handcuffs only not, so it took some time to work himself to his knees. He kept his head lowered in the gesture of "respect" demanded by his brutal captors. Even so, his eyes darted around the room to see what he could. In the corner, an Air Force First Lieutenant lay bleeding from his ears, nose and mouth. His eyes were open but he wasn't seeing a thing. Was he even alive? Yes. He moved just a bit and let a low groan escape his lips. He was missing teeth, and his hands and elbows were tied together behind his back. Cody knew from experience how much pain the man must be suffering. On the right, he saw the boots of another man in a brown uniform. He was new and not Vietnamese. Cody couldn't see any higher than the man's knees. A fat , sandaled foot slammed down before his eyes. Sergeant Pig Face.

"Good morning, Major Cody," said a voice. No! Not Captain Ho. Cody remembered him well from his stay at the Homestead. "I appreciate your position of respect. Please accept my apologies for the blood still on the floor, but your Australian comrade, Major Smythe-Gordon, wasn't as respectful. As far as the young Air Force officer in the corner, he was disrespectful and an uncooperative guest."

Sergeant Pig Face reached down and helped Cody to a chair, yanking him upwards by his hair and punching him in the face.

"This is Major Rojas from Cuba. His glorious country has joined our fight against Yankee imperialism." The Cuban was round-faced and sweaty, with an elaborate black mustache and an inevitable cigar between his teeth.

270

The cigar was unlit ... for the moment. The cruelty in his soul seeped out through his skin. Cody could smell it.

"Now, let us review your preliminary personnel record. We know a great deal about you, but not enough. You will tell us about your criminal acts against us in the past. We already know your name, rank, serial number and date of birth. You have told our comrades at the Homestead that you were a part of the 3rd Battalion 56th Air Defense Artillery Battalion. This is a 40 millimeter anti-aircraft unit on track vehicles which give anti-aircraft coverage and direct fire support for 1st Division supply convoys. Is that correct?"

Wild Bill Cody slumped in his chair, feeling more scared than wild at the moment. Captain Ho had already demonstrated in punishing detail that he had been well trained and was capable of unthinkable acts of torture. This session could easily be worse. Cody's mind raced through what he'd already "confessed" to Ho. At any cost, he could not reveal he was a part of the surface-to-air missile branch of Air Defense Artillery, particularly that he was involved with the SamD Program. It was a new branch, and they probably didn't know a lot about it, yet. What had they learned from their spies in Saigon? If he told them a story, would they buy it?

"Air Defense Artillery. Yes, sir." He could hardly speak.

"Your job in that unit?"

"Operations Officer S3, sir."

"I can see we're going to get along quite well," Ho continued. "Let's talk about the Hawk Missile System."

Here we go again. This is where Cody sheds his skin. Cody tried to prepare himself for the pain to come.

"I've never been in a Hawk unit, sir."

His head exploded as Sergeant Pig Face hit him from behind. He flew off the chair smashing into the floor on exactly the same shoulder and cheekbone.

"You've been in the service over 12 years," Ho stated mildly. "You were in a Hawk unit."

"No, sir," Cody said as Pig Face jerked him upward again by the metal collars around his wrists, pulled his arms toward the ceiling and dropped him back into the chair.

"I was in field artillery before air defense artillery, sir," he managed. "It's a new branch. They put us old field artillery types into forward area weapons like the 40 millimeter Duster and the newer Chaparral-Vulcan units. I have never been in a missile unit."

"Sergeant, it seems the major does not remember the penalty for lying."

One solid blow and Cody was back on the floor, dropping all his weight square on his backbone. The Sergeant stood on him and cranked the wrist cuffs a notch tighter. Ho waited until Cody stopped screaming and said, "Now, let's try again."

Stay with it, Cody reminded himself. "I've never been in Hawk, sir." The Cuban looked down at him through dark slitted eyes. Pig Face gave Cody another notch to his infected wrists. Blood flowed. Another scream.

Ho tried another angle. "Tell me about your training in Hawk or Nike Hercules Missile Systems." Cody knew he was fishing.

"No training, sir." The Cuban lost his patience. He found a piece of rubber hose on the floor and slammed it down as hard as he could on Cody's bleeding wrists. Bone showed through. The Cuban hit him twice in the shoulders, splitting the skin and letting more blood turn bright red on exposure to air. He then hit him once in the back of the head. Captain Ho signaled him to stop.

"The Hawk missile, Major? Tell me now and this will stop."

"No Hawk unit. No Hawk school, sir." He said it between gasps for air.

"Do you expect me to believe that you are a commissioned officer for 12 years and have not learned about Hawk or Hercules Missile Systems?"

"Yes, Sir. I was field artillery. Then air defense." He could barely see through the fog of pain and when he did make out objects, he didn't see them in color.

Ho made another motion, and Pig Face hauled the Air Force officer from the corner where he had managed to work himself into a ball. Pig Face deposited the officer in another chair opposite Cody. A few quick turns of baling wire, and the First Lieutenant was secure.

"It has become obvious," noted the Captain, "that your own well-being is not important to you. I admire that. However, this young Lieutenant might feel differently. As ranking officer, you are responsible for him, yes? Now, you were attached to what Hawk unit?"

It took all the strength Cody had left. "Hawk unit. No. Never."

The Cuban swung the rubber hose like Roger Maris going for the fences and hit the Lieutenant square on the bridge of the nose. Blood and tissue splattered across Cody's face and onto the walls some distance away. The man did not make a sound. He was in a coma and the next shot would probably kill him.

"Oh, my," Ho's soft voice had taken on an extra edge of sarcasm. "We need to get him some medical attention, don't we? We will, as soon as you tell us the truth. Once more, what training do you have in Hawk missiles?"

"None, sir." Cody stiffened as Pig Face gave him yet another notch on the metal cuffs. He almost passed out when the Cuban hit the Lieutenant in the face with the hose once, twice and again. He still didn't move.

Rojas shoved the Lieutenant's chair closer to Cody until the young man's ruined face filled what vision remained to him. Then he spoke. His English was accented but clear.

"You Americans." The Major spit on Cody. "You bring sickness to Cuba. And hunger. You should all die. But, I give you one more time to tell the truth." He pulled his pistol from his worn black belt.

Cody was barely conscious but he knew what was going to happen. He would be graciously given a choice. Either deliver his country's very latest tactical air defense secrets and its theater deployment strategy or watch this mad bastard spray the the young officer's brains all over the walls. He himself would be next. He closed his eyes and saw the faces of Carol and the kids.

"This is your last chance, Major," said Ho. "Tell me of your training in Hawk missiles." He made the question sound very final.

"No Hawk training. Sir. Field artillery training, sir. And Forward Area Weapons."

BLAM! The Lieutenant's face and brains sprayed toward Cody, coating him in sticky red blood. Cody started to spin into hysteria, but his mind saved itself, and he passed out instead.

Not even the Cuban's five or six punches to his face would revive him.

"Mierda," said Rojas. "He has gone away. I hope he comes back."

He turned to Captain Ho and lit his cigar. "You know, I don' think this man have the information you want. Anyway, he is finish for couple of days. Then maybe his brains is mix up."

"Major, do you know the English word 'hunch'? No? Then call it professional instinct. You understand? He is not telling us the truth. Amazing. I have never met one quite so strong."

"But look at his file." Rojas pulled a tattered brown folder off the sticky table. "Says nothing about missiles. It says field artillery and forward area weapons. He says field artillery and forward area weapons. Here is the record."

"The Americans are very good at faking this kind of thing. They're trying to protect him. And what he knows."

"You watch too much James Bond movies. You think they make fake files for all soldiers? He is a Major in field artillery, no mas. I think we stop with him. Give more time to other prisoner. They know more than this pendejo and they will talk. I tell my superiors this is over."

"As you like, sir. We're shipping him to Camp L711 at first light, anyway. Headquarters is sending a group of experts. They will butcher him."

"So? You do your best. A good job, I think. But he knows nothing. *Nada*. You have my compliments. I enjoy to watch your methods."

"At least, I have one more night with him before the boys from Hanoi get to him. Thank you for your help. A good job on the Lieutenant."

"Better luck next time," said Rojas with a smile. He had one dead American Lieutenant with his brains dripping down his shirt to his left, an insensible American Major, half out of his mind from abuse, to his right. He beamed. *"Buena suerte."*

"One request, Comrade Major. Please do not send your report until after tomorrow night. I want another chance to get the truth out of him."

"Certainly," said Major Rojas. "If you will allow me to watch."

∞∞

35

Two Peter Pilots, Just Summer Help

Grunt Air Headquarters
Udorn Air Force Base, Thailand
19 January, 1972

The mission wouldn't have a chance in Hell if the element of surprise was lost. That's why Roman was up at 0500 hours, working the phones, calling Fiddler, calling Kingfish. Was there any last-minute information that might affect their plans? The intelligence had to be right on. Not like that raid on Son Tay, when they went right into the outskirts of Hanoi, carried out the rescue mission perfectly and found all the cells empty. Great planning and execution ... but lousy intel.

The air was super-charged in the Ops room, the chatter level so high that nobody saw him come in. Good, because he wanted them doing exactly what they were doing. He surprised Abeel with a tap on the shoulder.

"That bridge east of the camp? How big is it?" Abeel could see the concern on Roman's face. The bridge was the only access to the area from the east and it carried supply trucks day and night. It was the one wild card that worried Roman.

"Don't worry, the four satchel charges will take care of the bridge," Abeel observed, looking at the map. Blowing the bridge would prevent any combat support from getting to the camp from the North Vietnam side. There was nothing they could do about troops responding from Sam Neua to the southwest. "Air Force and Navy have been trying to hit the damn thing for weeks. The other bridges, too. But look where they are." Roman had studied the map before but there was no harm in looking at it, again. There's no such thing as too much planning for a mission like this. "The whole bridge area is shielded from air attack by these two karsts. Our charges will take out the bridge for a couple of weeks, I guarantee."

Roman punched him once on the shoulder and moved on, pacing through the room like he an expectant father. He was, in fact, thinking of the little battle axiom Toothman had said during one of their many strategy sessions. "It's a good plan, but the beauty of an attack plan is in the eye of the beholder." *Better check my part of this thing, again, just to be sure I'm not blowing smoke up my own ass.*

The entire group moved to the B Frame for a quick breakfast, cooking it themselves because the Thai cook wouldn't get there until 0630 hours.

"Captain Roman?" The voice came from behind his back. He turned in his chair to discover Colonel Herbert and Major Fitzmorris standing at the door. "Your two replacement pilots have arrived." They'd put warrant officers W1 bars over their rank insignia. Roman realized he was sitting down and jumped to his feet. There was a full colonel in the room and the Aide de Camp to the Commanding General, at that.

"You now have two qualified 'Peter Pilots,'" Colonel Herbert announced to the room, "and I *expect* you to use us as copilots."

It was a good thing Fitzmorris spoke next, because Roman couldn't get a word out. "We're combat and Huey qualified, we know the details of the mission. Best two copilots you could ask for."

"Sir," Roman croaked to Herbert, "does the Commanding General know you're here for this mission?"

"Well ..." the Colonel scratched his head. "Yes and no. He knows I'm here to observe, but he thinks I'm flying with Archangel. As an observer, it's my opinion that the best vantage point is inside one of the mission aircraft."

"All due respect, Colonel, but you'll be wearing stars in a year. Why would you want to do something this ..."

"Dangerous? Stupid?"

"That was the word I was looking for, sir. If you get shot down and captured ... the bastards will pry the secrets out of your head with a crowbar."

"If your plan is as good as it looks, the risks are minimal. Don't think I could stay on the sidelines for this one."

Roman looked back and forth between the two men, Fitzmorris looking like he dared Roman to give him grief. "Okay. If you two are the best the American military can scrape up, we'll have to settle. Captain Toothman, 'Warrant Officer' Fitzmorris will fly with Lt. Dorsey and this one," pointing to Herbert, "will fly with you, on one condition. Jan, this is a direct order and I mean it very seriously. If you get shot down and are about to be captured, you and your crew are directed to kill Colonel Herbert. He's not to fall into enemy hands under any circumstances. You have a problem with that?"

Toothman just stared, then nodded. So did everyone else. They tried to avoid looking at Herbert until he cleared his throat.

"That's the way it's got to be. Frankly, it's better than getting tortured."
Everyone was silent.

"Coffee?" Roman chirped.

"Here is the camp as of 1610 hours yesterday," began Roman, starting the briefing exactly at 0800 hours. "A U-2 flew over it, and you're getting copies of this shot. Based on the photos and intelligence from Vang Pao, we've made the drawing here on the blackboard. There's a single, ten-foot-high, concrete and stucco wall with the traditional broken glass embedded in the top, covered by barbed-wire. It's 90 meters long running east/west and 65 meters deep, broken into three sections. Here's the admin office." Roman pointed to the southeast corner of the map. "There's one guard and, we're sure he'll be alone when we go in."

Roman took them through the place meter by meter. Two doors in the administration office, a double front door that goes into the open air reception area and one smaller door on the side. Only the outer gate on the right side was in use. The west gate was disabled except when trucks passed through. There were two tables and six chairs in the reception area for processing incoming prisoners.

"The southeast side is the sleeping quarters for the guards on duty. There will be four troops sleeping and possibly a sergeant of the guard, but we're told he doesn't always sleep through the night. Watch out for him. According to our recon teams, he's huge and he thoroughly enjoys beating the hell out of the POWs.

"In the center part of the compound," Roman said pointing with a black grease pencil, "you have the kitchen and mess hall on the east side. It's open air to the camp side and there's this wall in front of it. These two structures near the west wall are the isolation room and this larger building with four interrogation rooms. Our sources tell us they're very well equipped with the latest torture devices." The men shifted uneasily in their seats.

"There's a bamboo fence between here," Roman jabbed with his grease pencil, "and the rear prisoner containment area. There are two gates, one here by the interrogation area and the second in the center of the fence. There's a guard tower at the southeast corner of this area," Roman said as he pointed to it. "The trees come to within 10 meters of the tower. The guard has an AK-47 and a machine gun of some kind.

"In the prisoner containment area, we have a well and tank in the center and a cistern over here at the southwest end of the confinement building. The building has twelve cells on each side. We believe the Big Three are in the inside cells on the east end, but we're not sure, so you'll check every cell. We will not miss anyone who might be there. See this guard tower at the northeast corner? The trees come within 10 meters at the rear wall and 15 meters on the east wall, and they're really dense.

"The lights along the wall are turned off at night. The cell doors are lit by two floodlights. That's good news.

"We've made a slight change to the plan. When Three and Six Six take the teams in, the door gunner and crew chiefs will stay back at Site Eight Five to save weight. We're sending all five teams in on two birds for surprise and safety. They won't refuel until they get back from the insertion.

"Sergeant Major Panfil will go with Bravo, Charlie, and the scouts from Delta and Echo on Three. Alpha, Delta and Echo will go in with Six Six. The birds are real heavy with this loading. Take only what you absolutely need.

"This karst should minimize the helicopter noise at the compound. When you hit the ground, pay attention to where you are because we're putting you in at the alternate extraction point. You'll go in two groups, spread out as usual. Bravo and Charlie, with Delta's scout, will take the west route around the karst, in position by 0400 hours. Bravo on the west side. You'll take out the west guard tower, then over the wall. Charlie, with Delta's scout, will take out the guard in the admin office. Alpha, Delta and Echo will go the east route. Alpha will be on the northeast side and responsible for the northeast guard tower, then over the wall. Echo will take out the sleeping guards. Remember, the sergeant of the guard may or may not be there. If he is, kill the sadistic bastard. Delta will proceed to the bridge. When the aviation team is five mikes out, blow the bridge. Then lay out the bean bag lights on the road in front of the camp. Take up a defensive position fifty meters to the west of the pickup point in case of east bound traffic.

"Bravo and Charlie, take the isolation and torture buildings. As we have planned, Alpha will take the front cells and Echo take the rear. From the time we execute to pick up should not take more than 20 mikes, 15 if possible. Remember, *silence*! Guns make noise, knives don't. Keep it quiet and everybody'll get out alive.

Sergeant Major Panfil will divide the teams and prisoners evenly in the six Hueys going out. Remember, they'll be in bad shape, and you'll probably have to carry them. Medics will be waiting at Lima Site Five Niner. Make them comfortable, and don't give them anything but water and fruit cocktail from the C-rations.

"One final change. Archangel will stay at Lima Site Five Niner instead of Long Tieng, just in case Vang Pao doesn't send a plane to pick up the prisoners. Archangel will be on station at 0330 hours for reports. Use abbreviated squelch code as planned."

Alberts thought about the runway at Five Niner and shook his head. He visualized that oh-too-short runway at night, planning his departure, his power settings, his flaps, everything. He smiled to himself because it was challenging and dangerous, two things he liked best about Army Aviation.

"The CG and General Mattix have stuck their necks out a long way to get these prisoners out. They don't want to leave anyone behind when we get out of here and they don't want to sacrifice any of our men to Secretary Kissinger's negotiations. That's why we're here. It took a lot of balls to put this unit together and give us a chance to bring those men home alive. You know what you have to do, so let's roll." Chairs scraped as the men got to their feet and began shuffling out of the room. Roman motioned to Lieutenant Dorsey.

"Dorsey, I really tried to get you a decent copilot but this is the best I could come up with." He pointed to Fitzmorris.

"Well, sir, I'm sure we can work raw material."

"Good. Let's go preflight and get under way," Roman said.

It was a good hour before the first Huey was to take off for Two Zero Alpha, but crews were crawling over the choppers checking out every single system and part. They fired them up, watched the gauges, then shut them down. Sergeant Nolan took some extra time tweaking the voltage regulator on Toothman's bird. It had been within limits, but now it was perfect.

At 0945 hours, the recon teams marched out to the flight line fresh from yet another run-through of their part of the mission. Roman stopped for a second to watch them walk toward the flight line. None better, he thought.

"Well, Jake, looks like you're going to run through the bushes again," Roman said to Captain Best. He would never let him forget their college days and the job Cort Fraley and he did on Best that night in the woods.

Best put a huge hand on Roman's shoulder and squeezed a little too hard. "I still owe you for that one." He turned and started humping his gear into the chopper.

Crank time was 0955 hours. Roman and Toothman threw the switches, listening critically to the metallic click of the igniters and the sound of the turbines as they spun up.

Precisely at 1000 hours, Roman called Udorn Tower for takeoff clearance. The controller gave him traffic information, wind, visibility, altimeter settings and wished them a nice flight. Sure.

This was the part Roman liked best. The flying part. He pulled up on the collective and eased the cyclic forward, putting the nose down to slowly build up airspeed. With Toothman floating in the air to his left, they climbed to 4500 feet and glided north toward the mountains and Control Point Peter. Behind them, the other Hueys departed in ones and twos, out for a Sunday stroll. Nobody in the tower or on the ramp had any idea that history was about to be made.

Dorsey was the last to depart, letting Fitzmorris do all the flying so he could regain some feel for the aircraft before people started shooting at them. Fitz's face glowed with pleasure. He was back in the action, flying a chopper instead of a desk, and he was loving it. While Fitzmorris got his jollies with the machine, Dorsey busied himself writing the radio frequencies and call signs on the windscreen with his black grease pencil. They had to be easily readable when the shit hit the fan. Besides, it gave him something to do instead of fidgeting nervously in his seat.

As they glided above the deep green of the jungle, Dorsey made out the feature they called the Bottleneck, about ten nautical miles from Control Point Peter. In the back, his crew chief was scribbling maintenance notations in the log. The door gunner was checking his weapon one last time. Long Tieng was a short hop away.

"Mister Fitzmorris," Dorsey said, "you think you can fly this approach?"

"Don't press your luck, son," Fitz said. But he was smiling.

He did, in fact, fly the approach perfectly, settling the Huey on the ramp next to the other Grunt Air choppers at mid-field on the grassy area next to T28 parking area. A fuel truck rumbled up, and Fitzmorris and Dorsey immediately started reinspecting every moving part just to be double sure. Just as they climbed down from checking the rotor mast, a stocky man with a full black beard and immensely hairy arms and chest waddled toward them. He was nicely overweight, sweating and wearing a typical Saigon Correspondent Shirt. The existence of this base was a fairly well-kept secret, but here was a reporter from Saigon and he wanted to chat.

"Hi," he began with a genial smile. "I'm Jim Blackmore, touring the base with the Press Corps. What do you guys do here in Laos?"

Fitzmorris gave him the standard answer. Crash site team, inspecting areas where aircraft went down, blah, blah, blah.

"Then you're not a combat unit?" the hairy reporter asked, his bushy eyebrows lifting.

"That's a good one," Fitzmorris chuckled. "The Ambassador insists that we stay out of hostile situations."

"No combat, huh?" The sarcasm dribbled off his words. "Then, would you tell me what those armed guerrillas are doing as part of your unit?" He raised his chin toward the recon teams squatting on the ground and going over their gear.

"They're ground security, just in case. We land in some pretty nasty areas but they've never fired a shot. Have they, Mr. Dorsey?"

"Not a single one," Dorsey replied.

"Yeah," mused the reporter, craning his neck to watch them crawl around the top of the Huey. "But I bet you miss the real fighting with the others?"

"Not really. I saw my share of the action back in the Delta. Don't mind a little stroll in the park now and then." Blackmore grinned up at him.

"Major, you are so very full of shit. This is no place for crash site survey teams or non combat troops. But hey, I'll play along." He stomped over to the Air America Hueys that were cranking up for the hop to Skyline Ridge.

From the top of the Huey, Dorsey and Fitzmorris could see a gaggle of reporters and photographers climbing into helicopters and taking off for a tour of Skyline Ridge. Good. At the end of the flight line, Roman and Toothman stood with the other Grunt Air pilots, going over everything yet again, discussing all the events that could kill them on this mission. Gradually, the group broke up, the crews wandering back to their birds to get what sleep they could before departing in ones and twos to Site Eight Five, undetected if possible.

From Skyline Ridge came the sudden muffled *crump* of mortar shells. Then the staccato sound of machine gun fire drifted down. A Laotian sergeant ran out of the T-28 operations office, screaming.

"Incoming! Scramble! They shot up the reporters on Skyline Two. Medivac is on the way. You Army guys better scramble before the mortars make it over here!"

The Air America aircraft at the north end of the field began responding to the alert and scramble order. Roman was suddenly inspired. When his choppers cranked, the attack would hide their direction of flight. He ran to each chopper and gave the pilots a departure plan that would look like a normal scramble and allow them to fly to Site Eight Five without being noticed.

As he brought his Huey to a three-foot hover, he heard over the Tower frequency that the attack on the ridge was nothing more than NVA harassment fire. Major Nosavan, the commander of GM30, suffered a scalp wound right in the middle of his interview with the reporters. It scared them so badly that all the reporters jumped on one Huey and took off, leaving the wounded Major behind. The second press helicopter picked up Major Nosavan and took him for medical treatment.

Just after lift off from Two Zero Alpha, Roman radioed Archangel on his secure frequency, telling Alberts that he was using the attack as a diversion to sneak away. Alberts gave him some good news. Vang Pao's men had secured Site Eight Five with no fuss and no notice. There would be an intel update waiting when they arrived.

"That's great!" Roman said. "We can always use some current info."

Roman flew west of the PDJ out of sight of the NVA forces, then turned northeast at Peomon, staying low through the Nam Khan River Valley to Sop Khao, then north following the hill mass, which paralleled the highway at a safe distance. Soon he could see Site Eight Five in the distance. He came in low to hide behind the mountain known as Phou Pha Thi. Site Eight Five was on the southeastern down-slope side.

As Roman settled the chopper onto the airfield, he looked up at the mountaintop about 1500 feet above him. It had been the location of a Heavy Green base that directed air strikes in North Vietnam by radar until the NVA attacked and destroyed it in March, 1968. Base personnel had seen the attack coming and knew they'd be overrun, but somebody up the chain of command waited too long to order an evacuation. Eleven men died in the attack because somebody couldn't make up his mind. Roman found himself hoping that his mission wouldn't be the second screwup the mountain had seen.

Roman was last to land, and he was glad to see that refueling operations had already started, except on Dorsey's and Toothman's choppers. They had enough fuel to insert the teams and get back. At 4500 feet, aircraft weight was critical, so they'd refuel when they returned.

Three hours to moonrise, plenty of time to eat some cold C-rations. Roman was nervous, and visited each bird to verify that the circuit breaker on the red rotating beacon was pulled. It would be just his luck that some pilot forgot to turn off the switch on the overhead panel. Ryker and his crew had long ago modified the navigation lights so they could be seen by other aircraft at the same altitude or above, but not from the ground.

The time went quickly and before he knew it, Roman was watching the moon rise over the ridge to the east. He stopped for a second and uttered the aviator's prayer: "Please, God, don't let me fuck up." He asked himself why he let General Mattix talk him into this job, then, after a moment, admitted to himself that it was his own ego that drove him to it. For some reason, he was driven to do what people said couldn't be done, just to prove them wrong. Back in Kansas, at St. Johns Military School, he'd done the same thing. He loved to take on seemingly impossible tasks just to prove that if you tried, you could overcome anything. Now, he was going to do it, again.

The six Hueys were lined up facing the northeast even though the wind was out of the southeast. Carved out of a 680-foot ridge on the side of the mountain, the runway was only 45 feet wide with a big drop off 30 feet from the edge. Air America supply aircraft, like the Helo Courier, landed there by flying uphill on the runway then stopping just before hitting the trees and rocks. To take off, they ran downhill with only 600 feet to get airborne. If they didn't build enough airspeed in that distance, it was a thousand feet straight down to the first bounce.

Roman walked the choppers for the millionth time, convincing himself that they'd be safe enough flying completely blacked out. They had some navigation lights, but not many. The enemy on the ground wouldn't be able to see them. They'd have a hard enough time seeing each other.

Off to his left, Sergeant Major Panfil was relieving himself over the edge of the runway. Everything was go with the recon teams, and Panfil gave Roman a big smile as he buttoned himself up. The gesture lifted Roman's spirits a bit because Panfil had been in the Army for over 28 years. He'd seen the Utah Beach invasion during World War II, at age 17. He'd been in combat in Korea with the 187th Regimental Combat Team called "The Rokkasons." He went ashore at Inchon in September 1950. He made a combat parachute drop at Sukchon-Sunchon and the famous airborne assault at Munson-Ni. Now, he was in Vietnam on his third and final tour before retirement. All of his tours had been in Special Forces or Ranger units. and he'd garnered more awards for outstanding service and heroism than he could count. Roman looked upon him as the classic warrior. A man who embodied the true ideals of the military. He was 45 years old and leading men half his age into every high-risk mission he could get.

Roman wandered on, finding Eldon Barnes sitting on the edge of the cargo bay of his Huey and gazing up at the stars that were slowly appearing directly overhead.

"Are you trying to read the fate of the mission in the stars?" Roman asked.

"Nope. I'm praying to 'em. Mother always told me to pray to the North Star before every suicide mission, and it's worked so far. I'm still here. This mission is gonna make a great story for the grandkids."

"Hell," Roman remarked. "This is your second tour. You probably have plenty of stories already from IV Corp. Besides, you'd never give up all your girlfriends and get married."

"You're right. But, maybe I will … when I'm as old as Panfil."

Roman had been stationed with Barnes at Fort Bliss years before when they were both bachelors, running around as hard as they could with their "squeeze du jour." Once, they'd gone on a deer hunting expedition that neither of them would ever forget. Sands Missile Range covered thousands of square miles of desert and mountain areas, making it ideal for missile testing and a haven for deer, which bred like crazy in the wild. The range commander, along with some fish and wildlife people, decided to let hunters into the area for three days to thin the herd. Just about everybody on the base was dying to go out and shoot some deer so they held a drawing for the precious few hunting permits that were available. Roman and Barnes put their names in just for the hell of it. They didn't care about the event one way or the other and knew they wouldn't win ... but they did. Of course, to turn down the permits would be sacrilege, and they weren't transferable. So, they had to go.

Most of the diehard hunters had tents, but not Roman and Barnes. They rented a Winnebago the size of a semi trailer and equipped it with all the comforts, including a television for the football weekend that was coming up. Big games were going to be on Saturday and Sunday. Then, they dealt with the food and beverage concerns. Barnes was dating four women at the time, each of whom gave him casseroles, pies, snacks and assorted morsels. The men each kicked in a few hundred dollars for beer and liquor and they were ready. They even bought a box of ammunition for their rifles. Not that they would use the ammo.

They hadn't counted on the fact that the other hunters, who would be sleeping in tents during the cold desert nights, would descend on their camper and make it party central for three full days. The first night, the spirits flowed heavily enough to float an ark, allowing Roman about three hours of sleep. At first light, they trooped off, heads throbbing, to their assigned hunting positions. Freezing their balls off, they trooped right back to the Winnebago. They'd spent the morning cooking steak and eggs, then set themselves up in the captain's chairs for an afternoon football orgy. If a deer came up and knocked on the door, they'd probably shoot it, but otherwise, they were determined to leave the deer overpopulation problem to the others.

Every one of the mad-dog hunters bagged a deer that weekend and couldn't understand why Barnes and Roman didn't. Barnes told them it wasn't their lucky day or maybe they were bad shots or maybe they never left the camper. Besides, they didn't want to have to clean their rifles, much less a deer.

The two men sat in silence starring at the stars for a long while. "They look just like they did at White Sands," Roman observed.

"Yeah, except we don't have a Winnebago, and we're the deer." Barnes replied with a big smile.

The next stop was Toothman and Dorsey. "Don't even ask if we're ready," Jan said before Roman could speak. "Yes. We're fucking ready."

Roman grinned and sat down on the floor of the cargo bay with the two men. "Only question is, should Dorsey take the lead, or me? He's younger and his eyesight may be better. The moon won't be completely full when we insert so he may have an advantage. What do you think?"

"It's your call, Jan. You have about two mikes to make your decision before you depart," Roman said looking at his watch.

"Well," Toothman remarked. "I'll take age before beauty any day. My wobbly one and I will lead." He was referring to Colonel Herbert, his copilot for the big event.

Roman looked at his good friend long and hard. They were preparing for a dangerous operation, and the thought crossed both minds that they might never see each other again, alive. "Fine. Now get your ass in that bird and see if you can figure out how to make it fly. It's show time."

CE◯ED

36

Mom, Don't Cry During Bob Hope

Cody residence
Fort Bliss, Texas

At 10:14 in the evening, Calvin Dorsey put four quarters, a nickel and a dime into a pay phone at a 7-11 store a mile from the Pentagon. He listened to the chime sounds the coins made and waited for Carol Cody to pick up her phone in Texas.

"Carol, this is Cal," he said, just as he heard her hello. "I have to make this quick. Colonel Hurd got relieved of duty for taking sexual advantage of POW wives. They're deciding whether to court-martial him or force him out of the service."

"About damn time," Carol said. "Can you tell me how it happened?"

"It seems like somebody heard him propositioning you outside the conference room. One question led to another. The Judge Advocate's Office may be calling you for a statement. Now here's the big news. Don't say anything or ask me anything. He's alive in Laos. They move him frequently so it's hard to track him, but he's being watched almost constantly. That unit I told you about is going to try to get him, but it's a very high-risk mission. I hear that the unit commander is determined to get him out. Be patient and keep the faith. I may have more news in a week or two. Good night." He hung up without another word.

Carol Cody stood without moving an eyelash, then she slowly lowered the receiver into the cradle on the wall. She felt her body sway to the left and reached out to the wall for some support, but it didn't help. She slid on her back to the floor and stayed there half sitting, jolted by gasping, shuddering sobs.

"Mom! What is it!" Her son ran into the hallway leaving Bob Hope's Christmas special from Vietnam on the television in the background. Her daughter was right behind him. They got down on their knees at once, checking to see if she had cut or burned herself in the kitchen. The wailing sounds choked out of her.

It took about a minute but she got her breath and voice back. "No … no … these are happy tears. Your dad is alive! He's alive!" In seconds, all three of them were crying.

"They don't think he's a prisoner in Hanoi," she managed to continue. Carol let them help her up off the floor and she wiped her eyes. "So, there's hope. There's always hope."

Once the kids had quieted down and gone back to the Bob Hope show, Carol sat quietly in the darkened kitchen with a dish towel in hand just in case the tears started flowing again. She was having a conversation with herself. *I guess it's good he's not in Hanoi*, she thought, *but Laos may be worse. From what everybody tells me, the place is a bottomless pit. Prisoners who get sent to Laos never come out. God, I wish I could tell Charlie, but I can't. I've got to keep the faith with Cal. How the hell do you suppose he knows all this?*

∽∾

37

Anybody Need a Green Taxi?

Site Eight Five
Laos
20 January, 1972

Steve Dorsey lifted off ten seconds behind Toothman allowing for night separation. Roman then turned on his battery switch, energizing his radios. He squeezed the trigger mike switch on his cyclic and contacted Archangel, telling Alberts the insertion was on the go. Alberts responded with two quick clicks of his mike button.

In his Huey, Toothman flew low off the Site Eight Five runway to hide his bird from any NVA to the east and still have some moonlight to show him the walls of the valley. Covered with crushed limestone, the roads showed up nicely in the moonlight, and so did the Nam Yul River. Next to him, Colonel Herbert looked more like a tourist than a soldier who was flying low level at night, deep in enemy territory.

"You want to fly for a while?" Toothman asked.

Herbert's face lit up. "Sure."

"Okay, you have the aircraft. I'll navigate."

"Roger, I have the aircraft," Herbert responded, following strict procedure.

As they flew over the small village of Ban Sen Sam at the junction of three roads and two good-sized rivers, they were exactly on course and on schedule, flying no more than 25 to 50 feet off the ground. Herbert was good, making smooth course corrections to follow the river and the bright white limestone road to the northeast. The village of Ban Houel Ngoui flashed below them. "Hope they're still pro Vang Pao down there," Toothman remarked. "If not, they're reporting us to the NVA."

The crew chief reported that Dorsey was close behind and flying slightly higher so he could see their navigation lights. Ahead was another town and another fork in the road. This was Sop Y, where the course bore to the right. They continued up a branching valley, staying behind the mountains and karst that were providing cover. When they got to Ban Tat Lo, they turned hard back further to the right. Herbert flew carefully between the hills on either side. Toothman triggered his mike two times. It was returned by one click from Archangel. This told him they'd made the turn at Ban Tat Lo. They were still on time and on course.

Out of the valley area to the north now, and over a relatively more open but still mountainous area. They were staying low, concentrating and straining their eyes to avoid the small ridge lines, trees and limestone karsts that stuck up like jagged fingers reaching for their fragile machines. Toothman peered into the dim light, looking for the 4423-foot high mountain on their left and further ahead the 5315-foot mountain also on the left. He had every feature of the land memorized, seeing the map in his mind just as clearly as he saw it on the map table in the Grunt Air Ops Center. Suddenly they crossed Route 63, a north-south road that went into North Vietnam near Dien Bien Phu. A major supply route that didn't have any traffic for some reason. Was it luck or had they been compromised? Was there an ambush ahead? Toothman shook off the possible problems and went back to the mission.

They found their landmark, a small karst just ahead. Herbert gently pulled back on the cyclic and slightly reduced power on the collective, slowing down to land in a small clearing that the U-2 photos indicated was 30 meters north of the karst.

"I have the clearing in sight," Toothman said as he put his hands on the controls. "I have the aircraft."

"You have the aircraft," responded Herbert.

"Stay on the controls with me in case of trouble. I'm putting in a high left Deadman setting," Toothman said. Herbert could hear the tension in his voice even though Toothman's exceptional flying skills were apparent. He flared the big machine gracefully and touched down in the small clearing with hardly a bump. On the way out the cargo bay door, Gunny Thornhill patted him on the shoulder. The two recon teams were gone in three seconds and Toothman lifted off again, clicking his mike switch three times. Archangel got the message. The insertion was successful. No problems.

Toothman relaxed slightly, removed the Deadman setting and glanced over at Herbert who was examining the terrain ahead. "Okay, Peter Pilot, back to work. You have the controls."

"Roger, I have the controls," Herbert said with a grin that glowed in the moonlight. He was a happy warrior. Toothman watched Herbert's joy as he handled the Huey and hoped he himself would never get promoted that far up the line. He would miss the excitement of flying in combat and he sure as hell didn't want to be doomed to a desk for the rest of his career. Toothman was sure that Herbert would be a brigadier general in a year, if he survived the night's mission.

Herbert flew the Huey gracefully back to Site Eight Five and began the approach. Without lights, it would be tricky.

"You want the controls?" he asked.

"Naw. I'm too lazy. You're doing fine."

Herbert made a textbook approach, shut down the turbine and let the blades slowly spin to a stop. Before they turned off the radios and battery, they heard Roman in his aircraft send a coded message to Archangel informing Alberts that the two birds were back safely.

Bringing the C-47 down out of 12,000 feet, Alberts started looking for the infamous short strip at Lima Site Five Niner. It was less than 2000 feet long with a 300 foot sod overrun, making it a hairy operation even in the daylight. He took a few deep breaths and settled his butt in the seat, making a conscious effort to relax. If he nailed his approach speed, everything else would fall into place.

Lieutenant Davis was in the right seat, substituting for Captain Muang. Alberts wanted Davis to see what a night tactical landing was like. "There it is," said Davis, craning to see the white limestone runway ahead of them. It looked like nothing more than a small white scar on the side of a mountain.

The ground rose up on either side of them. There was plenty of space between the valley walls, but the drop-off at the near end of the runway was the big issue. Fortunately, there was no wind to contend with.

"Okay," Alberts said to Davis, "give me the gear and full flaps."

Davis pushed the gear handle down and an amber caution light came on above the unlit green lights. He heard and felt the landing gear go down into position and lock. The amber lights went out and the green lights came on. He then lowered the flaps lever to its full deployment position. "You have gear and flaps," he reported to Alberts, whose eyes were boring ahead into the near darkness. He had to put the big plane down at the very threshold of the runway or he'd be subjected to a sudden stop.

His hands delicately played the yoke toward him and away, adjusting his airspeed, keeping it just above a stall. He had to land at the slowest speed the C-47 was capable of. The aircraft flashed over the sod overrun, then the gravel-limestone runway was below them. He dropped the wheels down to contact the ground, pulled back to drop the tail wheel and stood up on the brakes. Plenty of room left ahead of them. Davis grinned and, in spite of himself, let out a small whoop.

After taxiing to the small ramp area, they bestowed the customary gifts on Vang Pao's wife. Her crew humped the barrels of AVGAS out of the cargo area and refueled the plane. They were ready and could catch some sleep, though one of the radio operators had to stay up to monitor the Grunt Air frequency in case of trouble.

The two hours of sleep seemed like two seconds. In no time, Davis was shaking Alberts by the shoulder telling him it was time to go. It was 0300 hours.

Alberts made his way to the cockpit and squirmed into the left seat. He immediately started his checklist, his hands running over every control, pointing to every switch, dial and gauge as if it were a graceful ballet.

"You want me up here, or Davis?" Captain U. Muang stuck his head into the cockpit.

"I'll need you for this take off," Alberts said.

"Too bad," U. Muang said, "it's safer in the back."

Their takeoff heading was 160 degrees, downhill into the dark. At the end of the runway, with the mighty engines of the C-47 droning in his ears, Alberts thought of all the takeoffs he'd made from this strip—in the daytime. This, he told himself, would be no different. He set the brakes and ran up both engines to check for malfunctions. He could tell by the sound that they were running well, and the instruments backed him up.

"Give me airspeed readouts," he told U. Muang.

"Roger."

With the brakes on, Alberts eased the throttles forward to max manifold pressure, feeling the C-47 shudder around him. When he had the power setting he wanted, he released the brakes, letting the plane roll forward slowly then rapidly gain speed. In just a few hundred feet, he pushed forward on the yoke to lift the tail wheel.

"Sixty knots … eighty … ninety … a hundred," U. Muang chanted, his eyes fixed on the airspeed indicator. Alberts eased back on the yoke. There was about two hundred feet of runway still in front of him and he was going to use all of it. Either by the force of nature or the force of will, the ancient C-47 lumbered into the sky, Alberts keeping it only a few feet off the ground. The runway suddenly disappeared altogether as they soared out over the cliff. He held it level to allow the airspeed to build up, then turned to follow the road down the valley, all the while easing back to gain altitude. Gradually, avoiding the mountains on both sides, he climbed to 10,500 feet to start his command and control function. Passing through 8,000 feet, he radioed,

"Archangel is up and ready for business." It was 0325 hours. He was five minutes early on station roll call.

"Alpha," was Captain Best's one word response. His team was in place and listening, ready to execute. The other four teams responded the same way.

"Six, this is Archangel with a go report, out."

"Give him two clicks," Roman told Dodson, who triggered his mike switch twice. Dodson was strapped in the chopper, ready to crank in an emergency. Each aircraft had one pilot already strapped in and ready to hit the battery and fuel-on switches for quick start. Even though the NVA were still unaware of their presence on Site Eight Five, they could be attacked at any moment.

The time was 0347 hours. Mission execution would be in 13 minutes. Everyone was in place, seated and strapped in, checking everything they could without actually cranking the engines. The night was spectacularly clear and, from his position on the mountainside, Roman could see for miles to the northeast, even to the glow of the lights of Hanoi on the horizon. The idea that he was so close to the enemy capital made his nerves tingle. Not many pilots would ever be able to say that they had seen the lights of Hanoi from a helicopter.

Forty kilometers to the east, Captain Jake Best watched Corporal Muong Ky as he crept through the night without a sound and climbed the wooden tower on the northeast side of the Big Casino. When he got to the top, he was four feet behind the guard and scarcely breathing. Waiting for the signal to execute, his eyes were divided between the guard and Captain Best.

Directly across the compound, Sgt. Mona Tong was doing the same thing, waiting low on the wall, his head close to the guard's feet. He glanced back and forth waiting for Gunny Thornhill to give him the go. He was so close to his victim he could smell the awful beer he'd been drinking. The Laotian brew was vile at its best, but Tong was glad to smell it. After all, an intoxicated guard would only help his mission.

In front of the compound, the two Hmong Corporals, Wang Sing Khan and Theng Pao Yap were ready, too. They were to take out the guard standing Charge of Quarters in the Administration Building. They would have to kill him quickly so that he couldn't call for help. Yap would knock at the door and tell the guard he was a courier with a message, then ask if the guard was authorized to accept a secret message. Meanwhile, Khan would come from behind through the side door and garrote him with his favorite piece of razor-sharp wire. Patiently, they waited for the sign.

Sergeant Yong Ton Pao was ready and waiting to slip into the NVA cadre quarters where four or five guards were asleep, unconsciously enjoying their last few moments of life. Next to him, Lieutenant Christian, Sergeant

Anderson and Sergeant Stibbens were prepared to shoot anyone who awoke before Pao could send them to meet Buddha. Fifteen seconds to go. Christian raised a finger.

Meanwhile, Delta Team had taken a slightly different route from the LZ to the bridge east of the Big Casino. Their march sent them past the abandoned village they called "Bon Houa Something," a place where the Pathet Lao and their NVA advisors killed everyone in the village as punishment for their pro-government sympathies. The younger men of the village had joined Vang Pao's forces before the slaughter. Even though the village was abandoned, Sergeant Krumins wasn't taking any chances, skirting the village instead of going through it. There was a slight chance someone would be there and sound the alarm.

Once they arrived at the bridge, it took only minutes to set the satchel charges and run the detonator wires back down the road. Sergeant Priest was detailed to stay behind and detonate the charges when he heard the inbound Hueys. He kept the team radio to report any major problems, such as troops heading their way, and had set a timer to blow the bridge ten minutes after the scheduled lift off. If he were killed or captured, the vital bridge would still come down.

From the bridge, Sergeants Krumins and Boynton moved west to where the road to the prison camp joined the main road. Their mission was to lay out the beanbag lights for the choppers.

Some distance away, inside a cave with flat iron bars across the entrance, Captain Bob Felderhoff and his cellmate, Navy Lieutenant Ed Mattingley, were awakened by the sweetest sound they'd ever heard—the rotors of a Huey helicopter. Since they'd been shot down and captured, they'd become increasingly sensitive to all the sounds around them because most of the noise they heard meant pain was coming their way.

Slowly, they crept to the mouth of the cave and peered into the darkness beyond the flat metal bars and toward the village of Muong Liet. The NVA guard who slept just out of arm's reach above them had not been awakened by the almost silent Hueys. They could see nothing but they knew now that there were Americans out there. In the Sam Neua area, there were over a hundred prisoners, but Felderhoff and Mattingley had been among the lucky ones. They were to be transferred out of their damp cave in the mountain to a new camp where they would soon be able to see sunlight once again. This was the good news. The bad news was that torture and disease would certainly come. They were both prizes for the NVA and Russians, and they knew it. Felderhoff, an F-105 Wild Weasel pilot, and Mattingley, an A-6 Intruder Bombardier Navigator, had advanced technical information the Russians would love to pry out of them. Felderhoff found himself praying into the night that the Hueys would get them out before the interrogations started.

"Where do you think they're going?" Mattingley whispered.

"Not here," said Felderhoff. "Not here, Goddamn it."

"Hey," replied Mattingley. "As long as we can hear choppers, we can hope. Right?" They listened intently for another hour, but heard nothing more.

Most temporary transit cells in the northern part of Laos were holes in the ground with bamboo and wood bars across the top. The regular cells were natural and manmade caves in the hundreds of limestone karsts that stuck up throughout the countryside. In Washington, the military and politicians argued endlessly over which caves were used and which weren't. Somehow, it was more important to debate that issue than to address the fact that living Americans were being imprisoned in them. They also spent a lot of time on the subject of how many were being held by the NVA and how many by the Pathet Lao. It was easier, somehow, to talk about numbers than people. The experts who debated these topics 8500 miles away from the cruel reality carefully avoided actually trying to help them. Those who tried lost their careers.

For once the CIA had some useful information, and when you sorted through it, the picture became much clearer. There was a series of caves in the Sam Neua area being used as prison camps. The people who really knew and actually cared at Headquarters 7th US Air Force believed the caves held about 100 POWs. Plus, they estimated another 120 or more were scattered in caves and camps throughout Northern Laos. Sam Neua was the headquarters for NVA forces in Northern Laos and they kept the valuable political pawns, called prisoners, close by.

The CIA had identified specific camps in the areas of Muong Liet, Ban Nakay, Than Sadet, Ban Tong, Muong Nong, Vieng Xai, Muong Hiet and as far east as Muong Soui. Most, with one or two exceptions, were extremely primitive and disease-ridden. In his negotiations, Kissinger solidly focused on Americans being held in North Vietnamese camps, especially the notorious Hanoi Hilton, but had apparently made the hard decision that prisoners in Laos probably wouldn't come home with the others. Kissinger, with great anguish, had to work with what he could get accomplished with the conniving North Vietnamese. The release of Americans in the Cambodian and Laotian prisons had to be negotiated separately with the Khamer Rouge and Pathet Lao, so said the North Vietnamese. That made General Coroneos' secret plan all the more necessary. The Grunt Air solution was, in the end, the only hope that Felderhoff, Mattingley, and the hundred others had. Unfortunately, the mission that had just begun would not include them. They would have to wait for another opportunity, if, in the unlikely event, they survived.

Roman pulled the starter trigger on his Huey and watched the gauges carefully. Turbine temperature good. N1 gauge coming up. As the N1 passed through the start threshold, he released the starter trigger and watched the temperature gauge to ensure he wouldn't get a hot start.

"Good start," he said to his copilot and crew chief. He immobilized the copilot attitude indicator with one hand, then switched on his AC inverter to power up the aircraft instruments. To his right, he could see that the other birds were ready. Giving no sign, he lifted off the runway and dropped down to the valley floor, turning northeast just as Toothman and Dorsey had done a few hours earlier. The others silently followed. His route would be the same, except he'd land on the road in front of the prison camp. They were under way!

Just as Roman was lifting off, Mona Tong got the go signal and, like a cat, sprung up to the side of the west guard tower, pounced on the back of the drunken guard, threw the wire around his neck and gave it a vicious pull. Nice thing about garrotes. They zip right through the windpipe and don't let the victim make a sound, except for perhaps a small surprised gurgle.

As the man fell before him, Mona Tong shot a quick look at the other tower. He hadn't been seen because Muong Ky had been as fast and deadly efficient as he was. Ky was scrambling down the tower to join his team. Tong did the same.

At the front of the Administration Office, Corporal Yap banged on the door. The sleepy guard opened it a crack and peeped through, showing Yap a yellow, bloodshot eye.

"I'm Corporal Yap with a secret dispatch for the camp commander," he said officiously. They'd received a number of important dispatches in recent days since Captain Ho and the new prisoners had arrived. The guard straightened up, stepped back and opened the office door the rest of the way. It was the last move he ever made. Corporal Kahn had entered silently through the side door, positioned himself behind the sleepy guard, and applied the garrote with a practiced and vicious twist of the wrist. The man fell to the floor inhaling his own blood.

Across the open air reception area in the cadre room, Sergeant Yong Ton Pao had, all by himself, swiftly and silently sent the four sleeping guards to join their ancestors. He took special pride in being able to kill all four without waking the guard next to the one being killed. The four he'd just dispatched brought his wartime total to 59. Lieutenant Christian had been standing just inside the door with his pistol drawn, ready to shoot any guard who woke up before Pao silenced them. Christian gave Pao a smiling nod and signaled him out the side door and into the reception area.

High above the bloody action, Archangel watched his clock. Three minutes had elapsed. It was time to make his first call to the teams with only three words.

"This is Archangel."

All the teams responded in a short pre-arranged code and each heard the reports of the others. Alpha and Bravo had killed their guards. Delta Scout was a decoy for Charlie, who got one. Delta had placed the charges at the bridge, and Echo had killed four. Echo reported "no SG," which meant the sadistic sergeant of the guard wasn't there. Now the teams would proceed with their individual tasks in the compound. All were watching for the sergeant of the guard and hoping for a crack at the sadistic bastard.

Alpha and Bravo crept into the compound area first, with Charlie and Echo close behind. Staying in the shadows, Echo immediately turned to the right and cleared the mess hall before heading to the cells in the back. Alpha had already begun checking each cell in the front.

Lieutenant Christian was the first in. In a cell near the center of the row, he peered through the bars and made out the shadow of a man crouched in the corner. One push on the bolt cutters was enough to cut the lock. As Christian walked in, the man scurried farther into the shadows. He was obviously terrified. Every time his cell door had opened in the past, pain came in.

"Hey. It's okay," Christian said quietly. "I'm an American. Let's go home." He could make out the man's eyes that opened wide in the shadows, then the emaciated form as it staggered toward him. "Major Reginald Smythe-Gordon, Royal Australian Air Force." He could barely speak as Christian put an arm around him and helped him into the hallway in front of the cells.

"Wait over there, Major. We're getting the others."

"Don't forget the missionaries," Smythe-Gordon croaked.

"What missionaries?"

"In the back cells. Three of them."

Christian nodded to Stibbens, who turned and ran down the hall and around to the back row of cells. Captain Best and his team were working toward him. Stibbens waved to Best and held up three fingers, then pointed to the last three cells. Best nodded. Stibbens had his own set of bolt cutters and got busy cutting the lock on the first cell in the row. He could barely see inside as he called out. "I'm an American."

From the shadow came the reply. "So am I."

"Good," Stibbens said. "Let's go home."

An elderly man emerged from the rear of the cell. His white hair had yellowed and was caked with filth.

"God bless you, son," he sobbed as he fell into the Sergeant's arms.

He led Stibbens to the next cell and waited while the Sergeant wrestled with the lock. The missionary walked in and came out carrying a badly beaten man in his late 30s. His eyes were blackened and nearly shut. Through swollen lips he managed to say, "Sister Jannette. She's next door, I think." Captain Best and his team got there first. From deep within came the soft moans and whimpering of a young woman.

"Don't be afraid," Best said as gently as he could. "We're Americans. We're here to take you home."

The older missionary stepped carefully into the cell, followed closely by Sergeant Lujan. The two men helped the woman to her feet, but she could not stand. Her right leg had been broken. She was so caked with blood and dirt they had to look twice to see that she was female.

"Who did this to her?" Best demanded.

"The big sergeant," replied the younger missionary.

"Okay, let's get them ready to move to the LZ," Best directed, moving off toward the door. Outside, in the main part of the confinement area, he found Sergeant Gryner and Spec5 Brindle carrying a body out of the isolation room. "Says he's Captain James Hansen, U.S. Air Force," said Gryner as they passed Best. Whoever it was, he couldn't walk and Best hoped it was only because his legs were numb and not broken. The room was too small for anyone to lay down or stand up. Prisoners spent days in a crouched or squatting position.

To the left, across the compound, Gunny Thornhill and Sergeant Richardson crept up on one of the interrogation rooms, trailed by Sergeant Ramirez. Thornhill counted on his fingers, holding up one, then two, then three. On three, the men burst through the door surprising the hell out of Captain Ho and the fat Sergeant. Both men stuck their hands up in the air without being told.

On the floor in front of them, Army Major Willard Cody knelt next to a blood-covered table, moaning in pain. He had been forced to the floor with his knees digging into a piece of iron rebar. They couldn't tell anything about him because his hands and face had been beaten into almost shapeless red masses. Thornhill lost whatever control he'd had over himself to that point and, before anyone could stop him, he lunged toward the Sergeant, grabbed his ears and ripped them completely off his head.

The Sergeant screamed in agony, ran into the wall in blinding pain and collided with Captain Ho, who had been propelled there by Richardson's rifle butt. Mason grabbed Ho, slammed him into the wall again, and rifled his pockets for his identification cards and wallet.

Ramirez concerned himself with the Major on the floor, putting his hands under the man's arms and lifting him slowly into a chair. He managed to cut through the ankle ropes just as Captain Best arrived.

"Major. Can you understand me?" Best asked, squatting in front of the man's chair.

"Yes," was his weak reply.

"We're here to take you home, Major."

"Home. Yes." The brutalized man tried to get to his feet, fell back in the chair and gamely tried, again.

Captain Ho's fortunes had been drastically reversed in a very short time. Richardson had him on his knees in the corner with his hands bound behind him. Ramirez handed him a bloody rag he found in the corner and Richardson shoved it into his mouth. Richardson noted the insignia on his uniform. NVA Intelligence Service. He would be a virtual gold mine of information.

"Okay, Captain, when this comes out of your mouth, you better be ready to recite your whole life story. If you don't, the boss will give you some encouragement. He's a mean son of a bitch. Do you understand?"

Captain Ho's eyes were the size of saucers. Like many people who delight in giving pain, the thought of receiving it terrified him. He nodded vigorously. The sight of Ramirez standing in the corner with the piece of rebar in his hand provided all the encouragement he needed.

They took Major Cody and Captain Ho outside. Gunny Thornhill and Sergeant Mason had managed to wrestle the fat Sergeant to the floor like a steer in a rodeo and tie his arms behind his back with his elbows touching. They were covered in his blood because the ears bleed more generously than almost any other part of the body. He was howling in pain and rolling around on the ground. The two men managed to drag him to his feet and stuff some rags in his mouth. "Look at this," Mason said, grabbing a rope that hung from a pulley on the ceiling. They both got the same idea at the same time. Thornhill grabbed the Sergeant's feet and, with some considerable effort, dragged him to the center of the room. Mason made a few quick twists of the rope, threaded it around the Sergeant's ankles and, in a matter of seconds, had him hanging upside down from the ceiling, blood dripping from his head onto the floor.

Mason got inspired and carried over the heavy wooden chair Cody had spent so much time in and tied it to the Sergeant's arms. In a few minutes, the chair would start getting heavy and, in a few hours, it would pull his arms out of the sockets. Gradually, the Sergeant would probably bleed to death, if he didn't have a stroke first.

"You sure you want to do that?" asked Jake Best. It was almost a rhetorical question. Thornhill walked slowly around the obese, hanging body.

"Not nearly as bad as what he's done to our boys," he observed. "Tell the truth, I think we're letting him off easy. I just ain't got the stomach to give him what he really deserves." They left him.

By the time Best went back outside, all the cells had been cleared and the teams were working their way back to the reception area to wait for the Hueys. They had recovered 11 people and one prized NVA Captain of Intelligence. So far, not a shot fired. When Best realized this, one of Toothman's axioms of combat immediately popped into his head. "If your attack is going really well, it's an ambush." *Well,* Best thought, *this must be an ambush, because it's going really well.*

Sergeant Pao was seething, off where nobody could see him. After looking at the female missionary and Major Cody, he couldn't help himself. Unobserved, he slipped back into the interrogation cell where the moaning fat Sergeant was hanging upside down like a slaughtered water buffalo. Pao looked at him for several minutes, breathing heavily and listening with wry pleasure to the Sergeant's moans.

Pao slipped his jungle knife out of his belt, which caused the Sergeant's moans and grunts to increase markedly in volume, and used it to cut the Grunt Air patch off his uniform. He stuck his knife through the patch with the insignia facing up and approached the hanging Sergeant. The man had blood coming out of his nose and the sticky, red liquid was still flowing from the gashes where his ears used to be. Pao lifted his knife, aimed carefully, and slammed it downward into the Sergeant's groin. As the hanging man convulsed and jerked in unspeakable agony, Pao adjusted the Grunt Air patch so it could be easily seen. He wanted whoever found the Sergeant to know that Grunt Air had been there.

"Animal. You are number 60." He regarded his handiwork one last time before walking out into the sticky, hot night air.

"What did you do in there?" Panfil asked him.

"You don't want to know," Pao replied.

Captain Best looked at his watch. It was 0416 hours. They were still good on time. Best could hear the *whup-whup* of the approaching Hueys in the distance, and, at the same time, the muffled sound of the bridge blowing up.

"Okay," Best said, "let's head to the road." The recon teams led the prisoners through the compound gates, across the parking area and into the trees on the other side of the road. Most could walk on their own, but Sister Janette and Major Cody had to be carried. The Major didn't like it at all. His pride made him struggle to walk, but he was too abused, too badly beaten. Sister Janette had the thousand-yard stare in her eyes, and Best could tell she'd never be the same, even if her body somehow managed to heal. He looked down at her lying on the stretcher that Lujan and Stibbens had made from a poncho and two pieces of bamboo from the fence. He couldn't even tell what she once might have looked like. He swallowed hard and blinked a few times. There was an emotional side to him that he never let anybody see.

The Hueys were close. Best and Thornhill carried the Major between them, trying to keep him from walking on his own. Richardson took pleasure in the burden of Captain Ho, who was slung over his shoulder like a freshly-killed deer. The Captain's life has just made a major detour, Best figured, and he may never get back on the road. Once Vang Pao gets hold of him, he's in for a bumpy ride. Best hoped the Dragon Lady would have a chance for an interview.

The six Hueys descended out of the darkness accompanied by huge noise and swirling dust. Sergeant Major Panfil had already organized the troops, prisoners and former captives into groups that climbed aboard with a minimum of confusion. Best and Thornhill brought up the rear, holding Cody between them. From his seat in the chopper, Roman silently screamed for them to hurry. Things had gone well and an encounter with the enemy would spoil the entire evening.

When Cody got close to the Hueys, he suddenly planted his feet and shrugged his arms off Best and Thornhill. Knowing he would fall, they lunged to grab him, but missed because he'd pulled himself upright and started to march to the helicopter like he was leading a Pass in Review Parade. Driven by pride and the self-esteem he'd managed to preserve during his ordeal, the Major would not be carried. He strode toward the Huey like a military officer.

Roman was squirming in his seat. He keyed his mike and called Bravo Team. "Gryner, go hurry that guy up, will you? I'm double parked and the cops are coming up the road giving tickets." But the Major had made it to Ditton's chopper on his own.

Suddenly, a pair of jeep lights appeared on the road ahead and to the left of Roman's lead Huey. In the rear of the jeep, two NVA soldiers with machine guns opened up on the first three Hueys. Roman's Huey was hit with only a few shots as the jeep sped past. Toothman's bird was not so lucky. The windshield exploded under the heavy fire. Toothman was hit in the chest, his blood splattering all over what remained of the windshield. The Huey suddenly began to rock in an unsteady manner as Jan fell forward against the shoulder straps and cyclic.

Gunny Thornhill and Captain Best jumped out of the Huey and returned the fire. The troops in the jeep were annihilated, but not before Thornhill was hit in the leg. As Best was attempting to get a very profane Thornhill back into the helicopter, an NVA soldier suddenly appeared out of nowhere carrying a RPG. He aimed at the last helicopter and fired before any-one saw him. The RPG missed the main cargo compartment by inches and hit the tailboom with a deafening explosion. Pieces of the destroyed tailboom flew up and severed the main rotor mast and blades. The blades, which were spin-ning at 320 revolutions per minute, launched off the bird and flew into the treetops. They went through the trees like a hot knife through butter.

The recently released captives were horrified by the noise and vio-lence. They were hesitant to move forward, but they lowered their heads and ran quickly to the waiting Hueys.

Roman turned in his seat and stuck his head out of the side window, trying to get a better look at the situation, when he heard Dorsey's voice over the radio. "The bastards shot up Toothman's bird and the RPG took out Dit-ton's. It's a goner, but everyone got out."

Roman activated his radio, "Panfil, get those people on the other birds and quick. This is starting to get bad. Jan, is everyone on your bird okay?" Silence.

After a couple of seconds, Colonel Herbert's subdued voice came over the radio. "Dan, they got Toothman in the chest. He's gone. Let's get outta here."

Roman could not believe what he had just heard. Jan couldn't be dead. There must be a mistake. He had to get the birds in the air. "Pitch pull, ready now," Roman transmitted as he lifted the heavily loaded Huey off the ground. The other four followed with uncommon precision despite the cum-bersome loads they carried.

"Archangel, Six. We're off and with a full load. Call off the Arclight strike!"

"Roger, Six. Standby. Cancellation acknowledged."

Roman climbed above the tree line before turning to the northwest. Off at 0419 hours. Up the road, he could see the twinkle of headlights com-ing from Sam Neua bunched up at the bridge. The enemy had gotten the word, but too late. They'd soon find all the guards with their throats cut and a dis-emboweled Sergeant hanging from the rafters, but no prisoners.

The scared and fatigued POWs were huddled together in the back of the Hueys, eating canned fruit cocktail and drinking large amounts of water. Still stunned from their sudden rescue and unsure of their fate, they contem-plated their surroundings while looking to their rescuers for reassurance. They were free and out of the torture chambers, and that's all that mattered.

The moon offered a friendly light as Roman, followed by the other five Grunt Air Hueys, flew west over Ban Keng Long, the village he had passed 28 minutes before. He stayed low and close to the big 6723-foot mountain just east of Lima Site Five Niner. As soon as he rounded the mountain, he could see the field. "Archangel, Grunt Air Six has the field in sight," Roman radioed as he removed his deadman setting.

"Roger, Six. Your Air America taxi is about two five mikes out."

"Good. I hope it's a stretch limo. We've got eleven passengers and a visitor from the east who wants to take singing lessons from Vang Pao," Roman said in a very sad voice. "Meet us at Alternate."

They landed just as they had departed. Troops led the freed prisoners toward the small airfield operations office while Charley and Alpha Teams, their work not yet done, set up a defensive perimeter around the aircraft. Bravo did the same around the rescued personnel. The wounded Gunny Thornhill, whose pride was hurt worse than his leg, put Captain Ho on the ground none too gently and stood guard over him with his CAR-15 rifle. Roman came up just as Best and Echo Team were putting Toothman's body in the back of the Huey. His lower lip began to quiver and his body shook as he watched his long time friend being wrapped up in a poncho. With tears running down his cheeks, Roman turned and headed towards the Operations office.

The rescuees were settling in the operations office, talking quietly, some in shock at their quick and unexpected release. They were trying to get their bearings. Roman, Colonel Herbert, Major Fitzmorris and Abeel squeezed in and were showered by greetings of gratitude. Roman held up his hand, and the noise died down.

"You've been rescued by a combined force of American and Laotian personnel. However, higher military command and the United States government do not know that this force exists. Our unit was unofficially established solely to rescue people like you who are trapped and essentially forgotten in the peace negotiations. There are over two hundred more just like you out there, and we can rescue them if you help. It's not too much to say that what happens to them from this point on is entirely up to you. Here's the choice you're faced with right now. If you tell anyone what happened tonight, if you tell them about our team, it will be over for us and we'll never be able to rescue anyone, again. I'm dead serious. If anyone ever finds out about us, our operation will be over.

"If you want to help and support our efforts, here's your story. You escaped when the truck you were riding in hit a tree, killing the driver. You walked west and found this airfield. The Laotian Commander, General Vang Pao, flew you from here to safety. That's your story. No matter who asks you. Generals, ambassadors, commanding officers … nobody knows about this unit, and they can't. We beg you to keep the faith with those who are still being held prisoner by the enemy. If you tell the truth about tonight, they will continue to be held prisoner and be tortured. If our secret gets out, they will die. Please help us complete our mission."

Silence, as the stunned prisoners struggled to come to grips with what they'd been told. The sudden rescue at four in the morning had been a lot to take in. And, now this officer was telling them to lie about it.

"The decision is yours and yours alone. Now you can discuss the matter between yourselves and give me your decision."

A weak voice came from the rear of the room. It was Sister Jannette, conscious after all, speaking for the first time in a thin but charming French accent.

"Is it a political consideration that forces you to hide the truth?"

"Yes, ma'am," Roman said gently.

"Since I was thirteen years old, I have not lied. I do not believe my Ecclesiastical order would approve if I started now."

Roman's heart sank. He didn't expect this to become a religious decision. He tried not to think of what he'd have to do if she didn't cooperate. Then she spoke again, her voice a bit stronger.

"However, I am certain my Order never thought our vow of truth would support the evils in the camps and cause the abandonment of the tortured souls still in them. I cannot allow those pigs to do to others what they have done to me. I feel compelled to respond to the calling of God. In this case, He is telling me to lie like a dog." The thin laughter broke the tension in the room and brought a smile to Roman's face.

"Thank you. I'm going to ask you to spend the next few minutes with Mr. Abeel. He'll fill you in on the details of the story that you're to tell the world. Please accept my personal thanks and the gratitude of all those who now have a chance to be recovered and returned home."

The last few words were difficult for him. He left before anyone could see the glistening at the corners of his eyes.

∽∾

38

All in a Day's Work

Landing Site Five Niner
Laos
20 January, 1972

Vang Pao sent Roman a C-7 Caribou transport, which was bigger than what he had requested. But that was fine with him because he had three additional passengers to transport.

The Caribou sat on the runway, its engines rumbling, as Abeel and Best led the former captives out of the office. Colonel Herbert and Major Fitzmorris stood with Roman next to the lead Huey and watched with concern as their flock made its way to the rear of the plane and up the loading ramp. Major Cody was last. Still trying to walk by himself, he needed the help of his comrades in arms, Reggie Smythe-Gordon and Captain Hansen. At the top of the ramp, the Major stepped back, turned to Roman and gave him the sharpest salute he could manage. But Roman's back was turned and Herbert saw him first.

"I think that's for you, Dan." Roman turned, saw Cody silhouetted in the vast opening of the Caribou's cargo bay, stood up and returned his salute. Cody disappeared inside, the ramp creaked upward and, in moments, the plane had roared into the air taking Cody and the rest to freedom, courtesy of Grunt Air.

"Dan," Herbert said quietly, "You couldn't have done anything differently that would have saved Toothman. You've got to treat it like any other combat loss, even if he was your friend." Roman's expression remained grim as he got up and gave Herbert a small smile and a knowing nod.

"You know, Colonel, we were *this close* to over a hundred other prisoners out there." He held his thumb and forefinger up, less than an inch apart. "This close. And all we got was a couple of them. I'm worried that something or someone will stop us before we can get the rest of them. There's a hundred in the caves, maybe more in the cages, and I can see the writing on the wall. The goddamned administration and higher headquarter jackasses will sacrifice these guys in a heartbeat if it gives them a quick political settlement to the war. That's a little hard for me to swallow. First thing tomorrow, I'm going to start working on a new plan. We're the only chance those poor guys have to go home. I can't see leaving them there just because of a bunch of goddamn—excuse me, sir—politicians."

Herbert measured Roman with his eyes, impressed by his deep convictions.

"Dan, the success of this mission was spectacular. The Major here and I had front row seats, and you can be damn sure the CG and the rest of the generals will know how well you pulled this off. I'm hoping we can get you your chance to keep doing what you're doing. You've obviously got the determination, you're just the right amount of crazy and there's no reason you shouldn't get the rest of those guys out of there." Herbert put his hand on Roman's shoulder and gave it an encouraging squeeze. "Now, let's go home. I'll buy you a beer at the B Frame."

"If you ask me, Dan" chimed in Fitzmorris, "people are going to be buying you drinks for a long time."

It took a while for them to get to the refueling stop at Long Tieng because they traveled in flights of ones and twos for security. During the refueling, they enjoyed watching the three-ring circus that had erupted in front of Vang Pao's Operations office. The returning prisoners were celebrities, and so was Vang Pao for his brave and daring recovery of the prisoners from his base at Landing Site Five Niner.

Alberts handed a Roman a decoded message. Generals Hamilton, Mattix and Geiger were at Udorn awaiting the return of the former prisoners and Grunt Air. All Grunt Air personnel were to go directly to their briefing room upon arrival. They were ordered to leave all maps, photos, flight plans, code books, everything but personal property in their aircraft, or turn it over to security personnel when they arrived. Everything relating to Grunt Air had to be surrendered. Roman handed the message to Colonel Herbert.

"I have no idea what this means," Herbert admitted after he'd read through it twice.

"Oh, well, let's go face the music," Roman said as he exhaled. "Crank 'em."

Thanks to Colonel Herbert's brief but pointed conversation with approach control coming into Udorn, all air traffic was cleared from the area allowing the Grunt Air flight to make an overhead approach. The five Hueys floated toward the runway in a tight echelon-right formation, precisely spaced and very military. Even the old C-47 was a loose part of the formation.

On the ground, base personnel shifted their eyes from the recently arrived prisoners to the sky above, admiring the highly unusual approach of the five Hueys and C-47. Along the side of the ramp, one airman said to another, "Look at this shit. All the big brass is here, we've got eleven free POWs and the Tower lets Grunt Air do a formation approach. Strange day." The other airman just nodded.

In the lead chopper, Roman radioed to the formation.

"Standby … and *break!*"

One by one, each Huey executed a sharp descending left turn for a downwind entry for landing. Even the C-47 followed suit but at a slightly greater distance because of its higher airspeed. The choppers formed back on Roman in a trail formation once they'd turned on to the final approach to the runway. It was a perfect and coordinated maneuver. All five Hueys came to a stop at the standard three-foot hover, then simultaneously turned right and hovered in a line to the parking area. Archangel landed shortly behind them, then taxied to his spot.

Before the blades stopped turning, two blue staff cars pulled up beside Roman's bird with Captain Mansen leaning out of the window, waving at Roman to get out quickly.

"Which chopper is Colonel Herbert in?" Mansen asked, without so much as a hello.

Roman pointed to what had been Toothman's bird.

"You and Colonel Herbert are to come with me, now. Send the rest of the crew to your briefing room as soon as they secure the Hueys and turn over all Grunt Air documents and material to the Air Police. You and your men have to hand over all maps, photos, anything that is a part of Grunt Air."

"I know. I got the message. Sergeant Decker, please go to each pilot and tell them what to do." Decker took off.

The Generals were waiting for them in the Base Commander's office. Mattix was the first to grab Roman and congratulate him, holding Roman's right hand in both of his.

"Outstanding, Dan. Absolutely outstanding. Perfect. One wounded and the loss of a great pilot. I'm sorry about Captain Toothman. I know how close you two were. But, congratulations are in order." Handshakes and congratulations continued until General Hamilton came into the room with Colonel Odom.

"I hate to be the bearer of bad news on this wonderful day," Hamilton said, "but I have to tell you that General Coroneos has been relieved of command by the President, effective at 0600 hours this morning." The room suddenly became very quiet. Herbert turned white.

"Because of us?" Roman asked quietly.

"No, Dan. It was because of the air strikes along the Cambodian border. The General felt that the damned Rules of Engagement the White House and Pentagon made us stick to cost us too many people. He had to do something, just like the action he took in putting Grunt Air together. He knew it could get him fired, but it was the only way to protect our air crews and get our boys back," the General said. "He asked me to personally convey his congratulations on this outstanding mission. He's prepared a special letter for you. Classified Top Secret, like everything else that has to do with Grunt Air. You have to destroy it after you read it. If the bastards find out about you guys on top of the Cambodia thing, they'll probably court-martial the General and the rest of us, too." He handed Roman a white business-sized envelope. Roman separated himself from the group, walked over to the window where the light was better and tore open the letter.

> *Dan,*
>
> *First let me extend my sympathy for your personal loss. I know you and Jan had been close friends for many years.*
>
> *I deeply regret not being able to be with you and Grunt Air to celebrate your outstanding achievement, but you understand why.*
>
> *Son, what you have done as a young officer under great secrecy, and extraordinary personal risk, will probably be the single greatest achievement of your military career. It was a remarkable operation from planning to execution.*
>
> *After 32 years of military service, I shall fondly remember this operation as one of the greatest in my career. You, Dan, will always be one of my personal favorites. If you don't shoot any staff officers you will wear stars.*
>
> *My warmest personal congratulations to you and those flying pirates you call Grunt Air.*
>
> *PPC*

Roman stood silent for a moment, staring out the window at the expanse of the base until General Hamilton spoke to Colonel Herbert.

"He leaves for the States in the morning and wants you to go with him. He's going via Hawaii to tell CINCPAC what this unit has accomplished here. Your first-hand knowledge will be helpful. Now, for Grunt Air," he said as he turned to Roman. "You are to stand down effective immediately." The statement caught Roman completely off guard. A hole opened in his gut.

"But General," Roman said, "we've just proven we can get those men out. We can't just abandon them now, sir."

"We must stand down until we get formal authorization. And we have to destroy or hide every bit of evidence that Grunt Air ever existed. If those assholes in Washington get wind of any of this, they'll bring charges against the old man just like that. We can't let that happen. There are a lot of people up the line who'd love to hang him out to dry because of those air strikes. I'm damned if I'll give them more ammunition.

"But … there's some good news. He's sending you and your whole unit to Clark Air Force Base in the Philippines. You'll be on 48-hour recall to this command for special missions, like the one you pulled off today. You'll devote all your time at Clark to training and to developing better procedures for this type of operation. For the moment, you won't have your chance to get the rest of those guys out of Laos, but that's the way it is. There are a lot of backdoor efforts being made to get full authorization for this unit and its mission. If we are successful, things could change and you'll get to back in after them. So you must be prepared to for such a mission. Start thinking about how to rescue those men in the caves.

"Just one more thing. Your unit will be augmented with other Army Aviation and Air Force personnel who will help document the way this unit works. General Coroneos has directed that you put together a detailed and comprehensive presentation to take to Washington so we can get authority to make four or five more Grunt Airs. Don't be disappointed, Dan. You and your people have proven the Grunt Air concept under fire. Now you'll put it on paper so it can be continued and promoted in the future."

"But, General. A staff job?" Roman was crushed.

"I know how much you hate staff jobs and officers, but I guarantee that General Cannon and I will assign qualified people to do the paperwork under your direct supervision. Your job is to stay combat ready on a 48-hour response time until this war is over. Kissinger could get it all wrapped up in eight or ten months, but until then, you're still on strip alert for deployment back to Laos, Cambodia or Vietnam. Can I count on you? Can General Coroneos count on you? Will you come through for us?"

Roman turned to look out the window, again. It was a glorious day. He'd been awake for … how long? Had flown a critical mission, was drained of all his physical strength and emotion. He remembered the shock he suffered when they briefed him about Grunt Air for the first time. He almost couldn't believe what he was hearing. This was the same.

"Deliver the goods? Of course, I will, sir."

"Outstanding," Lt. General Hamilton said. "Now, I want to meet your men."

∽∽∽

39

California Sunshine and Global Bullshit

Travis Air Force Base
Vacaville, California
23 January, 1972

The sun soaked through the windows of the C-141 Starlifter hot and white. Newly promoted Captain Steve Dorsey squinted against the glare and looked down on the approaching coastline of California. Major Roman had selected him to be the escort officer for the returning former POWs. General Geiger had made sure the Grunt Air commander would have a say in the matter. After all, someone had to make sure their trip across the Pacific and return home went smoothly. And, it was critical that their escort be able to handle the situation if anyone blurted out the truth about their rescue to the press. Roman had lost sleep thinking about that very real possibility.

As the plane landed and taxied to the ramp, Dorsey squinted some more at the crowd circulating in front of the Operations building. The flight was late because of bad winds at altitude, and many of them had been there for hours. Even from a distance, Dorsey could pick out flags and dozens of news cameras, all pointed in his direction. Flying the mission was a snap. Now comes the hard part. He twisted in his seat.

"Welcome home," he said to his little group, all looking much better after a few days of medical attention, food, and uninterrupted sleep. "I guess you can see the press is waiting for you. When we get off, I've been directed to say a few words of thanks to our friend, General Vang Pao, for helping us with your safe return. Then, it's your turn. I know I don't have to say this, but I'm going to anyway, just to be sure. Please keep the faith. Remember your story. There are hundreds of Americans who are going through what they did to you, and worse. Grunt Air can bring them home. Be careful what you say. Please."

The older missionary spoke up. "Son, you needn't tell us to keep the faith. We have faith in God, faith in those who are still being held, and faith in Grunt Air!" The applause rang in the small passenger cabin and lasted till the forward door opened.

A cheery Air Force major stuck his head into the cabin. "Welcome home," he said. "Major General Roberts and other dignitaries are outside to welcome you back. Please watch your step on the stairs. Don't want to lose any of you now." He gave a short laugh, but he was the only one. "Please follow the red carpet through the official receiving line. After that, the press would like to have a few words with you. Please be brief, and don't say anything that might hurt our efforts in Southeast Asia. Now, Captain Dorsey, would you be the last off and the first to speak at the press conference after General Roberts. I believe you've already been briefed."

"Yes, sir. Dorsey stood up. "I have my instructions from General Geiger."

"Yes, of course. Now let's get you back to your loved ones. By the way, for the three missionaries, the Bishop of the Archdiocese is here to personally greet you and take you to a clerical retreat."

Major Cody was first off, still being helped. It would be a long time before he could get rid of his cane. He stopped at the top of the stairs and tried to pick Carol out of the crowd, but there were too many people. Besides, as soon as he'd appeared in the doorway, the crowd started jumping up and down and the band banged into "The Stars and Stripes Forever."

Slowly, followed by the others, Major Cody limped along the carpet as Major General Roberts and the others came to greet him. Directly behind the General was Cody's wife, gorgeous, wonderful, smiling so hard he thought her face would break, and sobbing uncontrollably. Carol ran past the General and threw herself into his arms. It took all her control to keep from crushing him with a hug. As it was, she still made him wince. Behind her, Chris and Amy, also crying, impatiently waited their turn.

Cody whispered into Carol's neck, "Happy Birthday, dear." It was, in fact, Carol's birthday. She couldn't believe he remembered.

Charlie Hansen was more impulsive than Carol. By the time Carol had reached her husband, Charlie had already kissed Jim eight or nine times. With her clinging to him, he approached General Roberts and rendered a sloppy salute. The General let it pass. Then it was time. The General steered them toward the rope and a forest of silver microphones. As soon as they got close, the reporters started screaming questions at the former prisoners.

They quieted down, but just a little, when General Roberts made his remarks.

"On behalf of the President, Richard M. Nixon, let me be the first to welcome you back to the United States of America. This is a great day for this country to have you back from your ordeal. Captain Dorsey, the escort officer, has a few administrative remarks to make before your questions to these fine Americans."

"Thank you, General Roberts," Dorsey said as he looked out into the group. His father was standing toward the back, beaming at him. "As you can see by the canes, bandages and overall condition of these men and Sister Jannette, they've been through a terrible ordeal. Please understand that they are weak and tired after their long flight back." He was instantly overwhelmed with shouted questions.

"Major Cody," yelled a TV reporter, "how did you escape?"

"God gave us the strength to survive and endure. When the opportunity came, we were ready and we took it. I have no idea how General Vang Pao pulled it off, but we all owe our lives to him and our fine friends in Laos. Thank you." Carol helped him away from the crowd. She hadn't let go of him for a second.

On their way into the building, Carol brightened even more at the sight of Major Calvin Dorsey standing with his arm around his son. She would have hugged Cal, but she was holding on to her husband with all her might.

"Dear, this is Calvin Dorsey from the Pentagon. He's been our greatest friend through all this. We couldn't have made it without him."

"Absolutely not true," smiled the Major. "I wasn't the one who forced Hanoi to release the list of prisoners. That was you."

"This must be your son," Carol exclaimed, taking in the sight of Steve, still looking sharp, even after the eleven-hour flight. "How did you get the honor of escorting these heroes home?" Dorsey threw a glance at Bill Cody.

"Steve helped get us out," Cody whispered to Carol.

"But I thought the Laotians—

"Never mind. Just accept it."

Carol had her husband back. She was ready to accept anything.

"Now I get it!" The realization had dawned on her. "Cal, you're such a dog. This is where you got all that inside information."

"Shhh! Carol! You want to come visit us in Leavenworth?"

"Steve," she managed, "I'm so grateful. And so proud. You saved my husband, got promoted, you're at the start of a great career. Plus you've got a sensational father. I just wish he would stay in the service."

"Well, actually, Carol," Calvin Dorsey said, "I am. They selected me for lieutenant colonel. I just found out the other day. So, I guess I'll be around for a while."

They started toward the bus as soon as Jim and Charlie Hansen joined them. Back at the microphones, Sister Janette was being quizzed.

"Sister, said a local newspaper reporter, "all of you keep saying the same thing. 'Thank you, General Vang Pao.' That's great, but isn't there anything else you can tell us?"

"Yes, my son, there is. We were horribly abused by the North Vietnamese, in some cases aided by Cuban military officers. What happened to us is unimaginable. But there is one thing worse—the fact that over 200 more people just like us are still being held prisoner in Laos, suffering the horrors we have suffered, every day. We must get them back home. We must let the politicians know how we feel. God is working behind the scenes, and others are helping, too."

"Others? Asked the reporter. "What others? Can you explain that last comment?"

"Not in a million years," she said as she left.

⚭⚭

40

There is Always a Bounty on Staff Officers

Clark Air Force Base
The Philippines
30 January, 1972

It had been ten days since General Hamilton had hit him with the order to stand down at Udorn. Roman hefted his duffel bags and helmet from the rear of the C-141 Starlifter (the same aircraft, coincidentally, that had flown his former prisoners to the States) and let the sticky wet air of the tropics hit him in the face. Could be worse, he thought. He could be in Eareckson, Alaska, with Sweeney.

Walking down the ramp at the back of the plane, he thought of the Air Police and security geeks bagging up all his maps and charts and paperwork, his personal photos and letters, taking it all somewhere anonymous to be sanitized or destroyed. They had spent days turning in equipment, packing all of Grunt Air into boxes that were borne off by men he'd never seen before. The only documents that Archangel had carried to their new base were sanitized personnel records. No trace of Grunt Air remained at Udorn.

He looked down the ramp. The old C-47 squatted at the far end of the ramp. In a few days, Starlifters would fly the Hueys in, and Ryker could spend days joyously putting them back together. They were starting all over again, but still burdened by the blanket of secrecy.

He felt good and he felt bad. It gnawed at him that there were over two hundred souls still suffering under the kind of conditions they encountered at the Big Casino. He'd never gotten out of his chopper, but Gunny Thornhill, Richardson and others told him what they'd seen in horrific detail. Besides, all he had to do was look at the condition of Major Cody and the ten others and he could guess what had been done to them. *Give me one more chance over there*, he thought. *Just one more goddamn chance.*

Probably wouldn't happen. It was obvious from the articles in the *Stars and Stripes* that the prisoners in Laos and Cambodia would be abandoned by their own country. He started talking to himself about it, but Ryker broke in on his internal dialog.

"You know, Dan, if Jan were here he'd give us one of his axioms of war. Like, 'Things that must work together cannot be shipped together.'" Ryker's remark brought Roman back to the present and his current problems.

The base reception and assignment officer looked as much like a weenie as any rear echelon type.

"Well, Major Roman," he sniffed. "I see you have a bunch of Army pilots with you. That's good. They're in big demand over at the Army units here. I'm not sure what to do with you, yet."

"Sir, we're a special operations unit on a combat recall mission."

"Major, you don't decide where new personnel go. That's my job. I have no orders or information about an aviation unit of any kind. As far as the Army and Air Force are concerned, there is no special operations unit."

"Sir, would you excuse me for a moment, I need to speak to my executive officer outside." Roman hurried through the office door remembering another of Toothman's endless list of axioms. "Professional soldiers are predictable, but the world is full of amateurs." He was faced with an amateur. A very stupid one, at that.

Roman found Ryker first. "Take this paper. Call the first phone number. If it doesn't work, try the second. This asshole lieutenant colonel is trying to break us up and reassign us." Ryker disappeared in an instant, running to find a phone in strange surroundings.

Back in the office, Roman apologized in the most profuse terms.

"Thanks for your patience, sir. I just had to arrange for a phone call. By the way, do you like winter sports?"

"What? No. I hate cold weather. Now, back to you and your little crew ..."

The officer let Roman stand in front of his desk while he shuffled through a stack of files on the credenza behind him. It wasn't more than five minutes before a sergeant knocked on the door and said, "Sir, it's a call from Lieutenant General Hamilton at Headquarters 7th."

"Hamilton? The Vice Commanding General? Calling me?"

"Guess that's who it is, sir" the sergeant said, and closed the door.

Roman relaxed his stance a bit and tried to keep from smiling. This would be good.

"This is Lieutenant Colonel Potts speaking, sir," the officer said, unconsciously sitting up straighter in his chair. "Yes, sir. Yes, sir. I understand, sir. Yes, I know where Alaska is, sir. No problem, sir. Thank you, sir. Good bye, sir." Potts could barely get the receiver back in its cradle. His hands were trembling so hard. He tried to ignore the cold sweat rolling down the back of his neck.

"Do I like winter sports?" he sneered at Roman. "Now I get it. Okay. Your unit will remain intact and remain combat ready. You're dismissed, Major," Potts said bitterly.

Roman rendered a sloppy salute and left, grinning at the sergeant in the outside office. Ryker was waiting for him.

"What happened?" He was anxious.

Roman just shook his head and said, "Goddamned staff officer!"

⚬⚬⚬

For sales, editorial information, subsidiary rights information
or a catalog, please write or phone or e-mail

ibooks
1230 Park Avenue
New York, New York 10128, US
Sales: 1-800-68-BRICK
Tel: 212-427-7139 Fax: 212-860-8852
www.ibooksinc.com
email: bricktower@aol.com.

For sales in the United States, please contact
National Book Network
nbnbooks.com
Orders: 800-462-6420
Fax: 800-338-4550
custserv@nbnbooks.com

For sales in the UK and Europe please contact our distributor,
Gazelle Book Services
Falcon House, Queens Square
Lancaster, LA1 1RN, UK
Tel: (01524) 68765 Fax: (01524) 63232
email: gazelle4go@aol.com.

For Australian and New Zealand sales please contact
Bookwise International
174 Cormack Road, Wingfield, 5013, South Australia
Tel: 61 (0) 419 340056 Fax: 61 (0)8 8268 1010
email: karen.emmerson@bookwise.com.au